Also in the series:

MONTMORENCY

MONTMORENCY ON THE ROCKS

MONTMORENCY
⇥ AND THE ASSASSINS ⇤

⚜ ELEANOR UPDALE ⚜

ORCHARD BOOKS
AN IMPRINT OF SCHOLASTIC INC.
NEW YORK

LIBRARY OF CONGRESS CATALOGING-IN-PUBLICATION DATA
Updale, Eleanor.
Montmorency and the assassins / by Eleanor Updale.
—1st Orchard Books ed.
p. cm.
Summary: After twenty years as a gentleman, Montmorency
is glad to be free of Scarper, his wretched alter-ego,
but when a young friend is caught in the middle
of a murderous political plot, Montmorency
may have no choice but to call upon Scarper for help.
ISBN 0-439-68343-2 (reinforced lib. bdg.)
[1. Robbers and outlaws—Fiction. 2. Identity—Fiction.
3. London (England)—History—1800–1950—Fiction.
4. Great Britain—History—Victoria, 1837–1901—Fiction.]
I. Title.
PZ7.U4447Mj 2006
[Fic]—dc22   2005011980

10 9 8 7 6 5 4 3 2 1   06 07 08 09 10

Printed in the U.S.A.   23
Reinforced Binding for Library Use
First Orchard Books edition, February 2006
The display type was set in Aqualine.
The text type was set in 12.5-point Venetian301 BT.
Illustrations © 2005 by Nick Hardcastle
Book design by Tim Hall

Contents

AUTHOR'S NOTE

Many of the events in this story really happened. Others are made up, but it doesn't matter if you don't know which are which. There's nothing that couldn't have taken place in the years between 1898 and 1900, but this is a work of fiction.

There are real characters in here, too. Not only Montmorency (who is so real to me that I take him wherever I go) but others, including Thomas Edison, King Umberto and Queen Margherita, Empress Elizabeth, Gaetano Bresci, Puccini, and Little Tich. They lived long ago, and I have taken some liberties with their actions, words, and personal habits. We may never know if Professor Lombroso really picked his toenails.

I hope his descendants won't take offense, and that my own offspring — Andrew, Catherine, and Flora — and my husband, Jim, will enjoy the book enough to forgive me for neglecting them while it was written.

The guidebooks used by Montmorency on his travels were all published by Baedeker: *Handbook for Travellers: Central Italy and Rome*, 1886; *Handbook for Travellers: Northern Italy*, 1899; *Handbook for Travellers: The United States*, 1899.

The extracts from *The Times* appeared on January 13 and 15, 1900.

CHAPTER I

≫

THE *KNOCHENPRÜFER*, WÜRZBURG, GERMANY, MAY 1898

*I*n the darkened hospital room, Montmorency's skeleton lay illuminated on a flat board a few inches from the floor. Lord George Fox-Selwyn stood in reverential silence with his hat in his hands, looking down at the bones of his old friend. Beside him, Doctor Robert Farcett affectionately pointed out the many places where wounds had repaired themselves after Montmorency's catastrophic accident nearly a quarter of a century ago. He spoke softly, almost whispering in the gloom.

"I remember that one," he said, indicating a lump just above the elbow. "Thought it would never heal. Look at it now. It's probably one of the strongest limbs of the lot."

Fox-Selwyn bent forward to get a better view. Suddenly the bones on the slab started to shudder beneath him. The rib cage seemed to swell and twitch. Then the whole skeleton folded at the middle, twisted, and rose up in a spasm. Fox-Selwyn pulled back just in time to avoid being hit in the face. There was a gasping, rising groan, like bellows filling with air, and then a violent sneeze sent droplets of moisture cascading into the unearthly green light. A second later, after a creak, a rattle, and a click, the men were in total darkness. The skeleton had disappeared, but a voice came from its direction.

"Sorry!" cried Montmorency, with a sniff. "I was trying to hold it in. Have I ruined everything?"

Farcett tried the switch on the wall. No luck. He opened the door to let in some light from the corridor. It cast a monstrous silhouette high on the opposite wall: the irregular outline of a great machine. Farcett's shadow gently stroked the mechanism, checking that it was not irreparably damaged.

"No, I think it's all right," he said, relieved after a moment of frozen terror. "Nothing serious broken. It looks as if they'll just have to reattach a few wires. But you should have been more careful, Montmorency. These X-ray things are expensive. If the glass had smashed I'd have had a lot of apologizing to do. Professor Krauss didn't want to leave us alone in here with the *Knochenprüfer* in the first place. We'd better disconnect the power and get the technician back."

The real Montmorency had been suspended on a stretcher between the machine and the screen that had displayed his bones. As Montmorency struggled to slide his feet to the floor and steady himself upright, Doctor Farcett gingerly detached two thick wires from a large box in the middle of the room, putting them down well apart from each other, so that the circuit was definitely broken. Montmorency blew his nose into a big linen handkerchief.

"Better hang on to that," joked Fox-Selwyn. "We could take it downstairs to the laboratory and get it analyzed."

"Actually, we could," said Doctor Farcett, picking up Montmorency's wrist to feel his pulse. "This hospital has one of the best labs in Europe." He touched Montmorency's forehead gently. "You're very hot, you know. I hope you're not coming down with something serious."

Montmorency shrugged. "It's nothing," he insisted. "I'm just a bit achy and shaky after the journey. It was worth it, though. I've seen little X-ray pictures in London, of course, but this *Knochenprüfer* thing is wonderful."

"I'd love to have one at home," said Farcett. "Imagine, being able to look right inside the whole body at once without having to wait for plates to be developed. And to be able to see patients moving, too. Think what we could find out about the way the body works. If we could get the image a bit sharper we could probably even see your breakfast making its way down."

"And all with just electricity, glass tubes, some metal, and some wires," said Fox-Selwyn, looking at the component parts of the *Knochenprüfer*. "It's just a question of knowing how to put them together, I suppose."

"Don't touch, George!" said Farcett, sensing that his bear-like friend was about to have a go at repairing the machine. "It's not as simple as it looks. Why don't you two go back to the hotel and pack for your trip? I'll find Professor Krauss and own up about what's happened. See you at the station at four-thirty."

"You don't have to come and see us off, you know," said Montmorency. "We'll be back in London in a few weeks."

The doctor laughed. "Montmorency, I've known you two

for long enough to be well aware that your little foreign escapades never run according to plan. I'm not going to let you go to Italy without saying a proper good-bye."

"Four-thirty at the station, then," said Fox-Selwyn, gently nudging the stretcher to swing from the ropes that attached it to the ceiling. "It's a shame I didn't get a go under the *Knochenprüfer*. But to be honest, I was a bit worried about whether it would take my weight. And I don't think there would have been any breakfast left to see." He patted his ample tummy. "Fancy a spot of lunch, Montmorency?"

"Just a quick one. I've got a lot of packing to do."

"You and your luggage! When will you learn to travel light?"

"You never know what you might need on a job like this," Montmorency insisted. "And I like my comforts around me. You don't understand, George. You don't know what it's like to go without."

The two men left, joking with each other. Doctor Farcett watched from the dark room as the couple strode away along the bright corridor ahead of him. Lord George Fox-Selwyn was still as large and jolly in his mid-forties as he had been when they first met, some twenty years ago. Montmorency, though a year or two younger, had changed more. Farcett had first come across him as a ragged burglar. Clinging to life after a fall, he had been little more than a crushed pile of bones in bloodstained clothing. Doctor Farcett had returned him to health and strength in prison, and Montmorency had emerged as a lively, muscular man, charming those around him in high and low life with his easy manner and boyish dark good looks. Now the thick brown hair was beginning to recede. He had flecks of gray in his sideburns, and there were the beginnings of wrinkles around his eyes and across his forehead. In early middle age, Montmorency had an air of trustworthiness about him that belied his time as Scarper, the thief who had robbed his way across London using the sewers as his highway. But his fanatical preservation of his fitness kept his body straight and strong, and from the back, as Farcett watched him walking away, Montmorency looked much younger than his forty-odd years.

As he reached the end of the corridor, Montmorency stopped and dived for his pocket. Another loud sneeze echoed against the bare hospital walls. Montmorency had definitely caught something. Farcett hoped it wasn't the influenza that had been darting its way across London before they left. He went over to the basin and washed his hands thoroughly, just in case he had picked up any germs.

CHAPTER 2

≫

THE JOB

$\mathcal{I}$t wasn't the first time that Lord George Fox-Selwyn had taken a sick Montmorency on a train. More than ten years ago, he had watched his friend struggle with the effects of drug addiction on a painful journey from London to Scotland. This sneezing was nothing by comparison and didn't even seem to dent Montmorency's usual high spirits. But it made Fox-Selwyn gloomy for another reason. It brought back a fresher memory, of the suffering of his sister-in-law, Lorna, the late Duchess of Monaburn, who had been overtaken by influenza only a few months before.

Fox-Selwyn's brother, Gus, the Duke of Monaburn, had sent an urgent telegram calling George to Glendarvie Castle, and he had arrived in time to witness the duchess's last desperate struggle as her lungs filled with fluid and fever burned her speech into a delirious ramble. Her staring eyes spoke of her terror and anger at being dragged from the world too soon to guide her two adored sons through their early years of manhood. The family watched at her bedside as she wrestled for life, but without air she grew weak, eventually settled into quietness, and then faded into death. The duke — big, blustering Gus — who had always seemed offhand with her in public, was flattened by her loss.

George had become so worried that he had taken control of his brother's affairs. He had organized a foreign holiday for Gus and the boys, and they had been touring Europe together, trying to put the loss of their wife and mother out of their minds. Fox-Selwyn's latest commission, involving as it did a trip to Italy, was a welcome opportunity for him to check up on the family. They had arranged to meet in Florence. Lord George Fox-Selwyn was hopeful that he would find Gus in a better mood.

The train climbed through the Alps, crossing ravines spanned by dramatic viaducts, and plunging into tunnels carved into the rock at the cost of hundreds of human lives. Fox-Selwyn took down his portfolio from the overhead rack and spread out a dozen pieces of paper on the seat beside him. They were to be the guides for Montmorency and Fox-Selwyn on their new mission. There were samples of handwriting, diagrams, and lists of long Latin names. This was different from their usual work. In the past they had been used secretly by the British government to seek out enemies abroad, and once they'd tracked an elusive bomber in London itself. Few people knew of their real activities. Most assumed their excursions to the continent were purely for pleasure; and indeed, an outsider watching the two of them on their travels, and seeing the fun they both had, would not have thought of asking for a deeper reason for each trip. But some friends in high places knew of their skills, and the Commissioner of the Metropolitan

Police had recommended them, off the record, for a private job.

Their new employer was an amateur scientist, a member of both the House of Lords and the Scientific Society where Montmorency had been exhibited as a medical specimen long ago. Max, 2nd Baron Astleman, the wealthy son of a great international banker, was the proud owner of one of the largest private collections of natural history specimens in Europe. His imposing home in Dulwich in South London was so full of glass cases, jars, and stuffed animals that even the professionals at the great Natural History Museum sometimes turned to him for advice and information.

Members of the public could even arrange to visit, though they would be lucky to catch a glimpse of the baron himself. He was embarrassed by his short stature, and he could not bear the way some people would stare at the livid birthmark across his face, while others made a self-conscious show of ignoring it. He could not travel. Instead, he surrounded himself with tokens of exotic lands, learning every detail of each specimen's structure, searching all the time for the new and uncategorized, in the hope that one day some discovery might bear his name.

Early that year, after a week in bed with the flu, and restless dreams when he fancied he heard the muffled sound of carriage wheels in the rain, Lord Astleman had returned to his collection and noticed something odd about a display of jellyfish. To the untrained eye everything might have seemed in order. Each specimen was safe in a special jar, a tall cylinder filled with powerful preserving spirit and sealed with a flat glass lid. A paper label was pasted onto each one, detailing the precise name and categorization of the contents in Astleman's minute handwriting. The jars were evenly spaced on the shelves, and a less obsessive man might not have realized that anything was missing. But Lord Astleman sensed at once that the beautiful but lethal *Physalia utriculus* was not there. He had always been fond of it. A fellow enthusiast had sent it from Hawaii, and its bright blue body, flecked with touches of gold and yellow, retained some of its glory, despite its long journey in the pickling fluid.

Once he realized that the jellyfish was missing, Lord Astleman checked the rest of the collection. There were gaps everywhere. Fine examples of reptiles, amphibians, invertebrates, and mammals were gone. With a growing feeling of grief, he waited for his assistant, Mr. Lopello, to arrive. Together, they could draw up a full list of what was lost. By lunchtime he admitted to himself what he'd known in his heart for a while: Mr. Lopello would not be coming that day, or ever again. He was the thief.

Baron Astleman called the police. Respectful of his social status, they did their best. They searched Lopello's rooms in a dingy house among the ramshackle slums of Saffron Hill, where London's Italian immigrants clustered together. There was no sign of him. His neighbors pretended (the police thought) that they could not speak English. After three months of fruitless inquiries, often interrupted by new and more immediately exciting cases, the detectives abandoned the hunt.

Lord Astleman accepted that he might never see Lopello face justice. But he wanted his treasures back. He agreed with the police that the specimens had probably been stolen to order, and might well have gone abroad. He was horrified at the thought of traipsing around Europe looking for them, but the police commissioner regretfully insisted that Scotland Yard could not help him, and suggested that Lord George Fox-Selwyn and Montmorency might take on the job. They were intrigued by Astleman's invitation and, in a spring downpour, took Fox-Selwyn's carriage up the hills of South London to his home, hidden at the end of a winding drive through a garden rich in unusual plants.

Lord Astleman's maid answered the door, and helped Montmorency with his wet umbrella, shaking it out and placing it in a wide drum at the side of the front door. It was a few seconds before Montmorency realized that the umbrella stand was in fact the hollowed-out foot of an elephant, and the coat hooks were animal horns and tusks. The wildlife theme continued in the decor of the drawing room. Stuffed birds perched among the bookshelves, there was a splendid fan of peacock feathers above the fireplace, and the tiger-skin rug by the hearth included the beast's head, complete with ferocious teeth.

When the baron entered, Fox-Selwyn was facing the wall, inspecting a huge butterfly pinned out in a picture frame.

"That's a great favorite of mine," said Lord Astleman, as George spun around to face him. "I captured it myself. I must have been about ten. Father gave me a butterfly net for my birthday, and after that my interest in the natural world just grew and grew."

Fox-Selwyn did his best not to betray his shock at the sight of the purple splodge running from Astleman's right ear to the other side of his chin.

"How do you do, Lord Astleman. I was more of a stag beetle boy, myself. I'm George Fox-Selwyn. This is Montmorency."

Montmorency shook hands, groping for small talk. "I didn't really advance beyond worms, I'm afraid." He laughed, thinking of his poor, urban childhood, but not inclined to mention it in detail.

"Ah, but do not underestimate the humble worm, Mr. Montmorency. A peculiarly efficient creature. Can move several times its own body weight in soil every day. Did you know that our modern tunneling machines are based on the common earthworm? Without the worm we wouldn't have all our underground railways, pipes, and sewers."

The slightest flicker resonated between Fox-Selwyn and Montmorency. They were both thinking of Montmorency's old underground life, a world he wanted to forget, and managed to put out of his mind most of the time.

Lord Astleman continued: "I've got all sorts of worms in my collection. They don't take up much space, of course, though some of the longer ones are a bit tricky to display. I'll show you them when we go through to the museum. In fact, why don't we talk there? Then if the rain stops we can have some tea on the veranda afterward."

He took his visitors along a corridor and through high double doors into a barnlike structure that dwarfed the main house. The size of the collection astonished Montmorency and Fox-Selwyn.

"How on earth do you keep track of it all?" asked Montmorency, making conversation.

The answer told them all they needed to know about Lord Astleman's obsessive nature and passionate attention to detail. He opened a cabinet to reveal a series of leather-bound ledgers. Fox-Selwyn thought to himself that they looked like the huge cash books used in banks. Then he realized that that was exactly what they were, originally. Lord Astleman had adapted the tools of the family trade to accommodate his special enthusiasm. His punctiliousness in noting down the details of his collection was simply a different manifestation of his forefathers' care with money. The specimens were cross-referenced by species and subspecies, and a pencil note indicated where each was to be found within the museum, right down to its place on a shelf or position in a glass cabinet. Alongside the ledgers was a pile of loose sheets of paper. These were headed *"Missing, 1898,"* and showed exactly what had been taken.

Lord Astleman told them about the theft. "I've made you your own copy of the list, with some drawings of what the exhibits look like. If they've left the labels on, you should be

12

able to tell straightaway if something is mine. As you'll see, I have my own way of marking things."

They toured the exhibition. Every stuffed bird and animal had a small luggage label tied to its foot. Minute writing neatly told its Latin name, the date of its acquisition, and other coded symbols linking back to the ledgers. Visitors to the collection on its public open days often imagined that Lord Astleman must be a very dry and dreary man. But, as Fox-Selwyn and Montmorency were privileged to find out, having him as their personal guide, Astleman was boisterously in love with every item, and not afraid to show it. Indeed he was incapable of disguising it from people he trusted. And he had known from the moment of the stag beetle and worm conversation that he could depend on Fox-Selwyn and Montmorency.

"Now, gentlemen," he said when the tour was over, and he had shown them all the gaps. "It has stopped raining, so let's sit outside and discuss how you can get my things back. I'll ring for tea."

They sat looking out across the terraced garden. In the distance they could see the gray smoke of central London, but here, less than five miles away, they felt as if they were in the country. Lord Astleman started discussing tactics.

"I had thought of putting the word out in the natural history world. There aren't that many of us, you know. Someone might have heard or seen something. But I decided that was a bad idea."

Montmorency got his drift. "You mean the person who

robbed you — or arranged for you to be robbed — is likely to be a fellow enthusiast?"

"Exactly. If they know we're looking, they'll hide the stuff away. So I've thought of a plan. You're the professionals, of course, but tell me what you think of it."

The maid arrived with the tea. Montmorency took a sip and then balanced his cup on a side table made from the shell of a giant tortoise. A moment later he noticed ripples on top of the liquid, and a thick foot slowly emerged from under the dome. He rescued the cup and saucer as the shell moved away. Lord Astleman smiled.

"Oh, I should have warned you. Not all my treasures are dead. This chap wanders around at will. I sometimes think he's my very best friend. Seems to radiate wisdom. His name's Darwin. It's a bit of a private joke, you understand. Now this is my idea. I'd do it myself, but it involves traveling incognito, and as you can see, unlike most of the specimens in my collection, I am not a perfect example of my species. This disfigurement precludes any but the most grotesque disguise."

Astleman suggested that Montmorency and Fox-Selwyn should visit private and public collections across Europe, posing as amateur enthusiasts. They would check the displays for the specimens and, if they drew a blank, make a judgment about whether they could take the local curators into their confidence. That way they could set up a network of trustworthy people silently on the watch for Astleman's property. It was agreed that because of Lopello's background they would start in Italy, in Lopello's hometown of Florence, which boasted one of the oldest and best collections of natural curiosities: the museum known as La Specola.

Setting off across Europe, Fox-Selwyn and Montmorency were enjoying themselves. This job, with its unworldly scientists and spineless life-forms in glass jars, seemed to present none of the dangers of their usual political work. It was almost a holiday. They wanted to find Lord Astleman's specimens. They really would do their best, even if in their hearts they didn't expect much luck. But they intended to have some fun while they were trying, and by the time they crossed the Italian border, watching the sunlight playing on the lakes and mountains, Montmorency could tell that his cold was clearing up, too.

CHAPTER 3

≫

TARIMOND

*D*octer Farcett stayed on in Würzburg for longer than he had planned. The embarrassing incident of the broken X-ray machine turned out to be a blessing. Professor Krauss had been more amused than upset, and Farcett had watched carefully as the apparatus was checked over and put back together, noting how he might construct something similar himself. Farcett loved the professor. He had none of the arrogant swagger of some of the eminent men he knew in London. A stranger meeting Krauss away from his laboratory would have found it hard to believe that he had helped to achieve one of the greatest medical advances of the century.

In just a couple of years since its accidental discovery there in Würzburg, the X-ray had begun to transform diagnosis and surgery. It had captured the imagination of the press and the public all over the world. Scientists everywhere were racing to find new uses for the magic force. Farcett had become so absorbed in the subject that he had given up most of his formal medical responsibilities to work on it. Now he wanted to return to Britain, to develop his latest ideas.

But when he got to London, he found it hard to avoid interruptions, and the prying eyes of friends and former colleagues. He needed more privacy. And he had a place to go. Far away to the north, on the remote Scottish island of

Tarimond, he had other business. Lord George Fox-Selwyn had appointed him overseer of the infirmary he had built for the islanders, and Farcett visited it whenever he could to see that all was well. He felt uncomfortable if more than a few months passed without some contact with Maggie Goudie, the nurse who ran the infirmary. Under his instruction she was already operating his first X-ray machine, built the previous summer.

Now Farcett was off to Tarimond again. And he was taking with him materials for his new project. His boat was carrying spares for his electrical generator, some carefully blown and well-protected glass globes, and enough wires, tools, photographic plates, and fluorescent screens for what he had in mind. At the very least, if his new machine worked, he would have a more efficient means of examining patients with broken bones. If his theories about the therapeutic powers of X-rays were right, he might find cures for far more dangerous complaints: blood disorders, tumors — even tuberculosis.

And then there was the other possibility, an idea he was convinced was his alone, and which he guarded so carefully that he had not told even Professor Krauss about it. He had already given his invention a secret name: the Bodyscreener.

CHAPTER 4

≫

FLORENCE

*T*he locals at the station in Florence probably guessed that the three men standing at the end of the platform were related. The oldest, presumably the father, was large in all directions, and balding on top. The two younger ones, probably in their late teens or early twenties, had the height, but not the beard or the bulk. One was blond, his hair slicked down in a formal, sober style. The other had wild red hair and freckles. He was not cut out for sunshine. His face was burned to a painful shiny red, and his rolled-up shirtsleeves revealed skin peeling off his arms in rough patches. That alone was enough to suggest that the family might be British. The clumsy cut of the father's clothes and his heavy walking boots confirmed it. He had the patrician carriage of so many wealthy English tourists. No one guessed that he really was an aristocrat. This was Gus, the Duke of Monaburn, with his sons Alexander (now Marquess of Rosseley) and Lord Francis Fox-Selwyn (the one with ginger-colored hair). They had no luggage with them. Not traveling to Rome then. They must be meeting someone off the train from the north. Indeed they were. They were waiting for the boys' uncle George and his friend Montmorency.

Alexander and Francis were glad that Montmorency was coming. They had known him since they were small. He and

Lord George Fox-Selwyn had often visited their home at Glendarvie Castle in Scotland, full of stories of danger and adventure. Alexander (who had been granted leave from his history course at Oxford when his mother died) sometimes thought that those sessions, gathered around the globe in the library at Glendarvie, had given him his interest in international affairs.

Francis had enjoyed their childhood holidays at Uncle George's house on Tarimond. They had played with the local children and lived in a far more simple way than they were used to at home or at school. George's housekeeper on the island, Vi Evans, who'd been brought up in the slums of Covent Garden, entertained them with stories of her old backstreet life, and how she had met Montmorency and their uncle George in London years before. She had tried to stop herself, but had dropped enough hints about Montmorency's past to make him seem irresistibly glamorous. There were suggestions of poverty, crime, even prison. But the mystery was never fully explained. Montmorency just dodged questions by launching into tales of wild nights on the town, long days at the races, and evenings at the opera. Francis (who disliked his name, and preferred to be known as Frank these days) was looking forward to his seventeenth birthday. Montmorency had promised to celebrate it by taking him to Bargles, the gentlemen's club in London where some of the wilder tales of drink and gambling were set.

Waiting at the station in Florence, Frank hoped Montmorency would bring an injection of fun to the family's trek across Europe. The duke and his sons were weary of travel, and of each other's company. The formal hotels of France and Switzerland had failed to cheer them up. So Frank had been thrilled when a letter from Uncle George suggested diverting to Florence and sharing a flat.

In the distance the empty railway tracks seemed to bend and shimmer in the heat haze, then a small dot grew into a mighty engine, and a minute later the station was filled with steam and squealing wheels.

"See if you can find a porter, Frank," said Gus. "Montmorency always has a lot of luggage."

Gus and Alexander pushed their way through the crowd in search of the first-class carriages. The station was a tangle of people trying to get themselves and their baggage out of the train and onto the platform, and others desperate to get onboard before the train set off again.

In the melee, the Fox-Selwyn family's height came into its own. George spotted Gus first, and waved his walking stick in the air to attract his attention. Alexander saw the sign and steered his father in the right direction. The duke and his brother, Lord George Fox-Selwyn, greeted each other with real warmth in their eyes, but an embarrassed reserve in their bodies, shaking hands, and nodding slightly. Montmorency slapped Alexander on the back, shouting over the noise of the train.

"How are you, Alex?"

"Quite well, sir," said Alexander stiffly, unable to muster a public show of affection.

Frank arrived with the porter and threw his arms around Lord George Fox-Selwyn.

"Uncle George!" he cried. "I'm so glad you've come. And Montmorency." He shook hands powerfully. "You'll love it here. We've taken an apartment over the river. It's huge. We'll have a room each, and Florence is wonderful. Bars, theaters . . ."

Alexander interrupted him sternly: "And some of the finest art galleries and churches in the world."

"Oh yes, of course, those as well," said Frank, with a cheeky smile. "I'll get around to them in time, I'm sure. Give me a chance! We've only been here three days."

"And you, Gus?" asked Fox-Selwyn with an edge of concern in his voice. "Are you happy here?"

The duke sounded tired. "As happy as I could be anywhere, I suppose."

Fox-Selwyn saw that his brother still radiated grief from every pore. He tried some soothing words: "It's bound to take time. . . ."

But Gus cut short his attempt at consolation. He couldn't bear to risk talking about his dead wife for fear of making a public show of his distress.

"Let's go across to the flat," he said. "You'll want to get yourselves sorted out."

Alexander had arranged for a carriage to collect them at the station, but the luggage took up so much room that Montmorency and Frank had to walk. For Montmorency it was the best possible introduction to Florence, a city he had never visited before. In the evening sunlight, the buildings glowed in shades of yellow, gold, and orange. People, horses, and carts jostled around the Englishmen as they stopped halfway across a bridge to look at the reflections in the river.

"Nothing like the Thames, is it?" laughed Frank. "No fog here!"

"It's beautiful," said Montmorency, surprising himself with the genuine exhilaration of his feelings. His eye was taken by the next bridge along, a huge structure with high walls. He recognized it from the guidebook he had flicked through on the train.

"That's the Ponte Vecchio, isn't it?"

"Yes," said Frank. "It's amazing. Really ancient, apparently. There are shops all the way along it. When you cross the river there you forget you're on a bridge at all. Dad says there's a hidden corridor running along it, all muddled up with the other buildings. It's how the princes used to get around without being seen."

"Well, no one seems to be suspecting you of noble connections!" said Montmorency, laughing as Frank was forced out of the way by a man pushing a cart piled high with shoes.

"It's wonderful, you know," said Frank. "Being able to get about unrecognized. I've been all over town without anyone putting on airs and graces. And we don't have hordes of servants, either. Just a maid who comes in for a few hours each day, to do a bit of cooking and keep the apartment straight. I think word's getting around about Dad being a duke, though.

We had our first visiting card yesterday, from some contessa or other."

They walked down a narrow street to a small square with parched trees struggling to survive in the cobbled ground. In one corner, market traders were packing away their tattered stalls at the end of a day's work. Alongside, the austere walls of a church rose, high and forbidding. Montmorency was surprised by the quiet plainness of the square, after the bustle of the station and the bridge. Frank pushed open a pair of high wooden doors to reveal a wide marble entrance hall with a wrought-iron gate at one end. It was dark inside, but welcomingly cool. Then, beyond the gate, there was a courtyard filled with exquisite plants in terra-cotta pots. The dusty atmosphere of the square was replaced by a juicy greenness. A fountain in the middle seemed to calm everything down. Frank cupped his hands in the water and splashed his burning face. Montmorency could hear familiar voices above him. He looked up and saw George, Gus, and Alexander sitting in cane chairs on a balcony. George, already making himself at home, shouted a welcome.

"Come up and join us. You'll love this local wine."

Montmorency knew he would. He was sure he would be happy in Florence. He hoped that in time the magic of this place might make Gus happy again, too.

CHAPTER 5

≫

FAMILY BREAKFAST

*T*he next morning, Montmorency was woken by bells. No sooner had one clanged out its call to church than another started up a couple of streets away, and before long the loud deep sound of the nearest, just a few yards from his window, pulled him from his bed and into the dining room, where the maid was already serving coffee to Alexander and the duke.

"Welcome to Florence," said Gus. "These Italians certainly take their worshipping seriously. It's been like this every day since we got here. It was even worse on Sunday. I should imagine you could spend the whole day on your knees if you felt like it."

"Actually, I thought I might go to a few services," said Alex shyly, as Frank arrived, in his crumpled shirt from the day before, rubbing his eyes and yawning. Frank caught the end of the conversation and shook his head at his brother.

"What, go to church, on purpose?" he sneered, picking a roll from the basket on the table. "What do you want to do that for?"

"To get a sense of the place, to feel its history. This is one of the great religious centers of Europe. Faith has driven the art and architecture here for centuries."

Frank rolled his eyes to the ceiling. "Oh, spare me the

lecture," he said, letting crumbs fall from his mouth. "Anyway, you won't catch me in a church. I thought we might have lunch at that place in the next square. You'll love the food here, Montmorency. All sorts of things I've never seen anywhere else. They have these wonderful flat things, called pizzas. It's a sort of dough, covered in tomato sauce and cheese."

Alex corrected him: "And basil. It's the green herb on top. They have to have that to get the colors right."

"What on earth are you talking about?" said Frank. "What colors?"

"The colors of the Italian flag," said Alex. "Red, white, and green. It's a patriotic thing. The pizza's called a Margherita after the queen. It was invented specially in her honor. It's all in that guidebook you can't be bothered to read."

"Oh for goodness' sake," snapped Frank, exasperated. "Why do you have to turn every conversation into a history lesson? Can't we go anywhere without you digging up the background on everything?"

"Stop it, Frank," said Gus, from behind his newspaper. "Alex can't help being interested in more than just having fun. Perhaps you will be, too, one day."

"Meaning what, exactly?"

The duke just grunted, and Alexander answered for him. "Just that things look different when you grow up."

Montmorency felt awkward witnessing the spat and tried to leave the room, only to bump into Lord George Fox-Selwyn coming the other way, still in his pajamas.

George tried to defuse the gathering tension.

"Boys, boys! Leave each other alone. How can you be so touchy in this beautiful place? I'm so glad I got the room on the top floor. Do you know, when I opened the shutters this morning and looked across all those red-tiled roofs to the river and the towers and that wonderful dome on the cathedral, I thought I was near to heaven."

Frank laughed. "Try this bread, Uncle George, and you'll arrive there. Why can't we get bread like this at home?"

Alex came back with a serious answer. "It's the Italian flour. It comes from a special strain of wheat. The starch behaves differently when it's cooked."

"Oh Lord, Alex. I didn't want an answer!" said Frank, hurling a lump of bread at his brother. "Is there anything you don't know?"

"Not much."

"Then just learn to keep some of it to yourself. Some of us don't have space in our brains for all that stuff. It's enough for me to know that pizzas are tasty and the bread is soft. All right?"

"I think it's more a matter of standards," said Alexander. "If you bothered to smarten yourself up, and take an interest in the higher things in life, I might not find it so embarrassing to have you as a brother."

"And if you would just learn to relax and enjoy yourself, we might all find life a bit more bearable."

The duke folded his paper and slapped it down onto the

table. "That's enough, both of you! What would your mother think if she could see you bickering like this?"

There was an awkward hush. Mention of the duchess left all of them at a loss for what to say next. George broke the uncomfortable silence.

"Anything in the paper, Gus?"

"Nasty business in Milan," the duke replied. "Riots. It seems the army opened fire on protesters and the crowd panicked. Hundreds dead. Children among them, it says."

The news did nothing to lighten the atmosphere. Montmorency lamely tried to keep the conversation going. "What were they protesting about?"

"Bread, it seems," said the duke. Then he raised an eyebrow and looked at his sons. "Lack of, price of, rather than its chemical composition. Only in our family could *that* be cause for conflict."

Montmorency could see that living at close quarters on their European tour had worn down the duke and his sons. He thought they might welcome a day apart.

"Well, Frank," he said, "if Alexander is off to church, why don't you come with George and me? We've got work to do, and though it's mildly on the brainy side, you might find it interesting. We've got to visit a museum. It's called La Specola."

"A museum?" sighed Frank, disappointed.

"I'm afraid so, but for quite an unusual reason." And Montmorency, with the odd prompt from George and the help of their diagrams and notes, told the story of the missing specimens. Frank was gripped by the idea of the hunt and agreed to go with them to La Specola. He pushed the breakfast things to one end of the table and spread out a street map to find out exactly where the museum was, plonking down the saltshaker to mark the location of their apartment.

"Via Romana . . ." he muttered, tracing along the streets with a finger. "It can't be far away. . . . Look, here's the Ponte Vecchio. . . ."

Alexander interrupted, "A fascinating bridge. It dates right back to the fourteenth century, you know. Extraordinary, its having houses and shops along it like that. Though, of course, London Bridge was somewhat similar at one time."

Frank gave his brother a dirty look and continued, "Then the Pitti Palace . . ."

Alexander jumped in again. "Designed by the great architect Brunelleschi in the fifteenth century. The same man who built that great dome you so admire, Uncle George."

"Will you shut up!" Frank shouted. "I'm just showing them how to get to the museum. They don't need a guided tour of the whole city." Frank followed the map along a little farther. "And there's La Specola," he said, marking it with the sugar spoon. "It's less than five minutes' walk from here, I'd say, and quite close to that pizza place, too."

"Well, let's set off as soon as I'm dressed," said George. He put his hand on the duke's shoulder affectionately. "You take it easy, Gus. Why not have a quiet morning while

Alex tours the churches? We can all meet at lunchtime and see if these Margherita pizza things are all they're cracked up to be."

"And who knows," said Montmorency. "If we find Lord Astleman's treasures in La Specola, we can wrap the job up and have a proper holiday."

CHAPTER 6

≫

LA SPECOLA

La Specola turned out to be an ancient observatory, tucked away in part of the university. The museum itself was up several flights of stairs. Lord George Fox-Selwyn had to stop a couple of times on the way up, and they were all wheezing a bit when they paid the admission fee at the top. They were not surprised to find that they were the only visitors.

Astleman's museum in Dulwich had been in one huge barnlike hall, with galleries linked by spiral staircases. It was almost like being in a church. La Specola had a more domestic feel, even though the collection was much bigger. It was a series of little rooms, each containing one type of exhibit, labeled in luscious Italian, so that even the most humble of species sounded exotic to English ears. The first room held *spugne e coralli* (sponges and coral). Farther on, after the insects (*insetti*), rats and mice (*roditori*), and bats (*pipistrelli*), there were huge cases displaying the stuffed bodies of the *ippopotamo* (hippopotamus), *coccodrilli* (crocodiles), and all sorts of snakes and fish. The three of them walked around the whole thing quickly, to get an idea of the size of their task, pausing occasionally to stare into the eyes of a rhinoceros, an ostrich, or a monkey. Whoever had put the exhibits together and maintained them clearly shared Lord Astleman's obsessive skill. There was the same feeling of order, the same meticulous labeling, the same frozen poses of wild creatures caught by the hunter's gun.

Then, emerging from the sharks, Frank let out a cry that brought the others running. He had chanced upon the first of a series of rooms showing quite different exhibits that would have appalled Lord Astleman. Elegant glass cases housed human beings, naked and cut open to reveal their insides in intricate detail. The bodies pulsed with raw color, the flesh a damp, sweaty pink, the muscles bloody red, and the fat a glutinous yellowy orange, almost dripping from the raw incisions. From the throat of one corpse, delicate networks of arteries and veins were teased out across the pillow where the skinned head lay, as if asleep. The three men stood, horrified, imagining for a moment that these effigies might be real. Then Montmorency looked at the sign and consulted his dictionary. *Cere anatomiche.* They were waxworks.

The life-size figures were surrounded by other examples of body parts, like cuts of meat in a butcher's shop, with the skin peeled back to expose the organs: hearts, lungs, nerves, even detailed cross sections of babies in the womb. Montmorency tried translating a sign on the wall.

"They were made for medical students," he explained. "I think it was so that they didn't have to keep dissecting dead bodies to find out how people's insides work."

Fox-Selwyn was reading over his shoulder. "Yes, and they're really old, too, more than a hundred years. And yet they're so bright and realistic."

"Robert would adore this," said Montmorency, thinking of Doctor Farcett.

Frank had gone on ahead, and was leaning over the naked body of a young woman, complete with flowing hair and neat fingernails. "Look at this one," he cried. "It says they can take her apart piece by piece to show each level of tissues. She's even got a name, 'Venus Smantellata.'"

Montmorency dived into his dictionary. "'The Venus who can be dismantled,'" he translated. "It doesn't sound quite so enticing in English, does it?"

"Fascinating," George said with a sigh. "But not, I'm afraid, why we are here, gentlemen. We'll have to confine ourselves to the other rooms. Somewhere among those bottles, jars, and stuffed animals we may find what we're looking for. And there's only one way to do it."

"Systematically," said Montmorency wearily.

"Piece by piece, there's no other way. But at least there are three of us now. That's if you're still willing to help, Frank. I wouldn't blame you if you wanted to go off and do something more exciting."

"Not at all!" cried Frank, still poring over the waxworks. "I love this place. I could stay here forever."

"Well, just till lunchtime today, I think," said Montmorency. "If we're going to keep our concentration, we'll have to work in short bursts. And unless we strike it lucky early on, we're going to be coming here for quite a while."

Later, meeting Gus and Alexander in the pizzeria, Montmorency praised Frank's enthusiasm.

Gus pulled him away from the rest of the group. "Don't get too excited about it," he warned. "Frank's life is one wild project after another. You can't depend on him. Someone will wave another idea in front of him, and he'll be off."

But Montmorency didn't want to be deflated. He looked across and watched Frank trying to persuade his earnest brother of the thrills of the wax bodies in La Specola.

"Well, for now at least, it will be a joy to have an extra pair of hands."

"Come on, you two," called Frank, who was already sitting at the table. He beckoned the waiter. "*Pizza Margherita per cinque, per favore,*" he shouted. "*E vino rosso.*"

Alexander was embarrassed by his brother's ebullience. But George was glad to see at least one of the family emerging from the gloom of the duchess's death.

CHAPTER 7

≫

SLOG

*I*t was a difficult job. George, Montmorency, and Frank divided the rooms between them and meticulously scrutinized every exhibit, seeking a precise match for Astleman's diagrams and labels. They tried to be diligent, but Montmorency and Fox-Selwyn occasionally found themselves gazing out the window at the early summer sunshine; and every now and then Frank abandoned the glass jars and stuffed animals for a look at the wax models, particularly the ones depicting parts of the female anatomy that were quite new to him.

But although the work grew tedious, and their hopes of finding Lord Astleman's treasures flagged, they went to La Specola whenever it was open, which was only for a few short hours, three times a week. The staff were soon on nodding terms with them, obviously taking the two older men, as intended, for mildly eccentric Englishmen admiring Italy's greatest zoological collection, with the help of a younger, scruffier companion or employee. George warned Frank, and reminded Montmorency, not to reveal to anyone the true purpose of their visit. They would tell the head curator only if and when the time was right.

Frank thought it was just as important not to raise suspicions by being too tense and silent either, and so he was happy to engage in conversation with one of the attendants, a young student, not much older than himself, who made a little money on the side doing guard duty. He was shorter than Frank, with olive skin and bright eyes. His straight, dark, glossy hair flopped across his forehead, and from time to time he flicked it away from his eyes as he read his book. Frank was jealous of the dark stubble on his chin, which gave him a romantic, almost poetic air. The guard's job was to sit in a corner checking that visitors didn't touch anything, or break the delicate coffins of the wax models by leaning on the glass. Some days nobody came at all, and he could use the time to catch up on his reading. Most visitors dropped in and out, happy to leave with only the most general impression of the exhibition. But the attendant was intrigued by the young man who carefully checked the label of every exhibit against a long list in his notebook.

"You are English, no?" he asked.

Frank turned around and nodded, then thought he might have seemed rather rude, and replied, "Yes. I mean, *sì*."

"I learn English. Here at the university. To help me with my studies. It is good for me to have a chance to practice. Do you mind if I speak?"

"Oh no, go ahead. Though I should really be practicing my Italian, I suppose."

"I will speak English, and you will reply in Italian. What think you?"

Frank tried to correct him. "What do you think?"

"I think is good idea."

"No, I meant, you should say, 'What do you think?' Not 'What think you?'" He paused, working out how to say, "What do you think?" in Italian. *"Che cosa pensate?"*

"I think is good idea," repeated the Italian.

"Never mind," said Frank. "Let's just chat and see what comes out in the wash."

This time the guard launched confidently into a stock phrase he had been taught when he took on the job. "I am sorry, there are no public conveniences in this building, sir. Please try at the café opposite."

Frank tried to explain himself. "No. I meant let's just see how we get on. It's a figure of speech. I don't want to wash anything."

The guard looked bemused. Frank tried again.

"Ciò è un museo meraviglioso," he said, quickly adding his own translation. "This is a wonderful museum."

"Sì. Yes. We are very proud," said the Italian, delighted that they had at last got an exchange going. He held out his hand. "My name is Guido. How do you do?"

Frank was about to respond automatically with his full name, Lord Francis Fox-Selwyn, but realized that explaining the title and the hyphen might take him all afternoon.

"Frank," he said as they shook hands. *"Molto bene, grazie."*

"I am very well, too, thank you," said Guido.

It was a slow start, but they were off on a conversation and a friendship that would dominate Frank's time in Florence. Every evening Guido took Frank to meet his friends from the university. In a café on the other side of the river, in the shadow of the great domed cathedral, they drank into the small hours, playing cards, and sometimes talking seriously about politics. The students discussed subjects that were new to Frank, but he found himself gripped by their passion and certainty. The group were incensed by the massacre of the demonstrators in Milan. They were furious about the hold that bankers and industrialists had on the king and the government. They talked animatedly about workers' rights and fair shares for all. For as long as he was in their company, Frank was persuaded by what they had to say, even if he was happy to get back to the comforts of the apartment afterward.

Frank was glad he had not revealed his aristocratic background. When asked, he said that he was a student, too, stealing some of the details of Alexander's life at Oxford to give his story color and credibility.

"And these men you work with?" asked Guido.

Frank knew he couldn't tell the truth. "Oh, I met them in London. One of my teachers introduced us. They are fascinated by natural history, going all over Europe to visit the great collections. I do most of the work, of course. I write it all up at the end of each day. But I couldn't resist the chance to earn a bit of money, and travel."

He was surprised at how easy it was to lie. But he almost slipped up once. It was a hot night, and Frank was even more sweaty and disheveled than usual, having tripped in the street and torn the sleeve of his shirt. One of Guido's friends was railing on about the evils of an economic system that forced

some men to wait on others, when Frank found himself saying, in broken Italian, "Our servants always seem happy
enough!"

He'd meant it seriously, never having encountered resentment in the settled world of Glendarvie Castle, and had a
rush of horror as he heard the words leaving his mouth. But
his new friends assumed that the tatty young Englishman
was joking. One even congratulated him on managing to be
funny in a foreign language. There were more drinks, more
banter, and the conversation turned, as it often would,
from politics to girls and then to sport. That was when Frank
was at his happiest, feeling accepted by those bright young
men. He hoped his family would stay in Florence for a very
long time.

But one Thursday night, he couldn't meet his friends.
Alexander had accidentally got the whole family into a social
engagement none of them wanted to fulfill. While Frank had
been at the museum or in bars, Alex had continued his pursuit
of cultural enlightenment in the churches and galleries. In
the Renaissance grandeur of San Lorenzo, where he had gone
to admire the Medici tombs and a staircase by Michelangelo,
he was accosted by an elegant Englishwoman. She had introduced herself as the Contessa di Rogoli, widow of an Italian
aristocrat. She already knew that Alexander was Marquess of
Rosseley. A friend of hers owned the apartment hired by his
father, the duke, and she wished to show her fellow country-
men the delights of her adopted city. Before Alexander knew

it, she had her arm through his, and they were touring the church together.

Alexander was entranced by her descriptions of the sculptures and paintings. Somehow he found himself accepting an invitation for everyone to have dinner with her at her house high on a hill above the city. She had told him it would be unforgivable to visit Florence without taking in the view from her terrace. He thought it would be rude to say no. He liked her, and quite fancied seeing the city by moonlight, but as he walked home he realized that the rest of his family were unlikely to agree. He remembered his father tearing up her visiting card when they had first arrived in town.

When he got to the flat, Alexander tried to pluck up the courage to tell the duke about the invitation, but he put it off time and time again. He was just about to own up when the maid arrived carrying a large, stiff envelope on a tray. Alexander realized straightaway what it was. His father's expression shifted from mystification to exasperation and ended in alarm as he took out the embossed invitation and noted that it was for a dinner; that the dinner was the following night; and that the card was marked not *"R.S.V.P.,"* which would allow a polite expression of regret, but *"pour memoire"* implying that the invitation had already been verbally accepted. Alexander read his mind and came clean. His father was not amused. George and Montmorency, returning from a wearying and fruitless day at the museum, could hear him shouting as they crossed the courtyard below. When they reached the apartment, Gus thrust the invitation into his brother's hand, spitting in fury.

"Look what this blockhead has done!"

"I'm sorry," Alexander mumbled meekly. "She wouldn't take no for an answer."

"Go easy on the boy, Gus," said Montmorency. "Defying a determined woman can be difficult, you know."

"That's just it," said Gus. "She's obviously set on taking us up and showing us off to all her friends. I'm not prepared to become a status symbol for some impoverished Italian aristocrat on the make."

"She's not Italian," snapped Alex, in self-defense. "She's English, and a widow, and she's really very nice."

Montmorency and Fox-Selwyn exchanged a cheeky glance, which Alex caught out of the corner of his eye.

"It's nothing like that," he stuttered. "I just mean she's really pleasant."

"Well, it looks as if we've got to go," said George, examining the card. "All of us. I wonder how she got all our names so correctly?"

Alexander blushed. "I couldn't help it. She just got me talking."

"Oh, Alexander," said Montmorency, meaning to be kind. "You've got a lot to learn about women."

Alexander slammed the door as he left the room.

"Frank's not going to be very pleased," said George. "He'll miss a night out with Guido. But it will be good for you, Gus. Take you out of yourself."

"I don't need taking out of myself, and I don't want to go!" grumbled the duke.

"But we really must, you know," urged his brother gently. "It would be very bad form not to."

"Yes, I know," said Gus, with a sigh of resignation. "And perhaps it will teach Alexander a lesson. But just the one visit. I like it here, and the boys both want to stay, but we'll be off on our travels again if we start being pursued by social climbers. I'll come out tomorrow night. But after that, I want to be left alone."

CHAPTER 8

≫

DINNER ON THE HILL

*T*hey all crammed into one carriage. No one spoke, though Frank could occasionally be heard muttering angrily under his breath.

He prayed that none of his new friends would see him. He had told Guido that he had to go out to supper with his employers. He'd given the impression that it was a rather tedious, low-key affair. He dreaded to think what Guido and the other students would make of this gathering: one duke, a marquess, and two lords (one of them Frank himself) all in full evening dress and traveling in the company of a very rich man (Montmorency) to visit a contessa. Frank slumped in the corner, away from the window, so that there was no risk of being spotted. Opposite him, Alex's head was bowed, too. He could feel the disapproval of his entire family heavy upon him. Even Uncle George was down, worried about his brother's sadness. Montmorency had given up trying to persuade the others that they might enjoy the evening. They were determined not to, and now their misery had swamped his usual enthusiasm for meeting someone new.

They passed through huge rusty gates and up a twisting drive. The road meandered from one side of the hill to the other to make the incline easier for the horses. At the top, the house was classically square, with ancient cream paint peeling off the walls. In another mood, Gus would have thought it romantic. Now he just noticed the shabbiness — a sign of old money, run out. They caught up with another carriage and had to wait behind it at the front door.

"Oh dear!" groaned the duke. "She's invited other people as well. We're going to be expected to perform."

A middle-aged, perhaps even elderly, man stepped from the carriage to the house.

"Oh well, at least there's only one of them," said George, looking around. "And I can't see anyone else behind us. Come on now, everyone. Make an effort. This will all be over in a few hours."

The carriage rolled forward to take its place at the entrance, and the family pulled itself into public good humor. The duke led the way into the hall. To his surprise, the furnishings were not as threadbare as he had expected, and there were several agreeable pictures on the walls. At the foot of the stairs, alongside the other visitor, stood their hostess, statuesque and smiling, in a simple dress with a long embroidered coat over the top. Her hair was bound up in a purple turban that showed off her slim neck. She was wearing an unusual necklace, made of brightly colored glass beads. It matched her earrings, which dangled and swung as she walked to meet her guests. She looked younger than the duke had imagined, and more friendly, if rather unconventional. She smiled and held out her arms in a gesture of greeting.

"Your Grace, welcome. Forgive me for luring you here at such short notice."

"Not at all," lied Gus. "It is an honor to be here. May I introduce my brother, Lord George Fox-Selwyn?"

"Charmed," said George, taking the contessa's hand.

The duke continued. "And of course you have met my son Alexander. But not Francis." The boys stepped forward to be greeted.

"Poor Alexander," said the contessa. "I'm afraid I rather bullied him to get you all here. Have they been very hard on you for making them dress up and come out to dinner when they're on holiday?"

"Not a bit!" said Alex, rather too fast and too loud to be convincing. The contessa caught Frank's eye as he stifled a guffaw. She gave him a knowing wink. He started to believe that the evening might be bearable after all.

Lord George Fox-Selwyn changed the subject by continuing the introductions. "And this is our friend, Montmorency."

"So kind of you to invite me," said Montmorency.

"Ah!" laughed the contessa. "The intriguing Montmorency. I must say, the marquess painted a very exotic picture of you when we met yesterday. He tells me you have no Christian name."

"It is a little affectation of mine not to reveal it," said Montmorency. "I hope you will indulge me."

"Certainly," said the contessa. "But I have one, and I hope you will all feel free to call me Beatrice. And I have a feeling that my other guest may pry yours from you, Mr. Montmorency." She motioned to the man who had entered before them. He was tubby, with receding hair, a straggly white beard, and small, oval, gold-rimmed glasses. "May I introduce Cesare Lombroso? When I heard he was in town I couldn't resist inviting him. Professor Lombroso is a psychiatrist. He has a way of understanding people. My late husband was fascinated by his theories."

Montmorency shook the professor's hand. "Perhaps we had better watch ourselves over dinner. Will you be analyzing every word we say?"

The psychiatrist took in good part a question he must have been asked at every dinner party he had ever attended. "No, I am not on duty tonight."

A gong sounded from deep within the house. The contessa took the professor's arm.

"There we are. Time for dinner. Shall we go in?" she said. "How lucky for me to be the only woman among so many interesting men. I'm sure such a party would cause a sensation back in England, aren't you? Here, I find I can act more or less as I please. I'm the eccentric foreign widow up on the hill. It's wonderfully liberating. Now, tell me what you have all been doing since you got here."

A wave of relief passed through the guests as they made their way to the dining room. The professor was delighted to be in male company, and unlikely to be called upon to make small talk. Montmorency and the Fox-Selwyns were pleased to have their preconceptions about the contessa overturned. Headaches lifted, anxiety disappeared, and they tucked in to delicious food and wine with increasing happiness.

Then Montmorency and Lord George Fox-Selwyn froze

when the contessa revealed that Alexander had been far too free with information at San Lorenzo the day before.

"Alexander tells me that you are on the trail of a thief," she said casually, unaware that this was supposed to be a secret. George glowered at his nephew as Montmorency tried to answer.

"Not a thief so much as the proceeds of his crime," he said. "I'd rather not go into too much detail, but we have been asked to locate and return some stolen property. The owner is resigned to the idea that the criminal has got away."

"Do you know who carried out the theft?" asked the contessa.

"We're pretty sure. It's someone the victim trusted absolutely. He had no reason to suspect him."

"Ah, but if he had read Cesare's books, he might have had a warning. Cesare has proved that you can tell a criminal by the shape of his head."

"Really?" said George playfully, though inside he was worrying that the professor might be able to sense something about Montmorency's past.

"Oh yes," said Professor Lombroso. "I have studied the subject for years."

"And what does a real criminal look like?" asked Gus. He, too, was thinking about Montmorency's shameful career as a burglar, twenty years ago.

Lombroso pulled a notebook and pencil from his pocket

and began sketching a grotesque caricature of a "born criminal," listing the features as he worked. "The face will tend to be asymmetrical, the nose is usually twisted to one side, nostrils exaggerated, the ears at slightly different heights, the jaw square and dominating." He held up the picture. "This is the face of Ravachol, the anarchist who terrorized Paris a few years ago. I examined his body after his execution. He fitted a criminal type I have found all over the world."

All the dinner guests found themselves touching their noses and trying to judge the position of their ears. Alexander cupped his rather large chin in his hand.

"I'm sure no one here has anything to worry about!" laughed the contessa. "But Montmorency" — all eyes focused on him — "you should buy Cesare's book. It might help you in your work."

"Indeed I will," said Montmorency, relieved. "But tell me, Professor, don't you think other things drive people to crime?"

"Perhaps. There's poverty of course, but maybe the character traits that make a criminal also make a bad worker. And even if these communists and anarchists feel a real sense of social injustice, I'm convinced that the ones who bomb and riot are possessed by an inborn evil, and must be dealt with."

Frank, who had had a little too much to drink, was growing angry. Guido and his friends at the bar called themselves anarchists. He refused to believe they were criminals.

"What about all those people killed in Milan? The ones in the bread riot?" he asked aggressively. "Was it right that they were killed?"

The professor tried to be calm. "Perhaps they would not have been killed if their leaders had been in custody. They would not have been incited to illegal acts."

"And people like us could go on eating fabulous dinners without any idea of the plight of the poor. It stinks, your theory. You just want to oppress the masses."

"It's not a theory, young man. It's scientific fact," said Lombroso, as the duke glared at his impertinent son, and the contessa jumped in to change the mood.

"Well, shall we go onto the terrace for coffee?" she asked brightly. "I can't let you go home without showing you the view."

On the way out to the garden, Montmorency caught sight of himself in an ornate mirror. No doubt about it. The professor's theory was flawed.

Without the breathtaking vision of Florence from the hill, the meal might have ended as grumpily as it had begun, but the sight of the ancient city, lit by the moon and reflected in the glassy river, calmed everybody down. When the carriages returned to take them home, the guests parted on good terms, and Frank even forced himself to shake Lombroso's hand. The contessa insisted that everyone must come back again to see the view by day.

"Thank you so much," said the duke on behalf of his family. "That would be very pleasant indeed."

"And I could show you and Alexander parts of the city not mentioned in the guidebooks," she added.

"Too kind," said the duke. "We will look forward to that immensely."

That night there was a new air of contentment in the apartment. Everyone slept well into the following day.

CHAPTER 9

≫

THE CURATOR

*O*ver a very late breakfast, George admitted that the time had come to give up on La Specola. Astleman's things were not hidden in the elegant glass cupboards that lined its walls. They would take the curator into their confidence. They had seen him walking through the museum a few times. Even Guido snapped to attention when he was there, but it was a deference born of respect for the curator's eminence in his field. Antonio Moretti was not a domineering boss. He exuded gentleness. His interest in the minutiae of the natural world had given him stillness and an orderly manner, not unlike Lord Astleman's. He was a short, rotund man. Everything about him seemed to be circular, from the perfect bald patch on top of his head, to his round glasses and the wide sweep of his belt. Even his shoes rose up into domes above his toes.

"Not a natural criminal, I think!" joked George, thinking back to what Professor Lombroso had taught them the night before. "But he probably knows everyone in the natural history business in Italy, and I think we should trust him and ask him if he has any ideas on who might have wanted Astleman's specimens."

Frank was still sleeping off the effects of the dinner, so

Montmorency and George went to the museum alone. They asked at the desk at the top of the stairs, and Moretti came out of his office to greet them. "Ah, gentlemen!" he cried. "I was hoping you would call on me. I would love to hear your impressions of our collection. How does it compare with your Natural History Museum in London, would you say? You have a more flamboyant building, but I think we have an equally intriguing collection. Don't you agree?"

"Fascinating," said Fox-Selwyn. "But there is a matter on which I would welcome your advice. Is there anywhere private where we can talk?"

The curator showed them into his office. It was meticulously tidy, but crammed with pictures, maps, and exhibits that hadn't made it into the public displays. Fox-Selwyn told the story of Astleman's loss.

"Ah, Lord Astleman. I know his writings well," said the curator, taking a book on beetles from his shelf and casually flicking through the pages. "Poor man. I know how I would feel if anyone removed something from La Specola."

"Do you have any idea where the specimens may have gone?" asked Montmorency.

"Well, like you, I think they were probably stolen for a collector. Do you have details on what is missing? Depending on the nature of the pieces, I might be able to suggest a name."

Fox-Selwyn got out the diagrams and lists Astleman had given them. They were dirty, curling, and a little torn after so much handling, but the curator had no difficulty reading them. After his first look through he whistled and mopped some sweat from his bald patch, but he said nothing. The second time he swore quietly in Italian, then said, "Lord Fox-Selwyn, I fear you need look no farther. These items are here in Florence. In this very museum."

Montmorency and Fox-Selwyn were stunned. "I don't see how we could have missed them," said Montmorency, a little indignant at the thought that his hard work checking the cabinets had been in vain.

"We have a huge collection," explained Moretti. "Only a very small proportion is on display. Our vaults are full of crates containing duplicate items and damaged specimens. And only recently we received a gift of fine-quality things from a collector here. I regret to say that all the items on this list are included in that donation."

"Then we must speak to the man and find out where he got them," said Fox-Selwyn.

Moretti shook his head. "Too late, alas. It was a tragedy. He gave us his entire collection and soon after, he died. There was talk that he killed himself. But his family says he was ill. He must have known he was not long for this world."

"But it doesn't make sense," said Montmorency. "Why would he commission a theft if he knew he was dying?"

"I cannot imagine, but come downstairs with me and I will show you the things. Then we must sit down and work out what we are going to do."

They passed through the back door of the office and down a tight spiral staircase for floor after floor until they reached the cold cellar. Stacks of dusty packing cases lined the walls. The curator went straight over to a group of clean ones and pried off a lid. The first few objects he removed were unfamiliar and marked up in a thick Italian script, but lower down, packed in the straw, were things George and Montmorency had been looking for. They recognized Astleman's handwriting on the labels of the jars. Moretti carefully unwrapped a little bird, and there, dangling from its feet, was one of Astleman's luggage labels.

"We have not yet cataloged every item ourselves," said the curator. "I will make the facilities available for you to check everything against your list." He looked deflated. "We have examples of most of these things, of course, but there were a few I had my eye on for the display upstairs. I couldn't possibly take them now, of course. They must be returned to their rightful owner. This is extremely embarrassing. Will it have to be made public?"

"I don't think Lord Astleman will want to make a fuss," said Fox-Selwyn. "But let's not get ahead of ourselves. We must check to see how many of his things are here. Then we must write to tell him the circumstances of the find, and ask his directions on what to do."

"But there are so many unanswered questions," Montmorency continued. "Who was this benefactor of yours, and why did he steal the Astleman specimens only to give them away?"

"He was Carlo Pontini. He was quite famous years ago, when Italy was struggling to become a nation. As a young man he fought alongside Garibaldi. But he didn't like the way things turned out. A lot of idealists were disappointed to see how the old corruption resurfaced in the new Italy. Pontini gave up politics. Gave up people. He settled down in a big house over the bridge, near Santa Croce. Became something of a recluse, started collecting curiosities, and eventually turned away from the human world and took the natural world as his passion."

What is it about these collectors? thought Montmorency. *Why do they shut themselves away?*

Moretti continued. "I'm one of the few people Pontini ever allowed in to see what he'd got. In our terms it's a fairly undistinguished collection, but some of his snakes will fill important gaps in our own display. When he gave us everything, I was more excited about the new things I hadn't seen before. But it looks as if I may be losing them now."

"But this recluse. Did he tell you why he was giving away his collection?" asked Fox-Selwyn.

"Just wrote a letter when he sent in the crates. Said he trusted us to take care of it all. It was a bit inconvenient, actually. As you can see, we're short of space down here. But we couldn't say no. Anyway, a few weeks later, he was gone."

"Well, it's a mystery, but not our immediate concern," said Fox-Selwyn, slapping the side of one of the crates. "Our job was to recover the stuff, and we'd better start examining it all, to see how much we've got."

"But perhaps that could wait until tomorrow," said Montmorency wearily.

"Of course, gentlemen, everything is safe here, and no one knows about it but us. May I take you for a drink?"

CHAPTER 10

≫

ISLAND INVENTIONS

$\mathcal{D}$octor Robert Farcett was looking at a perfect example of a young seagull. Its plumage was beautifully preserved, with no sign of damage by weather or fights. The webbed feet were posed like something out of a textbook. But Farcett's bird wasn't stuffed like the ones at Lord Astleman's house or La Specola. It nodded its head, spread its wings, and took off for a circuit of the bay. If you wanted to study wildlife on Tarimond you had to catch it about its business, on foot or on the wing. The only static examples were the mangled victims of age, disease, or bloody predators.

A boy joined him on the cliff top to admire the bird. "She's a beauty, right enough," he said.

"You know, Jimmy," said the doctor, "when I see sights like that, I wonder why I ever go back to London."

Farcett never visited the island without checking on Jimmy McLean. Now a young teenager, he had been the first child on Tarimond to survive infancy after the mysterious poisoning of a generation. Farcett and Maggie Goudie had helped at Jimmy's birth and nursed him in his early months.

The gull came inland again and settled on one of a row of tiny graves. Lettie, a few months younger than Jimmy, was tending the flowers that paid tribute to the older brothers and sisters she had never met. Born into an old island family, Lettie was the second of the new Tarimond children. Her name was short for Violet. She'd been christened in honor of Farcett's old friend Vi Evans: now long established as Maggie's assistant and housekeeper at Lord George Fox-Selwyn's holiday home. That was by far the largest house on the island: built high up by the church, with a spectacular view of sunsets over the sea. Vi lived there with her son, Tom.

And it was twelve-year-old Tom to whom Farcett found himself most specially drawn. A lively, intelligent child, he had spent his whole life on Tarimond, spoke with the strong local accent, and fitted in perfectly with the rural life around him. Yet Farcett always fancied that there was something more to this boy. He noticed his speed at arithmetic; his interest in the workings of everything around him; his kindness to others, particularly anyone in distress. He enjoyed Tom's cheekiness, his scams and schemes, and laughed when Vi told how he had made himself a private world, a "hidden" den in one of Tarimond's many caves. The child had his mother's eyes, and her long elegant limbs. But his glossy brown curls came from someone else. Secretly, the doctor, who had never married, had put aside a considerable sum for Tom in his will.

Up on the cliff, Farcett was taking a break from his work in the infirmary. It had been a busy morning. He had removed a rusty nail from a little boy's hand. He had listened to the wheezing of an ancient farmer, not long for this world, and he had confirmed that Elsie McFairley was expecting her first child. Now Farcett was hoping for a quieter afternoon. He wanted to get back to work on the Bodyscreener. He had managed to rig up an improved electric power source (though it was exhausting turning the handle to generate enough current) and he was trying to coordinate the beams from a series of X-ray tubes to cover the full length of a patient. So far the results on his fluorescent screen were too fuzzy to be of any use, but he was sure he was on the right track. In the meantime, he was trying other experiments. He wondered if the lump on John McLean's neck could be cured by a blast of the rays, and was preparing to offer his old friend this experimental treatment, though in truth he had no idea whether it would work.

Maggie Goudie appeared from inside, carrying a tray. "Bread and cheese, Robert? It's such a lovely day, I thought it would be nice to sit in the sun." She sat down beside him and poured some beer from a jug.

"I was just wondering about John," he said. "Do you think I should try the X-rays on him?"

"I shouldn't imagine it would do any harm. And we've both seen lumps like that before. We know what they can lead to."

"Poor Jimmy, about to lose his father, when he's never had a mother. I'd do anything to avoid that." Farcett looked out over the waves into the distance. "But, you know, Maggie, if I'm honest with myself, that's not the only reason I want to do it. Imagine if I could discover a new treatment. I could really make a mark on the profession."

Maggie laughed. "You mean you want your great machine to be called Farcett's Apparatus! I thought you'd got that kind of vanity out of your system."

"I should, I know," said Farcett. "But Maggie, I feel I could make a difference. When I'm in London, I see so many doctors with money, power, and status just because of who they know, or who they treat. I want to be famous because I've made a contribution to the human race."

"You make a contribution here. You make a difference to Tarimond. Forget London. It's only because you keep going back that you have these ambitions. It doesn't matter. This is real life. Why don't you commit yourself, move here and dedicate yourself to Tarimond?"

"But going to London keeps me up to date. If I hadn't kept up my work there, we wouldn't have the X-ray machine at all. I wouldn't have been able to see exactly how Hamish's leg was broken. I need to keep up with what is going on there and bring it back for everyone's benefit here."

"So you'll be going away again soon, will you?"

"Yes, Maggie, I will. I may even go to Würzburg again to consult Professor Krauss. To be honest, if I had the chance, I'd go to America and see Thomas Edison. He's the one who's really making strides with the X-ray. He's invented something he calls a fluoroscope. It gives you a moving image instead of a still picture. But of course the picture goes away when it's switched off. Maggie, I'm working on something really special. I call it the Bodyscreener. I've kept it a secret till now, from everyone except George and Montmorency, but I want you to know all about it."

Maggie was flattered, but she saw the funny side, too, and teased Farcett a little. "Oh, Robert, I'm so touched that you trust me not to pass your idea on to the sheep."

"No, Maggie, I really do want you to know, then you can carry on my work when I am away."

Maggie pretended to be offended, and in truth she would have liked a sign that she was appreciated for more than just her professional skill. But while she waited for an expression of affection, he stuck to the facts.

"It's a wonderful idea. It came to me when I was watching a demonstration of moving pictures in Paris."

"Well, you couldn't have done that on Tarimond!"

"Not yet, Maggie. But one day, who knows? Anyway, seeing that film made me think. What if I could make a machine that combined three new inventions? If I could make a powerful X-ray that gave a full-body image, like Professor Krauss's *Knochenprüfer*; but showed it moving, like the fluoroscope; and then recorded it on film, like Edison's kinetoscope, I could teach students about the inner workings of real bodies. Edison knows about all these things individually. Perhaps he could show me how to make them work together. And he could help me out with my generator, too."

"We always managed without X-rays before, Robert."

"But you will manage so much better *with* them. And if

I can develop my new invention here, it will finally put Tarimond on the map."

"Robert, we don't want to be on the map. You don't understand, do you? Some of us have no ambition at all, beyond living in peace."

"I can't help it, Maggie. It's how I am. You'll just have to accept it."

"I know," said Maggie with a sigh. "I suppose we can only have you now and then."

She brushed the crumbs from her apron onto the grass. "Come on," she said, putting the empty mugs back on the tray. "You'd better return to your life's work."

They went back inside, and Maggie lay on the wooden rack between Farcett's machine and the fluorescent screen, while the doctor tinkered with the equipment, trying to get a clear image of her body.

"I've got an idea for a way of watching the blood go around," he said. "It doesn't show up on the X-ray now because the liquid lets the beams right through. Suppose I injected a substance — a metal perhaps — that would stop the beams, and made a trace on the image?"

"I'd rather you tried that one on an animal first," said Maggie. "What if your injection clogged up my heart?"

"I doubt it would," said Farcett. "But all right, I'll get Morag to sell me one of her pigs."

CHAPTER 11

≫

SIX IN THE CITY

When Montmorency and George returned from La Specola with the good news about their find, they discovered that there had been developments at the apartment, too. Frank was in the courtyard, smoking. When he saw them coming he angrily stubbed out his cigarette and threw the butt into the fountain, where it joined several others. He had obviously been there for some time. Montmorency assumed Frank was angry that they had gone to meet Antonio Moretti without him.

"No, it's not that," Frank moaned. "It's that crazy psychiatrist, Professor Lombroso. He was complaining last night that his hotel was noisy, and the contessa's persuaded Dad to let him move in with us."

"Well, we have got a spare room."

"But he's dreadful. He thinks people are born bad. You can't agree with that."

"No," George said gently, "I don't agree. But we can live and let live. And if your father wants company at last, you should be pleased for him. Anyway, we may not be here that much longer. It seems we may have found Astleman's stuff."

Frank perked up. "What? Which room was it in?"

George explained about the crates in the cellar and asked

Frank to join them in compiling an inventory of what was there.

"I'll help," said Frank. "But Uncle George, when that's finished, I'd really like to stay in Florence. I've got friends here. Do we have to move on?"

"I don't see why," said Montmorency. "After all, we're not going to have to go rummaging through any other museums. It all depends on your father, I suppose. The original plan was that you'd go on from Italy to Greece."

George coughed suggestively. "Gus is looking a bit happier today. Perhaps he's found a reason to stay, too. I think the contessa made quite an impression." He blushed and stuttered. "Not that anyone could take your mother's place, Frank."

Frank was getting irritated by the way people felt awkward whenever they accidentally said anything that might remind him of his mother. He hated the way they would change the subject, or offer clumsy words of consolation. Now, as so often, he ended up having to put *them* at their ease.

"Oh, don't worry. I'd give anything for Dad to cheer up."

Montmorency smiled. "Even put up with having the professor in the house?"

"Well, it's a bit much, but I'll try."

"Good lad," said George. "And anyway, I'll make sure you can spend lots of time with your friends once we've finished at the museum. You'll probably hardly notice he's here."

George couldn't have been more wrong. Professor Lombroso

had a huge effect on their lives, almost as great as the contessa, who arrived every morning to take the duke and Alexander on cultural tours of the town. Although Lombroso had his own room, he managed to spread his possessions everywhere. It became almost impossible to sit down without having to move papers, books, hats, jackets, or half-eaten bowls of food. The bathroom floor was always wet, the towels lurking in damp mounds wherever Lombroso had gone next, never back on the rail where they belonged. He sat on the veranda in his dressing gown, reading, picking at his toenails, and leaving the torn-off pieces on the floor around his chair. But his most annoying habit was starting conversations before arriving in a room, and leaving before he'd finished talking.

Gus and Alexander were chatting in the dining room. They heard the rumble of Lombroso's voice in the hall outside, gradually getting louder until they could make out the words. He swung through the door, saying, ". . . to the university, don't you think?"

Gus stopped his own conversation to ask, "What was that?"

Lombroso repeated himself forcefully, exasperated that they had not been listening. "I said I thought it would only take me a few minutes to walk to the university."

"Oh yes," said Alexander. "It doesn't take long to walk anywhere, actually."

"Well, I should get there in time, then. I have meetings all day. Is there . . . ?" His voice faded away as he left the room again.

"What did you say?" asked Alex, raising his voice to make sure Lombroso could hear him.

Lombroso was getting angrier and shouted back from the hall: "I. Was. Just. Asking. If. There. Was. Anything. I could. Do. For you. In. Town."

By now Alex had got up and was in the hall alongside the professor. "No, it's quite all right, thank you," he said softly, disguising his own annoyance at being interrupted. "I just couldn't hear you."

"It doesn't matter," said Lombroso huffily, grabbing his hat and slamming the door behind him.

By the time Alexander got back to the dining room, neither he nor his father could remember what they had been talking about before. It was a pattern that was repeated time and time again, with the professor leaving each disrupted domestic scene convinced that he had been slighted.

Sometimes his habit of inaudible talking caused real problems. One morning Gus was shaving. As usual he took no notice of the professor's distant muttering. He wandered from the bathroom in his underwear, only to find the contessa sitting in the drawing room.

"I told you she was here," said Lombroso testily, as the duke leaped away to get his clothes on.

Worst of all was the uncertainty about how long Lombroso was going to stay. Gus was sure he had been given the impression that the professor was visiting Florence for only a few days, attending a conference about criminology. But one evening, they all caught part of a sentence including the words ". . . be here a little while longer." No one dared ask him to be more precise. With the passage of time, the impact of his possessions on their apartment grew. The maid, who had managed looking after five men with little difficulty, found six impossible and handed in her notice.

George, Montmorency, and Frank soon established that everything they were looking for was in the crates at La Specola. George wrote to Lord Astleman with the good news, asking for further instructions. Then he and Montmorency at last dived into the pleasures of the ancient city, as they waited for Astleman's reply. When it arrived, they were resting on the veranda, serenaded by Lombroso, who was slumped, snoring, in a wicker chair, with a newspaper over his head. George read the letter aloud.

Dulwich

25 August 1898

My Dear Fox-Selwyn,
It is beyond my powers to express the sheer joy engendered by the receipt of your letter. I had feared my possessions lost forever, and had even begun filling their places on the shelves. I should have had more faith in you and Montmorency. I never doubted your diligence in your task, but it seemed such a difficult one, with so little information, and so many places to look. I can only assume that divine

inspiration led us to choose *La Specola* as your first port of call, and I must be grateful that the authorities there are people of such integrity that they led you to the goods, even when you could not find them yourselves.

It is in recognition of this that I ask you to invite the curator of the museum to choose one of the specimens for his own collection. He may take what he pleases, without regard to its value or rarity. I have contemplated life without any of the pieces. I can well adapt to being deprived of just one, whatever its quality, as a repayment for such kindness from a man whose learning and expertise I respect most highly.

You will appreciate that I wish to avoid any publicity in this matter. You have already handled everything with the utmost discretion, and I am sure I can rely on you to continue in this vein. I imagine that the authorities at *La Specola* also wish to avoid the embarrassment of public disclosure. To that end, I should be obliged if you would complete your efforts on my behalf by arranging safe shipment of the goods back to England, and not pursue the matter of the theft any further. I will, of course, reimburse all your expenses on your return.

If I were a traveling man (and I know you understand that I am not) I am sure I would take full advantage of being in Italy at this time of year. Please do not feel any obligation to rush back to London on my account, though I should be delighted if you would join me for a celebration of this happy outcome when you do come home.

> Yours in gratitude,
> Astleman

"It seems strange to leave it all there," said Montmorency, "with so many questions unanswered. Shouldn't we try and trace the thief, that Lopello, who worked for Astleman? And what about the collector, Pontini? Why did he bother to commission the theft if he was going to give it all away?"

"We can't let ourselves get interested in all that," said Fox-Selwyn. "We're working for Lord Astleman and he explicitly states that we shouldn't take it any further. In any case, what would we do if we found out more? Astleman doesn't want any fuss. If there were a trial it would only highlight the market in these specimens and make Astleman's collection even more of a target. To say nothing of the public exposure he'd face. You've met him. You know he couldn't bear that."

Montmorency persisted. "Isn't it a bit odd that Moretti came clean so quickly about having Astleman's stuff in his basement? Surely he could have hung on to it, and let us go on our way, searching all over Europe."

"What would have been the point in that? With us traveling on, putting the word out in the trade, he'd never have been able to put those specimens on display."

Montmorency changed tack. "But just suppose he's up to all sorts of shady business. Owning up to us about Astleman's stuff would be a good way to put us off the scent."

"What scent? Montmorency, we've absolutely no reason to doubt Moretti's story, and absolutely no duty to pursue the matter. You're just disappointed that this case hasn't been exciting enough for you. And anyway, you're neglecting something."

"Really? What?"

"Decency, Montmorency. Natural decency. It isn't a quality confined to Englishmen, you know. The professor here has described the criminal physique to us. I'd venture that Moretti is the embodiment of the higher qualities of human nature. He simply felt it was wrong to hang on to stolen goods."

"Maybe so," said Montmorency. "But this Pontini interests me."

Fox-Selwyn was losing patience. "His affairs are none of our business. Our job will be over as soon as Astleman's things are on their way to London."

"But why did Pontini commission the theft?"

There was a loud snort from Lombroso, as he pulled himself up into a sitting position, the cane of the chair creaking madly under the strain.

"What makes you think he did?" asked the professor.

"I beg your pardon?" said Fox-Selwyn, somewhat put out that Lombroso had been listening in while pretending to sleep.

"Might he not have bought the items innocently, and then discovered that he was ill?"

"Well, yes," said Montmorency. "But it seems a bit unlikely that the crook would steal the things on the off chance, and then come all the way to Italy to sell them."

"Why not?" Lombroso continued, as he wandered from the veranda into the drawing room. "He's Italian, he was a long way from home and charged with the care of valuable objects. He might have wanted the money for . . ." The professor's voice faded away as he rummaged in the pocket of his jacket on the back of a chair on the other side of the room. Montmorency and Fox-Selwyn exchanged exasperated looks as he mumbled on inaudibly. He reappeared, lighting himself a small cigar. They noted that he didn't offer them one, as he finished his point.

". . . or he might have been getting money and transport in the simplest way available to him, given his training, and his place of work. Perhaps it was a purely opportunistic crime."

"Which is exactly why we won't be taking it any further," Fox-Selwyn insisted. "We're going to have a nice holiday with Gus and the boys."

"And that brings me to another point," said the professor, picking some loose tobacco from his lip. "Young Frank."

"What about him?" said Fox-Selwyn, irritated that this stranger was delving into family affairs.

"You should watch the company he's keeping. I've seen him with his friends in town. They look like a bad lot."

"Oh, natural-born criminals, you mean!" said Montmorency facetiously.

"Precisely. I know what I'm talking about. I examined the men who killed the French president in '94, and the Spanish Prime Minister last year. I've studied bomb-throwers across Europe. . . ."

Fox-Selwyn rolled his eyes to heaven. He was heartily sick of hearing about the highlights of Lombroso's career.

"Those students show all the signs. Tattoos. Long arms. Everything. They'll get the boy into trouble with their . . ." He was off again, looking for an ashtray, returning with the words ". . . at a very impressionable age."

"I'll bear that in mind," said Fox-Selwyn, as politely as he could manage. "But Frank's all right. I walked past a café the other night, and they were just laughing and joking like young men everywhere. And it's doing wonders for his Italian. He's better than any of us now. Frank's old enough to choose his own friends, and that Guido seems to be a fine young man. We can't expect Frank to go around with Alex all the time. He might really be driven to violence then! The boy deserves a bit of fun after all the hard work he put in at the museum."

Lombroso went inside, muttering to himself.

"Infuriating man!" gasped Fox-Selwyn.

"All the same," said Montmorency. "Maybe we should pay Frank a bit more attention. I was thinking of going up to Milan. They're doing *La Bohème.* You know, the new Puccini opera. Perhaps I could take Frank with me."

"Well, it would give him a change of scenery. But count me out if you don't mind," said George. "I'm not too keen on that modern stuff. I'll stay here. I want to keep an eye on Gus and the contessa."

George closed his eyes and stretched out to soak up the sun. He was glad the Astleman job was finished, and looked forward to a lazy break. He couldn't have known that the Italian adventure was only just beginning.

CHAPTER 12

≫

LA BOHÈME

At first Frank wasn't too keen on the idea of an opera, but Montmorency won him over with the force of his enthusiasm. And anyway, Frank wanted to get away from the apartment, where his patience with the professor was wearing thin. At mealtimes he tried dropping hints that Lombroso was outstaying his welcome, but he was quickly put down by his father, who seemed extremely anxious not to offend the contessa's friend. Uncle George encouraged Frank to go to Milan, with amusing accounts of his own nights out with Montmorency at opera houses all over Europe.

"Just don't worry about trying to understand the story," he said reassuringly. "Sit back and let the music and the color wash over you. You'll have a great time."

In any case, thought Frank, they would be gone for only a few days, and he knew Montmorency would be an amusing companion, not forcing him to take in too many churches and paintings on the way. He mentioned the trip to Guido, without going into any details, and Guido asked if Frank would mind delivering a package to a friend in Milan. Frank was only too pleased to oblige.

They stayed at a grand hotel in the center of town, and while Montmorency was out at the shops, buying himself more clothes and shoes than any man could possibly need,

Frank went off to find Guido's friend. He lived in a tenement block near the train station. The stairwell was dark, which was probably just as well. It stopped Frank seeing exactly what the slimy rubbish at his feet was composed of. He couldn't block out the smell, though. It was a pungent mix of human fluids and decaying food. Eventually he found the right door and knocked politely. It was a while before anyone answered. When they did, they hardly opened the door at all. All Frank could see was the edge of a swarthy face, and one eye peering out through a curtain of greasy hair. Frank was proud of his Italian, but now he found that all he could come out with were stuttered phrasebook standbys.

"Buon giorno . . . mi scusi . . ." he started, hearing himself sounding like a bumbling tourist.

The man at the door looked him up and down. "You speak English? Are you from Paterson?" he asked suspiciously.

"No, Guido sent me. I'm looking for Malpensa. I have brought a package."

The character eyed him again, then opened the door a little wider, but still looked unfriendly.

"My name is Frank. I am a friend of Guido's from Florence. I have the package here." He took the small heavy parcel from his pocket. The man behind the door grabbed it, and seemed to be weighing it in his hand.

"You can come in," he said at last, limping across the dirty room to clear some old newspapers from the top of a packing case. He motioned to Frank to sit there and took another for himself. "How is Guido these days?"

They spoke in a mixture of English and Italian about Guido, and Frank's other friends from the bar. After a while Frank said he must go, and as Malpensa lifted himself up, his leg gave way underneath him. Frank steadied him before he hit the floor.

"Thank you," said Malpensa. "It's a gunshot wound. I was in the demonstration back in May. But I was the lucky one. A woman fell dead at my feet."

"I love your country," said Frank. "But bad things are happening here."

"Bad things are happening all over Europe," said Malpensa. "We cannot let the forces of oppression win. The aristocracy must die. The people must triumph."

Frank nodded silently, partly persuaded, and partly burdened with the secret knowledge that, through no fault of his own, he was a member of the European aristocracy.

"Will you take a letter back to Guido for me?" asked Malpensa. "I have some important, private, news for him. You will give it to him unopened?"

"Of course," Frank promised. He waited while Malpensa wrote his note, then ran back to the hotel to meet Montmorency. He was confused. The mysterious transaction in the filthy room had been curiously exciting. Now he was off to a wildly different world, a world in which he no longer felt entirely comfortable.

Montmorency was sitting at the café on the sidewalk outside the hotel. He was just beginning to worry when he saw Frank coming towards him in his scruffy clothes, and recognized something about the furtive look in his eye and the hunch of his shoulders. Frank looked like someone Montmorency hadn't seen for years. He was the image of Montmorency himself in his days as Scarper.

Should Montmorency ask what he had been up to? He gave himself a hundred reasons not to. Frank wasn't his son, and he didn't want to be landed with some secret that he'd have to pass on to Gus just when the duke was cheering up. There was probably a really simple explanation for Frank's absence and appearance. He had just been seeing the sights and lost track of time. At worst he might have fallen in with a shady woman, or been threatened by thugs. But he'd obviously survived. And anyway, they had to get to the opera; there was no time for a grand inquisition.

"Come on," said Montmorency with false cheeriness, as he contemplated where Frank might have been. "Let's get you upstairs for a bath. We've got to transform you into a man about town before the opera."

And in their grand suite, a ritual took place that Montmorency had acted out so many times before in his days at the Marimion Hotel. Half an hour later, Malpensa would never have recognized Lord Francis Fox-Selwyn.

On the way to the opera, Montmorency avoided the topic at the front of his mind by explaining a little of the plot of *La Bohème*.

"I missed it when it was on at Covent Garden last year. But according to the reviews, it's a really unusual piece. Most operas are about grand subjects: kings, princes, and so on. This one's about students — real Bohemians, not the rich sort like our contessa in Florence, playing with the idea of being different. These are real artists and writers, living in poverty in Paris. But it's a love story, too. You'll enjoy that."

When the curtain went up, Montmorency nudged Frank and whispered, "Amazing scenery. So realistic."

But Frank didn't think so. The set designer's idea of squalor had nothing on the real filth of Malpensa's smelly room only half a mile away. And yet he was attracted to the life he saw on the stage with its overtones of rebellion and individuality. He adored the slight, sickly, doomed heroine, with the beautiful voice, and joined Montmorency in wild cheers and applause at the end. He'd enjoyed the artificiality of the evening more than the raw menace of his encounter with real politics that afternoon. It felt safer.

Montmorency was proud of his protégé in the seat beside him. He sensed a special bond with Frank. He felt he had a duty to take care of this young man with all his enthusiasms. Montmorency knew all too well how easily he could be led into trouble. The professor might be annoying and impertinent, but perhaps he had a point. Frank was young and impressionable and at an age when hasty decisions and impulsive actions might unintentionally determine his whole future.

CHAPTER 13

≫

RIOT

*F*rank and Montmorency stayed on in Milan for a few days. When they got back to the apartment in Florence they were surprised to hear a woman's voice coming from the drawing room. She sounded agitated and upset. Montmorency knocked on the door and opened it gently, looking in to see if they would be welcome. The contessa was sitting red-eyed on the chaise longue by the window, clutching a damp handkerchief. Gus was standing over her, awkwardly trying to give some comfort. Montmorency caught his eye, and the duke beckoned him inside.

"I'm afraid we've had some very grave news," he whispered quietly.

The contessa held out a crumpled telegram. Montmorency struggled with the staccato message, written in Italian, but sent, he could see, from Switzerland.

The contessa explained it to him. "It's my dear friend, Elizabeth. She has been murdered."

Gus corrected her. "Assassinated. Elizabeth, Empress of Austria, stabbed to death."

"She was on holiday in Geneva," added the contessa. "How did they know she was there?" she asked, as if trying to make sense of the shocking news. "She was traveling under a false name. I know she was. She explained it all to me when she wrote asking me to go, too. Oh, if only I'd gone. Perhaps I could have prevented it."

"There's nothing you could have done," Gus insisted. "If some madman was determined to get to her, no one could have stopped him."

"Was it a madman?" asked Montmorency.

"This is all we know," said Gus, taking back the telegram. "A man stabbed her as she boarded a boat. She died from the bleeding."

"But who would want to do such a thing?" cried the contessa. "She is . . . was . . . such a gentle soul."

"That would mean nothing to the political fanatics that are around these days," spat the duke. "It will be those anarchists again, trying to bring down civilization. What do they have to replace it with? That's what I'd like to know. And where's George? He'd be able to find out what's going on."

"There's a message on the dining-room table," said Frank. "He's gone out with Alexander. They'll be looking at frescoes or something like that."

"Well, we need him here, now," said Gus. "Go and find them, and tell them to come home at once."

"I'll go, too," said Montmorency. "We'll split up and meet back here in an hour."

They went down into the square.

"You look on this side of the river," Montmorency told Frank. "I'll go over the bridge." He could see that Frank was bemused by the urgency in Montmorency's voice. "This is bad news, Frank. There are forces working to destroy the world as we know it. That poor woman may not be the last to die."

Upstairs in the apartment, the contessa was telling Gus more about her dead friend, a distant relative she had known since she was a little girl. It was common gossip that the aging empress, unhappy with her husband, and unimpressed by the Viennese court, lived a quiet, informal life away from Austria, hiding from the pressures of the throne. Now Gus learned that she had been a frequent visitor at the contessa's hillside home: resting, reading, and taking in the delights of Florence incognito. They had been through hard times together. The empress had turned to the contessa when her only son had committed suicide; and only a year before, when her sister had been killed in a fire, she had secretly taken refuge in Florence to restore her spirits.

Gus realized that the contessa had turned down Elizabeth's invitation to Switzerland because she wanted to be with him. He was flattered that she cared for him enough to disappoint an old friend. He had not, till that moment, acknowledged his own feelings for her. Though the contessa felt guilty that she had not been with the empress in her hour of need, he was relieved and grateful that she was safe. He sat down beside her and held her tenderly as she wept hot tears against his chest.

Montmorency looked in church after church for George and Alexander. As he went, he could sense a tension sweeping through the city. News of the assassination was coursing through the streets and cafés. He saw a boy taking his position at a street corner with a bundle of newspapers under his arm. A hastily written poster announced a special edition about the empress. He bought a copy, but could make out little more than what he already knew. *News must be coming in all the time,* he thought. He looked for the address of the newspaper's offices on the back page, and went there, hoping to find out more.

When he arrived, he saw that George had beaten him to it, and that he and Alex had made themselves at home in the editor's office where they were studying a telegram that had just arrived.

"A bad business," said George. "They've arrested someone. A known anarchist, someone called Luccheni. Sounds Italian. Maybe there's something we could do about all this."

Montmorency could see that his old friend was excited by the news: thrilled at the thought of getting back into the world he loved, dabbling in the underbelly of international politics.

"Actually, there is something you can do right now," he said. "It seems the empress was a friend of the contessa. She's with Gus at the apartment, and he wants you to come home and help with her."

"All right, I will," said George. "But first I want to telegraph Rome to offer our services to the British ambassador. This menace has got to be dealt with at its source."

>> >> >>

Frank was still looking for his uncle and brother at the main tourist attractions on his side of the river. Like Montmorency, he kept hearing snatches of conversation about the assassination. Most people reacted with gasps of horror as the news was broken. He saw some women, and at least one man, in tears. But others seemed energized by the news. Florence was usually steamy and sleepy in the late afternoon. Today was different. There was a buzz about the streets. People who would normally walk alone stopped and passed on what they knew. Strangers overheard, asked questions, and exchanged opinions, so that the narrow sidewalks became clogged with little groups of people, chatting more animatedly than usual. In the bigger spaces, larger crowds formed, inquisitive about why others had stopped. Facts were few, but they were embroidered and added to as the story was told and retold. Frank, pressing on alone as he searched for George and Alex, felt excluded from a special occasion.

He was outside the Pitti Palace, not far from La Specola, when he remembered the letter from Malpensa to Guido, still in his pocket, waiting to be delivered. He looked at his watch. La Specola might still be open, and it would not take him far out of his way to drop in and deliver the note at once. He dashed up the stairs to the museum entrance and found Guido there alone, with a huge bunch of keys, ready to lock up for the night. At last, Frank had an opportunity to become part of the rumor machine. He handed Guido

Malpensa's letter and broke the news that the empress Elizabeth was dead.

He should, perhaps, have been prepared for Guido's reaction. After all, hadn't he spent night after night listening to intoxicating talk about "The Revolution"? He had never thought for one minute that the upheaval his friends envisaged was any more than a romantic idea, that it might actually come to pass; but for Guido the assassination was clearly a dream come true. He was wildly elated, pacing furiously between the stuffed beasts and gory cadavers in the cases around him, muttering under his breath. He opened Malpensa's letter and read it quickly, smiling and punching the air with a clenched fist. Outside, the noise of a distant crowd was rumbling towards them. Something was happening. Something out of control. Something that excited Guido and terrified Frank.

Guido climbed up to look out the window and pulled Frank up to join him. A man with wild eyes was running down the street, pursued by police. As he got closer, Frank recognized him as one of Guido's friends from the bar: Milo, a student who had often stirred them all with drunken rages against the evils of the state and the rights of the masses. Moments later they could hear footsteps on stairs, first one set, fast and noisy, then many more, accompanied by shouts and whistles. Guido ran to the entrance and pulled Milo into the museum. Then he slammed the huge doors, locked them shut, and with Milo's help, dragged the huge desk across to reinforce them against the pressure from outside.

"Have you heard?" said the breathless man.

"Yes," said Guido, thrusting Malpensa's letter into Milo's hand. "It's started."

The two embraced and then, to Frank's horror and embarrassment, embraced him, too, as the shouts and thumps from the police outside grew louder and angrier. Frank realized that he was in danger and part of an enterprise he didn't understand. But the throbbing energy of the atmosphere gripped him, and he felt a rush of life sweep through his body. He didn't know what the new arrival had done, or why he was running from the police, but Frank knew he would support him, fight for him, against his pursuers. Together they piled up more and more furniture against the door. They were safe.

And then there was more noise out in the street. Guido went back to the window.

"There's hundreds of them," he said. "They've got a ladder. They're coming up."

The three of them looked around for something to use in self-defense. Frank pulled a strut from the back of Guido's chair. Guido grabbed the ring of keys and started struggling to open one of the specimen cases. He tried one key after another, with no luck. Then he slammed the whole bunch against the glass, smashing it into pointed shards. Frank thought he was going to use these as weapons, but Guido started loading up his arms with jars containing squid, worms, and starfish.

"Quick," he shouted to his mystified friends. "Have you got any matches?"

They both went through their pockets, and Frank handed some over.

"Give me the letter," Guido commanded Milo. And he started tearing the paper into strips. Then he pried the stoppers off the jars, and the acrid smell of the preserving spirit filled the room. Guido dipped a strip of paper into the top of each jar, lining them up on the windowsill, then slipped the catch on the window, and swung it open.

"Don't!" cried Frank. "They'll get in, you fool."

"No, they won't!" said Guido, striking a match and lighting the first of the paper fuses. The flame leaped as Guido hurled the first jar out into the crowd, where it landed in an explosion of light, surrounded by screams. Guido laughed and reached for another jar. His friend joined in, smashing another window and launching burning missiles into the street.

Frank shrank back, horrified and paralyzed with fear. Then he heard Guido shouting at him, calling for more jars. Frank couldn't resist. He didn't want to resist. He did as Guido instructed, passing the strange ammunition forward to the crazed men at the windows. One after another, the precious specimens hit the ground and burned to ashes. Guido and his friend kept on throwing them out well after the road had cleared. Then, following Guido's lead, all three of them swung themselves out the window and down the ladder the police had planned to use to capture them.

"Split up," shouted Guido as he reached the ground and ran to the right. Milo turned left, around a corner, and into the arms of the police.

Frank fled straight ahead. He could hear someone running behind him, but he dodged and ducked down side streets and alleyways until he was pretty sure he was on his own. Then he slowly made his way home, breathless and dirty, but trying to look calm as he turned into the square and opened the gates leading to the apartment.

He had hoped no one would be in, but as he opened the door he could hear voices coming from the drawing room. His father was there, with Alex and Uncle George, he could tell. Then a woman's voice. The contessa had not gone home. He couldn't let them see him like this. He crept along the passageway, trying to reach the bathroom without being noticed. But as he reached for the doorknob, the door opened of its own accord, and Montmorency came out. He realized at once that Frank was in some sort of trouble.

"Frank, what on earth has happened to you?"

Frank put his finger to his lips. "Don't tell Dad," he pleaded, and from the frantic look in Frank's eyes, Montmorency could tell that this was more than just a teenage scrape. He paused for a moment, persuading himself to go along with the cover-up.

"All right," he whispered, holding open the bathroom door.

"Get in there and have a wash. You can tell me about it later."

"Thanks," gasped Frank, scarcely able to believe what he had done that afternoon, but hoping that with Montmorency's help he might get away with it.

CHAPTER 14

≫

GETAWAY

*F*rank lay in the bath for as long as he dared, but in time his worry about having to answer questions was outweighed by the fear of rousing suspicion by staying there too long. In any case the skin on his fingers was wrinkling up, and the water had gone cold. His clothes were too dirty to put back on, so he took his father's bathrobe from the back of the door, and used Uncle George's brush to slick his wet hair back from his forehead. He couldn't get to his bedroom without passing the open door to the drawing room. George saw him and called him in.

"Frank! There you are! I didn't realize you were back. Come in and have a drink."

Frank entered, holding the robe tightly shut to avoid embarrassing the contessa. Montmorency turned to look out of the window, not wanting to get further involved in any subterfuge.

"I'm so sorry you had to waste your day looking for me," George continued. "Montmorency found me pretty quickly, but of course there was no way we could let you know. You must be exhausted after all that walking."

"Oh, it's quite all right, Uncle. I'm just glad you're here now."

"Well, I'm here, but not for long. I've had a telegram from

our ambassador in Rome. Apparently there's pressure for international action against these anarchists, and he wants me to visit him to talk about developments. Perhaps you boys would like to come, too. How about it, Alex?"

"Oh, I'd love to see Rome," said Alexander. Frank just smiled, not sure if he fancied being so close to the authorities.

He didn't have time to say anything. They were interrupted by the unmistakable sound of the professor coming home. They could hear the muffled jabber of his voice from the moment he slammed the door and dropped his key on the hall stand. As he approached the drawing room, and the sound grew louder, they could tell that he was very excited.

". . . explosions, and one policeman so badly burned that they think he may die. But at least they caught one of them. . . ."

"Slow down, Cesare," said the contessa calmly. "We missed the start of what you were saying. What's happened?"

Frank's heart was beating so hard at the news about the policeman that he feared the others must be able to tell something was wrong. He wanted to leave the room, so no one would notice his agitation, but he was desperate to hear what the professor had to say.

"The police cornered some of the anarchists. They tried to arrest one, who was raving to a crowd outside the Duomo, praising the killing of the empress Elizabeth. He got away, and the police and the crowd chased him right through the city, across the river, and down to the Via Romana. He led them straight to two more of the criminals, holed up in La Specola. You know that museum, I believe."

"Oh yes," said George. "We know it very well."

Montmorency was looking at Frank. Frank was looking at the floorboards.

The professor continued. "They threw firebombs down on the crowd. Cleared the street. Two of them got away, but the police caught the man they'd chased across town. I'm going down tonight to help them interview him. And one of the others was recognized. He's a student who worked part-time at the museum."

George immediately started talking about the staff at La Specola, inviting Montmorency and Frank to speculate on which of the young people they had met there might be a dangerous criminal.

"Perhaps it was that quiet one who sits in the rodent room," he suggested. "I always thought he had a bit of a rattish look himself."

"Maybe," said Frank. "I don't really know him. He never came out with us."

"You should ask Guido what he thinks about it all."

Montmorency rescued Frank from having to reply. "Possibly, but I think it would be best if you stayed in tonight, Frank. Things might get ugly in town."

"Of course," said George, returning to the subject of the likely suspects. Frank and Montmorency let him do most of the talking, Frank because he was afraid of giving anything away, and Montmorency because he saw the possibility that Frank was the third man.

George wanted more information from the professor. "And the two who got away, do you think they'll be captured?"

"They went in opposite directions. The police will be searching everywhere. All the bars and cafés the students use, all the sleazy slums where they live." Frank felt a little safer. Their own neighborhood would be spared a visit from the police. But he was soon scared again.

"And if the policeman dies?" asked George.

"The killer will go to prison for life," said the professor. "We don't have capital punishment here, you know. We would not want to create a martyr."

Gus was outraged. "No wonder you have all this trouble, if you don't execute killers," he said, defending the British system.

"And in England, Your Grace," the professor asked pointedly, "you find that hanging has cleared your streets of murderers, do you?"

Gus did not have an answer.

The professor continued. "We attack crime in different ways. Here, it is illegal to carry a firearm. At least those anarchists were not shooting into that crowd."

"Well, I still think they should be shot themselves," said the duke. "They're a danger to all of us, and to the whole civilized world. If they were in front of me now, I would shoot them without a moment's hesitation."

Frank looked at his father, unknowingly advocating his own son's execution. How could he explain that he had never meant to be part of the violence? That he hadn't imagined the fiery rhetoric of his drinking companions ever turning into something real? Then he thought back to the heavy parcel he had carried to Malpensa in Milan. He was only beginning to comprehend what he had got mixed up in.

The others were so excited by all the news that they didn't notice how little Frank contributed to their conversations throughout the rest of the evening. The discussion of international politics swept over him during dinner. He paid only the most scant attention to the professor's lengthy exposition of his theory about the criminal face and the assassin's mind. At the end of the evening, Gus and Alexander took the contessa home, and the professor went out to see if there were any new developments at police headquarters. Montmorency, George, and Frank were left together with a bottle of brandy. George was energized by the affair.

"Well, are you both going to join me in Rome, then? This is something we can really get our teeth into, Montmorency. You'll love it, Frank."

"George," said Montmorency, trying to calm him down. "I think Frank may have something to tell us."

Lord George Fox-Selwyn looked puzzled. Then his expression turned to shock as he realized what Montmorency was suggesting. Frank slumped in his chair, then looked up and tried to speak. He didn't know where to start.

Montmorency helped him. "I think Frank may have got out of his depth," he said.

George turned to Frank. "Were you involved in this terrible thing?"

Frank's head was in his hands, but he was nodding silently.

"You were at La Specola?"

Frank nodded again. George didn't want to believe it.

"But just by chance, surely," said George, trying to give Frank a way out, struggling for an explanation. "Just by chance. You were looking for me. It was a coincidence that you were there."

Frank looked up, relieved. "Yes. I just went to give Guido a letter."

"And you just happened to be there when the violence started."

"Yes."

"You weren't part of it at all."

"No. Except."

"Except what?"

"Except I was. I was." Frank was crying now. "I was in there, and I just couldn't help it. It seemed right at the time."

"Right to throw bombs?"

"I didn't actually throw any."

George sensed new hope. "So you weren't really involved."

"I just made them, and handed them over."

"Oh, Frank! Can't you see that's just as bad?"

"I know. I never said it wasn't. I wish I hadn't done it."

"Then why, Frank? Why?"

"I told you. They're my friends. It felt right." Frank's face was wet with tears and snot.

"Right? Right to murder, maim, and destroy?"

Montmorency put his hand on George's shoulder. "Go easy on the boy, George. I'm sure he'll tell us everything if we help him."

He turned to the sobbing figure in the chair, who suddenly looked very young and fragile. He knew how Frank must be feeling. He remembered only too well how, long after he had created his Montmorency self, his seedy alter ego, Scarper, had crept up on him time and again, luring him into all sorts of actions he now regretted. Montmorency believed he had conquered Scarper now. But he could see that, just as he had made the transition from the dark world to the light, Frank was in danger of traveling the other way.

"Frank, I don't see what's to be gained by you spending the rest of your life in an Italian jail," he said.

"It would break your father's heart," said George, outraged at his nephew's behavior. "How could you? How could you? Do you actually believe all this anarchist claptrap? Do you want to see your family annihilated?"

Frank mouthed a silent "No." He couldn't find the words to explain that his friends' vision hadn't seemed dangerous or unjust amid the camaraderie of the café, and was too powerful to resist in the museum.

"What are we going to do now?" hissed George, pacing the room and punching the furniture to defuse the anger he felt towards Frank. "We should turn you in to the authorities. But how can we? It would destroy Gus as surely as any bullet or knife."

"It would hurt all of us," said Montmorency, still striving for calm. "But Frank, if you will tell George what you know about these terrible people, I'm sure he will be able to do some good. He can help put them behind bars."

"But they're my friends," pleaded Frank.

"What sort of friend leads you into this kind of trouble?" asked George. "And how can they be real friends, anyway? You've only known them for a couple of months. We're your family. Don't you have a greater loyalty to us?"

"And to yourself, Frank," added Montmorency, passing him a handkerchief. "You deserve your freedom. We'll find a way out of this."

George was torn. "But we have a duty to pass on something to the authorities, surely. You know the name of the one who got away, don't you, Frank?"

There was no reply.

George raised his voice. "You do, don't you? Who was it?"

Frank's voice was barely audible as he muttered his friend's name into his chest. "Guido."

"Right," said George. "That's important information. We have to tell the police."

"Do we really?" said Montmorency. "Can we give them anything they won't find out elsewhere? We've already heard that Guido's been recognized. Surely the curator knows more about him than we do. He can give the police a description and tell them where he lives. He's probably already done it."

"What about the other man?" said George. "Lombroso said there were three of you."

"His name's Milo," said Frank. "I've met him before, but I don't really know anything about him. He's a student, like the others. He studies natural sciences. But the police will know all that. They've caught him."

"There you are," said Montmorency. "We really can't help the authorities. At least not without putting Frank in danger."

"Do the other two know your name?" asked George.

"They know I'm Frank. That's all. And of course Guido knows I've been working with you, but he thinks you're mad naturalists, and I'm a poor student making a bit of extra money by helping you with your research."

"Good," said George. "Though I'm not sure how I feel about being described as mad. But however little Guido knows about you, he'll be well aware that you know a lot about him. It's not just the police who might be on your trail."

"Maybe all three of us need to get out of town," said Montmorency.

"Come to Rome with me, both of you," said George. "That will get us out of the way."

"But not far enough, I fear," said Montmorency. "George, you take Alexander to Rome with you. Do what you can to fight the anarchists. And find a way of explaining everything to Gus. Water it down, if you like, but impress on him that he and Alex mustn't talk about Frank to anyone. We have to let Frank's friends believe that he's on his own, and he's run away. We can't risk his being recognized anywhere in Italy. I'm taking him back to Britain. I'm taking him to Tarimond."

CHAPTER 15

≫

SANCTUARY

*I*n the old days, almost every visitor to Tarimond had come as a complete surprise. Communications were slow and unreliable, and there was rarely time to warn the islanders that you were coming before taking the chance of a sea crossing to the far northwest. Now, better boats brought more regular supplies from the mainland, and though the telephone and telegraph were still unknown on Tarimond, and letters were still slow, the mail arrived more frequently, sometimes carrying news of a visit from Lord George Fox-Selwyn, Montmorency, and Doctor Farcett bringing injections of London gossip and news. Tarimond was still cut off, but it was rare now to see a boat arriving with no prior explanation, especially in the autumn when high winds and rough seas could cut off the island completely.

Jimmy McLean, the oldest of Tarimond's children, was playing football on the beach with Lettie and Tom when the boat carrying Montmorency and Frank came into view. They watched it come nearer, guessing who might be inside. In the end Frank's red hair gave the game away, then the quantity of luggage suggested that Montmorency was the other passenger. The children waded into the shallows to greet them. There were many hugs. Montmorency told them all how much they had grown. He opened his bag right there on the sand to get out a present he had brought them: Licorice Comfits — brightly colored sweets with black centers bought in London a week before. The children plunged their hands into the paper bag and stuffed their mouths with the hard, sugary lozenges.

Jimmy tried to speak. Lettie interrupted him. "Urrgh! You've sucked all the color off them!" she shouted.

"So have you!" said Jimmy, looking at the white lumps glistening on her tongue.

Tom pulled a sweet from his mouth and examined it. Without the color it looked like a tooth. He lined the rest up so that they stuck out between his lips, and he growled menacingly. Everybody laughed. Jimmy began crunching his sweets into little pieces. The licorice started to dissolve, and black saliva ran onto his chin. Lettie did the same and opened her mouth wide.

"Your teeth are all black!" shouted Tom.

"Oh no!" she said. "Will it come off? Me mam will go mad."

"Don't worry." Montmorency chuckled. "It will wear off. But you wait till I show you the cough candy. That will turn your tongues orange for hours!"

"Urrgh!" they all cried, loving the idea.

Montmorency turned to Violet. "Lettie, why don't you run on to the big house and tell Tom's mother that we're here. The boys can help me with all the bags."

Lettie scampered up the cliff, towards Tom's home: the grand new house that Lord George Fox-Selwyn had put up after his first visit to Tarimond. Tom's mother, Vi, would need to make up beds for the new arrivals.

Montmorency watched as Tom, Jimmy, and Frank formed a chain gang, passing the bags from hand to hand to get them to the top of the cliff. Usually, Frank and his brother stood out from the children on Tarimond, their pale skin making them look weak and fearful. Now Frank's Italian tan and his extra height gave him an air of command, but Jimmy and Tom really had grown, too. Montmorency watched Tom. He had an extra present for him at the bottom of his bag. It was a fine suit of clothes and a silk shirt from Italy. Something the boy could wear if he ever came to visit Montmorency in London. Montmorency had guessed the size, mentally allowing plenty of room for growth. From the look of him now, it wouldn't be long before Tom outgrew the outfit. Tom was like his mother in so many ways, with his cheeky delicate features, and his long limbs. But he was strong, too. Montmorency was proud to see him manhandling the baggage so easily and tousled his hair as they all got their breath back at the top.

Vi ran out to greet them. Her hair was starting to gray now, but she still had a girlish abandon about her. She flung her arms around Montmorency and let him twirl her around with her feet off the ground.

"Are you sure you've brought enough luggage?" she asked teasingly.

"We might be staying for quite a while, Vi," said Montmorency, not rising to the bait.

"Robert's here, you know," she added. "Up at the infirmary

till all hours, working on his invention. He's rigged up a machine that can make a picture of your bones."

"We knew he wasn't in London. Tried to visit him there, but his house was all closed up. I was hoping we'd find him here."

"And here I am," said a familiar voice. Doctor Farcett was approaching with Maggie Goudie, both of them overjoyed to see the new arrivals. "We heard you'd come. News travels fast on Tarimond, as you know."

"When did you two last have something to eat?" Maggie asked. "It's nearly suppertime. Vi, I'll give you a hand with a meal if you like, and Frank can tell us all about what he's been up to."

Frank panicked inside for a moment when he heard this, then realized she only wanted to leave Montmorency and Farcett alone together. All she expected from him was youthful babble about his foreign trip. To Maggie, Frank was still a child, the puny younger son of the duke: George Fox-Selwyn's little nephew. It hadn't occurred to her that the most interesting news — the thing she would not be told — actually centered on him.

"Come on in, children," Vi called. "Leave Doctor Farcett and Mr. Montmorency in peace. They probably want to talk."

Frank followed Lettie and Tom into the kitchen, and the two men paced around the garden catching up on developments since they had last seen each other, at the station in Würzburg.

"So, you found Astleman's specimens, then?" said Farcett.

"Oh yes. We were tremendously lucky. Our first lead paid off. It's an odd story, though. There's something about it I find a bit unsettling. A collector in Florence had bought them, then he gave them away and died."

"So what did he want them for? What does George think?"

"George thinks, and more to the point, Astleman insists, that it is none of our business. Anyway, George has more important things to worry about now. He's got involved in the fight against these anarchists. These maniacs who've been bombing their way all over Europe."

"Is that why he's not with you now?"

"Yes, there's a big international conference about it all in Italy. Twenty-one countries are taking part, and he's part of the British delegation."

"And why aren't you with him? You always work together."

Montmorency decided not to tell Robert about Frank's problems, and the real reason why he had come back to Tarimond.

"Oh well, George and Gus thought it would be a good chance for Alexander to see the workings of government at close quarters. The boy wants to be a diplomat or a politician, you know. He deserves to be in on history in the making."

"And so you're looking after young Francis?"

"Yes, though I think he'd rather you called him Frank these days. I don't think the idea of being shut in a conference hall with international statesmen would exactly appeal to him."

"Of course not. And what a good thing that you have come here. I can show you the new machine I'm working on. I think it may be one of the most powerful sources of X-rays in Europe. Mind you, I wish I'd known you were coming. There's a book I need. You could have picked it up in London."

"Oh, we got out of London as fast as we could. It was foggy and cold, and everyone was coughing and sneezing. It was so depressing after Florence."

"So the flu's getting a hold, is it? This is beginning to look like the start of another epidemic."

"Oh, Robert, calm down. Stop being a doctor for a minute! We just saw a few people sniffling, that's all."

Maggie Goudie came out, drying her hands on her apron. "Supper's ready!" she called. "Come and join us. We want to hear all about Italy."

For the first few days on Tarimond, both Montmorency and Frank slept a good deal. Then Montmorency started to spend more and more time at the infirmary with Doctor Farcett and Maggie Goudie. Farcett explained in detail his idea for making an educational film about the internal workings of the human body.

"You see, when X-rays were discovered, we all got excited, but we let them lead us astray. They give us a fixed picture of the bones, but in reality, the body is a heaving, moving, mobile thing. Everything inside us now is shifting, oozing, palpitating. . . ."

"Yes, Robert," said Montmorency squeamishly. "I get your point."

But Farcett continued: "You see, it all works together, and if we're not careful we're going to start thinking of all the parts as separate, all subject to diseases of their very own. You can see it now, in the big hospitals, more and more specialization. Big experts on little things. No one pulling it all together."

"And your film will do that."

"Yes, I want to show, for the first time, how the body really works. If I could create a film, thousands of copies could be made and distributed all over the world. Every doctor, every medical student in every country could see it."

"And every one of them would hear your name. You would be at the very top of your profession."

Farcett blushed, embarrassed at his obvious ambition. "Well, yes, but . . ."

"Oh, Robert," said Montmorency, "you never change!"

Weeks passed. The year was drawing to a close. Frank filled the short hours of daylight helping Tom and Jimmy with their work. The two island boys were finished with schooling, and the hard physical labor on their farmland distracted Frank from his worries about events in Italy. But the image of his last days there kept returning to his mind, violently colorful against the monochrome of the Tarimond winter. He could hardly believe that he had helped Guido pelt firebombs into a Florentine street. Had he really taken a package to that dingy room in Milan? Could it have contained a gun? Were the police after him? What had happened to Guido? What had happened to the injured policeman? Was Frank a murderer? Uncle George was attending a conference aimed at improving police cooperation across Europe. Would it lead to Frank's arrest, even though he was out of Italy? How long would he have to stay hidden on Tarimond?

He looked around him. It was beautiful, in a sparse, rugged sort of way. He loved the people, the first who had let him — forced him to — forget he was an aristocrat and behave normally. But could he live like this forever? Didn't he need something more? More excitement, more danger? He looked across at Tom, who was taking a break, leaning on his shovel, staring at the clouds.

"Do you think you'll live here all your life, Tom?"

"Aye, I suppose so," Tom replied. "But I might go to London someday."

"And what would you do there?" asked Frank, amused at the idea of this rough island boy walking down Piccadilly.

"You promise you won't tell my mam?" said Tom, dropping his voice, though there was no one about to hear.

"Promise," said Frank.

"I want to find my father," said Tom.

"Have you asked your mam who he was?"

"I tried, a long time ago. She just told me not to ask her, because it would break her heart to say. But Maggie let slip once that he was someone from London. She said she thought he might be dead, but I could tell she didn't really know. I want to go there and find him."

"London's a big place, Tom."

"I know, but I'll go there one day, when I'm old enough. I'll find him sometime. I want to know why he didn't marry my mam."

"Perhaps he was cruel to your mother, and that's why she ran away here. Maybe it would be better if you didn't know."

"But she said he was good, kind, and clever."

"Maybe she said it because that's how she wants you to turn out."

As soon as he'd said it, Frank wished he hadn't. He saw from the look on Tom's face that he was questioning the only description he'd had of his origins. Frank hurriedly changed the subject.

"Come on, it's getting dark. Let's get back and lend a hand with the Christmas decorations."

CHAPTER 16

≫

CHRISTMAS ON TARIMOND

*C*hristmas celebrations were another innovation on Tarimond. Before the Londoners started visiting, Christmas Day would be marked with nothing more than a few prayers in the austere church on the cliff, and perhaps some extra gravy or a special pie. On her first Christmas on the island, Vi had taken Maggie Goudie quite by surprise with a present: a handkerchief Vi had secretly embroidered with Maggie's initials, to say thank you for her welcome and support. Vi had covered up her disappointment at getting nothing in return. She had rarely been given anything of any value in her childhood in Covent Garden, but there had always been a little something (even if it might have been stolen), and plenty of fruit from the traders in the market. The guests in their lodging house would sometimes produce bottles of wine or gin. Vi remembered one very noisy party that had ended with her mother under the mistletoe with an aging actor dressed up as Santa Claus. All around London the shops had put up special decorations: paper snowflakes, holly, and sparkling lights.

For her second Christmas on Tarimond, with baby Tom at her side in Lord George Fox-Selwyn's brand-new house, Vi made some decorations of her own, using scraps of material, and odd pieces of wood. Later, she asked Fox-Selwyn and

Montmorency to see what they could pick up on their travels, and over the years they had brought her trinkets from all over Europe, including some fine Christmas tree ornaments from Austria. There weren't enough trees on Tarimond to justify wasting one by cutting it down to take inside, but from that year on, Vi always decorated a bush in the garden, and gradually some of the islanders had followed her example. Now there were always two splendid Christmas Day parties at Fox-Selwyn's house: one in the afternoon for the growing band of Tarimond children, and one in the evening, lasting well into the next morning, when the adults ate, drank, and sang a mixture of local ballads, traditional English Christmas carols taught by Vi, and her own repertoire of songs imported from the pubs of London.

This year, Montmorency had added to Vi's collection of ornaments with bits and pieces from Italy. There was a fine selection of silky ribbons; a gaudy china Madonna that had somehow survived the journey wrapped up in his (clean) underwear; and several colored postcards reproducing the artistic treasures of Florence. With a week to go, Vi was just getting into her stride, and when Frank and Tom got back to the house, the children from Maggie's school were gathered in the front parlor, happily cutting around the pictures and threading them onto strings. Vi was rummaging through the box where she stored the decorations from previous Christmases, gasping lovingly over her favorite objects, which had been out of sight for a year.

"Oh, Tom," she giggled, holding up a crooked wooden star.

"Do you remember making this? You must have been about six. Isn't it lovely, children?"

Tom couldn't see why she was so excited about such a dreadful attempt at a star shape. "Put it away, Mam," he said, embarrassed.

"I won't put it away," said Vi, hugging him and making his discomfort worse. "I'm proud of it, and I'm proud of you!"

Tom pushed her away. "Leave me alone!" he snapped, snatching the star and flinging it to the floor before stomping off into the kitchen. Vi set about trying to calm the children, who had been alarmed by Tom's burst of temper.

"Now then, wasn't that a silly fuss over that lovely star?" she said in the high-pitched voice of harassed teachers through the ages. "Let me have a look at what you are doing. Oh, that's lovely, Fiona, well done."

Frank picked up the star and watched, guiltily realizing he'd stirred up the emotions that had turned Tom against his mother. But he felt something else, too. At least Tom had a mother. This would be Frank's first Christmas without his. He'd thought he'd got over her death, but now he wanted only to be back at Glendarvie Castle, with the whole family around the fire and a sumptuous meal under construction in the kitchen. But he knew that could never be. His mother was gone, his father and brother and uncle were abroad, and he was in exile, miles from anywhere, permanently shamed because of his impulsive behavior in Florence. He slipped back out into the garden, hung the misshapen star onto the Christmas bush, and cried.

Montmorency and Doctor Farcett, approaching the house after a day of tinkering with machinery at the infirmary, spotted Frank in time to leave him in peace. Doctor Farcett guessed what was wrong.

"The poor young man must be missing his mother," he said.

"Yes," said Montmorency, keeping to himself all the other things that might be on Frank's mind.

A few hours later, all was calm again. At Frank's prompting, Tom apologized to Vi, and she said sorry to him for embarrassing him in front of the little ones. They continued the preparations together, and Montmorency chipped in with all sorts of ideas for the big party on Christmas Day, producing Italian sweetmeats and preserves from the depths of his luggage. He and Frank reminisced about Christmases at Glendarvie, and it was resolved that they would do what they had done so often there, and put on a play. They chose the story of Snow White, with seven of the children to play the part of the dwarfs, Vi as Snow White, and Maggie Goudie as the wicked stepmother with the poisoned apple. Doctor Farcett was pressed to take on the role of the King, Snow White's father; Montmorency volunteered for the dual role of the narrator and the huntsman, who takes Snow White into the woods but can't bear to kill her; and Frank was unanimously chosen as the Handsome Prince, who wakes Snow White with a kiss.

Tom wasn't sure he wanted to act at all and asked to be in

charge of the props, but they persuaded him to be the voice of the magic mirror as well. Like the rest of the children on Tarimond, he had never heard the story of Snow White. Perhaps for the first time in history, the pantomime was to be played to an audience who didn't know the ending. The dwarfs were told not to reveal it to their families and, fearing retribution from the wicked stepmother, they kept it secret to the very end.

On Christmas Eve, the islanders crammed into the sitting room at the big house. It seemed that every tablecloth, curtain, sheet, and blanket on Tarimond had been commandeered for use as capes, drapes, and set dressing. The cast was shut away in the kitchen, and a very nervous Tom took up his position behind a tall cheval mirror, brought down from Lord George Fox-Selwyn's bedroom just for the occasion.

Montmorency stepped forward to speak the prologue. The islanders had never before seen him dressed in his fancy city clothes. They whistled and giggled at him, and there were more whoops when Farcett and Maggie mimed a wedding scene, embracing lovingly (and very convincingly). Montmorency led the hisses and boos that greeted the Wicked Queen each time she spoke to her magic mirror, and they kept it up without him when he had to dash to the bathroom to change into the huntsman's costume, ready to take Snow White into the woods, kill her, and bring back her heart: a real one, supplied by a farmer who had slaughtered a pig that morning.

Montmorency made the most of his role, showing moving tenderness to Vi as Snow White (with some kisses that hadn't been in the original script) and letting blood drip from the heart onto the wicked stepmother's hands as she chortled over her triumph.

"Mirror, mirror, on the wall," chanted Maggie, accompanied by some of the audience, who were getting the idea. "Who is the fairest of them all?"

There were gasps as Tom replied from behind the mirror, "Mistress, you are beautiful, but Snow White has more beauty still."

Maggie Goudie's rage on hearing this shocked everyone, but they were soon laughing as she and Tom struggled off the stage and into the kitchen just as seven small people eagerly squashed and fought their way in.

The sweet little dwarfs were the stars of the show. Fourteen proud parents in the audience waved at them and smiled as they spoke their lines. Everyone pretended not to notice the damp patch that gradually spread across one pair of tiny trousers, and there was wild applause as the dwarfs made their exit, leaving Snow White alone. Frank, meanwhile, wishing he hadn't taken the part of the Handsome Prince who doesn't come on till the end, was outside in the cold with a cigarette, nervously pacing up and down.

When the wicked stepmother reappeared, disguised as an old woman, no one noticed that the poisoned apple was, in fact, a potato (apples being unavailable on Tarimond in December), and there were real tears when Snow White fell into her slumber, and the dwarfs gathered around her sleeping body.

Montmorency reappeared as the narrator, back in his best clothes.

"And so, Snow White slept on," he said. "No one could wake her, for only a handsome prince could break the spell. . . ."

This was the cue for the door to open and Frank to appear.

The door did open.

But it wasn't Frank.

A large, bearded man in a dripping wet cape walked in and bent over Snow White, taking her in his arms and kissing her passionately.

"George!" cried Snow White, as the room rocked with laughter. "What are you doing here?"

"Hello, everybody!" said Lord George Fox-Selwyn warmly. "I thought I'd come for Christmas."

It was the best ending the show could have had, and there were hugs and handshakes all around. Montmorency cornered George and asked quietly, "So the conference is over?"

"More or less, bar the paperwork," said George, as his beer mug was topped up by the father of one of the dwarfs. "I'll tell you all about it later."

CHAPTER 17

≫

CONFERENCE REPORT

Lord George Fox-Selwyn, Doctor Farcett, Montmorency, and Frank sat by the fire while Vi cleared up the mess left after the play. They were too tired to go upstairs to bed. Frank was desperate for his uncle to tell them the results of the Rome conference. Even as he and Montmorency had fled across Europe to Tarimond weeks ago, the papers of all the countries they crossed had been full of invective against the anarchists who had killed the empress, politicians, and scores of innocent bystanders over the past few years. Frank had read nervously of plans to coordinate the search for anarchist sympathizers across the continent. Here and there were references to the riot in Florence, and the hunt for the two firebombers who'd got away. Did they know who he really was? Was the whole of Europe looking for him? Would he be on the run forever?

When he had seen George making his way towards the house that night, Frank had wanted nothing more than to take him aside and find out, but it was almost time for him to burst in and rescue Snow White, and Uncle George had come up with the clever idea of taking his place, to surprise everyone. There had been no time for even the most cursory gesture of reassurance or warning. Then, at the party afterward, the moment was never right. George was surrounded by islanders with news of crops, animals, births, marriages, and deaths.

The room had emptied gradually. First the families with sleepy children took their leave; then Maggie Goudie (who was looking very weary), the elderly, and women with chores to do at home. A hard core of five men stayed, drinking and singing into the small hours. Doctor Farcett had dropped a few polite hints. Montmorency had tried a theatrical yawn or two. In the end it was Vi who decided the party was over.

"Get away to your beds now," she told the visitors, bossily taking their drinks away like a pub landlady at closing time. And they went, four of them carrying the unconscious fifth by his arms and legs, joking about the reception he would get from his angry wife.

Montmorency turned to George. "I hope you didn't mind us inviting everyone around."

"Not a bit," chortled Fox-Selwyn. "I'm only sorry I missed most of the play. It's delightful to see the house being used. And anyway, it's Christmas. It's good to see a bit of action, though I hope things will be a bit less frantic here than they were in Rome."

"So what was it like?" asked Doctor Farcett. "Nonstop meetings around a big table?"

"There was plenty of that. But the real work was done outside the conference chamber, quiet chats over lunch, trade-offs in the corridor. That sort of thing. Alexander loved it. He got to see some of the world's most important politicians and diplomats in action."

"Not exactly something you'd buy tickets for, Frank!" said Doctor Farcett, who had always been amused by the contrast between Frank and his older brother. "Anyway, George, did the conference achieve anything, or was it just a nice outing to Italy for the great and the good?"

"Some things were agreed, yes," said Fox-Selwyn. "In fact every country except one signed up to the final protocol. That's why I got away early. You see, it's us, Great Britain, who disagreed. I'm afraid we're not anyone's favorite nation now."

Frank felt a slight surge of relief. Perhaps he would be safe if he stayed in his own country.

"So why did we oppose the deal?" asked Montmorency.

"The Prime Minister felt it intruded too much on our traditional British liberties. And that if we give them up it should be because our own parliament decides to do it, not because a load of foreigners tell us to."

"I think I agree," said Farcett. "But what are the other countries going to do, exactly?"

"Well, they've worked out a definition of anarchism," said Fox-Selwyn, taking a crumpled piece of paper from his pocket and putting on his reading glasses. "It's any act 'having as its aim the destruction, through violent means, of all social organization.'"

As George rattled through the other main points, Frank assessed how each measure applied to him.

"All countries will prohibit the illegitimate possession and use of explosives. . . ."

Frank thought back to the package he had delivered to Malpensa in Milan. *What might it have contained?*

". . . It will be a crime to belong to anarchist organizations. . . ."

Well, he hadn't exactly joined. . . .

". . . To distribute anarchist propaganda . . ."

Frank thought back to a jovial night's drunken flyer-posting with his friends in Florence.

". . . or to render assistance to anarchists . . ."

Frank could feel the weight of the lethal spirit bombs in his hand at La Specola — he recalled the thrill of watching them fly through the window.

". . . And the death penalty should be mandatory for all assassinations of heads of state. . . ."

At last, relief — no one could accuse him of that.

"Sounds quite sensible, actually," said Farcett.

"Oh, and there's another thing," added Fox-Selwyn, folding away the paper. "You'll like this, Montmorency. Our friend Professor Lombroso was there. Quite a star of the occasion, actually. Everyone seemed entirely convinced by his theory of the criminal physiognomy. He had all sorts of charts and drawings showing the typical anarchist face and bone structure. It led on to another plan. They're going to work out a way of describing suspects by a series of measurements and symbols. The size of the head, position of the eyes, shape of the ears, everything, will be reduced to a sort of code that can be sent around the world by telegraph or telephone."

"That sounds like a good idea," said Doctor Farcett. "But this professor of yours, does he really believe there is such a thing as a criminal face? We could prove to him that that isn't true!"

George coughed and nodded slightly in Frank's direction, reminding Farcett that the boy was there, and had no idea about Montmorency's criminal past. Frank took the gesture as a reference to himself and wondered whether the doctor was in on his own secret. But it was the merest beat in their conversation. Montmorency shifted the subject effortlessly.

"I think the professor probably has the fewest social graces of anyone I've ever met," he said, launching off on a description of Lombroso's protruding nasal hair and his annoying little habits, which had them all in stitches. George acted out a typical breakfast in the Florence apartment. It started with Lombroso entering the room while other people were talking, and, with the words "I won't interrupt," starting a new topic of conversation, while absentmindedly picking tidbits off other people's plates. Then he'd get up and walk from the room, still talking, expecting replies to questions nobody could hear. George mimed Lombroso scrubbing his teeth and talking at the same time, then returning to the table and asking, "Don't you agree?" to a bemused audience who had absolutely no idea what he had been talking about.

"Sometimes he'd storm out, furious that we 'hadn't been listening.' He treated us like naughty students."

Frank added to the picture. "And all the time he was wandering from room to room, muttering, he'd be picking things up, moving them, or putting them in his pockets. That's where we found the lost pepper shaker, remember, Uncle?"

"And those train tickets to Milan." Montmorency laughed. "Do you remember the fuss when they disappeared from the hall table at the last minute?"

"He'd put them on the bookcase, sandwiched between two books for safekeeping," said George.

"Only he couldn't remember which books, of course. It took ages to find them. We only just caught the train."

"So why did Gus let him stay with you?" asked the doctor. "Lombroso must have some redeeming features."

"Well, as I saw at the conference, he is very eminent in his field," said George. "And of course he is a friend of the contessa. My brother has found a lady friend in Florence."

"I wouldn't be surprised if he stayed there for quite some time, just to be near her," added Montmorency.

Farcett was intrigued. "She must be quite a woman. I wouldn't mind making a trip to Florence just to see her. Are you all planning to return soon? I'll come with you."

There was a frisson between the other three, well aware that Florence was the last place Frank could visit.

"I think we'll stay put for a while," said Montmorency.

"Rubbish," said Farcett. "You can't stay in one place for long. I bet you're on your travels again in the New Year. But I'm off to bed. And if you'll take a doctor's advice, you three will do the same."

"I'm sure we will, Robert," said George. "You have the bathroom first, and we'll follow you up."

Robert left the room. They heard him say good night to Vi, who was still washing up in the kitchen. Then, when Fox-Selwyn could tell from his footsteps on the stairs that he was out of earshot, he spoke.

"You haven't told Robert about Frank?"

"No. Nobody here knows. I thought that was the safest thing," Montmorency replied.

"Safe and simple on Tarimond, perhaps, but Farcett is going to have to know if we go back to London, or he might unintentionally say something that lands us all in the soup."

"Are we going to London?" asked Frank.

George turned to his nephew. "Yes, Frank, we are," he said. "I know it's late, but we have got some serious talking to do."

CHAPTER 18

≫

INFORMATION

*Y*ou're a lucky man, Frank," said Fox-Selwyn sternly. "If Britain had signed up to that agreement, your description might be on its way to Scotland Yard now. As it is, I think we can be fairly confident that you've got away with your little escapade, at least as long as you stay away from Florence."

"Believe me, Uncle, I've got no intention of going back."

"But you are coming to London. I'm going to need your help with the rest of this investigation. I've done a lot of thinking while I've been on my own, and it seems to me we can't let the matter of Astleman's theft drop, even if he wants us to. That robbery never made sense, not as a purely criminal act."

"You mean, why did that collector, Pontini, commission the theft, only to give the goods away?" asked Montmorency.

"Well, that, but a lot of other things, too. I think the professor tried to alert us to it once. Don't you remember? Lombroso suggested that Pontini might have been an innocent dupe."

"But how does that change things?"

"It opens up the possibility that the theft had a political motive."

"What? Beetles, worms, and jellyfish — political?"

"No. Consider this. It's just a theory at the moment, but I

think it fits together. A group of political activists in Florence needs to raise some money. We already know that one of them is a student of natural science — the man arrested after the firebombing at La Specola. Perhaps he had links with another, a graduate working in London. . . ."

Montmorency saw where the story was going. "Lopello, Lord Astleman's assistant?"

"Exactly. Let's say that this Lopello is a driving force in this Italian anarchist group. They are planning something big — I don't know what — but they need money, and they need Lopello to come back to Florence to coordinate things. He comes up with a plan. One of his contacts in Florence poses as a dealer, offering Pontini new specimens for his collection. Pontini pays and covers the fare for Lopello to bring the items to Florence from London. The anarchists are reunited and have the cash to finance their plan."

"But why does Pontini give his collection away?" asked Montmorency.

Frank intervened. "Because he knew he was ill, and he wanted the collection properly looked after when he died."

"No, Frank," said George, "you're only partly right. I thought that, but if he'd known he was terminally ill, he'd never have bought the specimens in the first place. I think something happened. That he found out what was going on and either killed himself or was murdered."

Montmorency jumped in with an idea of his own. "Or perhaps the anarchists told him he was involved in a crime and blackmailed him until he took his own life."

Fox-Selwyn paused for a moment. "I hadn't thought of that. . . ." he said. "Yes, it's a possibility. That way the anarchists would raise even more money."

"But money for what?" said Frank. "What were they planning to do? One man stabbing the empress can't have cost a fortune. It wouldn't have been worth all those risks, and they wouldn't have had to bring someone over from England to do that."

George was glad that Frank had seen the point. "You're right, Frank. And you understand what that means? They may still be planning something."

"And we may be able to stop it," said Montmorency. "Shall we go back to Florence and tell the police?"

"No," said Fox-Selwyn. "We can't do that. You're forgetting that I was part of the delegation that turned its back on the Rome agreement. The Italian authorities are not going to look kindly on a half-baked freelance initiative by a couple of amateurs from England. We haven't enough evidence, and we can't risk exposing Frank's part in all this."

"But I didn't mean to do anything!" insisted Frank.

"You may not have meant to, Frank, but you did," said Fox-Selwyn sternly. "And you can make up for it by helping us. I had a discreet word with the authorities in London about it all. But it's not the same these days. They're all obsessed with events in Africa. They didn't want to hear about something new. Humored me. Pretended to listen. But they obviously thought I was deep into some fantasy. Said they were too busy to follow it up until they had something more concrete to go on. So we're on our own with this one. But I've got a powerful feeling about it. You know, Montmorency, that special twitch you feel when there's something out there?"

"Oh, I know all right. I had it right back at the beginning, remember? I was the one who wanted to ignore Lord Astleman and dig a bit deeper."

"Well, let's not get into a competition about our instincts. Perhaps I was wrong then. But if you're with me now, I think we'd better get down to work. We'll have to go gently. We haven't got any official cover this time."

Montmorency turned to Frank. "Oh, I'm all for it. But George is right, Frank. We won't be able to do it without you. You've got more inside information on the Italians than either of us."

George agreed. "I've got some questions to ask you now, and then when we can get a boat back to the mainland, you're coming with us to London. We've got to get inside the Italian community there, and your command of the language is good enough now for you to be able to help. But first, I want you to think back to those nights you spent with your 'friends' in Florence. Tell me everything, no matter how trivial it seems to you. Who did they talk about? What did they say? What did you do?"

And, ashamed at how stupid his youthful fun sounded when spelled out in retrospect, Frank told George and Montmorency about the firebrands in the bar. He described the flyer-posting. He even admitted to his meeting with Malpensa in Milan.

Fox-Selwyn turned on Montmorency. "You let him go off on his own in Milan?" he shouted. "You were supposed to be looking after him!"

Frank came to Montmorency's defense. "He knew nothing about it. And Uncle George, you've got to accept that I'm not a child."

Fox-Selwyn looked at his nephew. The skinny redheaded boy had matured into a strapping young man. But Frank still had a lot to learn. He could not be blamed for his naïveté in the face of sophisticated political activists. Frank's European tour with his father and brother was his first excursion outside the gentle world of Glendarvie and the narrow confines of a Scottish private school. Fox-Selwyn wondered if Frank had given his exciting friends a clue to his real identity. Was it possible that as well as being wanted by the police, he could be the target of the anarchists, wanting his money, or worse still, planning to silence him?

"No, Uncle. They knew me only as Frank. I didn't tell them where I lived. I just enjoyed their company, and I think they enjoyed mine. It was nice to be with people who wanted to be my friends because of me — not just because of my name."

"But you know you must tell me all about them. However affectionate you felt towards them, whatever loyalty you feel, it's important that you don't hold anything back. Did they ever mention money, or contacts abroad?"

Frank thought hard. "They talked a lot about someone called Paterson. They used to send things to him. Magazines, newspapers, books, and so on." Frank paused. He'd heard that name "Paterson" somewhere else. It suddenly came back to him. "I remember when I went to see Malpensa in Milan, he asked me if Paterson had sent me."

"And who is this Paterson? Where does he live?" asked George, getting excited.

"I don't know. But I remember them saying that the postage was expensive when they sent him parcels."

"Concentrate, Frank. Did they say anything else about where those parcels were going? Did they ever get anything from him?"

Frank closed his eyes and imagined himself back in a smoky bar in Florence. He could remember sharing some soft salty bread with his friends, dipping it into fragrant olive oil spiced with crushed peppercorns, and washing it down with rough red wine. "They were expecting something, I think," he said. "I remember someone saying something about a boat being delayed."

"A boat. So this thing he was sending was coming by sea," said George.

"Across the Mediterranean?" wondered Montmorency. "Or the Adriatic?"

"But this man's called Paterson," said George. "Isn't it much more likely that he's English?"

"And that the boat was crossing the Channel?"

"That would explain the high cost of postage. They'd have

to pay more to get things to England than to mainland Europe," said George. "Well done, Frank, you've given us a lead. And tomorrow we'll start planning what we're going to do about it."

"So Robert was right," said Montmorency, as he rose to go up to bed at last. "We're on the move again."

CHAPTER 19

≫

DEPARTURE

*T*he next morning, Christmas Day, everyone felt the worse for wear, but they blamed it on the party, and bore their headaches with good grace. George had brought presents from London and gave them out over a very late breakfast. Vi was thrilled with her earrings and kept them on even when she went out to feed the chickens. Maggie Goudie gratefully wrapped herself in a soft paisley shawl. Montmorency and Doctor Farcett put aside the bottles of wine he gave them for a time when everyone felt better able to face alcohol again. Frank was grateful for a new pair of gloves, though the leather was far too fine for him to contemplate using them on Tarimond. George himself was subdued, and as everyone else's spirits rose during the day, his declined further. He went to bed early, and the next day Robert Farcett diagnosed his high temperature, aching joints, and shivering as the early stages of the flu. He broke the news gently, well aware of the feelings it would arouse in Frank, who had lost his mother to the disease less than a year before. He took Montmorency aside.

"You're going to have to put off your trip to London. George won't be fit to travel for a while, and anyway, I may need you here. He's brought a very nasty bug to the island, and that party last night will have been the ideal place to spread it. I think we should stand by for an epidemic, and I'm not sure if Maggie and I will be able to cope on our own."

Montmorency was torn. Fox-Selwyn had whetted his appetite for getting back to London, and like George, he sensed that they might be on to something important, even if they had no real evidence to prove it. What if some dangerous plot were under way, and they had it in their power to stop it? Could he ever forgive himself for staying on Tarimond? Should he leave George and carry on in London alone? He told Farcett the whole story and asked his advice. The doctor was sure of his reply.

"You have to balance priorities, Montmorency. You know that there is trouble here on Tarimond; that people, people you know, may — probably will — die if you don't stay and help. Your dearest friend is sick. He needs you. Against this, you have the pursuit of a theory that may be right, and which may — *may* — manage to undermine some political plot. If it exists."

"Ah, but if it does exist, it may be of tremendous consequence," said Montmorency. "It may bring its own trail of death, to countless people, who knows, perhaps more than the whole population of Tarimond."

"Yes, but one is certain, the other is not. It's your choice," said the doctor.

Montmorency walked out to the cliff top and watched the sea pounding the ancient rocks. After half an hour, he made his way back to the infirmary. "I'll stay and help," he said. "But what if we catch the flu, too?"

"We'll cross that bridge when we come to it," said Farcett, gratefully clasping his friend's shoulders. "But it's a funny thing, you know. We medical men have a way of escaping these things. I think we must build up immunity from seeing so many patients. But island people pay a high price for being protected from the diseases we meet all the time. When a new illness strikes, it strikes hard."

Robert was right. The virus passed rapidly across the island. By the time Lord George Fox-Selwyn started to feel better, most of his party guests were taking to their beds. Montmorency, Frank, and Vi stayed well, but Maggie Goudie, though never going under completely, grew pale and weak. Nevertheless, she continued visiting the sick with herbal remedies and comforting words. Doctor Farcett was so busy that Maggie didn't trouble him with her own symptoms. Beneath her clothes, her skin was dry and peeling. When she combed her hair, white strands came away. She was feeling her age, but with so much suffering around her, she struggled not to show it.

The flu was worst for the very old and the very young. Montmorency's old friend Morag, who had led him to Tarimond years ago, lost both her grandparents. Their joint funeral was a sad occasion for everybody. But the worst moment came with the death of a baby. There was a time on

Tarimond when infant deaths had been expected. For seven years, none had survived, until Doctor Farcett had arrived from London and found the cause. Now the island had gone for more than a decade without losing a child.

The sight of a tiny coffin being lowered into the ground was too much for some of the islanders to bear. For a few, it brought a change in their attitude to the visitors. The gratitude towards them for saving a generation was replaced by resentment of Lord George Fox-Selwyn for introducing the killer disease. There was criticism of his grand house on the headland, and suggestions that Tarimond had been better off before the newcomers arrived. Even so, George, Montmorency, and Frank stayed on the island well after George was fit enough to travel, helping Maggie, Vi, and Doctor Farcett to tend the sick and comfort the bereaved.

But they were glad when at last, in the earliest days of spring, there were no new cases. The surviving victims were recovering, and it seemed safe for them to set off for the mainland.

"Do you mind if I go with them?" Doctor Farcett asked Maggie. "I want to get the latest X-ray journals and some new tubes and electrodes. I might even get a cine camera, too. I think we're almost at the point where we can start experimenting with committing images to film. And of course I could write about our experiences here. There's a new medical magazine that would probably be interested in a study of infection in a closed community. . . ."

Maggie could see that no word from her could keep Robert

on the island. She had always loved his enthusiasm, even his ambition, though at times she had thought that it stopped him living in the moment and enjoying what he already had. She had heard Farcett's fine words to Montmorency about priorities when George had first fallen ill, and had hoped it signified a shift in his own way of looking at the world. But she knew he had already made up his mind to leave and calmly interrupted him.

"It's fine, Robert. You go. I can cope perfectly well now." She managed to keep an even tone of voice, though she had to turn and pretend to start sorting bandages in the store cupboard to hide her true feelings.

"Right, then, I'll just go and tell the others," said Farcett, grabbing his hat and setting off for the big house, his mind humming with the things he could do in London.

Maggie sat down and rocked her body gently to try to lessen the pain in her chest.

Montmorency was just as excited about going, and he wanted to add someone else to the party. He thought it was time that Vi's son, Tom, had a chance to see London, his mother's hometown. Montmorency had sat night after night at Tom's bedside while he had struggled with the flu and had promised himself that he would look after the boy if he survived. Like so many young people, Tom had bounced back in no time. Montmorency asked Vi if she would let Tom go. At first her face drained at the idea of losing her little boy, but then she thought for a minute, smiled, and answered.

"He can go. But on one condition."

"And what's that?"

"Only if he wants to, and so long as I can come as well."

She was surprised at the eagerness with which Tom agreed to the idea. But she was glad and started making mental shopping lists straightaway.

So the six of them — George, Montmorency, Frank, Robert Farcett, Vi, and Tom — prepared to leave. The big house would be empty for the first time ever, and Vi was busy for two days: cleaning, tidying, and covering the furniture with dust sheets. There were so many passengers that they needed two boats to get them to another island where they could pick up a steamer. Despite all their efforts packing and planning, in the end it was a scramble to catch the tide. Morag and several other friends came to the beach to see them off. At the last minute, with one boat gone, and Vi and Tom already onboard the second, a small boy arrived with a note from Maggie Goudie, saying she felt unwell, and was sorry she could not be there.

"I should go and see her," said Doctor Farcett. "I wonder what's wrong?"

"Come along!" shouted the boatman. "We must leave now, or you'll have to wait till tomorrow."

"Get in, Robert," called Vi, unaware of the note or its contents.

"I'll go to Maggie straightaway," said Morag reassuringly. "She's probably just a bit tired."

Tom joined in his mother's urgent yelling, and Farcett gave Morag a chaste farewell hug.

"Tell Maggie I'll be back soon," he said. "And make sure she gets plenty of rest. She must be exhausted after all her hard work."

"Of course," said Morag. "I'll take her a nice bowl of soup. She'll be her old self in a couple of days. Now you get off, before the tide turns."

"Good-bye, Morag," shouted Robert, as he finally clambered in. "Tell Maggie I'll write."

The boatman pulled on the oars, and they were away.

CHAPTER 20

≫

LONDON

*O*n the way to London, everyone tried to prepare Tom for the big city, warning him about the traffic, the dirt, and the noise. Lord George Fox-Selwyn, Doctor Farcett, and Montmorency all told him about how they had first met his mother, in her Covent Garden days. The three stories didn't quite match up, and Tom sensed that there were things they didn't want him to know. He wondered if any of them knew who his father was and what had happened to him, but he could never bring himself to ask. Sometimes he thought one of them was about to tell him. Then they would pull back and change the subject. Vi had already explained to him that Fox-Selwyn and Montmorency were involved in secret work. She had warned him of the dangers of accidentally giving away information. It was better, she said, not to ask and not to tell.

"And anyway," she'd added, "I've told you what my mum, your Granny Evans, used to say. 'Them as asks no questions isn't told no lies.' She was right there."

Tom was unconvinced. *Them as asks no questions isn't told anything at all,* he thought. But he got the message and decided to look and listen for clues about the past, rather than ask anyone directly.

They might have tried to warn Tom about the city, and his brief stops in Aberdeen and Edinburgh on the way to London might have given him some idea of what to expect, but Tom was completely overwhelmed by his first experience of London. He clung to his mother's coat as they walked through the enormous station, with lines of giant railway engines letting off violent hisses of steam. He had never seen so many people, and in such a hurry, pushing and jostling one another without a word of apology. The street outside was clogged with horses pulling omnibuses, carriages, and carts. The travelers hurriedly split into groups of two and took three cabs between them. Fox-Selwyn squashed in beside Vi, Farcett and Frank took the next one, and Montmorency told the driver of the third to go to Lord George Fox-Selwyn's house by way of the main tourist sites.

Tom had seen pictures of London in a book Doctor Farcett had once given him for a birthday, but everything looked different in the bright spring sunshine. Nevertheless he chipped in with tidbits his mother had told him about London over the years. As they passed through Parliament Square, with Big Ben to one side of them and Westminster Abbey to the other, Tom came out with the fact that the huge church had been founded by Edward the Confessor. But he quickly dropped the subject when he saw his first motorcar, driven by a man wearing goggles and a flowing scarf, who was honking his horn in a vain attempt to make the horses and carriages clear out of his way. A bit farther along, at the side of the road, a gang of men were hauling up buckets through a hole in the pavement.

"What are they doing?" asked Tom.

"They're cleaning out the sewers. They have to keep the underground pipes clean so all the sewage can run smoothly out to sea."

"What's sewage?" asked Tom.

"It's waste — you know, the stuff that goes down the lavatory. In London it runs away underground, through huge tunnels. Otherwise the streets would be full of filth."

"But the streets *are* full of filth!" said Tom, looking around at the horse droppings, mud, and paper that littered their path.

"Well, all I can tell you is that it could be worse. It's amazing down in the sewers. If you think the streets are full of rubbish, you should see what's down there. All sorts of things turn up in the sludge: clothes, tools, dead animals. . . ."

"How on earth could you know that? You're just making it up to frighten me!" said Tom.

"No, I've been down there. And your mother has, too."

"Don't be daft, she'd have told me that!"

Montmorency changed the subject, realizing that he had got perilously close to letting Tom into his deepest secret, and grateful for the knowledge that Vi had protected it. "Look," he said. "Buckingham Palace! That's where the queen lives when she's in London. They fly a flag from the top to show when she's there."

Tom was disappointed to see that the flagpole was bare.

"We won't be seeing the queen today, then."

As Montmorency spoke, a policeman stopped the traffic, and a carriage emerged from the main gates. A fat, elderly-looking man with a big bushy beard was inside. He waved limply to a gaggle of pedestrians on the sidewalk.

"Good heavens. That's the Prince of Wales!" said Montmorency. "People live here for a lifetime and never see him, and you've got a glimpse in your first half hour!"

Tom was impressed, far more excited by the man in the carriage than the stately building behind him. "Mam says he's called Edward the Caresser." He giggled, and Montmorency realized that Vi's lesson about the founder of the Abbey had been an explanation of her joke about the racy habits of the heir to the throne. He had a feeling that he and Tom could have a lot of fun exploring parts of London that didn't make it into the guidebooks.

When they arrived at George's house, they were greeted by Chivers, Fox-Selwyn's aging manservant. He seemed intrigued to make the acquaintance of Vi's child, studying his face with particular interest.

"Lunch is served, sir," he said to Montmorency, taking his hat and coat. "I think they may have started without you."

Montmorency made for the dining room. "Come on, Tom," he called to the bemused boy who was standing quite still, gazing at the paintings, the grand staircase, and the huge chandelier that hung in the entrance hall.

On Tarimond, Tom had often been teased by the other children for his lavish lifestyle. Living with Vi in Fox-Selwyn's specially built island hideaway, he had grown used to luxuries his friends could only imagine. The architect had added on a high "lookout tower" whose main purpose was actually to hide a water tank, giving the flow from a local spring enough pressure to power the shower and flush the lavatories that spewed their contents over the cliff and into the sea. People on Tarimond still spoke of the day Fox-Selwyn's furniture had arrived from the mainland and been hauled up the cliff on pulleys. Tom knew all about fire screens, antimacassars, and humidors for cigars. But the big house on Tarimond was primitive compared with Fox-Selwyn's home in town. Montmorency remembered his own awe when he, only a little older than Tom was now, had seen the trappings of high society for the first time. Now he hardly noticed them. How things had changed. Part of him longed to show this country boy the finer side of life. But he wondered for a moment if it might not do more harm than good, and whether he might be about to upset Tom's contented existence forever.

CHAPTER 21

≫

BACK TO BARGLES

*O*ver lunch, Vi went on and on about how much London had changed in the thirteen years she had been away. Afterward, Doctor Farcett left for his own house, and Vi volunteered to help Chivers with everyone's unpacking, taking Tom upstairs with her and leaving the others free to talk in private.

"We'd better get straight down to work," said Fox-Selwyn. "I'll have a word with some of my contacts at Scotland Yard about this man Paterson. See if they've got anything about him on file. In the meantime, Frank, you and Montmorency can look for Astleman's assistant, Lopello. I'll dig out the notes I made about him when we met Astleman. We had an address, somewhere north of Holborn, though the police couldn't find anyone who'd own up to knowing him. We need to get stuck in there to get results. It's a pretty poor area — mainly Italians."

"Perhaps I could get a job there?" suggested Montmorency.

Frank spluttered into his coffee. "*You?* Get a job? Fit in, in a rough area? I'd like to see it!"

"I think you'll be surprised at what Montmorency can do." Fox-Selwyn laughed. He turned to Montmorency. "Perhaps you'd better introduce Frank to our old friend Scarper."

"It's been a long time since I've seen him myself," said

Montmorency. "His clothes are all locked away in a trunk at Bargles. I hope they'll still fit."

Frank was confused by their conversation, but picked up at the mention of Bargles. Uncle George and Montmorency had often joked about wild nights they'd spent at that London gentlemen's club, where Montmorency had a room. "Bargles!" he cried. "Can I come with you to fetch them?"

"We'll all go," said Fox-Selwyn. "I left a hat there when I dropped in on my way through London after the conference. I might as well pick it up."

So they all set off, through the park, to the tiny door that led to Bargles's secret world. Unusually, there was no one in the little kiosk by the entrance to greet them and check that only members and their guests came in.

"I'll sign for you anyway," George said to Frank, reaching over the desk and filling in the visitors' book. There were no other entries for that day. "Looks a bit quiet," mused George. "I wonder where everyone is?"

A flustered servant rushed through a door at the end of the passage, wiping his hands on his apron.

"Good afternoon, my lord, and Mr. Montmorency, sir," he said. "How nice to see you again."

"You, too, Sam," said Fox-Selwyn. "And may I introduce my nephew Lord Francis Fox-Selwyn." Sam nodded deferentially to Frank as George continued, "But what's up? Where's Sam?" he said, indicating the empty kiosk.

"Sick," said Sam. "We're terribly shorthanded. Half the

staff are off with the flu. Quite a few of the members, too, sir, though at least that means it's quieter than usual."

"Well, we won't be troubling you for much. Montmorency just needs to get something from his room."

"I think you'll find Sam's up on the top corridor with the keys. Otherwise he'll be mopping in Ploppers, or laying out in Eats Major. We're all doubling up, you see," said Sam.

Montmorency could see that Frank was confused, and whispered some explanations. "All the servants are called Sam; Ploppers is the lavatory downstairs, Eats Major is the big dining room."

"I see," said Frank. Though he wasn't sure he did.

They made their way upstairs to the bedrooms, where an elderly man was tottering along the hall carrying a pile of clean sheets that took up the whole of the space between his arms and his chin. He welcomed Montmorency, trying to execute a servile nod without dropping the linen. His eyes betrayed his panic as he asked, "Will you be staying, sir? Would you like me to make up your bed?"

"It's all right, Sam," said Fox-Selwyn. "I think Montmorency will be more comfortable staying with me for the time being. We just need to get some things from his room now. May I introduce my nephew Lord Francis Fox-Selwyn? He's only visiting today, but who knows, he may be a member in time."

"Honored to meet you, sir," said this other Sam. "I'm sorry your introduction to Bargles is in such unsatisfactory circumstances." The man sounded a little hurt at George's implied slur on his housekeeping. He propped himself against the wall and fumbled for a large bunch of keys that swung from his belt. "I'll just let you in, sir. I'm afraid I didn't know you were coming, or I'd have made a point of catching up on the dusting, sir." And the old man burst into a fit of coughing, bringing up phlegm, and swallowing it again, embarrassed at having nowhere to spit, and his betters looking on.

Frank held back a few steps along the hall watching and beginning to wonder whether he was really so keen to become a member of this ramshackle place. Another part of himself was appalled that Montmorency and his uncle were content for such a frail person to be burdened with so many tasks on their behalf. He was too shy to offer to help by taking the keys or the sheets. After all, he had never met this "Sam" before. But the others seemed to know him well, and they knew as well as he that the poor soul had to clean the lavatories and set the tables before his work was done.

When the door finally opened, after Sam's protracted efforts to find the keyhole, George and Montmorency pushed their way in past him, already chatting to each other about something else. It was left to Frank to thank the old man. He was horrified at the pathetic gratitude with which Sam acknowledged his words and took his leave, still carrying his unwieldy burden, off to make up beds in other rooms along the corridor, ready for any members who found themselves too drunk at the end of the evening to find their way to their own homes.

Inside Montmorency's room, the lid of the trunk was up, and Montmorency was throwing clothes onto the bed.

"What did you keep it all for?" asked Frank. "It's rubbish."

"Because it *is* rubbish," said Montmorency. "And as souvenirs, and — you know, 'just in case.'"

"Just in case of what?" asked Frank, amused by what looked like a dressing-up box for adults.

"Sometimes, in our line of work, we have to disguise ourselves," said Fox-Selwyn. "Montmorency does a good line in lowlife." He held up a smelly pair of trousers that could have done with a wash before they were packed away. "Go on, Montmorency. Put them on and show Frank."

Montmorency stripped to his underwear and started pulling on the old clothes. It wasn't long before he was regretting a hundred good dinners. There was no hope of the buttons fastening. "Oh well," he said. "It looks as if I'll have to get some more from somewhere. But you get the idea, Frank."

Fox-Selwyn held a jacket up against his nephew. "I think this would fit *you,* though, Frank. Why don't you have a go?"

Frank blushed at the idea of undressing in front of the others. George read his mind. "We won't look," he said, pulling Montmorency around to face the wall. "Give us a shout when you're ready."

Frank chose a shirt to go with the trousers and the jacket. He found a cap and a filthy neckerchief. He looked at himself in the mirror, made a few adjustments, and was pleased with the result. He felt comfortable dressed like this, more truly himself than in the starched collar and shiny shoes he had just taken off.

"All right," he said to the others, putting on a cockney accent. "You can look now. What do you think?"

Montmorency and Lord George Fox-Selwyn were speechless. Montmorency was reminded of the grubby character who had loped towards him at the sidewalk café in Milan. Fox-Selwyn recognized the man who stood before him, too. But it wasn't Frank. It was the young Scarper, all over again.

CHAPTER 22

≫

DRESSING DOWN

*V*i offered to go with Montmorency to buy replacements for his rough clothes. They went to a street market near where she used to live, and she squawked constantly, recognizing old haunts and criticizing new developments. Montmorency supplied the money but stood back as Vi haggled over the price of secondhand cloth caps, braces, and waistcoats. At first the traders laughed at her Scottish accent and tried to outsmart her in the bargaining, but she had lost none of her old London savvy, and stood her ground. Within a couple of hours her old voice was back, softened just a little by the gentleness of the north, and she was able to give Montmorency plenty of change. They disappeared around a corner for him to try on the boots she'd chosen, and once she knew the size was right, she got a couple more pairs. She even bought him underwear, just to be convincing: graying long johns and union suits with buttonholes all down the front, and not enough buttons to meet them. Montmorency didn't let himself think where the stains might have come from. They bought a tatty holdall to carry it all back to Fox-Selwyn's, and Vi insisted on a fashion parade in the very room where she had first dressed up for the men, years before.

Montmorency showed Frank how to change the way he walked, stood, placed his feet, used his hands. How to obliterate the habits, formed over years of unconscious training in the upper-class world, so that his new persona would be convincing.

"How do you know all this?" asked Frank, innocently reminding Montmorency of that other Frank — Freakshow — who had taught Montmorency how to achieve the reverse effect, years ago, in prison.

George instantly picked up on Montmorency's discomfort, recognizing the sudden stab of guilt about Freakshow's death that halted the conversation for the briefest of moments. He stepped into the gap.

"I've seen Montmorency in all sorts of guises," he said, jovially launching into an old story about posing as monks in the Balkans. "He's got a gift. He should have been an actor."

"I think I'd rather have been a singer. Imagine what it must be like to dress up and sing Verdi's *Otello*," and he burst into a rousing aria for a few seconds, until the others shut him up.

"But that's all earrings and armor," said Fox-Selwyn. "Tramps like you two don't get to sing the lead in grand opera."

"Yes, they do, Uncle George," Frank insisted. "*La Bohème* is full of people dressed up like this."

"I'm glad I didn't go all the way to Milan to see it, then," said George. "I can see plenty of people like you outside the opera house. I don't need to pay money for tickets to get in!"

"But Frank's got a point, George," said Montmorency. "And

it would be a good idea, Frank, to think back to that show. Remember what was convincing about the performances, and more important, what wasn't. Copy their good points, but avoid the mistakes."

Frank recalled the scene in the garret at the opening of the opera. He remembered the incongruity of the ragged clothes and the well-cut hair. But he also remembered the real squalor of Malpensa in his dingy room, the suspicion that had animated Malpensa's every movement, the threatening atmosphere he had generated with the tiniest gesture: denying eye contact when it was sought, enforcing it when it was not. Malpensa, he privately decided, would be his model for his foray into London's Italian society. He would be nice or obliging when it suited his needs: to get a job, a room, or meal; but he knew he might have to steal some of Malpensa's terrifying magnetism to get to the people with the information he really needed; the ones who might lead him to the elusive Mr. Paterson.

When he got back to his room that night, he put on Scarper's clothes and practiced in front of the mirror. He got the walk, the roll of the shoulders, the defensive, excluding snarl. But why did he find himself taking aim with an imaginary gun and jolting backward with the force of the recoil as he fired?

The next morning, Montmorency and Frank took an underground train to Farringdon Street Station, and walked north into the heart of London's Italian community. They had a clear plan, based on the way the old Scarper had operated, years before. The first task was to find a base, a room where their comings and goings would be masked by the activities of others. They would pose as father and son. Their command of spoken Italian was not good enough for them to pretend to be Italians, or even (with Frank's red hair) of Italian descent, but they were glad they could both understand the language well enough to listen to conversations around them. It would even be an advantage if other people believed they could not. So there was a ban on speaking Italian. No showing off, no practicing. They were native Englishmen, down on their luck.

But in reality, fortune was on their side. No sooner had Montmorency handed over the rent for the first week in a lodging house overlooking a railway track, than a chance came up.

"We're looking for work. I don't suppose you know of anything?" he asked as the landlord turned to go.

The old man eyed them up, assessing whether he could recommend these English strangers to a relative. "You don't mind an early start?"

"No. Not if we're paid for it. It will have to be enough to cover the rent, food, and so on."

The landlord still looked thoughtful. But in the end the promise of regular money from his new tenants outweighed the risk. "My cousin has an ice-cream factory. You can walk there from here. Turn right at the pub and then along the lane to the blue door. Tell him Giuseppe sent you." He shut the door behind him and shuffled down the stairs.

Frank was beaming. "An ice-cream factory! I think we've come to heaven."

Montmorency looked around the filthy room. Something black and crusty was skittering across the floor. He crushed it with his foot. "Not my idea of heaven, exactly. Do you want the top bunk?"

"Oh yes, please!" said Frank, swinging his backpack up onto his bed and raising a cloud of gray dust from the mattress. "Shall we go to the factory straightaway?"

"Might as well," said Montmorency, who was struggling with the window in the hope of freshening the stale air. "Don't get your hopes too high. They might not have any vacancies." He considered warning Frank about the likely physical appearance of the "factory," but thought it better for him to discover the reality of working life for himself. There was no point in lowering his spirits now.

So they set off, past the pub, down the lane, and came upon a door in a high brick wall. The paint was peeling off, but had, they thought, originally been blue. This must be the place. Montmorency turned the handle, and the door swung open on the one hinge that was still attached to the frame. It revealed a cobbled courtyard crammed with battered carts. In the far corner was another door with a dirty glass window to one side. Montmorency rubbed at it with his sleeve until he could see through. In the far distance, at the end of a corridor, he thought he could make out the shadows of people moving to and fro. The door wasn't locked.

"Follow me," he said to Frank. "Let's go in."

This time Montmorency was keen and Frank reluctant. Frank had imagined a sparkling tiled kitchen, enlivened by the chatter of Italian maidens, as they stirred huge pots of delicious creamy foam. This place was dark, it was damp, and it was dirty.

Montmorency saw his disappointment. "Come on," he said with more enthusiasm than he really felt. "This is perfect. Let's see if they'll take us on."

At the end of the corridor they found a messy office. Inside, at a desk facing the door, sat the owner, Signor Rossi, a fat man with greasy sideburns and a nasty rash on the hand he was using to hold a bulky, half-eaten sandwich. His other hand was ticking off entries in a large ledger. He finished the column before looking up at the unexpected visitors.

"We're looking for work," said Montmorency. "Giuseppe sent us." Rossi looked skeptical at first but was swayed by the mention of Giuseppe.

"I need strong men who won't complain — to load the stockroom, sweep up, and help on the carts," he said. "You staying at Giuseppe's?"

"Yes," said Montmorency. "The rent is . . ."

"I'll pay your rent direct and give you fourpence a day, every day I need you."

"Fourpence!" gasped Frank, too horrified to hold his tongue.

"We'll take it," said Montmorency, silencing Frank. He could see that Rossi wouldn't bargain. The grubby entrepreneur knew that the men would be cheaper to hire if he paid their rent direct and that they would be locked in as both workers and tenants by the deal.

Of course, the pay was irrelevant to them. What mattered was getting inside this community and mixing with people. But Montmorency was pleased by Frank's involuntary outburst. Rossi would have thought it showed how much they needed cash; even though for Frank the shock really lay in finding out how little money ordinary people were paid.

Two large men appeared at the doorway, all muscles, sweat, and hair. They had truncheons hanging from their belts, but they couldn't have looked less like policemen. They scowled at Montmorency and Frank.

"Sorry, Boss," said one. "Just slipped out for a minute. Must have missed these two getting in. I'll shift them for you." And he lumbered menacingly towards Frank, rolling up his sleeves.

"It's all right," said Rossi. "They're from Giuseppe. Looking for work." He turned to Montmorency. "Come back tomorrow morning. We start at four o'clock. You can help collect the ice from the docks."

Rossi's minders hustled Montmorency and Frank back to the gate.

"Yes, come back tomorrow, but watch yourselves. If you want to talk to the boss, you come through us, right?" said one.

"But you won't be causing us any trouble, will you?" sneered the other, cracking the joints in his fingers.

"We just want work," said Montmorency, with deliberate meekness.

"Four o'clock tomorrow, then. And don't be late, or you'll be out."

CHAPTER 23

≫

THE ICE-CREAM MEN

$\mathcal{J}$t had never occurred to Frank to wonder where the ice for ice cream came from. At Glendarvie, the servants harvested it when the ponds and streams were frozen and stored it for months in a deep, dark underground icehouse. Very occasionally, he and Alexander had been allowed to go down inside to bring out enough for Cook to use to keep utensils cold when she was making special desserts. In very hot summers the whole supply melted, and they had dared each other to venture through the tiny door into the empty, brooding cave. Here in London there were no crystal springs, and the quantities of ice required for industrial production must be massive. Rossi had mentioned the docks. Could it really be true that they got their ice from overseas?

They didn't have to wait long to find out, though it seemed an endless night. Montmorency couldn't sleep because of strange itches caused, he thought, by wildlife sharing his sagging mattress. On the top bunk, Frank was so afraid he would oversleep that he woke at every sound and counted the chimes of all the local clocks every hour. As it turned out, he had nothing to worry about. They weren't the only tenants who worked at Rossi's, and the whole house came alive in the half hour before they were due at the factory. They introduced themselves to the others at the front door. It was hard to tell if the coolness of their welcome was born of suspicion or just the early hour. As their little group made its way down the street they were joined by more and more workers. They were mainly Italian immigrants, but a handful of desperate Londoners were working at Rossi's, too. There were a few conversations and muted greetings, but the main sound was of boots on cobbles, as the reluctant workforce assembled for the day.

Asked his name, Montmorency reverted to one made up for him by Vi, years ago in Covent Garden. He was Bert. Frank was Frank.

"Surname?"

"Scarper," said Frank, before Montmorency could stop him.

They were told to help a man who was harnessing an elderly horse to a large wooden cart. When all was ready, they sat in the back as their boss for the day drove them towards the river. They avoided answering his questions by replying with questions of their own. Carlo was pleased to have someone to share his experience with.

"Where does the ice come from?" asked Frank.

"Norway," said Carlo. "They chop it up into chunks and send it across in huge ships."

"Doesn't it melt on the way?"

"It's all stored in holds under the water. The sea keeps it cold. We'll have to be quick getting back here though. Rossi doesn't want to pay to wash the streets of London."

Montmorency hadn't been back to the docks since his first days as Scarper, searching for tools for his life in the sewers.

Not much had changed, though the boats were bigger and the range of foreign accents wider than before. The Norwegian ship, with its precious cargo of ice, was already unloading. A huge claw was being maneuvered by a crane driver to pull out heavy blocks of ice from the bowels of the vessel. Carts were lined up along the quayside, ready to collect their loads. Most of them were adorned with the Rossi name.

"Blimey, how much ice does it take to produce ice cream?" asked Frank, wondering how on earth so much ice could be stored in the grubby little factory.

"It's not all for the works," said Carlo. "Most of it goes into Rossi's big ice well near the canal. He sells it to restaurants and hotels. Clever really. He persuades them to buy his ice cream, and then he makes them pay extra for the ice they need to stop it running away. Our load is for the factory, though. We'll smash it all up when we get back and put some in the sales carts and the rest in the kitchen."

They raced back with their load and set to work at once with hammers and chisels, breaking down the ice blocks into manageable chunks. The ice was hard and slippery, the chisels were heavy and sharp, and shards of ice found their way into their clothes, melting against their skin and leaving them wet and cold. Frank's hands were chapped and bleeding as he carried his first delivery into the kitchen. His arrival was greeted with loud whoops and cackles, as the women inside spotted a new face. One broke off from churning her creamy mixture and came across to him, stroking his face with her dirty hand.

"Ecco un bell 'inglese!" she giggled. Frank pretended he could not understand the compliment, and she obliged with a translation. "What a handsome Englishman you are!" She laughed, he blushed, and the others started teasing him about his red hair and his freckles. There were brief introductions and blown kisses. Frank was embarrassed at being the center of attention, but he knew he would have to put up with it if he was to get in with these women, close enough to hear about their other lives, beyond the factory, and whether any of them knew of Lopello or Mr. Paterson. He was pleased to see that they all assumed he could not understand Italian, even if so far the only secret he was able to find out by listening in was that at least one of the women really did find him attractive.

Suddenly the laughter stopped. The two ugly men he'd seen in Rossi's office the day before strode in, slapping truncheons against their palms, shouting in Italian. The jolly women shrank into cowed and frightened beings, frantically beating the mixture in their bowls to make up for lost time. Rossi's men toured the room, cursing at the girls to work faster, prodding and pushing them for no apparent reason. Frank was embarrassed to have been the cause of the trouble and tried to slip out unnoticed, but one of the men grabbed him by the hair and struck him across the back with his stick.

"Get out of here, you! Get back to the ice room. Any more of this and we'll cut your wages. And you can do an extra half an hour tonight as well."

An old woman caught Frank's eye, and her look of sympathy told him that the pain and humiliation were worth it. After the way he'd been treated, he would be accepted by the rest of them and be able to find out how this tight community worked.

For the rest of the afternoon, he came and went in silence, but he had the feeling he was among friends. At the end of the day, one woman took a chance and spoke again: just a few words of motherly encouragement to the boy. She could see he was exhausted after his first shift at Rossi's. But when she dipped her finger into a bowl of pink mixture and offered it to his lips, he had to resist. It wasn't just that her finger was dirty, or that he had seen her using it to pick her nose only a moment before. He could see one of her coarse black hairs floating in the thick liquid. Ice cream was beginning to seem less like the food of the gods.

The next day, Montmorency's taste for the stuff was lost forever, too. He was sent out with one of the street salesmen, to help on a regular pitch near the zoo. He could remember buying penny cones there years before, when Frank and Alexander were little and had visited their uncle George in town. How different it looked from the other side of the little three-wheeled cart. The ice-cream man taught him well, showing exactly how to measure out the right amount for each customer and how to position it in the paper tub so that it looked generous even though each scoop was calculated to produce the maximum profit for Signor Rossi. As he changed from one flavor to another, he wiped the spoon on a rag. To the customer this looked like a gesture of cleanliness. As the day wore on Montmorency saw that rag was used to wipe various parts of the ice cream man's body as well. The next day he was out again with the same man and the same unlaundered rag.

Over time, each of them got little bits of knowledge about the people they worked with and the lives they led. Montmorency and Frank swapped horror stories about their jobs. Frank described the kitchen, and some of the more unpleasant practices he had seen there. The bright pink of strawberry ice cream came not from fruit, but from a chemical dye in a bottle. The tiny seeds which made the raspberry variety seem so authentic were in fact wood shavings added specially for the purpose. Even the basic ingredients were suspect. The cream arrived in dirty pails, and the sugar stood in huge open tubs, which showed signs of being visited by vermin at night. Within a week, Montmorency, helping with the trade deliveries, had found out where Bargles Club and the Marimion Hotel got their ice-cream supplies. He thought back to expensive desserts he had eaten over the years at both establishments. Sometimes he had even asked for second helpings. Never again. But despite their disillusionment, Montmorency and Frank were pleased that they had found themselves in the ice-cream trade. Their fellow workers took them to their hearts and gradually introduced them to the activities of Italian émigrés in London.

They split up, making friends in different parts of the factory. Montmorency drank with the older men and played cards with them after work. Rossi's enforcers seemed to pick on Frank whatever he did, and he drew sympathy from other young workers, many of whom had been victimized themselves. After hours, they told him of their anger with Rossi, and their dreams of fighting back, or breaking away. But in the mornings their need for work and shelter kept them rising early to trudge down to the factory yet again.

"It's not fair," said Frank, as he told Montmorency yet another story of oppression.

"Of course it isn't. But it's the same everywhere, Frank."

"But it shouldn't be. It's wrong. Something should be done."

"Frank."

"What?"

"Be careful."

"I am careful. Rossi's men haven't caught me doing anything wrong this week."

"I mean, be careful with your friends. Watch you don't get sucked in to their cause. Remember what happened in Florence. We're here to observe, not to take part."

Frank understood. But he was still angry.

"I know," he said. "I can keep myself under control. But it still isn't fair."

One night they both came home with news of exciting invitations. Montmorency's was for the next Sunday. The driver on the delivery round had asked Montmorency to bring Frank and join his family for the Festival of Our Lady of Mount Carmel: the Italian community's big day for dressing up and eating fine food.

"It should be an excellent chance to talk," said Montmorency. "We can get them reminiscing about Italy and then steer them around to politics." He was proud of himself. "You never know what they might let slip when they've had a bit to drink."

But Frank thought he could go one better. "I'm going to a pub," he said.

"But you do that every night," teased Montmorency.

"No, not just any pub," said Frank. "Not the one down the road. I'm going to the White Hart." Montmorency looked unimpressed, and Frank continued. "The White Hart," he repeated, emphasizing each word. "On Tuesday." It was clear this meant nothing to Montmorency. "Don't you know who meets there on Tuesdays?"

Montmorency had to admit that this piece of information had not come his way.

"It's the Unione Sociale Italiana," said Frank.

"And what's that, then?" asked Montmorency lazily, still a bit peeved that Frank was so unexcited by his own news, that he'd wangled their way into the biggest Italian social event in London.

"Unione Sociale Italiana," Frank repeated. "You really don't know what it is, do you?"

"Should I?"

"Hasn't anyone at the factory told you? It's the welfare organization for the Italian workforce. It gives grants to the poor and tries to improve conditions. But there's more to it than that."

"And why should we get excited about it?"

"Because, Montmorency, it's the cover name for the anarchists! If anyone's going to give us a lead to this mysterious Mr. Paterson, they should, don't you think?"

CHAPTER 24

≫

CATCHING UP

They had planned, in any case, to pay a visit to Lord George Fox-Selwyn that night, to report on how things were going. Now the visit was more urgent, because Montmorency needed to commission Vi to get more secondhand clothes. He and Frank needed something respectable enough for St. Peter's Italian Church. Better clothes than their working outfits but not as fine as the things they normally wore. Vi understood at once and had great fun measuring up Frank with the tape from Doctor Farcett's bag.

She laughed. "I remember you measuring me and Mum with this once, Robert."

"What was he doing that for, Mam?" asked Tom.

Vi had forgotten her son was in the room and didn't fancy getting into a long explanation of her past relationship with the doctor. "We were dressing up. Helping Montmorency and George catch some villains."

"What sort of villains?"

"Bombers. One of them had stayed at my house."

"Weren't you scared?" asked Tom, a little frightened himself.

"Oh no. I didn't know who he was while he was with me. I was just involved because I could recognize him. I was never in any danger," she lied, as the memory of her desperate flight from the angry man started playing in her head. She tried to smile as she felt again the terror of cowering in the sewers with Montmorency, while the man ran about above, threatening to kill her. "Where is he now?" she asked Fox-Selwyn, trying to sound casual, though her mind was already running away with the thought that he might be on the loose in London, looking for her once again.

"Still safely inside," said George, recognizing her fear and patting her on the arm. "In fact, I went to see him the other day. He's been so good with information over the years, I wondered if he could shed any light on this Paterson man."

"And could he?" asked Montmorency.

"Not at all. He knew of a Paterson in prison, but that was the same man Scotland Yard put me on to. A swindler. Cheated old ladies out of their life savings. And anyway, he was locked up all through the time Frank's friends were sending things from Italy."

"Maybe they were posting them to the prison," suggested Frank.

"No, I checked all the records just in case. The only thing that man received was a Bible from his old vicar. He hadn't even been visited. I think our Mr. Paterson is someone else. Still on the loose."

"But Scotland Yard don't know him?" asked Farcett.

"Drawn a complete blank. Just as they did with Lopello. There's nothing in their files. I tried fishing at a drinks party at the Italian embassy, but got nowhere. They seem pretty confident that the Italian community here is hardworking and docile. Not much insurrection here, in their view."

"Well, they would say that, wouldn't they?" said Vi, putting into words what everyone else was thinking.

"It doesn't mean they're not right," said Montmorency. "We've been working pretty hard, haven't we, Frank?"

"They're all too tired to fight back, if you ask me."

And the conversation turned to the inner workings of the ice-cream industry. By the end, Vi was regretting buying Tom a cornet outside the Tower of London. She spent the rest of the evening waiting for him to be sick.

"Don't be silly, Vi," said Doctor Farcett. "The boy has a wonderful constitution. It will take more than a scoop of ice cream to knock him out. Look at the way he fought off the flu on Tarimond."

"Just as well he had it there," said Fox-Selwyn. "It's still rampaging through Bargles."

"It's the very end of the infection," said Farcett. "It should die down now until next winter. I don't think we'll be losing anybody else. And by the way, I've had some good news today. The editor of *The Physician* has accepted my article about influenza on Tarimond for his next edition. He said the statistical analysis was first-rate." He could see Montmorency's lips curving into a smile and, realizing that he was slipping back into his old, ambitious ways, changed the subject. "And I'm sure that ice cream has done Tom here no harm at all."

Even so, Farcett inconspicuously kept an eye on him for the rest of the evening.

Far away, on Tarimond, Morag was writing a letter. It was the hardest she had ever had to compose. In the little island school her teacher, and later friend, Maggie Goudie, had assigned copying tasks using a textbook that gave examples of all sorts of correspondence, covering occasions the children of Tarimond were never likely to meet. Thanks to Maggie, Morag knew exactly how to book a hotel room, complain about shoddy service, or accept a formal wedding invitation. But she was struggling now. She had never had to break news like this. After several false starts, she decided that a straightforward beginning, getting the bad news into the open, would be best.

Tarimond
16 July 1899

Dear Doctor Farcett,
It is with great pain that I write to tell you that our dear Maggie is dead. She passed away just before dawn this morning. I hope it will be of some comfort for you to know that her last words were of love for you.

I know that you left Tarimond believing that Maggie had caught the flu while nursing the sick. I feel it is my duty, since you are a medical man, to tell you in detail exactly how she died. For it is my opinion that she did not have the flu and that you may be able to tell from her symptoms exactly what was wrong.

After you left, her tiredness and shortness of breath grew with every day. Her hair thinned, and every morning strands lay across the pillow, until at last I had to cover her bald head with a cap. Her skin flaked away, too. When I washed her I could see that it was as if her body had been burned. There were blisters and infection and no sign of healing no matter how many creams and lotions I applied. None of the flu victims looked like that.

Maggie's last days were full of pain, though the Good Lord took away her reason at the very last, and I am sure that her suffering was lessened by her confusion. By the end, she did not know me, but she still talked of you, lovingly, and constantly.

I am very sad to be the person who must send you this news. Maggie will be buried in the churchyard tomorrow. By the time you get this letter her death will be well in the past, but I shall still be thinking of you and praying for you every day, and trust that your own heartache at this news will be supportable.

I had always secretly hoped that you might marry Maggie and settle here with us. I know Maggie understood how important your work is to you, and she would never have wanted to stand in your way. But in case she never told you, I feel I must take it upon myself now to let you know on her behalf how much she loved you, and how much she would still wish you to be happy, however upset you may be by her loss.

Please forgive me for talking so straight, but I feel I owe it to my old friend Maggie. Passing on her love is the final service I can do for her.

I would be grateful if you would be so kind as to take on the task

of breaking this sad news to Lord George Fox-Selwyn, Mr.
Montmorency, and our other friends who are with you in London.

    I am, sir, your most humble servant,

    Morag

Morag sealed and addressed the letter, rightly guessing that the most certain way to get it to Doctor Farcett was to send it care of Lord George Fox-Selwyn in London. As dinner was being served to the happy gathering in that smart London house that night, Morag put the envelope in her apron, ready to pass it on to the next person setting off in the direction of the mainland. Once or twice she wondered if she should rewrite it, cutting out the part at the end, which she knew was more forward than might be thought appropriate. But she still had it with her when she heard a boat was leaving, and she handed it over intact. Deep in a damp wool pocket under a waterproof cape, the letter started its long, uncertain journey on its way to break a heart.

CHAPTER 25

≫

FITTING IN

After three months' hard work at the factory, the Festival of Our Lady of Mount Carmel marked the full acceptance of Montmorency and Frank by their new Italian friends. It centered on a new church, St. Peter's in Clerkenwell Road, snuggled in amid the slums, but built in the grand continental style, with pillars, arches, and statues. The choir included several professional singers, and for Montmorency, the smell of the incense and intensity of the music made him feel as if he were actually performing in one of his beloved Italian operas. There was a huge procession through the streets, with cheap Italian wine on sale everywhere, and then a vast lunch, shared by all the generations, with course after course taking them happily into the evening. Frank and Montmorency staggered back to their little room full of affection for their workmates, who would share their hangovers at work in the morning. But though they had picked up all sorts of useful background there were no mentions of Lopello, or the mysterious Mr. Paterson, and no sign of anyone who might be he. Indeed, Montmorency and Frank were flattered to see that they were just about the only Englishmen allowed anywhere near the feast.

≫ ≫ ≫

Monday was hard. Tuesday was even harder for Frank, who had a long day, driving around London on a cart, with fresh supplies for the street vendors, selling ice cream to hot tourists all over London. It was a battle to keep everything cold in the searing July heat. Frank stuffed old rags under the melting ice and used them, one by one, to mop his face as he labored through the traffic. Even so, his eyes stung as the salty sweat dribbled into them. All the long day he was thinking about the pub that night, hoping that at last there would be a breakthrough, that they could move on to the next stage of their hunt, and that he would not be an ice-cream deliveryman forever.

"Why can't I come?" said Montmorency angrily, as Frank started getting ready to go to the White Hart.

"It just wouldn't look right."

"But I can understand the language, I could listen in. With two of us there, there'd be twice the chance of picking something up."

"Montmorency, I know you don't want to miss it, but can't you see, I've got to go on my own. They think you're my father."

"So?" said Montmorency.

"You don't go to the White Hart with your father. It's for young people."

"Are you saying I'm old?"

"Yes . . . no." Frank didn't want to hurt Montmorency's feelings. "Not really old. Just too old for this. And anyway,

Luigi has asked me as his friend, not for any political reason. I think he just wants to show off a bit. If you're not there, they're less likely to suspect me; more likely to think that I'm just a stupid boy; that I haven't picked up enough Italian to work out what they're talking about."

"Perhaps you've got a point there," said Montmorency, flinging himself down onto the bottom bunk. "All right, I'll stay here. But be careful. Don't do or say anything that might give away who you really are. And try to be back by eleven, or I'll worry."

"All right . . . Dad." Frank laughed. "But you don't need to worry. You can trust me. I can look after myself."

Montmorency lay back with his hands behind his head. He didn't feel old, but he had to admit that the youngsters were getting older. Here was Frank, off on his first solo mission; and young Tom was growing up, too. Montmorency hoped he'd have time, when he left the ice-cream world, to show Tom more of London, perhaps even tell him a bit more about his own past, and see if he fancied coming along on a job or two.

At first Frank was a bit disappointed. The White Hart wasn't seething with danger and menace; it was full of jovial people out for a drink after a hard day's work. In the summer heat, some had spilled out onto the sidewalk, bringing a table with them, and a crowd was gathering around a game of cards. It took him a while to find Luigi, his friend from the factory, who bought him a beer and chatted easily about his family, and the heat. Then some slightly older men arrived, and the mood changed. The volume of chatter dropped and drinkers moved cautiously out of the way of the new arrivals, so they could get to the bar. The men went upstairs with their drinks, and Luigi nudged Frank gently, indicating that they should follow. The narrow stairs led to a small room with a large table in the middle. There weren't enough chairs, and Frank and Luigi were sent down to get some stools from the bar. Frank was surprised to find how willingly the drinkers parted with their seats, as if he had a perfect right to take them. The men upstairs certainly commanded respect. Possibly even fear.

One of the men took out a large leather-bound book and a pencil, and entered the date on a new page. At the head of the table a muscular man in a dirty shirt seemed ready to take charge. He looked around, taking in who was there. He stopped when he got to Frank, concentrating on his face and then casting his eyes towards Luigi, who gave the smallest of nods. It was enough to vouch for Frank's trustworthiness, and the chairman threw Frank a welcoming smile. Then he called the meeting to order, speaking in very fast Italian and asking the man with the ledger to speak about donations given to the local poor. As each family was mentioned, people around the table chipped in with bits of gossip. Apparently there had been some domestic dramas during the celebrations on Sunday. Husbands had walked out, wives had been slapped, engagements had been announced, and a baby had been born prematurely. That family needed money for a decent

171

funeral. It didn't sound very political to Frank, and he began to think that his hopes for the evening had been too high.

Then there was a furtive tap on the door, and the chairman went over and opened it a crack. There were mumbles, and he left the room. The mundane atmosphere of the meeting turned to a mixture of excitement and confusion. It seemed that the inner circle, who had arrived with the chairman, were expecting something. They sat silent while others tried to start conversations to fill the quiet. Down below there was a click from the back gate, the creak of a door, and then irregular footsteps on the stairs. The chairman reappeared. "He's here!" he whispered, and the men around the table bristled with excitement as a tall figure entered, though many, including Luigi, seemed uncertain as to what was going on, or who this visitor was. The newcomer's face was obscured by a wide-brimmed hat. He walked with a limp and a stick. Someone quickly gave up a chair to let him sit down. The silence continued, tinged with a hushed reverence. The man took off his hat and laid it on the table. There was no introduction. None was needed. The men recognized him from photographs or assumed from the reaction of their fellows that he was someone very important indeed.

It was obvious to Frank that they were being visited by a true celebrity — probably a wanted man, on the run in the interests of their cause. It could have been awkward for Frank, the only person there who had no means of guessing who this special person might be. Except Frank did know, and his head was spinning with competing ideas about how to react.

The moment the man took his hat off, Frank recognized him from the filthy flat in Milan. It was Malpensa.

As pleasantries were exchanged around the table, Frank was racking his brains to reconstruct the story he had told his friend. He had cultivated their friendship at the factory, when he saw that Luigi was an organizer, a complainer, the sort of person who might be in with political agitators. To sustain the link, Frank had painted himself as a malcontent, too, but the identity he had given himself had been entirely English. He'd said he'd never been to Italy. What if Malpensa recognized him and spoke of their meeting in Milan? Would that add to his credibility or leave him utterly exposed as a liar and possible spy? He kept quiet and listened, hoping that if Malpensa spotted him he would register only familiarity and not remember the context in which they had met before. With luck, all would be well. He must calm down and pay attention. He might learn something to report back to Montmorency after all.

"So, Malpensa," said the chairman, in thick Italian, "what news do you bring from Milan?"

"Our organization is still compromised after the riots. We have to go carefully. We know we are being watched. We are confining ourselves to supporting those who lost loved ones in the outrage last year. Thank you for your own contributions to the relief effort."

"We will give more, if you need it," said the chairman, to general agreement from the meeting.

The man with the ledger started adding a column of

figures. He took off his hat and turned it upside down. "Our funds are low, perhaps we can have a collection now," he said, putting his hand into his pocket and pulling out a few coins before passing around the hat.

"Thank you. The savage attack by the army on an unarmed crowd has left many victims," said Malpensa, raising his walking stick. "I myself was wounded, as you can see. Our brothers in Florence have taken on much of our work."

Did he give Frank a special look? Frank wasn't sure. He struggled to seem no more or less interested in the news than anyone else. Malpensa continued: "We lost one brother, Milo, jailed for life after the death of a policeman in September." Frank realized at once that he must be wanted for murder, too, and that Guido must still be on the run.

Malpensa confirmed it: "Our comrade, Guido, escaped; along with a British man."

There was a pause. Malpensa really did look at Frank this time. Frank could feel his face coloring up as others followed Malpensa's gaze. He fought to stay calm, not to reveal a flicker of reaction. He said nothing. He sensed approval from Malpensa. Frank hoped his silence was interpreted by Malpensa as strength — a sign that, here in London, he had not risked betraying his colleagues by boasting of his exploits in Florence.

Malpensa spoke again, sending Frank a coded message of recognition and confidence. "We believe the Englishman has left Italy, and that he has not talked." Now Frank fought not to show his relief.

Someone spoke from the floor: "And Guido?"

"Guido is safe," said Malpensa. "He will be able to help us with our revenge. We sent him to Paterson."

Paterson. At last, a mention of the man Frank had been trying so long, and so fruitlessly, to trace. His mind started racing. Should he try to collar Malpensa after the meeting to find out more about Paterson, perhaps even arrange an introduction? For now he continued listening as Malpensa launched into a polemic about the need to keep the memory of the Milan atrocity alive, to avenge it, and to support those working for the cause. The hat was filling up with coins. Frank dipped into his own pocket and gave generously, desperate to fit in.

"Now, let us talk of your own plans," said Malpensa, calming down. "Is everything in place for the strike?"

"We have not fixed a date, but it will be soon," said the chairman. "We want to hit Rossi in the summer, when he makes most of his profit. The will is there. All his workers suffer from his meanness and his greed. Our problem is fear. So many at the factory live in rooms that belong to Rossi's cousin. If they lose their jobs, they lose their homes as well."

"But Rossi must be crushed," insisted Malpensa. "He works against us here, and his family undermines us in Italy. He makes the workers afraid to stand up against oppression everywhere."

Malpensa spoke on, and Frank found himself caught up in the force of his oratory. Even in that shabby room back in Milan, Frank had found Malpensa's sour resentfulness intoxicating. In front of this bigger audience Malpensa had more charisma, using all the music of the Italian language to champion the rights of the small man, the worker, and condemn the crushing profiteering of the rich, sucking the energy from the souls of the masses. Frank fought at first to hold back, to stay an observer, but after his own experiences working for Rossi he agreed with much of what Malpensa said, and effortlessly joined in the shouts of agreement from the men around him. He even found himself thumping the table when Malpensa railed against the role of governments, all governments, in stifling the potential of the people. He felt the old excitement that had gripped him while drinking in the bars of Florence and passing firebombs to Guido at the window of La Specola. Luigi wrapped an arm around Frank's shoulders, and they exchanged a look of exhilarated defiance. Frank fit in perfectly. Because he didn't have to act.

But the revolutionary spell was broken by a scream from down in the bar, and a rush of heavy footfalls on the stairs. Frank feared that the police had come to break up the meeting, but as the door swung back hard against the wall he saw two familiar faces: the hard men who protected Signor Rossi as he went about his day. The men around the table panicked. Someone wrenched off the tablecloth and threw it over Malpensa to try to disguise him. Others leaped from the open windows into the street.

Frank dived down into the dark under the table just as the heavy leather-bound book hit the ground beside him, displaced by the flying cloth. He grabbed the book and whacked the legs of one of the heavies advancing on Malpensa, forcing him to the floor. Malpensa was hustled over the flailing man and out to the stairs. Frank stayed where he was and tripped Rossi's men again as they tried to reach the door. He heard the click of the back gate and knew that Malpensa had got away. Rossi's henchmen were back on their feet now, one chasing down the stairs in vain pursuit of Malpensa, the other lashing out at the Italians who were left in the room. Frank stayed where he was, watching the frantic men pressing towards the windows. He rolled and shuffled himself to the door and down the stairs. Soon he was out of the back gate, too, still clutching the book. He ran home, ready to tell Montmorency everything he had heard.

"We must go," he gasped, as he ran into the room. "We must leave here. Immediately."

Montmorency got up from his bunk and tried to calm Frank. "Sit down and get your breath back, and tell me everything, slowly."

Frank ran through the events in the pub, telling the story backward, starting with the raid by Rossi's men. Montmorency tried to piece it all together in a logical order.

"So this Malpensa. Why had he come?"

"To get money, I think. For revenge against the Italian government. Because of the riots in Milan. You know, when all those people were killed in the street. Do you remember? It happened just after you arrived in Italy."

"Yes, I remember. And what form is this revenge to take exactly?"

"I don't know, but it may be something to do with that man Paterson. Malpensa mentioned him. And they're planning something else, here at the factory. They're going to have a strike."

"So that's why Rossi sent in his men to break up the meeting."

"I suppose so. But we won't be here to see it. We have to get away. The people at the meeting are bound to wonder what I was doing there. It looks a bit fishy, me there for the first time just when they get raided by Rossi. They're bound to think I betrayed them. They'll be after me. And Malpensa — I'm sure he recognized me. After tonight he might be thinking I let Milo and Guido down, too. I must get away."

Montmorency thought for a moment. "Yes, you must. We both should. But not straightaway. Frank, you are going to have to be brave. We are both going to the factory tomorrow."

"But why? Luigi, or Luigi's friends, will kill me."

"You only think that because you're panicking. They have no reason to suppose you were behind the raid. It's far more likely that they were betrayed by one of their own: someone who was in on the strike plan. You weren't, and they know that. They won't suspect you if you stay."

"So what do I do? What do I say to Luigi when I see him again?"

"You support him. You help foment the strike. We have to keep on good terms with these people if we are going to track their movements and find out who this Paterson is. Don't forget, your friend Luigi doesn't know how good your Italian really is. He probably thinks you only picked up the mood of the meeting, not the details. He'll be much less suspicious of you if you go into work tomorrow, and if I go, too. But I can promise you that it won't be for very long."

"Why?"

"Because, Frank, you and I are going to get the sack."

CHAPTER 26

≫

THE MORNING AFTER

*A*nd they did. And Frank enjoyed that day more than any other at the factory. He was nervous on the way to work. Would he be the only man from the night before to bother to turn up? Would that make him even more of a suspect?

At the factory gate, Rossi's two hard men were quietly angry, both nursing bruises. There was no sign that they recognized Frank from the pub. He'd woken several times in the night wondering what would happen when they saw him, refusing to let himself believe that he had not been spotted under the table. But it was true. They hadn't seen him. Today they were scouring the new arrivals for Italian faces, the people they had fought in the upstairs room. They lurched towards some and turned them away from the factory for good. But several, Luigi among them, had got out the window in time to avoid being spotted, and they were all getting down to their work, with an extra incentive to bring down Rossi's empire now.

In the yard, Frank saw Luigi tightening the straps on a delivery cart. They instinctively knew not to speak, but the look on Luigi's face said: *Glad you're here. Great to see you got out safely.* Montmorency had been right, by turning up for work, Frank dispelled any suspicion on Luigi's part.

The foreman put Frank and Montmorency to work carrying

heavy sacks of sugar from the underground storeroom up rickety wooden stairs to the kitchen. In their short stay at the factory they had seen several workers injured by heavy weights or falls as they lugged the supplies around. Montmorency got out his penknife and nicked the bottom of each sack, so that they laid a white trail all along their route. The storeroom supervisor noticed and followed him into the kitchen. Montmorency examined the sack he was carrying, deliberately letting more sugar onto the floor.

"Must be the rats!" he said, pointing out the hole.

"Sweep it up, and put it in the vat. We can't let it go to waste," said the stern fat woman, another of Rossi's cousins, who spent her day cataloging the arrival and departure of all the raw materials and criticizing everyone around her. She was renowned throughout the factory as a ruthless slave driver.

"Do it yourself," said Montmorency, swinging the sack around so that it clouted her across the chest before falling to the ground. "I'm not going to put dirt from the floor into the ice cream."

The woman thrust a broom and a dustpan into Montmorency's hand. He broke the broom over his knee. "Do it yourself," he said again, muttering a very rude Italian insult he had picked up on the wagons.

The women in the kitchen had never seen such defiance. They stopped their laborious stirring to watch the encounter. Frank arrived, with another sack over his shoulder, spouting a cascade of white granules behind him.

"You, too!" shouted the woman. "Stop that. Put it down!"

Frank dropped the sack from his shoulders, accidentally on purpose knocking over a tall churn of cream. The liquid crept across the floor, soaking up the sugar. He made as if to right the churn and brought down another. This one vomited its contents straight into the supervisor's face, down her apron, and onto her shoes. There was laughter from the workbenches.

"Silence!" cried the supervisor. "Get back to your work!"

But now Frank and Montmorency were finding more things to topple. A box of chocolate shavings, a pail of raspberry juice, and a bowl of nuts, painstakingly chopped that morning, all found their way into the slimy mix on the floor. The noise from the kitchen brought in men from the yard. Luigi leaped onto the worktop and started ranting, repeating Malpensa's message from the night before. The supervisor lunged towards him and found herself sliding down into an undignified heap on the floor. The workforce roared at the sight of their oppressor humiliated.

"Come on!" shouted Luigi. "This is our chance. Rossi can't make money without us. Stick together and we can't be defeated. Strike! Everyone get out now!"

"That's right. What have we got to lose?" shouted another man Frank recognized from the pub. One of the kitchen girls rose from her place, theatrically tying on a head scarf.

"I'm going! I won't work for Rossi anymore," she shouted, spitting on the supervisor in the slime.

"Me, too," said another, following her lead.

Soon all the women were up and leaving, smashing pots and overturning buckets as they went.

Rossi's minders arrived, tripped, and slipped to join the floundering woman on the floor. Two of the men from the pub started kicking them in retaliation for the night before. Rossi himself appeared at the door. There was a moment's pause as he tried and failed to exert his authority. Then a young girl, barely more than a child, scooped some ice cream onto a plate, and shoved it into his face like a custard pie. Everyone laughed and ran, followed by others from all over the factory. On the way up the lane, Luigi grabbed Frank.

"Get away. You and your dad get out of here. Our families will care for us, but you two stand out too much. Hide. If you need me, ask at the White Hart. But be careful. Lie low."

The press of the crowd split Frank and Luigi apart. Frank was exhilarated, thrilled by Rossi's downfall, and by Luigi's permission to leave the scene. But Montmorency felt guilty. He knew that when the rush of liberation wore off, the workers would realize that they had lost their homes as well as their jobs, and that a life of even greater poverty and oppression lay before many of them. They would never know that they were victims not just of Rossi and his like, but of a quick plan designed to save the skins of Frank and Montmorency: two men who were working to undermine the very movement some of them looked to for support.

Frank and Montmorency rushed back to their room to

gather up their few belongings. Montmorency wrapped his coat around the leather-bound ledger from the White Hart and tucked it under his arm. Then they took a bus to Lord George Fox-Selwyn's house and went in through the back door.

It was a hot summer's day in London, but no one could buy an ice cream.

CHAPTER 27

≫

THE BOOK

*N*ot exactly subtle!" scoffed Fox-Selwyn, as Frank babbled away to him about the events of the morning. "And if you don't mind me saying so, you two stink! Get yourselves off for a bath and I'll have a look at this book of yours. At least you didn't come away empty-handed."

Montmorency and Frank went up to their rooms with Chivers the manservant to find clean clothes. After many years in Fox-Selwyn's service, Chivers knew better than to ask questions, and as the men passed him their soiled rags he handled them as delicately as if they were silk and satin. He made sure both the upstairs bathrooms had copious supplies of shampoo, soap, shaving cream, and towels. It took an hour for Montmorency and Frank to turn themselves back into upper-class gentlemen, and their hair was still a little wet as they walked down the stairs together to join Fox-Selwyn in the library for a prelunch drink.

"You look better!" he said.

"Actually, I feel really strange in these stiff clothes," said Frank. "I liked living more simply. I was really comfortable."

"You won't think that after a night's sleep in a featherbed!" Montmorency laughed. "I think you'll find you get used to luxury again pretty quickly. What's for lunch?"

"I'm not sure," said Fox-Selwyn. "Cook's been banging

about down there for hours. She didn't know you were coming, and I'm afraid you've rather upset her plans. Whatever it is, please praise it. She's been under a lot of pressure what with Vi and young Tom staying here, and rushing off at all hours to see the sights. Not to mention Robert, who drops in to visit whenever he feels like it. Cook's not getting any younger, and she doesn't like her numbers going up and down all the time."

"Just as long as it isn't ice cream for dessert!" said Montmorency. "I think it will be a long time before I eat that again, even if Cook makes her own."

"So how did you get on with the ledger?" asked Frank. "We never got a chance to have a proper look at it."

"It's very interesting," said Fox-Selwyn. "Very interesting indeed. A lot of it seems to be in some kind of cipher, and even the straightforward bits are in Italian of course. But I'm sure an expert could find out a lot about how this movement is funded, and what they really get up to. I can't be absolutely certain, but I think I've worked something out."

"And what's that?" asked Montmorency.

"It's this Paterson."

"Have you discovered who he is?"

"Not who *he* is. No."

"You think it's a woman?"

"That might explain why we've been having so much trouble finding him," said Frank.

"No, not a woman," said George. "I don't think it's a person at all."

Montmorency and Frank were downcast. All that work for nothing. George continued: "I don't think it's a person. I think it might be a place. A town somewhere, perhaps. You see, there are references to sending people to Paterson, or getting things *from* Paterson, but some of these sentences seem to translate as *in* Paterson. Unless he's smuggling some kind of contraband in his stomach, I think it has to be a place. I was just going to get out the atlas when you came back down." He handed Montmorency the book. "See what you can make of this entry. The name comes up elsewhere, too."

Montmorency took the book, and Frank leaned over him as he struggled to decipher the cramped, foreign handwriting. The doorbell rang, and a familiar voice answered Chivers's formal greeting. Doctor Robert Farcett strode into the room with a jovial grin.

"Tom and Vi will be here in a minute," he said, accepting Fox-Selwyn's offer of a drink. "They've just stopped off to do a bit of shopping."

"Oh no. More parcels!" said Fox-Selwyn. "That boy will be quite spoiled by the time he gets back to Tarimond."

"And Cook's not going to be too pleased, either," said Frank, as Vi's familiar laugh floated in from outside the window.

They knew at once that Cook had seen the new arrivals pass her basement kitchen. They could sense her anger by the way she pounded the lunch gong. They dropped everything and made for the dining room immediately. No one wanted to risk Cook's wrath by being late.

After the meal, Frank went down to the kitchen to thank Cook. After his first experience of the world of work, he was beginning to realize the unacknowledged effort that went in to looking after his family, and felt a little embarrassed at putting so many unpredictable tasks onto the shoulders of this elderly woman.

"Well done, Cook. Delicious. And so good of you to cater for us all at so little notice."

Cook was grateful for his kind words. "Thank you, my lord," she said, with a little bob of a curtsy.

Frank was uncomfortable. It was a long time since anyone had addressed him by his title. Was this the same jolly woman who had let him help her when he had visited his uncle as a small boy? The one who had chatted happily about her past and rapped his fingers gently when he dipped them into the cake mixture? Was it right that she should be slaving in the kitchen while he was lounging around upstairs? Perhaps Malpensa had a point.

When he got back, Robert was on the library steps getting down the atlas. It was almost out of his reach, and he set off an avalanche of other books as he tried to pull it down.

Tom laughed. "Why do you have so many books? Have you read them all?"

"Of course," said George defensively, as Tom picked one up.

"What's this one about?" asked Tom mischievously, trying to sound out a long Latin name.

"Ah, well. Let me think. . . ." said George, playing for time.

"And this one? It's all in funny writing."

George looked closer. "Ah, that's Greek," he said. "We learned it at school."

"Why?" said Tom. "In case you ever went to Greece?"

"Well, no, actually. It's ancient Greek. No one speaks it anymore. You don't learn modern Greek at school."

"Why not?" asked Tom. "Seems silly. Anyway what's it about?"

"I think I'll need my glasses. . . ." mumbled George.

Frank intervened. "Uncle George, don't bother with your glasses! You haven't actually read any of these books, have you?"

"Well, not all of them . . . not many of them, to be honest. They belonged to my father, and to his father before him. But they do make the room look nice, don't you agree?"

"Someone's read this one, I think," said Tom, picking up a well-worn, dog-eared volume. "Or at least looked at it. Look." He laughed, holding it up for all to see. "It's pictures of naked ladies!"

Fox-Selwyn snatched the book away, blushing. "Oh, that one, yes. I think that was one of my father's particular favorites. I didn't realize it was still here."

Vi nudged Tom to stop him from giggling, and the boy

carefully noted exactly where Fox-Selwyn had replaced the book on the shelf.

"Anyway," said Fox-Selwyn, "let's have a go at that atlas, Robert. Is there anywhere called Paterson?"

Doctor Farcett ran his finger down a column of tiny print. "Quite a few, actually. Paterson, Australia; Paterson, South Africa; Paterson Bay in the South Pacific; and some in America: Paterson Ford, Missouri; Paterson, New Jersey; Paterson, Washington."

"Well, that's not much help," said Montmorency. "We could go all around the world looking for it."

"And no doubt some of them would turn out to be just muddy swamps with the odd tin hut," said George.

"Are there any other clues in the book?" Farcett asked.

They took it in turns to look at the ledger, wading through accounts and minutes of meetings. Every now and then someone would come across the word *Paterson*, and they would all gather around, but it was almost teatime before they found what they were looking for: a clear reference to a donation to workers who were trying to set up a political newspaper in Paterson, New Jersey, USA.

Doctor Farcett turned to the page in the atlas that would show them where Paterson, New Jersey, was. He could see at once that it was somewhere near New York, and traced along the grid lines until he found the precise spot. "There," he said. "There's your Paterson! And look at this. Almost next door. It's West Orange."

"Sorry?" said George. "West Orange. Funny name. Should I have heard of it?"

"It's where Thomas Edison has his headquarters."

"What, Edison the inventor?" asked Montmorency. "The lightbulb man?"

"Yes, and I know he's done work on X-rays and on moving pictures. Let's go there. He might be able to make my Bodyscreener work! We simply have to go."

"We can't just dash off to America," said Fox-Selwyn. "We've got things to do here. What about Gus and Alexander? We can't just go off to another continent and leave them languishing in Italy."

"Why not?" asked Frank. "Dad and Alex seemed perfectly happy when we left them. Not languishing at all. And anyway, what about me? I can't go back to Italy. I'm a wanted man there, remember?"

"You may be a wanted man here, too," said Montmorency. "Wanted by Rossi and some very nasty people. Remember what Luigi said about keeping your head down."

"What could be better cover than a trip to America?" insisted Frank. "No one would know who I was there. We could travel with Robert and tell people we had come to help him with his research. No one would be looking for three respectable Englishmen."

Vi intervened. "No one would ask any questions at all if you were traveling with a woman," she said. "Maybe Tom and I could come along, too?"

"Would you like to come to New Jersey, Tom?" asked Farcett.

"You could see New York as well; I've always wanted to go there," said Montmorency. "What do you think, Tom?"

"I'd love to go," he said, as his mother gave him a huge, excited hug.

"But will it be safe?" said Fox-Selwyn, uncharacteristically concerned about the sea voyage. "I'll worry about you, Tom."

Vi brushed his reservations aside. "He'll be fine. He'll have all of us to look after him. Oh, go on, George. You come, too."

Fox-Selwyn thought for a minute and then made his decision. "No, I mustn't come. We're losing sight of what we are trying to achieve here. These anarchists may be plotting something spectacular in Europe. We have to have someone on the case here, even if we get good leads from the United States. I want to stay on this side of the Atlantic anyway. I want to visit Gus, and that will give me a chance to do some more investigations in Italy. Montmorency, we'll have to split up on this one. But maybe you can teach Frank and Tom a few tricks of the trade."

And so it was decided. Robert, Vi, Montmorency, Frank, and Tom started whirlwind preparations for their voyage. Montmorency visited the shipping office, organized all the tickets for the steamer *Campania*, and booked hotels in New York and New Jersey. Vi supplied everyone with fine and tatty clothes in an orgy of shopping that left her happier than she had ever been. George did some quiet checking with contacts at the Foreign Office, to see what they knew about Paterson, New Jersey, and anarchists in America. It turned out to be almost nothing, and they asked him to let them know what Montmorency had found out when he returned. Then George packed his own bag ready to travel light to Florence. When he went to the bookcase to get his favorite book for the journey, he was disappointed, and then amused, to find that it wasn't there. Tom certainly was growing up. It pleased him to think of Tom on his travels with that special book under his pillow, like generations of Fox-Selwyns before him.

On the day of their departure to catch the boat at Liverpool, the house was a riot of activity. At last they said good-bye to Chivers, who was to close up the house, go to visit his sister in the country, and then take up a temporary position as butler to the Countess of Morbury while Fox-Selwyn was away. He slipped a lucky charm into Tom's pocket at the last minute. Cook was going on a sort of holiday, too: to the seaside where she would care for an even more elderly maiden aunt. Despite all her complaining during that overworked summer, she was sorry that it was coming to an end. Secretly she was worried that she would not live to see them all come back. As she squeezed a final, special slab of toffee into the top of Lord George Fox-Selwyn's bag, her eyes stung with tears.

But everyone else was in high spirits right up to the end. When the house was empty, Chivers turned the key in the last lock and set off for his well-earned rest. A week later, the postman pushed an envelope through the letterbox. It was addressed to Doctor Farcett and had come all the way from Tarimond. The news of Maggie Goudie's death lay on the doormat all the time they were away.

CHAPTER 28

≫

SEA STORIES

They all had different ideas about what to expect onboard ship, but they shared an expectation of luxury. Vi and Montmorency found it, and Vi in particular adored the long days of drinking, dancing, and dining in first-class splendor, meeting rich and interesting people from all over the world. In no time the last remains of the Scottish islander were gone, and in their place was a more sophisticated version of Vi's old, carefree London self. It was different for the others.

Farcett was right. The flu was dying out in London. But in its last flickers it had infected an elderly man who was off to visit relatives in America. The boat sailed before he realized he was ill. He sneezed as the steward was showing him his cabin, and that steward coughed as he played cards with a friend who worked among the third-class passengers in the bowels of the ship. A few days out at sea the *Campania*'s doctor was being called for too often to cope alone. The captain consulted his passenger list to see if there were any other medics on board. He approached Doctor Farcett, who was only too pleased to oblige, delighted to have another example of viral transmission in a closed community to put alongside his study of the Tarimond case. However much fun Vi and Montmorency might be having, for Farcett this was a working trip.

Like many other passengers who had been exposed to the flu before, Farcett and his friends escaped the disease, but that did not ensure them a comfortable passage. There was another illness onboard, and one that wasn't catching: seasickness. From the very start Frank felt as if his head was full of metallic jelly. He was disorientated, hardly able to walk in a straight line, even when he was rushing to the side of the ship to vomit into the sea. The crew and seasoned travelers took pity on him, offering conflicting advice.

"Drink plenty of water," said one.

"Whatever you do, avoid water. Sip brandy, slowly," insisted another.

"Stay on deck and focus your eyes on the horizon."

"Lie down in the dark."

"Eggs will settle your stomach."

"What you need is ice cream."

This last suggestion had him back leaning over the side.

To everyone's surprise, Tom, the child of the isles, who could sway around in small boats all day without the slightest wobble, was also defeated by the pitch and roll of the big ship when the ocean got rough. He joined Frank lying down in his cabin with a couple of buckets on the floor between them. Montmorency popped in to see how they were getting on. The scene, and the smell, triggered off a memory of his days in prison, but he managed to overcome his initial physical revulsion to give the two invalids comfort. They didn't want the light on, so he told them stories, making them up as he went along, drawing on his experiences of high and low life all over Europe.

"Was that one true?" asked Tom, as Montmorency came to the end of a tale about a spy on the run.

"Not really. Some of it happened, though."

"Happened to you?" asked Frank.

"To me, and to your uncle George. But if I told you my *real* life story you wouldn't believe it." Montmorency's mind was racing: Why had he said that? Was he inviting them to ask him about his secret life?

"What do you mean?" asked Frank. "Why wouldn't we believe it?"

"Well, you see . . ." said Montmorency, as the ship lurched and Tom dived for the bucket. Montmorency took a damp flannel and wiped the boy's mouth, smoothed his hair, and helped him settle back down.

Perhaps that was a sign. The interruption had come just in time. He must change the subject.

But Tom wanted to know. "What is your real story? Mam always says she doesn't know. But she does, doesn't she?"

"She knows some of it, but I asked her not to tell anyone, and I'm pleased to hear that she hasn't."

"But you have to tell us now," urged Frank. "You can't just say you've got a secret and then not tell us what it is. It isn't fair."

Frank was right. It wasn't fair, and Montmorency knew he had gone too far to stay silent. They might just run to Vi and pump it out of her. He would give them an edited version of the truth.

"I haven't always lived like this," he began. "I'm not like you and your family, Frank. I was born poor."

"Like me?" asked Tom.

"Far poorer than you, Tom. You had the natural riches of Tarimond and the blessing of your mother's love. I never knew my mother. She gave me away to an orphanage when I was born. I don't even know my real name. They changed it when they took me in."

"Changed it to what?" asked Tom.

"Never you mind," said Montmorency. "It never really was my name, and now I've left it behind forever."

Tom didn't want to let that go, but Frank jumped in with another question, keen to get to the meat of the story.

"So how did you get rich?" He looked at Montmorency's downcast face in the pause that followed. "Did you steal your money?"

"At the beginning, yes. Then after that I put what I had to work for me. I was lucky on the horses, things like that. Once you've got a bit of money you can make it grow, and if you're careful it just goes on growing. It's that first injection of cash that's important."

"Of someone else's cash," said Frank, intrigued, but a bit disappointed, too. "I hope you only stole from really nasty people, or really rich people who wouldn't notice it was gone."

"I did steal from people like that," said Montmorency. "But not only them. I'm not proud of what I did."

"And that's why you're so good at pretending to be poor," said Frank, working it all out. "Because you really were." He rattled off a huge list of questions, about the orphanage, about how Montmorency had met Uncle George, not noticing that Tom was silent in the bed opposite. "Did you ever go to prison?"

"Yes, Frank, I have been in prison. And my advice is to do everything you can to stay out of it."

Montmorency took refuge in this part of the story, acting out scenes from prison life, describing the awfulness of the food, the viciousness of some of the other prisoners, talking about the dark, the damp, the smell, and the constant crushing hopelessness of losing freedom. In the back of his mind was the hope that Frank might remember this picture if he were ever seduced again by the verve of the political activists he found so alluring. But he knew how strong the glamour of a forbidden act could be, how easy it was to fall in a moment, despite the best of intentions, and the good sense a conscience could wallow in when there was no temptation on hand.

Frank kept up the questioning as Tom became more quiet and thoughtful. Eventually the younger boy spoke.

"And when you got out of prison? Is that when you met my mother?"

"Yes, Tom," said Montmorency with a jovial laugh. "I met

her on my first day of freedom. I've known her since she was about your age. On and off."

"So," said Tom, stuttering a little, "do you know who my father is?"

Montmorency had been expecting that question for a long time. He'd always been relieved when a visit to Tarimond ended without it being asked. He'd imagined himself having to explain things to a much younger child, but Tom had never raised the matter. Montmorency had persuaded himself that Vi must have given her son some sort of assurance that had satisfied his curiosity. But he had always known, somewhere inside himself, that she hadn't; that she, like him, had avoided the embarrassment of addressing the question. They had both relied on giving out enough signals of discomfort to stop Tom from asking, pretending to themselves that he didn't really think about it, that he wasn't curious about his roots.

And yet Montmorency could remember only too well the many nights he had lain on his hard bed in the Foundling Hospital, wondering who his own parents had been, imagining a woman somewhere pondering what might have happened to the child she had given away. He had stared at strangers all his life, looking for physical signs of a family link. He had fantasized about princes, sportsmen, and actors. He had stopped only when he realized that thieves, cheats, and murderers were just as likely, perhaps even more so, to share his blood. And now here was this boy before him, so like his mother that it was hard to imagine more than one person was responsible for his existence. And yet Montmorency felt such powerful kinship, such love for Tom, who was, after all, possibly the only blood relative he had ever met. He wanted Tom to be his son. But he couldn't be sure.

Tom was looking at the floor, shamefully dreading the answer to his question.

"Has your mother never told you?" asked Montmorency, blandly, trying to hide his own discomfort with the subject.

"I can't ask her," said Tom. "She doesn't like to talk about it."

"Well, it really is a matter for her, Tom," said Montmorency, relieved to have found a way of avoiding details. "Perhaps she thinks it's best that you don't know, or perhaps she's waiting till you are older."

Tom pretended to be satisfied with that thin answer. The awkwardness was broken by Frank, vomiting yet again, and Tom filling his own bucket, as if by a reflex.

Montmorency continued talking as he made them both comfortable again. "Anyway," he said with false jollity, "there are advantages in not having a father. No one's ever run my life for me, not since I got out of prison. I've been able to choose who I was and what I would do, and I haven't got any aged parents to look after." Now he noticed it was Frank who looked glum, and he thought again about Frank's dead mother. But he couldn't find the words to say anything of comfort. Instead, Montmorency changed the subject completely.

"Now, what you'll really want to hear about is how I met your uncle George, Frank!" And he embarked on a rambunctious account of his life at the Marimion Hotel and Bargles Club.

Frank had heard most of it before, and relaxed in the familiarity of the tales of London high life. He loved the part about Cissie, the grotesque daughter of the hotel manager, who had pursued Montmorency with dreams of marriage. Montmorency minced about the cabin, imitating her walk and her lisp, making both boys laugh, though all three of them really had their minds on other things. When the door opened, and Doctor Farcett appeared to check on them, he was pleased to see that their spirits were high, even if their stomachs were still troubled.

"Good news," he said. "The captain's told me there's calm water ahead. We'll soon have you two running around on deck."

With that the ship rolled, and the boys grabbed their buckets once again.

Later on, after dinner, when Frank and Tom were asleep, Montmorency joined Farcett for a cigarette under the stars. Side by side, leaning on the guardrail and looking down into the waves, they could talk without having to meet each other's eyes. Montmorency raised the subject that had sat, unspoken, between them for fourteen years.

"Tom asked if I knew who his father was," he said, trying to sound relaxed.

"What did you tell him?" asked Farcett, even more casually than he had intended.

"I said it was a matter for Vi," said Montmorency.

"Of course. Yes. Of course it is. It's not for us to tell him." Farcett was relieved that such an important piece of information had not been revealed by Montmorency. He would find his own time and place for it, one day.

Each man felt reassured by the other; and a little better for the acknowledgment, however coded, of what they each believed to be the truth. It was a relief. They wouldn't need to raise the matter again.

Far away, in Florence, Lord George Fox-Selwyn was playing chess with his earnest nephew Alexander, and found his thoughts straying to the transatlantic steamer and its precious cargo. He wished he was with them, and he wondered what Tom would make of New York.

Deep in the English countryside, Chivers was outside his sister's house. He hoped she had already gone to bed, so the nagging about how long he had spent at the pub could wait until the morning. He was missing London and the excitements of life in Lord George Fox-Selwyn's household. He looked up at the same moon that shone over the mighty *Campania*, halfway across the ocean. He hoped Vi was safe. And that lovely boy of hers with his soft brown curls.

CHAPTER 29

≫

AMERICA

*M*ontmorency had a guidebook, and had read to everybody the description of the approach to New York. The ship was decorated with photographs of the main tourist attractions. By the end of their weeklong voyage, they felt as if they already knew this city of high buildings and bustling streets. But after everyone had repacked their cabin baggage, tipped the stewards, and prepared to land on Manhattan, nothing about their arrival went according to plan. Wrapped up against the cold morning, they went on deck longing for their first sight of the huge new Statue of Liberty. But there was nothing to be seen. A thick fog had wrapped itself around the *Campania*, and her warning horn howled out forlornly into a gray nothingness.

The pilot's launch came out to meet them, and the captain and the ship's doctor broke the news of the flu outbreak onboard. The pilot returned with the port's medical officer, who spent ages checking over those who had been ill and making sure that they would not be infecting anyone on land. Doctor Farcett was invited to join in the consultations and returned to the others in the lounge with bad news. "They may keep us out here in quarantine until they're sure everyone is all right," he explained.

"But no one's really ill, are they?" asked Montmorency.

"No, but you can't blame them for being concerned," said Farcett.

"But what are we supposed to do?" Frank complained, unbuttoning his heavy overcoat and slumping down into a chair. "They've closed all the restaurants and bars. Are we going to be stuck here with nothing to eat or drink?"

"And how long is it going to take?" asked Montmorency. "Surely they'll never be certain that everyone's in the clear. We can't just sit here waiting for new cases to emerge."

"I'll go and ask Harrison," said Vi.

"Who on earth is that?" said Montmorency, who had found it hard to keep up with Vi's shipboard friendships.

"Harrison Bayfield," said Vi, sashaying off into the adjacent bar. "He's a major shareholder of the shipping company. I was dancing with him last night. I'm sure he'll know what to do."

Farcett laughed. "Do you think Vi has the slightest idea what a major shareholder is?" he joked.

"No," said Montmorency, "but I bet you this Bayfield man has been boasting to her about how powerful he is, and how he can get things done around here."

"Let's hope he's right," said Frank. "I want to get back onto dry land."

Vi returned with a tall man, brimming with self-importance.

"Gentlemen," he said in a refined American accent, as Vi introduced him to her friends, "as a major shareholder of the shipping company, may I apologize for this delay in our arrival. We always joke about your London fog, but here we are with a pea-souper of our own."

"Not at all," said Montmorency, making an effort to sound polite, though he had taken an instant dislike to the man's pomposity. "We can hardly hold you responsible for the weather or the flu."

"Indeed not," said Bayfield. "But I can at least ensure that the wait is not unpleasant. The captain should keep us informed." Bayfield looked pleased with himself when, a second later, the captain did arrive and made a contrite announcement to his first-class passengers.

"I do apologize for the delay. We were hoping the authorities would let us dock, but they are insisting that we must wait until the morning to see if there are any new cases of influenza. In any event, the fog is against us. We will have to stay where we are."

"How about something to eat?" shouted an angry voice from one corner of the room.

"And drink," said another, as a babble of complaints started to build. The captain held up his hand to quiet them.

"I have asked the crew to reopen the bars. We are sending out for more supplies, but you will appreciate that food is short at the moment. The galley staff are doing what they can."

"Oh, how exciting," said a blowsy American matron, who had been the life and soul of late-night parties throughout the voyage. "We're cast adrift on survival rations!"

"Not exactly," said the captain sternly, as a champagne

cork popped behind the bar. "We will make you as comfortable as possible."

He hoped the promise of a party would placate his most privileged passengers, but he was wondering how he was going to keep order in the belly of the ship, in the hungry crush of third class. There, a thousand people were desperate for dry land, many of them clinging to dreams of opportunity in the New World, and terrified that they would be sent home again if they were found to be sick. The captain hoped they would not be kept at sea for long. Even with the engines still, just keeping the boat warm took a lot of coal. There wasn't much left after the long journey, and the stokers were angry about keeping going when they expected to be having fun, spending their wages onshore.

"Well, we'll just have to make the best of it," said Montmorency, taking a pack of cards from his coat pocket. At the prospect of a game, Harrison Bayfield sat down and joined them without asking, and they were soon laughing together and forgetting their disappointment.

"Are you staying in New York for long?" he asked them.

"No," said Frank, as he dealt the next round of cards. "We're just stopping over until we can organize transport to another place. It's called Paterson, New Jersey."

"Well, I'll be!" cried Bayfield. "My brother lives there. How extraordinary. To think you have come all the way from England to see Paterson. Now why on earth would anyone do that?"

He had, unwittingly, hit on a flaw in their plan. It was a

question none of them could answer convincingly. The cover story they'd made up before they left depended on them turning up in Paterson almost accidentally: tourists passing by on a trip through North America. They'd imagined themselves getting their bearings at a hotel before Montmorency and Frank went undercover. Now Frank had revealed that seeing Paterson was the whole point of their visit. But why would they want to go there? They could hardly say they were on the trail of an anarchist cell.

Montmorency thought of something as he organized his hand of cards. "The scenery," he said. "We've been told it's quite sublime."

"Well, there is the waterfall, I suppose," said Bayfield, half mockingly. "It's why there's so much industry there. You could say it's the industrial capital of the USA now. Fabrics. Silks. That's my brother's trade. He's one of the biggest manufacturers in the state."

Farcett saw an opening for another explanation. "Yes, industry. We're interested in industry. We've got a feeling you Americans could teach us a thing or two. And science. I am hoping to visit the Edison works. I gather that they're nearby."

"They are, and you are in luck," boasted Bayfield. "I've known Thomas Alva Edison for years. I've seen him through some of his biggest projects. The lightbulb. The phonograph. I've backed them, and I've bought them. He couldn't have got anywhere without me!"

Is there anything this man won't boast about? thought Montmorency. *Is there anyone he doesn't know?*

Bayfield continued. "I can get you all the introductions you need," he said. "My brother has an English wife. She'll be delighted to meet you. What the heck, my business in Manhattan can wait a few days. I'll show you the place myself. That is, if we ever get off this ship."

Montmorency and Farcett exchanged glances. Did they want a chaperone? Should they accept his offer? Neither could think of a way of brushing Bayfield off.

"That's too kind of you," said Montmorency. "I'm sure Vi would be glad of a companion to show her the softer side of things while we are studying the local industry." Vi actually looked as if she might.

"And I could show your boys a thing or two as well," said Bayfield. "Keep them out of trouble."

Montmorency realized that however little he liked this man, Bayfield was actually offering them a service they needed. They had to get under the skin of that Paterson place. They had imagined themselves doing it from the bottom, infiltrating the working quarters and asking questions in the underworld. Perhaps that wasn't the only way. Perhaps it might be better, or just as good, to start at the top.

"Thank you, Mr. Bayfield," he said.

"Please. Call me Harrison."

"Thanks, Harry," said Vi cheekily, well on her way to drunkenness.

They were in for a long afternoon.

It was long, but it was profitable, and not just because Montmorency had a run of good luck with the cards. Forcing himself to overcome his first impressions of Bayfield, Montmorency made an effort to talk to him nicely, at first making polite conversation, but then realized that he had found a comfortable way of learning about Paterson without the effort of walking its streets. Bayfield told them all about the silk industry there and how it was sustained by cheap immigrant workers from Europe.

"We used to depend on the Irish," said Bayfield. "Now it's more Italians. They're good. They do silk over there. They bring their skills to us and send their wages back to Italy. Can't understand a word most of them say, though. If you go downtown after work it's like being in Milan."

Montmorency was glad of the confirmation that they were probably on the right track. Frank was even more convinced of it. Migrant labor, exploited by fat bosses in a foreign land. He knew what that could lead to. He knew why so many of the Italian underground had been "sent to Paterson." And he guessed that it wasn't just money they were sending back to Italy, but ideas and activists — even arms as well.

Next morning, Bayfield called on them early, in their cabins, to break the news that the fog had lifted. They dressed quickly to get on deck. Farcett was already up. He had been talking with the captain and a representative of the City

Health Department. All first-class passengers were to be allowed to disembark as soon as the ship berthed. Those in second and third class would be examined as they left, and any found to be ailing would be sent home again on the next ship.

"But why should first-class people be any less infectious than the others?" asked Frank.

"I know, Frank, it doesn't seem fair," said Montmorency. "But then some of those people would be going into very cramped and overcrowded conditions, where the disease could spread quickly."

"And anyway," said Frank, "the authorities wouldn't want to upset the likes of us and our friend Mr. Bayfield."

"No, Frank, they wouldn't. And you should be glad of that. You don't want to spend a fortnight cooped up on ship, do you?"

"No, but I still say it's not fair," said Frank.

Tom was the first up the staircase to the deck. The sun was out, and his scream of joy as he looked around him brought the others rushing out into the open. There was the view, just as it was in the ship's photographs, but in radiant color, instead of black and white. The proud figure of Liberty Enlightening the World held her torch aloft before them, and in the distance grand buildings, towers, domes, and spires reached for the sky. The architecture recalled all the grace and majesty of the best of Europe but on a superhuman scale. Montmorency brought out his guidebook, and with Bayfield's help, pointed out one landmark after another:

"'The Produce Exchange,'" he read, "'with its square Florentine tower 225 feet high . . .'"

"We didn't see anything as tall as that in Florence!" laughed Frank, as Montmorency continued.

"'The Bowling Green Building — 16 stories, designed by English architects and built with English capital . . .'"

"That's it there," said Bayfield, pointing, "and there's Trinity Church, and the St. Paul, and see that dome —"

Montmorency interrupted him. He'd found it in the book: "It's 'the lofty gilded dome of the World Building (310 feet — view)'."

Montmorency's readings from his guidebook were to be a feature of the trip. He became an instant expert, regaling them all with facts as if he had always known them, when he'd really only found out that instant. Sometimes it was as if reading the book was more important than seeing the sights. Now, for instance, he was looking up information about the Produce Exchange — "view (see p. 26) — huge brick and terra-cotta structure in the Italian Renaissance style (offices)" — instead of looking at it in front of him.

The engines rumbled into action beneath them, and the massive structures seemed to grow bigger all the time as they pulled towards the wharf. But it was a long time before they set foot on American soil. Halfway across, the ship stopped at an island, where the exhausted mass of third-class passengers were put off for their medical checks, some excited, some in fear.

"Poor souls," said Frank. But he was brusquely shut up by Bayfield.

"Don't waste your sympathy on them. No one makes them come here. They'll get work, and a better life in America than they ever would have had where they've come from."

"Where have they come from?" asked Vi.

"Some got on at Liverpool, most of them when we stopped at Ireland," Bayfield told her. "But see that boat over there?" He pointed to a smaller, tattier vessel than their own. "It's come from Italy. They're moving in everywhere. Running away from poverty and taking over whole neighborhoods. We'll see our fair share of them in Paterson, I can assure you."

"Do we get off here?" asked Tom.

"Oh no!" Bayfield laughed, aghast at the idea of mingling with the huddled masses. "We don't need delousing and medical checks! We go right in to Manhattan. That's the real heart of New York."

They might not have needed delousing, but getting off the boat still seemed quite an arduous affair. Once they were tied up at the quay, with the gangplanks down, the first-class passengers made their way to the customs shed, struggled to find their luggage, and lined up in rough alphabetical order. The baggage of Vi and Tom Evans and Doctor Robert Farcett was neatly stacked, not too far apart. But some of Frank's luggage had been placed under "F" for Fox, and some under "S" for Selwyn. Montmorency's many cases and trunks were somewhere in between. Montmorency's guidebook told him that arrangements could be made to transport luggage directly to the larger hotels. It took him ages to work out how to do it, and then, even with Bayfield's help, to find taxis to get themselves to the palatial comfort of the Waldorf-Astoria, where they were to stay the night before setting out for Paterson. All around them, passengers were fanning out across the city and to train stations where they could set out for more distant locations.

Within a week, people were catching the flu all over northeast America.

CHAPTER 30

≫

THE HAPPY DUKE

Lord George Fox-Selwyn's journey to Florence was as relaxed as the American trip was stressful. He had taken it gently, breaking it into easily manageable chunks, and stopping off at comfortable hotels along the way. He had only himself to take care of, knew where he was going, and, better still, had something to look forward to. His brother's letters had become more and more cheerful of late. George could tell that Gus was starting, at last, to get over the death of his wife. The contessa was mentioned only in passing, but he was pretty sure that she was responsible for the change of mood. George had meant what he said when he turned down the chance to visit America. He really did want to delve further into the world of the Italian anarchists, in the hope of finding out their next target, but he had another reason for visiting Florence. He wanted to see Gus and Alexander even more.

Gus was sitting on the veranda, reading in the cool autumn sunlight, as George crossed the courtyard to the door of the apartment. "George! Welcome!" he shouted, jumping up from his wicker chair. "You're early. We were going to come and meet you with a carriage at the station."

"I was lucky with the trains. And I walked over the bridge," said Fox-Selwyn, lifting up his small bag to show that he was traveling light. "I haven't got much luggage. Doesn't Florence look beautiful in this light?"

"It's wonderful, George. I wouldn't want to live anywhere else. And from the size of that bag, I imagine you'll be wanting to borrow a pair of my pajamas?"

"That and a few other bits and pieces if you don't mind," said George. "No point in lugging clothes halfway across Europe when you've got a brother just your size."

Alexander appeared behind his father through the French windows. "I'm beginning to wonder if *I've* got a brother at all," he said. "How is Frank? Has he started behaving himself at last?"

"He's been a great help, actually," said George. "I'll tell you all about it when I get upstairs."

As soon as the door was opened, George felt there was something different about his brother's holiday home. It was tidy, for a start. "I see Professor Lombroso has gone, then?" he said, looking around. "And you've got a piano. And flowers. Do I detect a woman's touch?"

Gus and Alexander both blushed. "Beatrice has been helping us out a bit on the domestic side," muttered the duke.

"Beatrice . . .? Oh, the contessa!" said George, pretending he had not known her first name before. "How kind of her. Do you see her often?"

"Oh, almost every day!" said Alex cheerily. "And we've met lots of her friends. Writers. Artists. Really interesting people."

"She's invited you to dine with us all tonight," said Gus,

"if you feel up to it, that is. Of course she knows why you're really here, so she's asked the chief of police as well. And a couple of others. Some sort of composer, I think, and your old friend the curator from La Specola. What's his name? Morelli, Marini . . . ?"

"Antonio Moretti. Has he recovered from that horrible business with the firebombs?" asked George, trying to sound detached, though the contessa's intervention alarmed him. He didn't want to draw attention to his inquiries in Florence. He wanted to operate under the cover of a family visit.

Alex answered. "Yes, I went to the museum the other day, and apparently everything is back to normal. They replaced the lost specimens from their reserve stock."

"Anyway," said Gus, "Beatrice thought you would like to catch up with Moretti. You seemed to get along with him so well last time you were here."

"Yes, I did. He's rather an impressive man. So knowledge-able, and yet so unassuming. I would like to see him again."

"So you'll come?"

"Of course I'll come," said George. "But don't expect me to go into detail about the investigation. Not in front of that composer. You never know who you can trust. You have to be careful, especially with those arty types. And Alexander, you asked about Frank earlier. He's safe. But remember, you mustn't mention him to anyone here. No one must know that he's part of our family; otherwise he could be in hiding forever. The safest thing is just to keep him out of your con-versation. Even among friends. If you do find yourself saying that you have a brother, call him Lord Francis Fox-Selwyn, not Frank, and don't say that he's been in Florence. The Frank who helped us at the museum was an employee. He's moved on now, and we don't know where he is."

"Understood," said Alex. "And we have been careful, haven't we, Dad?"

"Oh yes," said Gus. "But it's good to be reminded. And I'll have a word with Beatrice about it, too, though she's always discreet. She just wants to give you the chance to make contact with the police chief, and maybe get him out on the terrace for a private word. And he might want to hear from you about what's going on in London. It sounded from your letter as if things are heating up."

"Well, it's been a long slog — especially for Frank and Montmorency — but we've established beyond doubt that there are international links between the anarchists. I've got no idea what they're planning, but my gut tells me that this is where the ringleaders are. The money may be coming from America and Britain, but the really dangerous men — the killers — are in Italy. We're finding more and more pieces of the jigsaw, all over the world, but this is where we'll put them together."

"Even without a picture on the box?" said Alex.

"You're right," said George. "There isn't a picture. But if there were, I fear it would be of a monarch or a statesman in a pool of blood. It's our job to make sure that that picture is never completed."

"Your job, not mine," said Gus. "I'll introduce you to some

useful people, but I don't want to get involved. And just you make sure that the picture isn't of *you* with a knife in your back."

"Don't be silly, Gus. No one's going to come after a fat old bumbler like me. Even the people in Florence who already know me think I'm just a rich Englishman with too much time on his hands and a passion for natural history. I intend to keep it that way. That's why I can be useful here. And my aim is for everyone to end up alive, including myself. Don't you worry about that."

"I'm very pleased to hear it, Uncle George!" Alex laughed. "Can I get you a drink?"

"So long as your father isn't frightened of me dying from alcohol poisoning!" George giggled. "After all, I'm far more likely to be carried off by my own bad habits than by some foreign criminal, don't you think?"

They all laughed, and Alexander opened a bottle of wine. Then Gus dug out some spare clothes for George to wear to the contessa's dinner. Their jolly progress up the hill to see her could not have been more unlike their first trip there, sulking and squabbling, more than a year before.

CHAPTER 31

≫

PATERSON

*I*n America it was only lunchtime, and Montmorency and the others were getting ready to leave for Paterson. It meant another (brief) boat ride and then their first experience of the American railroad. Montmorency read to them from his guidebook.

"'In America, the traveler is left to rely upon his own common sense still more freely than in England, and no attempt is made to take care of him in the patriarchal fashion of Continental railways. . . . Names of stations are not clearly marked. . . . The brakeman is supposed to call them out but can be indistinct. . . .'"

"I think we can cope with that!" Frank laughed. "Whoever wrote that must think we're complete babies!"

"And we'll have Harrison to show us what to do," added Vi. "He'll make sure we get off at the right stop."

"Ah!" said Montmorency, still leafing through the book. "But will he behave himself? It says here, 'The average Englishman will probably find the chief physical discomforts in the dirt of the city streets, the roughness of the country roads, the winter overheating of hotels and railway-cars, and (in many places) the habit of spitting on the floor, but the Americans are now keenly alive to these weak points and are doing their best to remove them.'"

"I'm sure Harrison would never spit!" insisted Vi, defending her friend.

"And of course, you never, ever see people spitting in England!" Montmorency joked. "Oh no!"

"You'd better not let Mr. Bayfield see what that book says about his country," said Tom. "It's so rude."

"Not all the way through," said Montmorency. "This bit's better. 'The first requisites for the enjoyment of a tour in the United States are an absence of prejudice and a willingness to accommodate oneself to the customs of the country.' If we stick to that we shouldn't go far wrong."

"So shall we all have a good spit in the hotel lobby before we leave?" suggested Frank.

"No, let's leave that for the dirty street," said Montmorency, laughing.

"Or the rough country road," said Vi.

"Or even the overheated railway car!" cried Tom.

"Let's just keep it for when we're brushing our teeth!" said Doctor Farcett. "We are sophisticated Europeans, after all!"

They were in high spirits on the long ride down in the fancy elevator.

"What does it say about Paterson in your book, Montmorency?" asked Frank.

"Nothing. It's marked on the map, but that's all."

"It's just as well we've got Harrison, then, isn't it?" said Vi.

"Yes, Vi," said Montmorency suggestively, nudging her in the ribs and knocking her hat askew. "We're going to be very dependent on him . . . you'll be pleased to hear."

"Shut up!" she squawked, playfully whacking at him with her handbag, just as the door opened in front of a very correct-looking American woman, who joined them in the elevator, making it clear she thought these English tourists were impossibly unrefined.

Frank whispered to Montmorency, "Perhaps your book's a bit out of date. I think we'd better mind our manners."

"Yes, sonny, you should!" bellowed the woman. "And don't whisper in elevators. It's impolite."

She got out three floors below. Very soon everyone else realized why. The stink in the elevator was quite unmissable by the time the doors opened onto the crowded lobby. The English party got out, letting in more well-dressed Americans. You could tell from the look on their faces exactly what they were thinking: These rough Europeans definitely didn't know how to behave.

Harrison Bayfield was waiting far enough away not to notice their discomfort. He strode towards Vi and took her arm. "I have arranged some cabs. The luggage is already on its way. Let's get along now."

Montmorency and Doctor Farcett were both a little put out by Bayfield's interest in Vi. But they had to admit that it was useful to have someone to steer them through the practicalities of life in this extraordinary country.

Montmorency's *Handbook for Travelers* had missed out on the most important thing about American trains. They were bigger and far, far more fun than their English counterparts. The engine, with its pointed cowcatcher and its loud bell, seemed to have a personality, and even, if you looked at it in the right way, a face. It was strange not having platforms at the stations, but Vi loved the little steps that came down to help you board. In England, passengers sat in tight compartments, facing one another in silence. Here the long carriages had a central aisle with seats on either side, and a babble of chatter from the passengers and the conductor selling refreshments along the way. It was lighter, airier, and easier to look out on the countryside, which, like the buildings and the trains, seemed somehow larger, more impressive than the scenery they were used to.

Frank wandered through the train, out of the first-class accommodations to the cheaper seats, where he noticed at once the music of strong Italian voices. These were the workers Bayfield had talked about, coming to the Silk City to make their fortunes. He listened in for a while, overhearing conversations about Italy, families, and food. There was apprehension in the air, but also an excitement and a profound sense of hope. Frank wondered if it was justified. What would the factories these immigrants were going to really be like? Would life in urban America offer them more than rural Italy? He would do his best to find out. He and Montmorency had already worked out a plan, based on their successful infiltration of Rossi's empire in London. Frank would go undercover again and work alongside these people. Originally they were going to repeat their "father and son" act, but since they'd become entangled with Harrison Bayfield, Montmorency had decided to stay as he was and find out about any insurrection in the workforce from a boss's-eye view.

"There you are, Frank!" said Vi when she spotted him coming back into their carriage, as the train slowed down. "I was panicking. I thought we'd lost you. It's a good thing I didn't send Tom after you; we'd have lost him, too."

"We haven't lost anyone, Vi," said Montmorency. "Keep calm. The train hasn't even stopped yet!"

When it did, the brakeman shouted out "Paterson!" quite clearly several times, so that even if they hadn't had Bayfield with them they would have had no doubt they were in the right place. Harrison had wired ahead for transport, and soon they were installed in the town's best hotel: a long way from the standards of the Waldorf, but quite comfortable enough.

As soon as they walked in, they realized from the reaction of the hotel staff that Bayfield was a big, big name in this town. The deference to Harrison Bayfield was quickly extended to those who accompanied him, and the manager was just as obsequious towards Montmorency and his friends as his counterpart at the Marimion in London had been, all those years ago. When he finally left them alone upstairs, Montmorency wandered into Frank's room with the guidebook.

"I thought you said that thing wasn't going to be any use to us here," said Frank.

"I just wanted to read you something I left out this morning. It will make you laugh." Montmorency opened the book at the introduction. " 'The traveler in the United States should from the outset reconcile himself to the absence of deference or servility on the part of those he considers his social infe-riors.' I think we may be rewriting this book before we're done here, don't you think?"

"Perhaps," said Frank. "But let's see what things are like outside this hotel. There must be a reason why the anarchists send people here."

"You're probably right. Have you got your old clothes ready? You'll have to go out and find yourself a job tomorrow."

"Won't Harrison think it's a bit odd if I just disappear? It doesn't look as if he's going to keep his distance while we're here."

"I've thought of that. And I've got a plan. You get a room in town, and we'll say that you've gone off with Robert to find his inventor."

"So this is my last bath for a while," said Frank, turning on the taps.

"Yes, and make it a good one. Bayfield's taking us for din-ner at his brother's house. And it looks as if Bayfield's brother is the real 'Mr. Paterson'!"

CHAPTER 32

≫

PUCCINI

*G*us, darling!" said the contessa, reaching for his hands, and holding out her cheek for a kiss.

"Beatrice, how lovely!" replied the duke, brushing his whiskers against her soft skin, in a gesture of affection far in excess of anything George had seen him show to his first wife at Glendarvie.

Then it was his turn, as the contessa greeted him with almost equal warmth.

"And George! How wonderful to see you again. And Alex, too. I'm so glad you could come. I'm expecting some people you'll find very interesting."

"I told George about the police chief," said Gus.

"Oh, Mario. He's a real poppet! You'll adore him," Beatrice gushed, using a word George had never before heard applied to a policeman. "And I'm thrilled that Puccini can join us. You know, the opera composer? I got to know him through the dear, late empress."

"The man who wrote *La Bohème*?" said George, not mentioning that he had turned down the chance to see the opera last time he was in Italy.

"Yes, and he's working on something new. He was telling me all about it yesterday."

"What a pity Montmorency isn't here," said George,

thinking how much easier the dinner would be if his opera-mad companion were there to keep the conversation going.

"Yes, Gus was saying it's a long time since you two have been apart."

"We work together well," said George, "but he's had to go to America. It's quite exciting, really. We may be getting to the heart of this anarchist network. But, my dear contessa . . ."

"Oh, George, call me Beatrice!"

"Beatrice, I think I should say that . . ." George was about to explain that he didn't want to go into detail about his work in front of people he didn't know, but before he could get the words out they heard a carriage at the door, and the contessa had rushed forward to meet the new arrival. Fox-Selwyn hoped it would be the police chief. Then he could take him aside and have a quick word before the social chit-chat started. But no. And it wasn't the curator either. It was the composer.

He swept into the hall, handing his soft white gloves and fine ebony cane to the butler at the door. Like the others, he was dressed formally for dinner, but even the most insensitive observer could have spotted at once that they were English, and he was Italian. Their shirts were white and stiff, his was soft and of the finest cotton, topped with an elaborately embroidered waistcoat. The Englishmen wore small tight, white bow ties. His was a rich red, looped loosely around his stand-up collar. He was shorter than the others, with very dark features, accentuated by his black, waxed mustache, twirled to stand upward at the corners, so he appeared to

227

have a permanent smile. His eyes were bright, and darted between the Englishmen as the contessa introduced them: the Duke of Monaburn, the Marquess of Rosseley, and Lord George Fox-Selwyn.

"Don't be fooled by all the different names, Puccini!" she said. "They're all from the same family, as you can probably tell by looking."

"George and I are twins," said the duke. "And Alexander here is my son. Do call me Gus," he said, shaking Puccini's hand.

"I am Giacomo," said the composer. "But most people call me Puccini."

"George," said Fox-Selwyn, bowing and offering his hand.

"Please, Signor Puccini, call me Alex," said Alexander.

"Gus, George, Alex," confirmed Puccini. "I think I can remember that."

"And here's Antonio," said Beatrice, as Moretti, the museum curator, arrived. There was another round of handshakes, repeated again when the police chief walked in with a pretty young girl on his arm. He was older than the others, stocky, and running to fat slightly, now that his job kept him confined to an office.

"May I introduce my daughter, Angelina?" he said, showing her off proudly.

"Angelina!" said Beatrice. "How lovely that for once I am not the only woman at my table! I have seated you next to Alex." She turned to Alexander. "Angelina is passionate about history, Alexander. I'm sure she will be interested to hear of your own work at Oxford." The two young people exchanged an embarrassed greeting. Beatrice and Gus flashed each other patronizing smiles.

"Shall we go in to dinner?" said Beatrice, offering Gus her arm. "George, I've put you between Antonio and Puccini. George is a great fan of *La Bohème*, you know!"

Oh Lord, thought George. *I wish Montmorency was here. How do I get out of this one?*

He got out of it by turning the conversation on to the future. He thought it would be safe simply to ask Puccini about his next work. "Beatrice tells me you have a new opera opening soon."

"In Rome. In January. Yes. It's called *Tosca*. The queen is coming to the first night."

For a moment Fox-Selwyn imagined the ancient Queen Victoria making her way to Rome, then he realized Puccini was talking about the Italian queen, Margherita, the one who had a pizza named after her.

Puccini continued. "It's a nightmare, actually. There are rumors of a plot against her. There are going to be policemen everywhere. I fear that the evening will be all about the queen and not about my work."

"I'm sure the officers will be as discreet as possible," said the police chief, trying not to sound as offended as he felt. "We cannot be too careful. There are some dangerous people around."

"As we know too well," said the contessa. "Remember the poor empress, killed so savagely only a year ago."

"How could I forget," said Moretti. "That was the day of our own disaster at the museum."

And so there they were, only just beginning the soup course, and George had inadvertently set the conversation off on the very subject he had wanted to avoid. Gus and Alexander were both careful to steer around the subject of George's inquiries into the anarchist world, but the contessa plunged straight in. It seemed to George that she shouted it across the table to the police chief.

"You really must talk to George. He knows everything there is to know about the anarchists in London. He might have some clues about what they're plotting here."

George played for time: "I really don't know anything except what I read in the papers. . . ."

"Don't underestimate yourself, George. The British government wouldn't have asked you to go to that conference in Rome if you weren't in the thick of it."

"You were at the conference?" asked the police chief. "Such a shame that the British stood out against international cooperation."

"Well, that's not really a matter for me!" said George. "I was a humble observer."

"Don't believe him, Mario," said Beatrice, thinking she was helping George by building him up in the eyes of the police chief. "He's being far too English and modest. George has spent his whole life studying international politics, spying on governments all over Europe."

"Not spying, exactly . . ." said George, still trying to deflect the conversation.

"Well, whatever he calls it, he knows a lot more than you'd think. Gus has told me all about it."

George glared at his brother, who was staring into his soup.

"So you're an expert on these anarchists, then?" asked Puccini.

"No, not at all," said George. "In fact the whole point is that we know nothing about them. It's quite different from the international affairs I've been involved in before. You see, normally we know quite a lot about our enemies. When it's another government, we know who they are, where they are, and if our intelligence is any good, we know what weapons they've got. The problem is usually working out exactly what their intentions are."

"So what's the difference now?" asked the police chief.

"Now we know everything about their intentions. These anarchists want to bring down all organized, civilized states. What we don't know is who they are, where they are, and what means they have to do their dreadful deeds. That's why this situation is so much more dangerous than what we've faced before. There's no place for the normal negotiation of diplomatic life."

"And you think things are dangerous now?" asked Moretti.

"I fear so. Surely Mario would know more," said George, trying to pass the baton to the police chief.

"There are rumors and threats all the time," he said. "No doubt that is why the police in Rome are worried about the queen's visit to your opera, Puccini."

The contessa intervened, still in her jolly mood, and picking up on none of Fox-Selwyn's discomfort. "You should go to Rome, George, and see what happens."

"Perhaps I will," replied George, trying to close the conversation down.

"I will arrange a ticket for you," said Puccini.

"Too kind," said Fox-Selwyn, though inside he was wondering whether Montmorency might be back in Europe by then, and able to go in his place. He made one more attempt at changing the subject. "So, tell us, Puccini, what is this new work of yours about?"

"It's about politics, actually," said Puccini. "An idealist fighting a despot."

Oh dear, thought George. *Why can't we talk about anything else?*

"But it's about love as well. The heroine is an opera singer. But she's a killer, too."

"Perhaps you could play us some of the tunes after dinner?" said the contessa.

"Delighted," said the composer, barely disguising his weariness at being asked to perform when he thought he was having a night off.

"And anyway, we must be boring Antonio and these two young people with all our talk of politics," Beatrice continued, as the fish course was brought in. "Alexander, tell us about your plans. Are you hoping to return to Oxford?"

"It rather depends on Father," he said, "but in any case I can't resume my studies until next autumn, when the new academic year begins. They've given me time off till then."

"Well, that's good news for us, isn't it?" said Beatrice. "We'll have you here for a good few months."

Angelina said nothing. But she agreed. It was very good news indeed.

CHAPTER 33

≫

MRS. CURTIS BAYFIELD

*I*n Paterson, Montmorency, Farcett, Frank, Tom, and Vi were preparing for dinner. No one was quite sure what to expect, and whether people in these parts dressed formally for their evening meal, but Vi remembered that Harrison had mentioned that his brother had an English wife, and they all agreed to put on evening wear, hoping it would be better to be over- rather than underdressed.

Montmorency went downstairs early, and got into a conversation with the barman. The stooped, sour man made him revise his view that Americans were just as deferential as the British to their betters. In the twenty minutes before the others joined him, Montmorency learned a great deal more about their host. Harrison Bayfield's older brother, Curtis, was, as Montmorency had suspected, one of the leading men in Paterson. He owned several of the largest factories; whole estates of houses; shops; offices; and even the hotel they were staying in. There were photographs of Paterson landmarks on the walls, and the barman talked Montmorency through them, eventually pointing out a picture of a mighty waterfall. It was the source of the power that had made Paterson rich, and towering over it was a grand mansion, built like a medieval fortress.

"That's the Bayfield house," he said. "Built by Curtis

Bayfield's father. He came here with nothing and bought up business after business until he became one of the richest men in America. They say you can see right across the town from up there, though the likes of me will never get in to check. Curtis Bayfield can stand at his window and watch his whole empire at work. There's almost nothing that happens in Paterson that doesn't make money for Mr. Bayfield. He'll be buying your dinner tonight with the money you pay to stay at this hotel. They ought to rename the city. A hundred years ago they called it after William Paterson. A great man. One of the Founding Fathers. Signed the American Constitution. They had a dream of making this place a source of riches for everyone. Now it just makes money for a few. And it makes the most for Curtis Bayfield, through the sweat and toil of the rest of us. This place shouldn't be called Paterson. It should be called Bayfield."

Montmorency was shocked at the man's indiscretion. He doubted if a barman in London would talk to a guest so openly, and with such ill-disguised contempt for his employer. He noted that the barman didn't seem to put much "sweat and toil" into his work, as he aimlessly rubbed the bar top with a grubby cloth. Montmorency wondered if he should mention it to Harrison, or even to Curtis Bayfield himself when he met him later, but he knew that it was more important to make a friend of this barman. He might be a very useful source of information in days to come.

The others gradually assembled downstairs, and Harrison Bayfield arrived to escort them to his brother's home.

"Curtis is sending down a couple of automobiles to collect us. I sent a note telling him I was bringing some friends from England. He says his wife, Cecilia, can't wait to meet you. She hasn't seen anyone from her homeland in quite a while."

They heard the cars arriving, as the drivers honked their horns to frighten the local children out of the way. Montmorency and his friends had all seen cars before, and everyone except Vi and Tom had even been in a few in England, but these gleaming metal constructions were far bigger than anything they had come across in Europe. It was a fine evening, and the hoods on the broad, high vehicles were folded down. The two chauffeurs, dressed in identical uniforms and wearing goggles that made them look quite terrifying, got out and moved in unison to open the doors for their passengers and help them up into the stiffly uphol- stered green leather seats. Harrison climbed in alongside Vi, squashing up against her to make room for Tom on his other side. Montmorency and Farcett had more space in the car behind, with Frank sitting up front by the chauffeur, men- tally pretending that he was doing the driving.

It was an uphill journey. It reminded Montmorency of their first ride to the contessa's house in Florence, and how that wonderful city had been laid out before them in all its splendor when they reached the top. But this was different. In Florence the view grew more breathtaking with every inch of the climb, and the city seemed to be a triumph of man working with nature to produce a greater beauty than had been there before. In Paterson, the countryside was ravishing, with its lush trees and the thunderous waterfall plummeting into the ravine, but man's hand had been rough on the landscape below. It was a dark scene of mean houses cramped together, and giant factories, way out of scale with everything else. A smoky haze hung over the town. Florence had radiated noble human spirit. Paterson seemed to blanket its people with a depressing fog. Or had Montmorency simply paid too much attention to the sullen barman, who had poisoned his mind against Curtis Bayfield before they had even met?

But Montmorency's first glimpse of Curtis confirmed his preconceptions. He was standing, with a hand in one pocket, gazing out across his terraced garden to the town below. He had a proprietorial air, and Montmorency could well imagine what he was thinking. All the activity in the valley was making money for him. So long as everyone down there kept working he would be secure in his mansion on top of the hill. Montmorency looked across to Frank, to see if he was thinking the same. Far from it. Frank was loving his car ride, and was more obviously happy than Montmorency had seen him for a very long time.

Curtis turned to greet them as the cars drew to a stop. "Welcome to Bayfield!" he shouted over the noise of the engines.

For a moment Montmorency thought the renaming must have happened, then he understood that Bayfield was the name of the house, not the town (yet).

Harrison proudly introduced his new friends to his brother, and Curtis shook their hands with great bonhomie. His eyes visibly lit when he heard Frank's title "Lord Francis Fox-Selwyn," and he seemed pleased to hear that Farcett was a doctor.

"Come upstairs and meet Mrs. Bayfield. She's just getting ready. She got real excited when I told her Harry was bringing some English people. Have you come from London?"

"London and Scotland, yes," said Montmorency.

"Cecilia's a London girl herself," said Curtis. "Though she's been here quite a while. She was a widow when I married her. Her first husband met her in London, and brought her over about fifteen years ago. Come inside and say hello."

They went through the high double doors into a grand hall that seemed more like the entrance to a public building or a museum than a home. Then they filed through one interconnecting room after another, each with high windows looking out over the waterfall to the town below and portraits on the walls: seventeenth- and eighteenth-century pictures of English grandees, which looked to Montmorency as if they must have been shipped to America as a job lot, to give the impression of a solid, aristocratic past. At the end of the line was a huge room with a marble fireplace at the far end opposite the door. From a distance, they could see a statuesque woman with an elegant blond coiffure standing with her back to them, staring into the flames. As they drew closer, she heard their footsteps and began to turn. It was a movement of consummate grace. A sapphire bracelet dripped from her wrist as she lifted her arm, and her sky-blue silk dress clung softly to the curves of her figure, rustling quietly as she moved. She lifted her head, smiling, ready to meet the strangers from her homeland.

She noticed Vi first. Striking and open, well dressed, but perhaps a little tired after her long journey. She could tell that the younger boy was Vi's son. He shared her fine bones, and her natural smile. The other boy, the tallest of the group, with wiry red hair, freckles, and gangly limbs, had all the awkwardness of adolescence. He didn't share any of the features of the two older men, who had the same trim but muscular build, and might be brothers. One of them looked faintly familiar. She kept her composure as her mind raced back through the years. As they got closer, Montmorency recognized something about her eyes. Her plump cheeks were familiar, even if the smooth, flattering hairstyle hid their full size. There was a tiny scar, hidden by skillful makeup, alongside her nose. He could picture the hairy lump that had been cut away. He could hardly believe it, but it must be true.

It was Cissie.

The raucous, clumsy girl who had persecuted him with passion at the Marimion Hotel was now the glamorous wife of an American millionaire. How she had changed.

Neither Montmorency nor Cissie could hear them, but Harrison and Curtis had begun the introductions. Cissie mechanically shook hands with Doctor Farcett, saying, "Pleased to meet you" in the same American accent as her husband and brother-in-law. She was charming to Vi and Tom. When Harrison announced, "Lord Francis Fox-Selwyn," she took Frank's hand warmly, saying, "I believe I knew your father some years ago. I didn't know he had any children."

Montmorency cut into the conversation. "It is his uncle you remember, Lord George Fox-Selwyn. Frank is the son of the Duke of Monaburn."

It was sweet to see that her snobbery had not died, and Montmorency was amused by the way her top lip quivered as she heard this news. "And I hope you remember me," he said, not really meaning it, but nevertheless intrigued to know if he still looked like his younger self.

"Mr. Montmorency!" she said charmingly, without the old lisp she had used, just for him. "Of course I remember you. Curtis, Mr. Montmorency is an old friend of mine from London. How clever of you, Harrison, to bring him here."

Montmorency was too polite to challenge her claim to friendship, too much of a gentleman to point out that he had been a paying customer at the hotel managed by her father. He imagined that she had given her second husband an idealized version of her British origins. And who was he to talk, anyway? He was not what he seemed either. He was fascinated by her transformation, and wondered if she now felt completely comfortable in her new identity, just as he did in his.

They had drinks, and then a meal. Montmorency noticed that everything ran extremely smoothly. Cissie, or Cecilia as he tried to remember to call her, had developed into a great organizer. Her home ran with all the surface efficiency of a grand hotel.

"Tell me, gentlemen, what brings you to Paterson?" asked Curtis Bayfield. "We don't often see the English aristocracy out here."

Montmorency was ready with his answer. He had worked it out with Frank and Farcett at the Waldorf-Astoria in New York. Even after the encounter with Harrison, he hadn't expected such a perfect audience, so likely to be flattered by and to believe his tale. "We are interested in industry, sir. We know that Britain has a lot to learn from your country, where you do everything in such a modern way with none of the snobbery and pomposity we find at home."

"My family has always made its money as landowners," added Frank. "Commerce has always been frowned upon by people of my class. But I feel that the future is in manufacturing, and that a nation's real wealth comes from the activities of people such as yourself."

The Bayfields lapped it up. "So you have heard of Paterson in England?" asked Curtis.

"Heard *of* it, but heard little *about* it," said Montmorency. "That is why we have come. To see for ourselves, and to learn."

Doctor Farcett chimed in, rescuing Montmorency from having to go into detail about his (nonexistent) industrial interests in England. "I, however, am en route elsewhere," he said. "I have come from England to seek out Mr. Edison, the great inventor. I have a project involving medical technology on which I wish to seek his advice."

"Well, he's just down the road here," said Curtis, waving

his hand in a rough westerly direction. "His invention factory churns out miracles all the time, and we get them first here in Paterson. I'll play you my phonograph after dinner, and when you get back to the hotel, I'll call you on the telephone. Edison designed the generators in my factories, and we use his bulbs in our electric lights. Gentlemen, you have come to the right place. Now tell me, Doctor Farcett. What is this medical machine of yours?"

"I wonder if the dinner table is an appropriate place to talk about it," said Robert coyly. "Especially with such a charming lady present."

Cissie blushed. *Still a sponge for compliments,* Montmorency noted.

"Doctor Farcett, all sorts of things have been discussed at this dinner table. This invention of yours, it could make money, right?"

"I suppose it could, though of course that is not my prime motivation."

"Listen, Doctor —"

"Please, call me Robert."

"Robert. You're not going to get anywhere with anything without money. Now what is this machine of yours?"

Farcett didn't want to reveal all his secrets, but somehow, faced with Curtis Bayfield's relentless persistence, he found himself describing the Bodyscreener, and his dream of making moving pictures of the inner workings of the human body; getting quite carried away with his vision of what a brilliant teaching aid it could be in medical schools. "But I can't get the image large and sharp enough to film it," he said. "That's where I'm hoping Edison can help."

"I'll lend you a driver to get you over there, if you like," said Curtis. "He could drop you off on the way to take Harrison back to New York tomorrow. I'll send him to pick you up at the hotel in the morning. Say nine o'clock?"

Farcett was overwhelmed by Curtis's can-do attitude. Everything seemed to move so fast for these men. He didn't feel he had the right to do anything but accept. "Well, yes, thank you, that would be most kind."

"And keep me posted on developments. Who knows, I may want to invest in this invention of yours."

"We could call it the 'Paterson People Picture.'" Harrison laughed.

"Or the 'Bayfield Body Box,'" said Curtis. "Imagine the fun people could have, looking inside themselves. They'd be queuing up for miles."

Farcett smiled politely. But hated to hear his idea discussed like that. The sooner he was away from Paterson, the better.

Cissie changed the subject, asking Vi about her plans. By the time they were taking coffee in the drawing room they had agreed to go shopping together in New York. Cecilia would introduce Vi to the top fashion houses of the big city, and show Tom the sights. Montmorency was glad Vi would be out of the way while he investigated the low politics of Paterson, even though he knew he would end up paying for a trunkful of new clothes. And he also knew that he would have to spend a lot of time in the company of Curtis Bayfield, as he showed off the glories of his savage commercial empire.

Montmorency, Farcett, and Frank stayed up late that night, talking in Montmorency's room. First he had to explain to them about Cissie. Farcett could hardly believe that the elegant and composed woman they had met at dinner was the same person whose gross habits Montmorency impersonated before them.

"'Mithter Montmorenthy,'" he lisped, wiggling his hips and pouting. "'Mithter Montmorenthy, pleath help Thithie find her likkle kittin!'"

Frank was choking with laughter. But after a good cough, he brought the others down to earth. "Now, how am I going to get away from all this high life to see what's really going on in this town?" he asked.

"We agreed. We'll say that you've gone to West Orange with Robert to see Edison."

"But Robert's being driven there now, isn't he? I'm really going to have to go with him, if that story's going to stick."

"Oh dear," said Montmorency. "You're right."

"You can come with me, and then you can make your own way back," Doctor Farcett suggested.

"How? How will I know the way?" Frank asked anxiously.

Montmorency got out his guidebook and unfolded the map from the section on New Jersey. They pored over it together, trying to find Paterson, and then West Orange. "It's not too far. There seems to be some sort of a road. You can do it, Frank, I know you can. Take some working clothes with you when you leave with Robert, change when you get there, and set off back again. But don't come here. Go straight to get a job. We can leave messages for each other at the post office. Now that Bayfield knows what you look like, we can't risk being seen together. I promise I'll check every day. Do you think you can manage on your own?"

Frank suddenly looked very young and very naive, and Montmorency wondered whether he really had the right to expect such courage from the son of his friend.

"Of course I'll do it," said Frank. "It's why we've come all this way, isn't it? We didn't come to eat lobster with rich Americans; we wanted to find out what the anarchists are planning. And if we fail, innocent lives may be lost."

Montmorency clapped him on the back. "Well said, my boy. You're very brave."

"But now get to bed," said Robert, using his "doctor's" voice. "We've got an early start in the morning and another ride in one of those wonderful motorcars."

CHAPTER 34

≫

EDISON

*D*octor Farcett had intended to write to Edison, warning of his arrival, and politely asking for an interview. But Bayfield's generosity with the car meant there was no time for that, and he turned up unannounced. He and Frank thanked the driver, said good-bye to Harrison, and waved him off. Then Frank nipped into some bushes by the side of the road, changed his clothes, and gave his bag to Farcett.

"Good luck," said Farcett, wanting to shake hands or even hug him, but holding back in case they were seen. "Keep in touch. We'll be worrying about you."

"I will," said Frank. "And don't worry. I'll be all right."

Then he set off, back down the road they had come on, alone.

Farcett turned and faced the huge factory where Edison worked. He had seen pictures of it before, in books and magazines about the man who must be the most famous scientist in the world. Even so, like so many things in America, it turned out to be far larger than he'd expected, with separate buildings for each of Edison's enthusiasms: electronics, chemistry, sound, and light, rather than just laboratories for the inventing teams Edison had gathered around him. There were real factories, too, manufacturing the fruits of their ingenuity for sale all over the world. Farcett could hardly believe that he was really there, on the very spot where some of the greatest advances of modern civilization had taken place. He wouldn't blame the great man if he resented the intrusion and sent him back, following Frank on the lonely road to Paterson, but he hoped he wouldn't. He wanted more than anything to meet Edison, to be in the presence of someone who had really made a difference, someone who got things done.

He approached a man at the gate. "Excuse me," he said, hearing his voice coming back to him, ludicrously English and mannered. "My name is Doctor Robert Farcett. I have come from England to see Mr. Edison."

The guard was chewing tobacco, and golden spittle trickled down onto his chin as he spoke.

"You got an appointment?" he drawled.

"Well, no, actually," Farcett stuttered. "I had intended to write, but I got here sooner than I expected. Mr. Bayfield kindly offered me the use of his car."

"You're from Bayfield? You might as well go in. Don't know where he is right now, though. Try the machine shop." The man gestured with a limp wave, and Farcett walked uncertainly in the rough direction of his arm. He had seen pictures of Edison, so he knew vaguely who he was looking for, but he had no idea of the character of the man. Would he be offended by the unannounced approach, contemptuous of Farcett's amateur attempts at invention, outraged at his presumption in disturbing him at his work?

And there was plenty of work going on. Farcett entered

what looked like a barn. Inside, it was brightly lit by Edison's own invention: strings of lightbulbs were draped from the ceiling, powered by one of his own generators. All around, men were carrying equipment, drilling holes, and sending showers of sparks into the air with welding torches. At one end, there was a hubbub of activity, punctuated by the odd blast of musical notes. About twenty men were carrying phonographs like the one Farcett had seen the night before at Curtis Bayfield's house. They set them up on a tier of wooden staging, their huge metal horns arranged in a semicircle, pointing towards a band of musicians sitting in their shirt-sleeves, armed with trumpets, euphoniums, trombones, French horns, and cornets. It was as if the phonographs were an audience, here to listen to a concert. Farcett stood well back, careful not to interrupt.

The operation was directed by a man Farcett suspected to be Edison himself. In his mid-fifties, he looked like the eager, round-faced man Farcett had seen in so many photographs, but where those formal portraits had shown him in well-pressed clothes, with a long jacket over a smart waistcoat and with a black bow tie fastened around a high collar, the man before him wore no coat at all. His shirt was coming out from his trousers, the collar was open, and the sleeves were rolled to his elbows. He was busily checking the position of each machine, running his hand through his hair to brush his unruly fringe from his eyes as he adjusted the distance between the phonographs and the band, ordering his assistants about, but always checking what they did, and constantly encouraging the musicians with assurances that all would be ready soon.

This was the Edison Farcett had read about: the energetic proprietor who had lost none of his appetite for work as he had grown rich. And Farcett realized what must be going on now. They were making new cylinders for sale to the owners of phonographs.

Eventually Edison was satisfied.

"Silence!" he called, and another man blew a whistle, which signaled everyone within earshot to lay down their tools. A man stood behind each phonograph ready to set the cylinder spinning against the needle that would carve the tracks of musical vibration into the wax. Edison held up his hand. The conductor anxiously turned between him and the band, nervous in case he should start them playing too early, so that the opening failed to record, or late, wasting precious space on the cylinders. The bandsmen themselves shared his apprehension. They each knew that one wrong note could be immortalized forever, to be heard over and over again. But everything worked perfectly. Edison dropped his hand and the conductor leaned towards the bank of recording machines, bellowing:

"*America's Glory March*, by the Edison Military Band."

Then he spun around and whipped the players into action. They belted out a rousing tune at high volume, coming to a halt after a couple of minutes, and waiting for Edison's hand to rise again. When it did, they relaxed and the workmen removed the cylinders from the phonographs. Farcett wondered if this might be a good moment to move in and introduce himself, but Edison was calling everyone to order again.

"Well done. That was good. Stay where you are. We'll just do the changeover and go for the next recording."

The assistants frantically loaded up the machines with new cylinders. Edison raised his hand, lowered it, and the conductor made the same booming announcement again.

"*America's Glory March*, by the Edison Military Band."

The same tune rocked the warehouse, with the same gusto as before. The process was repeated over and over again. After an hour of it, by which time about a hundred recorded cylinders had been neatly stacked away, Edison called out, "OK, take a break. We'll do another batch after coffee."

By then, Farcett wouldn't have minded if he never heard that stomping tune again. He had a feeling it would be echoing in his head for a good while to come. He gingerly made his way towards the phonographs, where Edison was making a few adjustments.

"I wonder if I might introduce myself," he said.

There was no sign of any response from Edison, and Farcett tried again.

"I am most reluctant to disturb you, but I have come all the way from England, and would very much like to talk."

This time Edison replied, without turning around. "Well, if you've come that far, you might as well make yourself useful," he said, reaching out an arm behind him. "Pass me that spanner."

Farcett picked it up and placed it into Edison's hand.

"Thanks. And what brings you all the way from England?" continued the inventor, still not looking at his visitor.

Farcett suddenly felt very stupid, talking about his own ideas to one of the most fruitful minds in the world. "I wanted to ask your advice. It's about an idea I've got."

"Screwdriver," Edison interrupted, reaching out behind him again. "And what makes you think I'll give you advice? If you've got a good idea you should work on it, patent it, and produce it. I'm not in the business of refining ideas so you can make your fortune."

"Oh, I'm not looking to make a fortune, Mr. Edison. In fact, my idea isn't really mine at all. It's something you could do. Something that would bring together two of your projects. I've been trying, but I can't seem to make it work."

Now Edison sounded quite sarcastic, still busying himself with his machine. "And you've been doing this out of the kindness of your heart, for the benefit of mankind, I suppose."

"Well, yes, actually," said Farcett, embarrassed. "You see, I'm a medical doctor, and I can see great potential in bringing together the X-ray and the moving picture. I want to make films of the internal organs. For teaching purposes."

Edison at last looked around to see his unexpected visitor. Farcett held out his hand, and the inventor wiped his on a rag before accepting the approach.

"I'm Doctor Robert Farcett."

"You from London?"

"I do work in London, yes. I have arrangements with various London institutions, and I lecture and teach. But I work in Scotland, too. That's where I do most of my research on X-rays."

"In Edinburgh?"

"No, on an island, actually. It's called Tarimond."

"So that other people can't interfere with you, and steal your ideas?"

Edison had cut straight to the heart of Farcett's ambivalence about his X-ray project. He was forcing him to admit that he did want to take the credit if his idea worked. There was a pause before the doctor replied, trying to justify himself.

"Yes, I suppose I must admit to a certain amount of ambition. But I do other work on Tarimond, too. I am in charge of the island's health care. I moved my X-ray work there because I have good facilities, and a particularly able assistant." As he spoke, he thought of Maggie for the first time since the start of the trip. He wondered if she had recovered from the flu yet.

Edison brought him back to the subject in hand. "And this idea of yours?"

"I'm trying to devise a way of producing an X-ray image of the whole body. Clear enough to show more than just the bones. Something that will reveal the inner workings of the organs as they happen. Then I want to commit that image to film, so that it can be shown at medical schools. So doctors won't need to learn by cutting up dead bodies. They'll be able to see how a live, healthy person functions. From the inside. I call it the Bodyscreener."

Edison was looking closely at Farcett now. He seemed to like something about him. He picked up one of the recorded cylinders. "Come into my office. I want to go somewhere quiet to hear how this has turned out. We can talk more privately there, too."

They walked through the vast grounds of the factory, stopping here and there for Edison to check on the progress of work.

"What's your latest project?" asked Farcett politely.

"I want to find a way of reproducing these things," said Edison, holding up the cylinder. "You've seen how long it takes to record them separately. Just imagine how many we could make if we could produce a master recording, and then just copy them off. I can see a day when every house will have a phonograph and whole libraries of tunes they can play as often as they like."

Somehow Farcett couldn't quite imagine such a thing, but he admired Edison's enthusiasm; the way he kept thinking ahead, even though he had already invented enough things to make him a rich man.

They reached the office, and Edison set up the cylinder to play back. The rousing beat of *America's Glory March* started up again, crackly and distant now, compared with the echoing *oompah* of the band in the flesh. Still, it sounded quite miraculous to Farcett, who had heard very few recordings before. "I was listening to some of your cylinders last night," he said. "At the home of Mr. Curtis Bayfield." He hoped that the mention of a man who had boasted of being one of Edison's greatest patrons would help to make Edison accept him. He was wrong.

Edison snarled back. "You're a friend of Bayfield? Did he send you here?"

"He said he was a great admirer of yours."

"I bet he did. Did he tell you how he's trying to get a share of my profits?"

"N-no," stuttered Farcett, trying to distance himself from Bayfield. "And I only met him yesterday. I was just passing through Paterson on my way here."

"Well, my advice is to keep away from him. And don't tell him anything about this idea of yours. He'll claim it as his own before you know it."

Farcett didn't mention that Bayfield already knew. "I understand," he said. "What do you think of the idea, Mr. Edison? Do you think it could work? I know you did a lot of work on X-rays when you developed the fluoroscope. I so admire you for not taking any profits from it. For donating it to medical science."

Edison went quiet again, then reached for his hat.

"Come with me, Doctor Farcett. I want to show you something," he said. And Farcett followed him out of the factory, wondering what new invention he might be about to see.

CHAPTER 35

≫

THE HOSPITAL

*E*dison walked quickly, and Farcett was quite breathless trying to keep up. Soon they were outside a hospital. Doctor Farcett wondered if Edison had already hit upon the Bodyscreener idea himself, and that he might be about to see it in action — all his own secret efforts having been for nothing. He felt a deep disappointment inside himself, and acknowledged more than ever before how much he had wanted the glory of being first with the idea. Edison stayed silent as they climbed the steps and went inside.

But he didn't lead Farcett to a laboratory. They went together into a long, quiet ward, where sick men lay pale against crisp sheets. An efficient woman in a smart white uniform greeted them in a whisper.

"Good afternoon, Mr. Edison. I'm afraid he is rather poorly today."

"Oh dear," said the inventor. "May we visit for just a few minutes? This is Doctor Robert Farcett, from London."

The sister looked at Farcett with increased respect. "Just a moment, please," she said. "I will go and make him comfortable." She went ahead of them to the bed farthest from the door, and busied herself tucking in the already immaculate blankets. Then she turned and nodded to them, encouraging them to approach.

The patient in the bed was a shriveled old man, bald and wrinkled, barely able to open his eyelids to see them. He raised one finger of his left hand in a gesture of greeting. His other arm was tightly bandaged from shoulder to fingertips. Edison sat on the bed and took the patient's left hand. Farcett wondered why Edison had brought him here. Did he want a second opinion on the old man's care? Was it an elderly relative perhaps? Someone Edison loved, and could not bear the idea of losing even though his life was obviously slipping away? Farcett stood awkwardly at the end of the bed as Edison's eyes filled with tears. The patient wheezed and spluttered for breath, and the sister swooped in to help him.

"I think perhaps you had better leave him. The excitement might be too much."

Edison squeezed the old man's left hand and rose mournfully from the bed. "It won't be long now," whispered the sister as they turned to leave. "He'll soon be at peace."

Outside in the corridor, Farcett still felt awkward. He agreed with the sister. The man was close to death. He appeared to be suffering from a wasting disease that had affected his lungs. Farcett felt he must say something to the distressed scientist.

"A relative of yours?" he asked.

"No, not a relative. An assistant. One of the most able men I have ever worked with. How old would you say he is?"

"Seventy, seventy-five?" guessed Farcett, thinking back to the sunken cheeks and shadowed eye sockets staring out from the pillow.

"Thirty-nine," said Edison. "Hans Schmidt is thirty-nine years old. And he's dying. He'll leave a young widow and three children with no father to care for them."

"What's wrong with him? What do the doctors say?"

"The doctors don't put a name to it, but I know why he is suffering," said Edison. "I watched him decline. First his eyes began to ache and burn, then his skin started to flake, and his hair fell out. Then this dreadful illness entered his very bones. It was as if he was being burned away from within."

"Did he catch something?" asked Farcett, wondering if there were strange germs in America producing new diseases he had not come across at home.

"No. He was a healthy man. Healthy until he started working for me, that is. Doctor Farcett, I hired that man when he came to America from Germany looking for a new and prosperous life. He had worked in Würzburg. At the Institute —"

Farcett interrupted. "The institute where they're developing X-rays? I was there only a year or so ago."

"Yes, there. And I put him to work here, helping me devise new X-ray machines. He spent hours in my laboratory, testing out designs for the fluoroscope. I used him as a technician, an adviser, and he volunteered himself as a mock patient. I exposed every inch of his body to the rays. Between us we invented that cute piece of machinery that can show a doctor a crack in a bone, or the position of a bullet in a heart. I know that what we did will save lives. But Doctor Farcett, I suspect now that this wonderful new ray has its dangers, too.

Maybe not for a single patient who might be exposed for a minute or two in a lifetime, but for people who work with it day in, day out. I think we could be on the verge of an epidemic within the medical profession itself. That poor man may be only one of the first. Who knows, I may follow, though in truth I left all the hands-on work to him. I took the credit for what he did, but he was the man who sacrificed his life to working day after day to perfect the fluoroscope. Now his body is riddled with tumors. There is no hope for him."

"But we have been experimenting with the power of X-rays to *shrink* tumors!" insisted Farcett, hoping desperately that Edison was wrong. "We are convinced that X-rays are a bringer of health, not disease. They are widely used in Europe now. No invention has spread so quickly. Three years ago we didn't even know they existed, and now you can even look down a machine in a fairground, and see your toes wiggling, just for fun."

"The man in there invented that machine," said Edison. "We saw it first as a medical instrument, and that's why we didn't patent it. I didn't want to profit from something that could benefit mankind. Then other people picked it up and turned it into a toy. Do you know who the main investor in those peep shows is?" he asked, looking into Farcett's eyes.

"I've no idea," said Farcett, noticing that Edison was still gently crying.

"Curtis Bayfield! Your friend from Paterson is making money from the fruits of our research."

"Have you told him about the dangers? Have you shown him the man you have just shown me?"

"I have written, and he has written back dismissing my concerns. He insists that most people aren't at risk. He says that it's the endless long-term exposure that did it for my man. He's probably right. After all, I'm not ill, and neither is anyone else at West Orange, but then none of us has had as much continuous exposure, over so many years, as Schmidt. Think about it, Farcett. Are you willing to submit yourself to the danger of ending up like him? You tell me that you have an assistant carrying out experiments when you are away from that island of yours. He, too, will be exposed."

"It's not a man," said Farcett. "It's a woman."

"And she has been working with X-rays?"

"Every day, and in massive quantities." Farcett was thinking of Maggie, and his mind began to race over the danger she might be facing. "We have been increasing the strength of the rays to get a better picture. We've had whole rows of tubes working together to try to capture the entire body. I got the idea from Professor Krauss in Würzburg. He's been working on trying to get a full body image, though his is only a static picture." Farcett paused for a moment, thinking of Professor Krauss. "Do you know, I heard before we left for America that he was ill. I thought it must just be this flu that has been sweeping Europe. Suppose he's in danger, too? We must warn everyone. Everybody working in this field."

"But how?"

"We must get papers into the medical journals. I can write

something for your magazines here, and spread the word as fast as I can."

"But look at the good X-rays are doing, look at the people they've saved. The bones that have been mended, the illnesses detected. Think of the uses my portable fluoroscope might have at the scenes of accidents, on battlefields. We can't risk starting a panic that would put an end to all that. If we're going to spread the word about the dangers of overexposure we have to do it in a way that won't frighten people off X-rays completely. That's why I've waited. I've started looking into ways of shielding doctors and technicians from the rays as they work. I don't want to raise the alarm before I've devised a way to reassure as well."

"But all this time Maggie is working with my machines!" cried Farcett, imagining her carrying out the long list of experiments he had set out in the infirmary log before rushing away from Tarimond. "I told her to make sure she did something every day, so that when I got back there would be real progress. I thought perhaps she might perfect the image so that it could be captured on film."

"Perhaps she has," said Edison, sensing Farcett's concern for his assistant. "Perhaps she has made a real breakthrough."

"But at what cost? She may be ill already." Farcett paused. "She was feeling ill when I left. I thought it was just tiredness. She'd been working so hard. I didn't even say a final good-bye. I must get a message to her telling her to stop."

"Send a cable," said Edison, moved by Farcett's distress,

and guessing that his relationship with this female assistant went beyond the professional.

"But she's on an island. They don't have the telegraph there. I write her letters, of course, but I have no idea whether she gets them; and there's no hope of me getting hers, with all this traveling around. I really must go myself."

"And how long will that take?" asked Edison. "You'd have to cross the Atlantic first. We will find a way to get the message through. In the meantime, I want you to stay here and study Schmidt. Watch him through his final days, and work out what is wrong, and why. Then you can write about it and tell the world. Doctor Farcett, your Bodyscreener may be a way off still, but believe me, it is a good idea, and its day will come. In the meantime, you must help to make this new science safe. I beg you to stay and do it here. If you run away to Scotland, you will help one researcher, who may be perfectly well. Here you have a case to study. You can provide real evidence, which might save many lives. Or you may find that I am wrong, that Schmidt has some other disease, unrelated to his work, and a panic can be avoided. That way, X-rays can continue to develop, your own project may go ahead, and even more lives can be saved. Doctor Farcett, you have a duty to stay here."

Farcett considered his options. His heart wanted to rush to Tarimond, however long it took, to wrench Maggie from the potential dangers of the tasks he had so rashly given her. But his head, his calm scientific head, agreed with Edison. It was a choice between racing to deal with a theoretical risk, or taking time to establish whether there was a genuine one. And who could tell? If X-rays turned out to be safe, maybe the Bodyscreener could still become a reality.

He made his decision. He would set about contacting Maggie Goudie at once. He could cable his friend Doctor Dougall at Great Ormond Street Hospital, explaining the situation, commanding Maggie to stop all X-ray work, and asking Dougall to forward the message to Tarimond by post. Farcett would have to keep it short. He didn't want to frighten the radiographers at Great Ormond Street. And anyway, even at its most terse, a complicated message could cost several dollars, and he would need to keep an eye on his cash if he was staying longer than expected. He would back the cable up with a proper letter, setting everything out in detail. A letter shouldn't take so very long to reach Tarimond. Just a few weeks at most, and then all would be well. Maggie would be safe, and Farcett could stay on to study Edison's assistant, and examine everyone else who had worked with X-rays in West Orange, New Jersey, USA.

He was soon glad he stayed. Visitors from New York had brought the flu virus with them. Within a week he had the chance of another epidemiological study, this time of the progress of the disease through a workforce. He really was becoming quite an expert on the communication of influenza. Perhaps he would be able to expand his articles for *The Physician* into a book.

CHAPTER 36

≫

THE *QUESTION*

*F*rank had not walked far down the road back to Paterson when a farmer offered him a lift on his cart. He was pleased to have company on his way to market, and pumped Frank for information about his background, asking what he was doing in New Jersey, so far from home. Frank had his story ready. He knew his accent would give him away, so he admitted to being from England, and said he was looking for work in the textile trade. The farmer told him where to go to find it, directing him straight to the heart of the Italian community in Paterson, in the slums huddled around the silk works. There, Frank found himself a room in a house that reminded him of his digs near the ice-cream factory in London. He drew heavily on his experiences working for Rossi when people asked him why he had come to America. It all fitted with what they knew of exploitation in Europe. They were not surprised he had come, and he was quickly absorbed into their world.

At work, in the factory, he started dropping quiet political hints that drew the attention of agitators against Bayfield's grip on the poor of Paterson. He was soon drinking with them. They found out that he could write in English and Italian, and within a week he was taken, after dark, to the cramped office where they produced a newspaper, the *Question*, which circulated among Italian immigrants, calling for the overthrow of the bosses, and justice for all. It was the perfect vantage point to observe the anarchists, and listen out for any plans for future atrocities.

But it was lonely. In London, Frank had had Montmorency at his side, to guide him in the skills of deception, and to encourage him when the rigors of factory work seemed too much. Here, he could not risk regular trips back to the hotel for baths and gossip. He and Montmorency exchanged notes almost every day: Frank would describe conditions and characters; Montmorency sent words of encouragement, chitchat about Vi and Tom, and the occasional tip, gleaned from Bayfield, about troublemakers among the workforce. Sometimes there were a few extra dollars in the envelope, too, and Frank could buy himself a good meal or warm clothes. He missed his friends, and wished he could visit them. But he couldn't: He was supposed to be in West Orange, with Farcett. So Montmorency, Vi, and Tom enjoyed the high life with the Bayfields on their own.

Perhaps, then, it wasn't surprising that with the passage of time Frank became less of an observer and more of a participant. He hadn't liked Bayfield face-to-face. He loathed him as a distant employer, mean with money and working conditions. And he needed company. The driven men and women who collected in the office of the *Question* night after night to exchange grievances and news from Europe soon became a substitute family. He was delighted when a familiar face appeared, a week or so after he first started working there.

Frank at once recognized the long fringe and the passionate eyes. It was Guido. The last time Frank had seen him he had been hurling burning jars from the museum building in Florence. They had run in opposite directions as they escaped. Frank knew Guido had been sent to Paterson, he had heard about it in London, but Guido was astounded to see his English friend here in America.

"Frank! What are you doing here?"

One of the others answered. "He works with us, Guido. He's from England. Do you know him?"

By now Guido was embracing Frank warmly. "I knew him in Florence. He is a good man."

"We know that. Look at the stuff he has been writing." Guido was shown that week's edition of the paper. A long article, condemning housing conditions in Paterson, ran under the byline "Franco Lupo."

Guido laughed. "I read this on the way back from New York. I've been away, Frank, doing some deliveries in Manhattan." There was a hint of a conspiratorial nod between Guido and the man setting up the printing press. Guido clasped Frank's arms and stared into his eyes. "So you are Franco Lupo?" He translated the Italian name. "Frank Wolf."

"Yes, that's my English name," said Frank, fibbing. He'd made up the pen name by playing on an irritating joke that was often made by dull people about his family surname. At last the clumsy transposition of Fox and Wolf had been use-ful. There was no need to mention the hyphen and the

Selwyn. "It's Wolfe with an 'e' on the end," said Frank, embroidering the deception. "Like the great general who beat the French at Quebec."

"Well, we Italians like anyone who beats the French!" Guido laughed. "That's something that will bind our two nations forever!" He said the name again. "Frank Wolfe. I never knew. Always thought of you as just young Frank in Florence. Frank Wolfe . . . You seem older now. More mature. And now you're Franco Lupo. It's a good name for a writer. Trips off the tongue. A good name for a man of action, too. How did you get here? How did you know where to find me?"

"I wasn't looking for you. I didn't know you were here," lied Frank. "I was sent here by Italian friends in London. I worked in an ice-cream factory there. Rossi's. You may have heard of it."

"Rossi's. Were you there for the strike? Everyone has heard of Rossi's."

"It's because of the strike I had to get away."

Guido was thrilled. "You are the Englishman who started it all. I've heard of you. Malpensa wrote about it. They feared you'd been arrested."

"No, I got away. But I was at a meeting where Malpensa spoke the night before. What a man! He was the real fire behind the strike. He inspired me to hit out at Rossi. I've never heard anyone like him."

"He's proud of you, too. They did so much damage to Rossi's factory that day that he went out of business. Hanged himself. Great result."

Frank smiled, but inside he shuddered. For the second time he had been indirectly responsible for someone's death, and much as he had despised Rossi, he had never meant to kill him. But at least his anarchist credentials were established to the people in the office and to Guido himself, who turned out to be one of the most fiery among them. From that moment any doubts Frank may have had about fitting in were dispelled. And in truth it became easier for him to act the part as Guido's seductive enthusiasm for political change took him over once again.

Up the hill, in the great house, Montmorency, Vi, and Tom were leading a very different life, seeing Paterson from the opposite perspective. If working at Rossi's had planted any radicalism in Montmorency's soul, it was all uprooted now. Sitting out on the terrace after dinner with fat cigars and glasses of bourbon, it was easy to accept Curtis Bayfield's picture of his immigrant workforce as a bunch of lazy troublemakers. Montmorency's pose as a British industrialist in search of advice from the American masters of the craft of moneymaking became more and more comfortable. In any case, Montmorency thought it was his duty to encourage his host to expand on the subject. After all, he might reveal just as much intelligence on the membership and plans of the anarchist movement as Frank's friends down in town. Sometimes, left alone with Cissie, there was a flicker of the old awkwardness from the Marimion. Cissie would get a little too close, or show a bit too much ankle. But in company she never let her guard drop, and he marveled at her transformation.

But something else made him happy in the Bayfields' company. At dinner one evening he sat next to the daughter of another industrial magnate, and found her more than just entertaining. Mary Gibson's family was one of the oldest in Paterson. Her grandfather had seen an opening for money-lending when the town was new, and through careful management — giving the occasional excessive loan here, seizing property as a penalty for late payment there — he had managed to secure himself an interest in all Paterson's most profitable enterprises. His son had built on his success, investing cleverly as Paterson grew. Mary and her siblings had been expensively educated. Her older sisters had already made glittering marriages. She was the last left at home, expected to stay there as a companion to her sickly mother. But now she was attracted to the handsome English visitor: even practicing Mary Montmorency's signature in the back of her diary.

Mary Gibson was naturally gifted with everything Cissie had acquired through determination and the beautician's art. Cissie cleverly covered her plump freckled arms in long tight white gloves. Mary could let her soft skin glow from her slender shoulders down to the tips of her graceful fingers. Cissie's corset took fifteen minutes to tighten, sometimes with two maids tugging at the strings. Mary's simply defined her natural shape. Cissie's hair was straightened with hot irons, pinned down, and waxed to tame its ebullient frizz. Its striking blondness was less obviously artificial than it had been in London, but her darker eyebrows still betrayed the secret that it was fake. Mary's heavy chestnut hair gleamed effortlessly, and hung dead straight, ready to be looped and twirled into charming styles with just a few well-placed combs and pins. Cissie's clothes were chosen for her by personal advisers at the very best shops in New York. Mary went to the same shops and effortlessly found by herself clothes that suited her physique and personality perfectly. Cissie knew the titles of all the most fashionable books. Mary had actually read them. Cissie was on the wrong side of thirty-five and married. Mary had rejected a series of suitors, and she was still in her twenties. Cissie knew when she was beaten. She might not be able to have Montmorency for herself, but she encouraged her friend, in the hope of keeping Montmorency close at hand.

Tom saw what was happening when Cissie, Mary, and Vi took him along on their shopping trips to Manhattan. While Vi was out of earshot trying on clothes, the American women would forget the boy was there as they chatted about Montmorency. Mary opened her heart to Cissie, who encouraged her to think a proposal was in the offing.

"But I couldn't go to Europe," said Mary. "Not with Mother so ill. She would never forgive me if I left her."

"Then make him stay here," said Cissie. "Tell him you'll have him, but only if he moves to Paterson, or at least New York. If he really loves you, he'll do that for you surely."

Tom was horrified. From then on he was always on the

alert for signs that Montmorency was growing keener on Mary. Vi was uncomfortable, too. She was unvaryingly polite to Cissie, but she saw through her early on. Americans might be charmed by the residue of Cissie's English accent, but Vi could tell that the refinement was false. After all, she was not above a bit of acting herself: The vague personal history she told Cissie on their shopping expeditions was even more unreal than Cissie's own. She could see that Cissie still had her eye on Montmorency, but like Tom she was more worried by Mary. They both admired the genteel American, but both feared that she would capture Montmorency, and take him away from them. Back on Tarimond they had often been separated from Montmorency as he lounged in London, or chased across Europe on his mysterious missions; but he was always theirs: writing letters, bringing back presents, and relaxing back into Tarimond life whenever he could.

Vi hoped that Frank would come up with something to send them rushing back to Europe before Montmorency's flirtation blossomed into something really serious. Tom did all he could to get in the way, somehow being there whenever Montmorency and Mary might have been hoping for time alone, and dropping hints about how nice it would be to get back home as soon as Montmorency's "business trip" was finished.

Montmorency understood none of this. At first he'd told himself that Mary was just an interesting diversion, keeping Cissie at bay while he waited for news from Frank, but just now and then he found himself imagining a more permanent life in America. He enjoyed taking Mary for walks and hearing about the big cities, New York and Boston, where she had been to school. He was amused when Mary teased him for picking up a little of her vocabulary and accent: saying "sidewalk" instead of "pavement" and slurring some of his words. And he knew, watching Cissie, that in America he really could put his old identity behind him. This was a land of new beginnings and forgiven pasts. He felt at home here.

Tom wanted to talk to someone about it. He didn't think his mother would understand. He couldn't find a way of forcing himself to ask her straight out if his suspicions were right and Montmorency was his father. It would be too hurtful to her if her vague hints about a fine man long dead were true. But his own heart would break if Montmorency decided to stay in America. He understood little of the political intrigue that had brought them all there. His own concerns seemed far more important, and he couldn't keep his anxieties to himself. There was only one person he could turn to. Frank would understand, he was sure. He knew Frank couldn't be seen with Montmorency or Vi, but Tom was only a child: Surely no one would remark on the two of them talking in the street?

He rummaged through his suitcase and found his most anonymous clothes. Then he set off down the hill to the smoky factories at the heart of town. He needed advice on how to stop Montmorency popping the question and becoming an American.

CHAPTER 37

≫

ROMANCE AND BETRAYAL

*I*t was nearly Christmas. In Florence, George, Gus, and Alex had great fun choosing presents to send to America. A friend of the contessa's was going to New York, and offered to post them on to Paterson from there. George included a long letter for Montmorency, summarizing his investigations, and asking for news from the American front. He thought back to the happy time they had spent on Tarimond a year before, and wondered what kind of celebrations people went in for in the United States. He put a silk scarf and a special tin of Italian sweetmeats into the parcel for Tom, with an affectionate note wishing him the very best for the New Year, and the new century that was about to begin. He saw a lace handkerchief in a shop window and had it wrapped to be sent to Maggie Goudie on Tarimond. He doubted whether it would ever arrive, but in the spirit of the season it was worth a try. The news of her death was still waiting on the doormat in London.

In Paterson, Frank was at Guido's sickbed, mopping his forehead with a damp rag. Guido was hot, but he was shivering, too, and was tucked up in the kitchen, close to a meager fire. By now the flu was on the march through Paterson, and it had hit Guido harder than most. The disease seemed to have gone straight to his lungs. Guido was lodging with a family from the silk works. He had caught the sickness from them. The Brescis had come to Paterson from Italy two years before. Gaetano, the husband, was already skilled in weaving, and got a job at the Paterson factory, though it paid barely enough to keep his wife and daughter. Gaetano Bresci was a quiet, dapper man with short, springy black hair, a neat mustache, and an open, trustworthy face. His home was orderly and respectable. Frank had been surprised to meet such a sober figure at the offices of the *Question*, and even more so when Guido told him that Bresci had been one of the founders of the paper.

"You'd better be careful," Bresci said to Frank, as he arrived home from work. "You might catch it, too." Bresci kissed his wife, and looked over at their child, sleeping in a makeshift cot, but recovering at last.

"It's all right. I've had it already, in Britain," said Frank. "It killed my mother."

"You poor boy," said Bresci's wife. "Is your father still alive?"

"Yes," said Frank, "but I haven't seen him for some time. I had to get away."

Frank's voice trailed off, and Bresci squeezed his shoulder sympathetically. He had heard about Frank's activities in Florence, and his flight from London.

The tears in Frank's eyes were real. He deeply mourned his mother, and missed his father. But he felt a fraud even so. He wasn't going to mention that his mother had been a duchess. He knew that his new friends were imagining her languishing in tattered sheets in a cold dingy room, not in the comfort of Glendarvie Castle, under the care of the best doctors that could be found.

"Still, I survived, and I'm sure Guido will, too," he said. "It was just bad luck."

"You must be lonely without her," said Bresci's wife. "You can spend Christmas with us if you like. We don't have much, but we will share it with you."

"Thank you," said Frank, genuinely moved by the invitation.

"You speak very good Italian," said Bresci. "Where did you learn it?"

"I read a bit when I was a student in Britain." It wasn't a complete lie. He had never been a real student, but he had been taught rudimentary languages by his governess at home in Scotland. "Then I learned to speak it when I went traveling with my father after my mother died." He realized that he might be giving the impression of wealth, and quickly dulled down the details. "He wanted a change of scene, and we went from place to place. We were in Italy when that terrible massacre happened in Milan."

"We heard about that here," said Bresci. "We sent money for the injured. But I wish we could do more."

"The injured are still suffering," said Frank, seeing a chance to steer the conversation off his own background. "Even Malpensa. He was hit in the leg. He was still using a stick when I saw him in London."

Guido was coming around, and joined in the story. "Can

you believe it? The king actually decorated the man who gave the order to fire on the crowd in Milan. It's a disgrace. We still don't have justice."

"Calm yourself, Guido," said Bresci's wife, bringing over a cup of water. "I'm sure someone is working on it. You just concentrate on getting better."

"Yes," said Bresci. "Keep calm. The victims of Milan will be avenged. Perhaps you will even do it yourself. Malpensa has a plan. Now get yourself better. We want you back on your feet when he comes to tell us about it."

Frank could hardly believe his luck. If he played his cards right he should be able to find out what was being plotted. But he didn't want to sound too inquisitive.

"If I can do anything to help, you know I will. Is Malpensa coming here?"

Bresci nodded. "I know you'll help," he whispered. "Let's not say too much here." He looked towards his wife, bending over a cooking pot with her back to them. Bresci indicated that he didn't trust her completely. Frank was overcome with a feeling of injustice. But it wasn't only rage at the fate of the innocent victims of the state in Italy. It was pity for this honest, loyal, kind woman, whose husband doubted her while confiding in a stranger who was really a spy.

Later, Frank left for the silk works alone. Guido was still too ill to work, and was likely to lose his job if he didn't put in an appearance soon. For now, Frank was trying to cover for him, shifting heavy bales of fabric twice as fast as usual, hoping that his friend would not be replaced. The work had made him stronger. Walking along the street he looked fit, even though he stooped with the natural reluctance of the night worker fighting the instinct to sleep. Bayfield didn't like to waste money. After his big investment in Edison's electric lights, he saw no reason to stop production after dark.

Tom was hiding in a shop doorway watching the night shift trudge to their jobs. He saw Frank coming and rushed to catch up with him. Frank flinched as a hand touched his arm.

"Frank, it's me, Tom."

Frank carried on walking, speaking out of the side of his mouth. "What are you doing here? I can't be seen with you."

"But no one knows who I am, and it's dark. I have to talk to you."

"I can't stop. I'll be late. What is it? Quick."

Tom gabbled out his story about Montmorency and Mary Gibson. After the intensity of the scene in the Brescis' brave but shabby household, Frank was impatient with this tale of love among the rich. He was angry with Tom for endangering him, just to tell him such trivia. What's more, he could see in an instant a perfectly easy way for Tom to sabotage Montmorency's marriage if he really wanted to.

They were just coming to the factory, and the klaxon was sounding out the start of the shift. Frank had to get inside quickly, or he'd lose a night's pay.

"So what should I do?" asked Tom desperately, as Frank picked up speed.

"Just tell her about him. You know. Everything he told us on the boat. That should do the trick."

The crowd of rushing workers carried Frank through the gates. Tom lost sight of him and turned to get back to the hotel before he was missed.

Inside the factory, Frank felt a rush of panic to his heart. He imagined Montmorency's world falling apart when the story of his life as a thief and a con man came out. Their mission could be threatened; Montmorency might make them all leave town just when they had something concrete to work on. Worse still, in the emotional and social explosion that might follow a revelation, Frank could lose contact with his friends. And he needed them more than ever, now that he was taking more chances and exposing himself to greater risks.

They might all be put in danger far from home. What had he done?

Tom was agitated, too, but he was determined to do as Frank advised. In his mind he had built up the risk of losing Montmorency into a certainty, and he felt he had no other option. He would tell Mary Gibson. They were going up to the Bayfields' again for another of those ghastly dinners, and she was bound to be there.

But she wasn't. She had sent Montmorency a note explaining that her mother's illness had worsened, and she could not leave the family home over Christmas. They would not be receiving visitors, so she and Montmorency might be apart till the New Year. Tom suspected that the letter ended with words of love. Montmorency wouldn't show it to anybody, but he put it in his pocket, and kept fingering it and pulling it out to read when he thought no one was looking.

Vi noticed, too. She didn't say anything to Tom, but he could tell she was anxious. Dinner was a quiet, sullen affair that night. Cissie seemed different with her beautiful proté-gée away. She was more forward, blowsier, and drank a little more than usual.

Vi whispered to Tom as they climbed into the car to go back to their hotel:

"The sooner we get out of here the better."

"What's that?" asked Montmorency, who hadn't caught what she said.

"I was just thinking it would be nice to have Christmas at home. Remember what a lovely time we had last year."

"There's no time to get back. Especially to Tarimond," snapped Montmorency. "And anyway it would be rude to leave before Mrs. Gibson recovers." He thought he had been a bit too obvious and added quickly, "And we've got to see what Frank comes up with, and get Robert away from West Orange. I think we'll be here for quite a while yet."

The rest of the drive took place in silence. In the front, Montmorency was lovesick. In the back, Vi and Tom were homesick. At the hotel Montmorency went straight upstairs without saying good night.

"I want to go home," said Tom.

"I know, love," said Vi, giving him a kiss on the cheek. "I

don't think this high living is doing any of us any good. Perhaps you and I could leave together."

"Oh no, we can't leave Montmorency on his own!"

"You're right. I think we'd better stay and keep an eye on him."

They were speaking in the old code that had served them so well all Tom's life. They were so close that things didn't need to be spelled out. Each felt they could read the other's mind. But there was a downside to that, too. They had never really talked, and that had left Tom with too many questions he felt he really couldn't ask.

Once the British visitors were in bed the hotel was locked for the night. It was still in darkness at 6:30, when Frank crept up to the front door. He had run there straight after the end of his shift. In the long hours at work he had thought the problem through, and decided to risk breaking the strictest rule Montmorency had set when Frank had been sent out into the slums. They were not supposed to contact each other directly. Communication was to be by means of letters left at the main post office, addressed in false names. But this was an emergency, and the post office was closed. Frank slipped the note under the door, hoping that he wasn't too late: that there hadn't been a fatal outburst from Tom the previous night.

Two hours later, Tom was the first up for breakfast. He saw the note on the front desk, addressed to Montmorency. He recognized Frank's handwriting, and opened it at once. It couldn't have been briefer, or more to the point:

Keep Tom away from Mary.

Tom was still angry with Frank for being so unsympathetic in the street. Reading the note, he was convinced that Frank wanted to spoil his plan just to get back at him for following him to work. Overnight he had thought through what he would say to Mary, and had persuaded himself that revealing Montmorency's past was the only way to secure his own happiness. He put the letter in the fire before Montmorency came downstairs.

Back at Bresci's house Guido's temperature had dropped. His breathing was smoother. He was asleep, but the chesty rattle that had reminded Frank so much of his mother was gone. Frank was surprised at how relieved he felt. Bresci was eating his breakfast. He was on the afternoon shift today, at home till two o'clock. His wife had taken the baby out. They were free to talk.

"Malpensa's coming on Christmas Day," he said. "The police should be off guard then. He's pretty sure he's being watched, but it will be easier for him to travel around when everyone's visiting family."

"Do you know what his plan is?"

"Not in detail. I've heard hints. It's something big. But it has to be organized from here because the police are infiltrating our groups all over Europe. I know it's happening in January. I'm pretty sure it's in Rome. But the boys in Florence are involved. That's why Guido was sending them stuff the other day. I think Malpensa is going to give us all tasks. But I've worked with him before. He believes in dealing with people one by one, so nobody knows the whole plan. That way, if we're caught, we can't give the whole picture away. A careless word in the wrong ear could cost us everything. What you don't know, you can't say."

Frank nodded, but he saw at once the flaw in Malpensa's method. It gave his men a false sense of security. No one felt they knew enough to be at risk of exposing the whole plot. So they traded tidbits among themselves like gossips everywhere. He silently committed to memory what Bresci himself had just revealed: action in January. Probably in Rome. And a visit to Paterson by Malpensa on Christmas Day. He would pass it all on to Montmorency in his next letter at the post office. He kept the conversation going, hoping for more details.

"Are you going on this January job?"

"I don't know. Maybe me, maybe Guido, maybe even you. I want to go, but we will see what Malpensa says. He might use us now, or save us up for something later. We are all going to have to be very brave. If someone disappears, we mustn't make a fuss. They will have their reasons, their task. Those of us who are left behind can help with money. We can look after the families while the men are away. Please, I want to ask you specially. My wife trusts you. I beg you, look after her and my little girl if anything should happen to me."

"I will," said Frank. And he meant it.

Bresci's wife returned, and the conversation shifted quickly to Guido's health. He woke to find the three of them leaning over him.

"Good morning," he said, blinking against the light. "I think I'm a bit better today."

Frank was delighted to hear it, even though he was about to betray his friends, sending Montmorency news of Malpensa's visit, and telling him to stand by for more details of a major international plot.

CHAPTER 38

≫

CHRISTMAS EVE, 1899

Doctor Farcett was sorry to be leaving West Orange, but he had promised the others he would join them in Paterson for Christmas. In any case, his investigations were complete. He had examined Edison's assistant in the hospital, and agreed that the appalling deterioration of his right hand and his loss of hair had probably been caused by repeated exposure to radiation. It seemed that the blood vessels in the hand had ceased to work, and that the problem was spreading upward. Farcett had advised an amputation. The man survived, and his arm couldn't get any worse, since it was no longer there. But there was no hope of real recovery. He would die before long.

Farcett had found few signs of illness in those who had worked with X-rays at Edison's factory. Some had unexplained skin lesions, and one had lost his mustache after sticking his head inside a fluoroscope for fun. Farcett had left instructions for them to be monitored in the future. His own view was that the rays were safe, except in the most enormous quantities, or when exposure had been repeated or extremely prolonged, as was the case with the amputee.

The flu study was over, too, and Farcett was looking forward to writing it up. If the others were ready to sail for England, the ship would be the perfect place to get that done.

Perhaps *The Physician* would take articles on both subjects. He could even do some lecturing about them, and, of course, find time to go to Tarimond and check on Maggie, too.

On Christmas Eve he went to Edison's office.

"Robert!" cried Edison, who had grown fond of this English enthusiast during his short stay. "I hope you haven't come to say good-bye. You've caught me wrapping up a few presents for you."

"I'm afraid I am off soon. Curtis Bayfield's sending a car for me."

"Bayfield!" spat Edison. "I can't think what these friends of yours are like if they want to be mixed up with him."

"He speaks very highly of you."

"Does he? Well, it is the season of goodwill. I'll throw in a cylinder or two for you to give him for his phonograph."

"That's very kind. But there's no need to give me anything. You've already been too generous with your time."

"It's just a couple of things to remember us by. I thought you might like this." Edison picked up a small pyramid-shaped device, no bigger than a shoe box. "It's our smallest portable fluoroscope. Gives you a quick look inside a tiny part of a patient. A hand, a foot, that sort of thing. I thought it might be useful in your surgery. You'll have to set up your own X-ray source, but it sounds as if you've got plenty of those on that island of yours. No good for the Bodyscreener, of course."

"Oh, I'm giving up on that idea."

"Don't give up. You've got a great brain, Robert, and I

think you've come up with the germ of something good. I hope you won't mind. I've done you a little sketch of how it might work."

Edison unrolled a large piece of paper. It was far more than a little sketch. It was an intricate depiction of exactly what equipment would be needed to realize Farcett's dream, from the banks of X-ray tubes to the positioning of the cine cameras and calculations of the precise power needed for each stage of the operation. That alone showed Farcett that the project was beyond the force of the generators he had installed on Tarimond, and the amount of X-ray equipment needed to produce a filmable image now only made him think of illness and death. But the picture was beautiful.

"Thank you so much. So you think it's a feasible idea?"

"Feasible, but expensive, Robert. And inadvisable, until we know it's safe."

"And you don't think it will be?"

"Not now, but science will find a way of making it so, in time."

"How long do you think?"

"Well, I'll bet on one thing. It won't be this century."

It took a moment for Robert to realize he was joking. The century had only a week left.

"And I won't see you again this century," he said, shaking Edison's hand, and picking up his box of presents. "But I'll send you copies of my articles as soon as they are written."

Bayfield's car drew up outside.

"Merry Christmas, Robert," said Edison, holding the door

for him. "Come back anytime. But if you are off for home, remember one thing. There's more to life than work. Even I have found time for two wives and some children. Perhaps you should take a second look at that assistant of yours."

Robert blushed. He hadn't thought his feelings for Maggie were that obvious. "You're right. I will. Who knows what might happen? I'll let you know."

"And bring her over to meet me after the wedding."

"Steady on." Farcett laughed. "I haven't even asked her yet!"

But he left Edison's office with a spring in his step.

It wasn't long before his mood flagged. His friends in Paterson were glad to see him, but there was no disguising their underlying gloom. Montmorency was annoyed that Mary was away, Vi and Tom were dreading Christmas dinner in the faux-posh atmosphere of the big house, and Frank wasn't there at all. His latest communication spoke of major developments that would keep him in town on Christmas Day. They would have to make up an explanation for his absence.

Vi came up with the idea of a girl in West Orange, even though she knew it would get Cissie dangerously excited and embarking on a whole new round of matrimonial plotting. Farcett promised to feign amnesia about the girl's name. It wouldn't be difficult, since she didn't exist. The doctor did at least manage to rouse Montmorency from his reveries about

Mary, by reminding him that Frank was his responsibility and might well be in danger.

"Are you sure you're not letting him get in too deep? It sounds as if he's in the thick of it with these plotters. What if they realize he's a spy? What if he gets carried away? He's going to be meeting that Malpensa again. Remember the effect that man's had on him in the past."

"I know," said Montmorency. "But Frank's older now. He knows the risks. And anyway, what can I do?"

"You could pull him out. Stop now before things get too dangerous. After all, he's found out that something's going to happen in January in Rome. Isn't that enough for George to work on?"

"No, Robert. It's not enough. Not when we're so close to finding out more. And you can tell from the note that Frank wants to stay on the case. We've come all this way. We can't stop now."

There was a brief outburst of excitement when George's parcel arrived. They gathered in Montmorency's room to open it. Vi gave out the presents, then decided that it would be unlucky to open them before Christmas Day itself, and collected them back up again. Everyone noticed that Tom had more than anyone else. Vi seemed particularly pleased that George had made a point of remembering him. Montmorency took the fat envelope containing George's letter. He had a quick look. It seemed to contain serious news. The authorities in Italy were sure that the anarchists were planning some spectacular action soon.

Vi was watching him, and saw the concern on his face. "What does it say?" she asked.

"It looks as if George has made some progress. It's something about a threatened attack."

"I don't mean that. What does he say about Gus? Is he still in love with the contessa?"

"How do you know about that?"

"Frank told me ages ago, back on Tarimond."

"Well," said Montmorency, flicking through the pages, "there does seem to be quite a lot about her. And it sounds as if Alex has found himself a girl as well. Daughter of the police chief. Very convenient for George."

"And is he going back to London?"

"No. In fact he's asking me to go to Italy." He read on. "The police are expecting an attack on the queen."

"Oh dear!" said Vi. "Who would attack an old lady like that?"

"Not our queen, theirs."

"I didn't know they had one."

"Oh yes. Margherita. She's got a pizza named after her."

"What's a pizza when it's at home?"

"Never mind. Anyway. She's going to the première of a new opera in Rome in January, and the police don't think she's safe."

"Rome in January," said Farcett. "That could be the plot Frank told you about."

"All the more reason for him to stay undercover now, don't you think?" said Montmorency.

"What else does George say?" asked Farcett.

Montmorency started reading again. "'. . . convinced the queen is in danger . . .'"

Vi interrupted. "Then they should stop her going."

"They can't do that. It would look weak, and anyway, they want to catch the criminals. They'll want them to think the queen's going to be there and see if they can intercept them. Set a trap. Arrest them. It's not enough just to take away their target. They'll only do something else some other time."

"So what's George going to do about it?"

"He's asking me to go there and help him. I wouldn't mind actually. It's Puccini's new opera, *Tosca*. I'd love to see it."

"He's asking you to travel thousands of miles to go to the opera?" said Farcett. "I know you're a fan, but even for you that sounds like a bit much!"

Their weak attempts at humor hung in the air. Montmorency reread the passage. He looked anxious.

"Well, perhaps I should go. I'm not sure. Excuse me a minute. I'd better read this through properly. I'll just take it outside for a moment." And Montmorency left the room, flustered, leaving the other three sitting on his bed.

"What was that about?" asked Tom. "Why is he so upset?"

"He's probably worrying about Frank," said Farcett. "Doesn't know whether he should leave him here on his own, to get more information, or take him back to Europe."

"More likely he's worried about leaving his lady friend," said Vi. "Hasn't he told you about this Mary? She's got him wrapped around her little finger."

"Really?" said Farcett. "I hadn't heard. Perhaps he could take her to Italy, too."

"Exactly what I was thinking!" said Montmorency, who was back in the doorway, and happy again. "I'll ask her as soon as she gets back."

But Farcett was already rethinking his suggestion, realizing the dangers of Montmorency becoming involved with someone outside their tight circle. He had almost forgotten the old problem of Montmorency's past. Could Montmorency keep the truth from someone he loved? Could he trust her to hold on to his secret and to help hide their real purpose in visiting Paterson? And in any case, was it right that Montmorency should be distracted from his work when a life — a royal life — was at stake?

Tom sat silent. The thoughts in his head were more muddled. He just didn't want to lose Montmorency, didn't want him diluted by love. He would do everything he could to stop it.

It was late at night. Down at the silk works, Frank and Guido were finishing their shift, the last before Bayfield reluctantly closed the factory down for Christmas Day, the only day of the year when the looms fell silent and no money was made. They were going on to the *Question* office afterward, to prepare for Malpensa's visit. Secretly, Frank thought it was a little absurd that the opponents of hierarchy were so concerned about tidying up for a visiting anarchist dignitary, particularly as he had had a glimpse of Malpensa's squalid home life once before. But he went along with the idea, not least because it gave him a chance to talk to Guido: to find out what he knew.

"What do you think he's going to say?" he asked as he swept the floor.

"I'm not sure," said Guido, pushing a cloth through a couple of years' worth of dust. "But I know there are lots of guns involved. They've been hiding them in Florence. I thought of a wonderful place. The last place in the world the police would look. And anyway, there's nothing to see."

"What do you mean? Where is this place?"

"It's somewhere you've been before."

"Oh, come on, Guido. Don't make it into a riddle. Just tell me."

"Somewhere you and I were together. Somewhere the police think they've cleaned out."

"La Specola?"

"I didn't say that."

"But it is there, isn't it?"

"I'm saying nothing. I've already said too much."

"But you can trust me, Guido, you know you can. And anyway, if I'm going to be involved in this thing, I'll have to know where to find the guns, won't I?"

"I don't think they'll send you. Not to Florence. You're wanted in Florence. For murder, remember, just like me.

Malpensa will use us for something else. For somewhere else. For London perhaps."

"London?"

"It's the biggest prize of all. Strike at the heart of the Empire. I think Malpensa is going to send you home."

"I'm wanted there, too."

"But only by Rossi's old mob. Not by the police. No one there knows you've anything to do with us. You're perfect for it. You know your way around."

"And you. Where do you think he'll send you?"

"I'm hoping he'll keep us together. To keep each other's courage up. To keep an eye out for each other. We're a good team. Together we could bring down the world."

"But not until we've brought down these cobwebs." Frank laughed, waving his broom up against a fat spider snoozing in the top corner of the window. Inside, he wasn't laughing. He was beginning to feel trapped. He was getting into something he didn't fully understand; and he might have Guido permanently at his side. How would he contact Montmorency then? How could he pass on even the information he had just received? The post office was closed for Christmas. He couldn't leave one of his regular letters. He would be stuck with Guido and the Brescis now until after Malpensa had gone. What if things moved too fast? How was he supposed to get away?

CHAPTER 39

≫

CHRISTMAS DAY

All over Paterson, families were waking up to a special day. The streets were quiet. The factory sirens were silent. Only the background noise of the rushing waterfall disturbed the peace, and that was so familiar as to be unnoticeable. At eight o'clock, the first church bells started summoning the faithful. Paterson had every shade of faith in its population, from the gaudy Catholics of the Italian quarter to the dour Lutherans from Germany to the smart Episcopalians on the hill. They each worshipped in their own way, before special lunches reminding them of the best food of their homelands. The rich feasted on goose and beef. The poor had saved extra vegetables, and hoarded flour for pasta and sauces. Everywhere there was cake: rich fruitcake for the northern Europeans, soft chocolate sponges for the southerners.

As the day wore on, the streets filled with happy family parties visiting relatives and friends. Drink was taken. The goodwill was punctuated by the occasional strident argument and slammed doors. The aggrieved walked alone with their bottles, nursing their resentments, too proud to go home. Musicians took to the streets. Little groups burst into impromptu songs in many languages. There was the occasional fight. The few police on duty turned a blind eye, just for today.

In mid-afternoon, as the light began to fade, Malpensa limped into town. Volunteers had been waiting for him all day at the offices of the *Question*. They made him welcome, and set off around the town, knocking on windows and discreetly luring men from their families. The tiny office filled with a dozen excited people, the hard core of anarchism in Paterson, clutching bottles and staring admiringly at their guest. Malpensa rose to speak. There was applause. He silenced it at once, and lowered his voice to little more than a whisper.

"No noise! We must not attract attention. My friends, this may be the most important meeting of your lives. We are about to enter a new century. We are to leave behind us a hundred years of oppression and injustice. Let us make the new century — the *twentieth* century — the century of the individual, the century of the people, the century of the workingman."

Again the audience moved to clap, but Malpensa stopped them and continued. In a reflex action, the men leaned closer, and the atmosphere of conspiracy heightened. Frank had heard much of what Malpensa said months before, on that night in London, but the force of it still gripped him, despite his nervousness about what was to come. Finally, Malpensa dropped his voice still lower and issued a challenge to all present.

"Tonight you must make a choice. Each of you must look into his heart and decide which side you are on. If you choose to stay with us, you must do so wholeheartedly. Completely.

There will be no way out. Things will be revealed that you must take to your graves. Any betrayal of those secrets will result in instant death. Some of you will be given small tasks. They may seem insignificant to you, but do not be offended. Without your humble efforts, the grand gestures cannot be made. Your time may come in the future, if you prove yourselves trustworthy. If you fail, even in the simplest of tasks, you will die. Some of you will be sent away. You will not see your families for months — maybe never again. In return you will be rewarded in your own hearts with the knowledge that you have served your fellow men. That you have fought the forces of evil in the cause of a fairer world for all. You may have to guard that knowledge for the rest of your lives. You may never be able to tell anyone what you have done, and if you fall, if you die, your bravery may go unremarked. I am looking for heroes. I do not expect you all to volunteer. If you know yourself to be weak, leave now. There is no way out later." He looked around him. Almost all the eyes still burned with admiration and passion. One man was fingering his hat. Malpensa knew at once what to say.

"Leave, sir. You do not have the stomach for the fight. You are right to admit it now. But we have let you come this far. You know too much. You will be watched. And if you betray us you will be dealt with." There was a click from under Malpensa's cape, and he drew out a revolver, pointing it at the terrified man, who till that day had happily set the type on the printing press. Malpensa let the gun fall onto the table, as a warning to everyone. "Look at me," he shouted to the man, who was staring at his feet, quivering. Malpensa paused, then softened his tone again: "I am not a cruel man. You may go. But remember, you will always be watched."

The printer ran from the room and down the stairs to the street. There was silence.

"Does anyone else wish to follow him?" asked Malpensa. "If you do, go now. Your names will be taken. If you don't, you must be prepared to sacrifice everything for a life of glory."

No one else dared leave. Very few wanted to. Even Frank was hypnotized, though he was still memorizing everything Malpensa said, ready to pass it on to Montmorency. If he ever saw him again.

"Now," said Malpensa. "I am going to talk to you one by one. You will each be given a task. You must not tell anyone else precisely what that task is, though some of you may be working together. Each member of a team will know only that which is necessary for his part in the plan."

He pulled a list from his pocket. It held the name of everyone in the room. The name of the nervous printer was already crossed through. Someone had briefed Malpensa well. He already knew exactly what he could demand of each of his volunteers.

"Giovanni Pretti!" he called, and a fat man proudly put up his hand. "Stay here," Malpensa ordered. "The rest of you, outside!"

The others crammed onto the staircase, hushed, trying to hear what was being said; but they could make out nothing. After five minutes, Pretti emerged, sweating, and pushed his way past the other men without a word.

"Bruno Carollo!" came the next summons, and a tall thin man made his entrance. The roll call continued, and one after another the men entered and left Malpensa's lair, with varying degrees of enthusiasm and terror. Finally, only Frank, Guido, and Bresci were left. Bresci was in and out very quickly. He shook their hands as he passed them on the stairs as if he were saying farewell. Malpensa called Frank and Guido in together. He was looking tired now, and stretched to ease the pain in his leg as they sat down before him. He drank from one of the wine bottles, and passed it on to them. Guido took a swig. Frank declined.

"Not thirsty?"

"I want to keep a clear head."

"Good. Good. I was told you were a cool one. I saw it for myself at that meeting in London. You did not boast that you knew me. I was impressed. Do you want to know why I kept you two till last?" They nodded silently. "It's because you are going to do the real work. Everyone else here will be servicing your mission in ways you will never know. You are to work in London. The job is planned down to the last detail."

"But why us?" asked Frank. "You have supporters on the spot. I've met them. I know how strongly they feel." Malpensa's look scared him. He hoped he hadn't sounded frightened, as if he wanted a way out, and added quickly, "But of course I will do exactly as you say."

Malpensa nodded. "Yes, you will. Our London organization is not secure. I saw that myself when we were raided in the summer. They are being watched. There may even be police infiltrators among them. Their logbook has disappeared. The authorities know names. It is not safe."

"But no one in London will be looking for *us*," said Guido.

"Exactly. And none of our people there know you are coming. The deed will be simple. But you must do it on a certain day, and at a certain time. Too soon and you will jeopardize our actions elsewhere. Too late and the British authorities will have been alerted to the possible danger."

"What is the date?" asked Guido.

"January 14th."

"Three weeks from now?"

"Yes. In the evening. At seven o'clock, London time."

"Why then?"

"Because at that moment we will hit the Teatro Costanzi in Rome. The Queen of Italy will be there. We will take her out along with the worst of the swaggering nobility. In London, too, we can scare the people who have the real power: the financiers, the investors, and the corrupters of morals, the people who think they can buy the hearts of the masses with fripperies and stunts. And we're going to make it worse for them by hitting a place where they play, where they think they are safe. And best of all, by coordinating the two attacks we will be showing how strong we are, that we are everywhere, that they can never relax."

"So what are we going to do?" asked Guido.

Frank's mind was racing ahead. "How do we get to London?"

Malpensa brought out a leather briefcase, and took out a bundle of papers tied with green ribbon. "Here are tickets for a boat leaving New York in three days' time. I have passports for you in false names, and money. Your clothes are being collected now by other members of the team."

"So we are not going home?" asked Frank, horrified that his worst fears were being confirmed.

"I warned you of sacrifices and isolation. We cannot risk letting you out of our sight now until we know you are safely onboard ship in New York."

"I understand," said Frank bravely, totally unable to think of a way out.

Malpensa shuffled through his papers and pulled out a scrap torn from a newspaper. It was written in English. Frank recognized the typeface of the London *Times*. Malpensa passed it over. It was the section advertising forthcoming entertainments. Frank scanned the columns. There was to be a concert by the band of the Grenadier Guards at the Royal Albert Hall at 2 p.m. on January 14. On the 20th, Sir Arthur Sullivan would conduct "the Largest Orchestra in the World." But one large announcement was circled in black ink. Frank read it out:

THE LONDON HIPPODROME
Cranbourne Street — Leicester Square
Managing Director Mr. H. E. Moss
GRAND OPENING
Monday, January 15 at 7:45 p.m. Doors open 7:15
A SOUVENIR WILL BE PRESENTED
TO EVERY MEMBER OF THE AUDIENCE
AT THE FIRST PERFORMANCE
A structure unlike any other in London.
An entertainment of unprecedented type.
A moving stage.
A rising and sinking Arena.
MADAME BELLE COLE WILL SING THE
NATIONAL ANTHEM
FOLLOWED BY
The grand spectacular Aquatic Carnival
GIDDY OSTEND or the Absent-minded Millionaire
FEATURING
LITTLE TICH
Thereafter TWICE DAILY at 2 and 8 p.m.

"The Hippodrome," said Frank. "I know where that is. They've been building it for ages. They say it's going to be one of the wonders of the world. A cross between a theater and a circus. They can get elephants in there, and there's going to be a great water tank with fountains, and things like that."

Malpensa crushed Frank's excitement. "They may think that's what it's going to be like. In fact, all they're going to get is a very expensive pile of rubble."

Guido realized what he was saying. "We're going to blow it up?"

"Yes. You two will destroy it. The night before this Grand Opening they're boasting about. Just as our friends attack the première of *Tosca* in Rome."

"But they're going to kill Queen Margherita. Shouldn't we go for Queen Victoria, or the Prince of Wales?" said Guido, carried away by the idea. For a heartbeat Frank agreed with him. Then he realized the enormity of what Guido was suggesting.

Malpensa had obviously studied the Court Circular in *The Times* as well as the entertainments page.

"The British royal family are all over the place. Victoria is old and ill, and hiding away on the Isle of Wight. Her son is in somewhere called Norfolk. They have princes and dukes on their travels all over the world: everywhere from Singapore to St. Petersburg. We could try hitting them there, picking them off one by one, but what we need now is a big impact at a particular moment. We can always get royalty in the future. Perhaps they will all be together at Victoria's funeral before too long. For now, this Hippodrome is what we need. It's a different kind of palace. And by bringing it down we can strike a blow on behalf of all the workers who have given their life and health to building it."

"What if they're still there, the night before the opening, finishing off?" asked Frank. "What if the performers are having a last-minute rehearsal?"

"Then they will die in a worthy cause. On behalf of their fellow workers everywhere."

Guido looked convinced and raised a clenched fist. Frank did his best to seem happy, too, as Malpensa continued.

"Now. To the details. The materials you will need are already hidden in locations around London. My men did it when we were there in the summer. I have a map here which you must memorize and destroy." He opened out a sheet. Frank recognized several familiar landmarks.

"We will go over the procedure several times before you leave here for your ship. You will know your parts so well that there will be no possibility of failure."

"And afterward?" asked Frank.

"Afterward you will disappear. Split up. Find work. Blend in. After six months, make contact again, through this address in Paris." He dipped his pen in the inkwell and wrote it on his hand, showed it to each of them just long enough for them to read it, then licked it away, leaving a blue-black stain across his palm.

"And if anything goes wrong?" asked Frank nervously.

"Your equipment will include revolvers. We expect you to be ready to use them. If necessary on yourselves."

"Thank you," said Guido. "This is my dream. We will not let you down."

CHAPTER 40

≫

CHRISTMAS NIGHT

*U*p on the hill, the Bayfields' Christmas dinner party was not a success. The sudden departure of the Gibsons had disrupted Cissie's seating plan, and to have asked replacements at such short notice would have smacked of desperation. Cissie had considered it, but Curtis pointed out that the new guests would know they were substitutes, and be insulted not to have been invited earlier. Anyone worth inviting was bound to have a prior engagement on Christmas night anyway. They would have to do their best with what they had: a bunch of people who had already worn themselves out with one another's company. At least Doctor Farcett was back. Cissie hadn't seen him since that first night, before he rushed off to visit Edison. She looked forward to hearing about his trip, and the details of Frank's strange liaison with a West Orange girl, but the doctor was whisked away from the table when a kitchen maid cut herself, and spent most of the evening binding up her wound and eating below stairs.

Montmorency was low, very low. He'd started off quite buoyant, with talk about going to Italy, and possibly taking Mary with him. Cissie said she was sure Mary would agree, and that she herself might join the party. But then the talk turned to Frank, and Cissie teased Montmorency for being a bad guardian, knowing so little about his whereabouts.

"Really it's too bad, you know. I'm sure this West Orange girl is from a fine family, but Montmorency, you're supposed to be looking after Lord Francis Fox-Selwyn on behalf of the Duke of Monaburn! Don't you think you should have taken more care of him? I mean, you can't say exactly where he is, and it's Christmas Day!"

Montmorency tried to laugh it off. "Oh, don't worry, Doctor Farcett has met the girl's family. He's content that Frank is in good hands."

While Cissie giggled politely at the unintentional sauciness of his reply, Montmorency descended into gloom. Cissie had touched his conscience, in spite of being way off the mark.

Vi seemed uneasy throughout the meal. Her usually witty remarks had a sour cutting edge. Perhaps she was worrying about Tom, who was even quieter than usual. Meanwhile Curtis wouldn't settle. He kept getting up and wandering over to the window, looking down on to Paterson, and his dark factories, silenced for the day, idle until the arrival of the first morning shift at 6 a.m.

"God knows what's going on over there," he said, as he stared into the night. "They'll all be drunk tomorrow. Who knows how many won't even bother to turn up? It will take ages to get back to full production. And then we've got the New Year in a week. They'll be drunk, they'll be tired. It all leads to sloppiness and accidents."

"That's probably what's behind the upset in the kitchen,"

said Cissie. "I wonder how poor Doctor Farcett is getting on?"

"I'm sure he's coping splendidly," said Montmorency. "But I fear that when he has finished, we had better be getting along. It's not fair to keep the hotel staff up late on Christmas Day."

"They're being paid to do it, you know," said Curtis. "They're not serving you out of the kindness of their hearts."

"Still, perhaps they deserve a little extra consideration today," said Montmorency, rather more firmly than he had intended. "Ah, here's Robert now."

"Sorry to be so long. It's a nasty cut and she was very shocked. It might be a good idea to get her to hospital in the morning, just to have it checked."

"Do you people think I'm made of money?" mumbled Curtis under his breath.

"Yes," whispered Vi, still managing to keep a grin on her face as she stood to join the movement towards the door. "Thank you so much, Cecilia," she gushed, motioning to kiss Cissie on both cheeks, but managing to miss twice.

"Yes. Thank you, and Merry Christmas," said Montmorency, trying too hard to hide his urge to get away. His kisses landed on target, and he got a mouthful of makeup for his pains.

"Good night," said Curtis, brusquely, eager to get to bed. "I'll call the car around."

"Oh, don't bother," said Montmorency. "The walk will do us good."

So they walked all the way down the steep hill to the hotel. Vi was furious. Her dress was dragging in the mud and she had to take off her shoes to go at anything more than a snail's pace. But Montmorency didn't notice. Once they were out of earshot of the house he said what had been bothering him. In a way, Cissie had been right. He had let Frank down.

"How can I have let things slip like this? I'm just overwhelmed by the thought that we have no idea where Frank is. His note said something important was happening tonight, and that was why he couldn't be here. But suppose it was something dangerous. How could he let us know?"

Vi chimed in, "I've had a feeling all day that something's wrong, you know."

"Can't we go and find him?" said Farcett. "You know where he's living, don't you?"

"Yes. But we can't go dressed like this, and if he is in danger, two old foreigners turning up isn't going to do him any good, is it?"

Tom spoke up. "I'll go, Montmorency. I want to. There's something I want to ask Frank about anyway."

Vi objected: "It's late, Tom. I'm not having you in danger, too."

"Then come with me, Mam. We can dirty ourselves up a bit, easy enough. We can blend in."

"I'm halfway there already," said Vi, pulling at a run in her muddy stocking. "People will just think we've been out having a good time."

"If only!" said Montmorency. "Would you go, Vi? It would put my mind at rest."

"Of course. I'd love to see Frank. Today of all days. I've really missed him. And if he's all right you can sleep easy tonight."

Doctor Farcett and Montmorency took Tom's jacket and tie, and Vi's fur wrap. They were both chilly, and Vi took Tom's jacket back again and put it on herself. It did the trick, making her look like a disheveled partygoer rather than a wealthy woman. Tom had no option but to put up with the cold. He dragged his shiny shoes in the mud, but they still looked too smart, so he took them off completely, and rolled up his trousers to his knees. He looked a bit odd, but the clothes looked stolen rather than posh. Nobody with money would go around on a winter's night dressed like that.

They soon found Frank's building, a ramshackle dwelling house not far from the factory. Frank's window was dark. Perhaps he was out or asleep. Then there was the flicker of a match and the glow of a candle cast a shadow on the wall inside. Someone was in the room. Another candle borrowed flame from the first, and another shadow appeared. Perhaps Frank had somebody with him. For a moment Vi thought — hoped even — that it might be a woman. But it wasn't a woman, and neither of the shadows looked like Frank either. They were bulky male figures, busying themselves about the room.

Tom thought aloud. "Frank's being burgled!"

The candles went out, and Vi pulled Tom hard against the wall where they couldn't be seen. Two men, smaller than the shadows, but matching them in build, came out furtively, one of them carrying a bag Vi recognized as Frank's. The men strode up the street, and Vi and Tom followed at a safe distance. They stepped over drunks, dodged gaggles of happy revelers, and even exchanged Christmas greetings with a few of them. It was the one night of the year when such an oddly dressed mother and son didn't look out of place on the street at that hour. Neither did the men with the bag. They walked on without anyone remarking on them. Then they came to a building where a light was burning upstairs. They knocked on the door and were let inside.

"What do we do now?" whispered Tom.

"Find out if Frank's in there, I suppose."

The window was too high for them to see in, even when Vi tried jumping. They walked around the side of the building. There was another window at the back. It was open slightly, perhaps for ventilation, perhaps because it couldn't really close. There was a low wall behind. Tom bent down and let Vi climb onto his back. From there she could pull herself up and stand on top of the bricks. There was a gap of only about two feet between the wall and the building. If she leaned across, she thought she might be able to . . . Yes! She could see into the room inside.

It was a dingy place, lit by one dim central oil light. The walls were covered in a chaos of posters, notices, and scribbled notes. A typewriter balanced on a stack of newspapers.

Three figures were huddled around a small square table in the middle of the room, studying some documents. The largest, wearing a broad-brimmed hat and swathed in a dark cape, had his back to her, and almost obscured the other two, who were younger, and looked as if they were taking a lesson from a teacher. She recognized Frank at once. He was thinner than when she had last seen him, and was concentrating hard. The other man's face was obscured by his hair as he leaned forward to study the paper in front of him.

Vi knew at once that it would be a mistake to knock on the window. Although she could not make out the details of the muttered conversation, she knew from the tone that dark matters were being discussed. She stayed still, watching and waiting. Down on the ground, Tom was getting impatient. He wanted to know what Vi could see. She put a finger to her lips, hoping he could tell from her face that something might be wrong. Now and again she wobbled slightly. Her arms started to ache with the effort of supporting her weight against the wall. She tried shifting her feet, but could make only the slightest movements without causing a sound. She was cold, even with the benefit of Tom's jacket. Looking down, she could see that he was shivering in his shirtsleeves and socks.

The men in the room seemed locked into position, too. Vi longed for Frank to look up, so she could make a sign to show that she was there. She dreaded one of the others catching sight of her, hated to think what consequences that could bring for poor Frank. He had always been such a happy boy, so unlike his serious older brother. Yet he had never resembled Alexander as much as he did now, talking with these two strangers, thousands of miles from home.

There was no sign of the two men Vi and Tom had followed to the office, but the bag they had been carrying was in the room, against the side wall. They must have dropped it off and left. Was Frank going somewhere? Had they been sent to get his luggage? She was wondering why he hadn't packed it himself, whether he was perhaps being abducted, when the large caped man rose from his chair, as if in response to a knock on the door. He let in two slight, rather frightened-looking figures, who had brought another bag. The young man sitting alongside Frank rose, too, and turned to greet them, opening the bag, and starting to rummage through it. For the first time, Frank was the only one facing the window. Vi took her chance, and tapped gently. Frank looked up. There was a momentary flash of amazement across his face, then he picked up something from the table and walked quietly over. He pressed the paper to the glass. It was only there for a moment, but long enough for Vi to see what it was: a third-class ticket for the SS *St. Louis* from New York to Southampton on December 28. Frank turned away, placed the ticket back down, and picked up a newspaper, opening it out over the top of the other documents on the desk. The two newcomers left, and the others spun around towards the window again.

Vi ducked down so that there would be no danger of her being seen. But she could hear. The voices were louder after the interruption. They were speaking Italian. Vi could make out only the vaguest gist of what was being said. It sounded at first as if Frank was being scolded. She felt suddenly hot. Her sweaty hands were almost slipping against the bricks. But then there was laughter, congratulations even. Frank was being praised for his presence of mind in covering over the things on the table while the visitors were in the room.

"I didn't want to risk those two seeing anything. I mean, I trust them. I know they're on our side, but if they don't have the facts, they can't tell, can they, however hard people try to make them?"

"Absolutely right," said Malpensa. "That's the attitude you've both got to have from now on. Don't trust anyone. Don't tell anyone anything they don't need to know, no matter how friendly they seem. You never know who they might really be working for."

You're right, thought Frank, *but if only you knew the real weak link in this chain. You've told me too much already.*

He'd won Malpensa's trust. But would Vi understand what to make of the ticket? Had she had time to read it? Even if she had, would his friends be able to do anything about it, to rescue him from these people?

Frank was very, very scared.

CHAPTER 41

≫

DISENGAGING

*M*ontmorency and Farcett stayed up waiting for Vi and Tom to come home. The doctor's room overlooked the wide drive up to the hotel door, and they took turns watching out for their friends. Montmorency leaned against the window, his bow tie undone and his collar stud out, waistcoat open and shirt untucked.

"I should never have let them go," he said. "It's much too dangerous. They'll never fit in down there."

"They'll be all right. Vi's very resourceful, you know. If any of us can find Frank, it's her."

"But there's not much chance, is there? Even for Vi. I've made a real mess of this job. I've let myself get completely sidetracked by life up here, leaving Frank to do all the dangerous work."

"I should have helped more," said Farcett. "I got carried away with Edison and my own enthusiasms."

"But that's why you came. I was here with a specific mission: to find out what the anarchists plan to do next. What have I got to show for it? A detailed knowledge of American big business, and a bulging waistline!"

As he spoke a couple rounded the corner at the bottom of the drive. Vi had her arm around her son's shoulders. Montmorency and Farcett both noticed how tall the boy was becoming. From this distance the mother and son looked more like young lovers on the way back from a wild night. Each carried a wine bottle, and stopped every now and again for another swig. Vi's stockings had now disintegrated completely, and her bare legs were starkly white in the moonlight. She had hitched her long skirt right up, annoyed by the way it trailed in the dirt on the long walk home.

Vi waved up to the window. Montmorency beckoned them to speed up, trying to judge from her face whether they'd had any success. There was no sign of Frank.

"That doesn't necessarily mean they didn't find him," said Farcett. "He might be coming separately. Might not want to be seen with them."

"Or he might be ill. Or maybe they didn't find him. Or perhaps they just abandoned the search and joined in the fun on the streets. They look merry enough. How can it be taking them so long to walk here?"

"They're tired. I'm sure they've done their best. They'll be here in a minute."

They soon heard Vi shout a tipsy greeting to the doorman. He really had been celebrating, and didn't even open his eyes to reply. Then Vi and Tom clattered up the stairs, and Farcett opened his door to let them in. Vi suddenly looked extremely sober. Montmorency realized that he had misjudged them. They hadn't been having a good time in town. The revelry of their homecoming had been for the benefit of anyone watching. Vi had rightly decided that on Christmas night in Paterson, it was the least suspicious way to behave.

"Did you find him?" he asked, as soon as the door was closed.

"Yes," said Tom.

"Thank heavens," said Montmorency. "Thank goodness he's safe. I'd been imagining . . ."

Vi interrupted. "We saw him, but we couldn't talk to him. And I think he's in trouble."

She described the tiny newspaper office, the strange conspiratorial meeting, and the ticket Frank had held up to the window.

"Sounds as if they're taking him to England," said Farcett. "Perhaps we can catch him at his digs tomorrow and find out what's going on."

"His room's been cleaned out. All his stuff is in a bag at the office. If you ask me they're keeping him with them until they leave the country."

Farcett wanted to see for himself. "Couldn't we go downtown and rescue him?"

"The door's locked, and there are bars at the window," said Tom. "Anyway, he's not on his own."

"Tom's right," said Vi. "We might just put him in more danger. And what if they've moved on already? Perhaps he's not even in Paterson anymore."

"So our only chance of getting to him will be if we catch that boat, too," said Farcett. "I can go and get the tickets tomorrow. Then we could all meet in New York on the 28th. There's time."

Montmorency was thoughtful. Vi guessed why. He was

unhappy about leaving Mary Gibson, or possibly wondering how he could persuade her to come with them.

"Don't you worry about leaving that Mary," she said, emphasizing where she thought his loyalties should lie. "I'm sure she'll get in touch if she really likes you. Surely Frank comes first."

"Yes," said Montmorency, unconvincingly. "But perhaps we don't need to leave just yet. Let's talk about it in the morning. I'm going to bed."

As soon as he'd left the room, Robert turned to Vi.

"I'm not going to give him the chance to change my mind. I'll leave for Manhattan first thing in the morning, and get tickets for the four of us. And Vi, I want you to do everything you can to keep him away from that woman. We can't risk him staying behind, or her coming with us."

"I don't understand," said Vi. "How can he put her before Frank? How can he ignore what George says? George needs him in Italy."

"If George were here, I'm sure Montmorency wouldn't have gone off the rails like this," said Farcett. "But I've seen it before. Sometimes Montmorency just makes bad decisions. He can let people down just when they need him most. We're going to have to do his thinking for him and make sure he's on that boat. Promise me you'll get him to New York for the 28th."

"I'll do whatever it takes, I promise."

"And remember, don't let him have any contact with Mary Gibson."

"He's safe with me."

They had both forgotten that Tom was in the room. He was just as determined as them to get Montmorency back to England unattached.

"I'd better get some sleep, too," Tom said, hurrying to his own room, where he took out a pen and paper and started compiling a list of Montmorency's falsehoods and faults, ready to show Mary the next day.

Vi helped Farcett with his packing and went to bed. She was too tired to sleep, and spent the restless hours sorting her own things and working out how to keep Mary and Montmorency apart. In the morning, she suggested that Montmorency should go up to the big house to apologize for his boorish behavior the night before. As soon as he left, she moved into his room and prepared everything for a quick departure. Then she asked the desk clerk to show her the Gibsons' house on the map. It was on the other side of the river, a fair step away, but Vi had made up her mind. She had decided to get to Mary before Montmorency could. She would tell her that Montmorency had already gone and had sent only a perfunctory, secondhand message of farewell.

Vi rang the doorbell. The upstairs curtains were still closed, and for a moment she wondered if Mrs. Gibson had died. But when the maid opened the door, she could hear an old woman's nagging voice. She knew from that tone alone that Mary would be unlikely to leave Paterson. Her mother would not allow herself to be abandoned. If Vi was to have a fight on her hands it would be to keep Montmorency from staying. She planned to call on Mary's selflessness and good nature: Montmorency had obligations in England. He must be allowed to go. She ran through her opening sentence in her mind. But she never got a chance to say it. The maid's response to her first question — "Good morning. Is Miss Mary Gibson at home?" — told her why Mary's mother was so cross, and that her own walk across town had been a big mistake.

"Miss Gibson is at Bayfield, ma'am. Mrs. Bayfield sent a car for her this morning."

Vi turned and looked back the way she had come. She faced an uphill climb, and at the end of it she would find Mary and Montmorency together already.

So Vi was tired and flustered when Cissie's butler showed her into the Bayfields' morning room. Cissie was there alone, but a large teapot and three used cups showed that she had already had visitors. A chill blast from the French windows told Vi that Montmorency and Mary must be in the garden.

"Forgive me, Cecilia," she said, walking towards the open door. "I must see Montmorency."

Cissie was not going to let her. After the disastrous Christmas dinner she had guessed that Montmorency might be leaving town soon. She had prised Mary away from her mother to tell her to press him to stay. Montmorency's own unexpected arrival had moved her plan forward even more quickly than she had hoped. Now she wanted to give Montmorency time to propose, and Mary a chance to accept on condition that they would live in America.

"I don't think he wants to be disturbed just at present," she said, turning to the butler. "Take away this tray, Jones, and bring fresh cups and more tea."

Then she took Vi by the hand, in what the servant must have interpreted as a friendly gesture. He couldn't have seen how she dug her nails into Vi's palm, and pulled her forcefully towards a chair, her face fixed in a smile, her voice still sweet and light.

"Vi, dear, do sit down. You look exhausted. How pleasant for us to have a chance to talk alone for a change."

Vi made an attempt to stand up, but Cissie leaned on her shoulder until she was sitting again. Through the window, Vi could see two dark figures weaving between the flowerbeds, arm in arm, their heads close in intense conversation.

Cissie played for time, confecting a genteel conversation while they waited for the tea. She wanted to know more about Vi, whom she instinctively felt to be a threat to her plans. There were questions she hadn't been able to ask with Tom in tow on their shopping trips. Both of them were hiding the truth about themselves.

"Have you known Mr. Montmorency long, Mrs. Evans?"

"Oh yes," said Vi. "Let's see. It must be nearly twenty years. I was only a girl when we met. And you?"

"About the same, I suppose. We met at the Marimion Hotel, in London. Do you know it?"

"Indeed I do. I have stayed there, in fact. In the Parkview Suite."

Cissie, whose father had been the manager of the Marimion, was impressed. She knew how much the Parkview Suite cost. And yet this independent, worldly wise woman, with her hybrid accent, somehow didn't seem like the Marimion's usual clients.

Vi knew all about Cissie's background, and couldn't resist teasing her, to see how far her lies would go. "When were you at the Marimion, Mrs. Bayfield?"

Cissie tried to look as if she was searching her memory, though the hotel had been her home for many years. "I was last there in '86. My first husband, Cornelius Delahaye Newhaven Junior, and I had our wedding reception in the ballroom."

"Charming. I was there in '86, too. And what a coincidence. The manager's daughter had just married an American."

"Really?" said Cissie. "What a coincidence indeed."

"The staff told me she was very lucky to get him. She was a real gold digger, apparently."

"Oh, now you mention her, I think I heard something of the girl. But it can't be the same person. This one was quite a beauty apparently. Admired by many of the guests."

"Indeed? Well, let us hope that she settled happily. I was told that her American husband was worth at least a quarter of a million dollars."

"Oh, far more than that!" said Cissie, before she had time to think, adding, "So I was told. Assuming we're talking about the same person, of course."

The butler returned with the tea.

Vi smiled gracefully, staying on the subject, but appearing to change it.

"And your first husband, Mrs. Bayfield, he was in pig meat, was he not?"

"The food industry, yes. I inherited his business." Cissie fiddled with a large diamond ring on her right hand, and then the engraved gold wedding band on her left. "It's now incorporated with Curtis's fabric enterprise, of course."

Vi held back from making a joke about a silk purse and a sow's ear, but she tucked it away at the back of her mind to try on the others later.

The figures in the garden had gone out of sight.

Cissie probed gently on the subject of Vi's confusing marital status.

"And Mr. Evans, Tom's father . . ." Cissie smiled and paused, leaving a space for Vi to correct that assumption. The opportunity was not taken up.

"Mr. Evans. Is he dead? Are you a widow, too?"

"Evans is my maiden name," said Vi, not admitting that she was unmarried, and not giving anything away.

Cissie tried to get information from another angle. "You are not originally from Scotland?"

"No," said Vi, leaving it at that, and subtly digging back at Cissie. "We were in the hotel trade." She didn't say where or when, or who "we" were. In fact she was thinking of her mother, and the sleazy boardinghouse in Covent Garden where she had spent her childhood.

"How interesting." Cissie smiled, still not admitting her own background.

They sipped in silence for a little longer. Vi was growing restless. She wanted to get outside. Every time she tried to rise, Cissie stood over her, refilling her cup. The two women were managing to stay on the right side of insults, but the refinement was beginning to slip.

"You have no children, Mrs. Bayfield?"

"My husband and I have not been so blessed. Unlike you and . . . er . . . Mr. . . . ?"

Vi didn't rise to the bait. "Tom is indeed a blessing to me."

"He must remind you so much of his father."

Vi didn't know what to read into the remark. She hit back with a low blow about the Marimion Hotel. "Just as you remind me of yours."

Cissie froze for a moment. Just long enough for Vi to stand at last. But Cissie grabbed her, more roughly this time, to keep her in the room.

"Mrs. Evans . . . Vi, dear. I do so admire your dress. I adored it the moment we saw it in the shop. But, forgive me for mentioning it, the hooks at the back of the neck have come undone. Do allow me to fasten them for you."

"Oh please, don't trouble yourself," said Vi. But Cissie held on to her, fiddling with the fastenings, and "accidentally" pulling the fine hair at the nape of Vi's neck as she undid the clips, which had been perfectly tight all along.

Vi's shoe crunched down on Cissie's toes. She pointed to Cissie's reflection on the mirror over the mantelpiece.

"I couldn't help noticing that one of your combs has worked loose."

She tugged on a loop of hair, and a hank of artificial curls came away in her hand.

"Oh, I'm so sorry." Once again, Vi tried to make for the garden, but this time Cissie had her by the chin, firmly wiping away an invisible smudge of soot with her thumb. It was a long time since Vi had fought with a woman, but in the Covent Garden slums she had not been above solving problems with physical force. Now she saw that if she couldn't get outside to rescue Montmorency, she did at least have a way of getting him to come in. Hadn't Doctor Farcett said she was to do anything to get Montmorency away from Mary? She did the only thing she could think of and tilted her cup just enough to pour a stream of tea down Cissie's dress.

"Forgive me. An accident. I'm sure it will wash out."

"No need, I can get a new dress whenever I want."

"Just as well," said Vi, ripping a panel of lace from the bodice.

Cissie squealed and lashed back, tearing away a sleeve. Vi yelled as loud as she could, hoping to lure the lovers inside, lurching at Cissie, who was screaming, too, now, while Vi tried to keep her at arm's length, pushing against her head and kicking her shins.

In the garden, Mary knew that Montmorency was on the verge of asking for her hand, but he was interrupted by the commotion. The expletives and insults grew louder, as the two shrill voices lapsed further and further back into the coarse London accents the women had grown up with. By the time Montmorency and Mary reached the French windows, Cissie and Vi were rolling on the floor, showing their corsets and bloomers, tugging at each other's hair and spitting.

"Cecilia!" shouted Mary. "What's happening?"

Montmorency dived between the two women and pulled Vi off Cissie, holding her tightly as she struggled to get her breath back. Cissie tried to regain her composure, but she could not think what to say, and resorted to tears. Mary took off her own shawl and wrapped it around Cissie's tattered clothing. Vi tried to get Montmorency away, hoping he had not had time to make any promises to Mary.

"Take me back to the hotel," she said indignantly. "I will not be treated like this. We must leave Paterson at once."

But Montmorency didn't move and still held her so firmly that she couldn't make the grand exit she intended. Cissie, outraged at the collapse of the dignity she had spent so long acquiring, found her voice.

"Yes. Leave. Leave our town." She turned to her friend. "Mary. You cannot marry this man. Look at the company he keeps. That hussy just flew at me!"

Vi rejoiced. Somehow she and Cissie had become allies. But her relief was short-lived. Mary looked at Montmorency.

"No. Stay. I'm sure there must be an explanation."

Vi could see the danger. Montmorency might be even more inclined to stay, wanting to put things right. She tried appealing to his sense of duty. "Montmorency, you must come with me. We must return to England. You have important obligations to others."

Montmorency stood silent, torn between Mary's emotion and Vi's good sense, but Cissie, in her ferocious anger, still wanted revenge on Vi for sabotaging her carefully constructed respectability. For the moment, keeping the man both she and Mary wanted didn't matter to her. She wanted to inflict a humiliation as great as her own.

"She's right, Mary. He has obligations. Mary, for the sake of your own honor, you cannot stay with him. He has obligations, all right. He has obligations to a child. Mary, he has a son. By this trollop. I bet he never told you that in all his courting and romancing!"

They all froze. Montmorency could only return Mary's questioning gaze with bemused panic. He looked at Vi. She was panicking, too.

"Is it true?" said Mary.

Montmorency couldn't answer, and Vi's face gave him no guidance. His silence seemed to give Mary the confirmation she feared, as Cissie pressed on.

"And what have they been up to, traveling halfway around the world together? Ask yourself that, Mary."

Mary was in tears now, clinging to Cissie as Montmorency stuttered and stumbled his way through incoherent denials that just made him seem more guilty.

Cissie shouted to the butler she knew must be waiting outside the door, attracted by the unprecedented racket of the fight.

"Jones! Kindly see Mr. Montmorency and Mrs. Evans out. They are leaving."

She repelled Montmorency's attempt to approach Mary, and Vi pulled him towards the door. The butler escorted them all the way to the gates in silence.

CHAPTER 42

≫

OUT IN THE OPEN

*I*t was cold out on the hill, but after walking a few yards in silence, they both knew they had to stop and talk before returning to the hotel, where Tom was waiting.

"Is it true?" said Montmorency. "Is Tom my son?"

"Yes," said Vi quietly, amazed to hear the fact emerging from her lips so easily after all the years.

"But you never said. You never told me."

"You never asked. I waited. And then it was too late."

"But I wasn't sure. I thought . . ." He realized the implied insult in what he'd said.

"I know. You thought it might be someone else. And I did, too, sometimes. And how could I ask you to support me when he might be someone else's boy? You had your own life. If you'd really cared you would have offered."

"But what about Tom? Didn't he have a right to know?"

"I told him enough to stop him asking. And anyway. He got close to other people. People who sent him presents, and cared about his future. It wouldn't have been fair to cut him off from them."

"But we must tell him, Vi. We must tell him today, now, as soon as we get back."

"And then set off for the ship?"

"Yes. I'm coming with you. We will find Frank."

≫ ≫ ≫

When they reached the hotel, Montmorency gallantly distracted the doorman so that Vi could get upstairs without him seeing the state of her clothes. He needed to talk to the man anyway, sorting out train times and the transport of their baggage to the station.

Vi knocked on the door of Tom's room. There was no reply. Inside, Tom was still sleeping, overwhelmed by exhaustion from the night before. After his exploits in town he had stayed up far too late, writing down all the negative points about Montmorency, ready for his confrontation with Mary. The pages lay scattered on the floor by his bed, where he had dropped them as he finally fell asleep. Vi picked them up and tidied them into a heap on the table, before noticing what they said. She took them to her own room and read what her son had to say about his father.

Montmorency knocked, ready to go with her to acknowledge Tom as his own. She handed him the list. He read with a mixture of horror and self-disgust. It was an accurate exposition of all his shortcomings.

"So this is what my son thinks of me," he said. "How can we tell him the truth now?"

Vi wanted to reassure Montmorency that he had many fine characteristics, not mentioned by Tom, but part of her was glad that they might be spared the duty of making the revelation straightaway.

"Perhaps this is not the time. Perhaps we can wait."

"Wait until he has seen me do something praiseworthy,"

said Montmorency. "Wait for him to see me show truthfulness, unselfishness, reliability — and all the other qualities he says I lack."

"And you can show them straightaway, can't you? Put Mary behind you and help us find Frank."

"Of course. There's a train at two o'clock."

Vi went back to Tom's room, and put the papers back on the floor, then she roused her son, trying not to show the emotions of that tumultuous morning.

"Wake up, sleepyhead! We're going home."

Montmorency went to his own room, sat down on his luggage, and wept.

CHAPTER 43

≫

PASSENGERS

Doctor Farcett was lucky to get tickets for the SS *St. Louis*. There was only one double cabin left, in first class. When the others arrived in New York, Farcett persuaded Montmorency to share the cabin with him, and he arranged for Vi and Tom to go back to the Waldorf-Astoria. In some ways it was the perfect arrangement. If it turned out that Frank was not onboard, at least someone was left in the United States to try and find him. Montmorency would cable the Waldorf as soon as they reached land; and if Frank was safe, Vi and Tom would get the next boat home.

The clerk in the shipping office had explained to Farcett that it was a busy time, with people returning from Christmas holidays and romantics wanting to see in the new century at sea.

"If it's space you're after, you'd do better to try steerage!" he said. "It's always full on the way here, with all those poor souls looking for a better life. We don't get so many making the trip the other way."

He was right. But even so, conditions in the hold shocked Frank, as he and Guido settled in. He said nothing, of course. This was how Guido had come to America in the first place: crammed in with hundreds of others, sleeping in tightly packed bunks, with no privacy and only the most basic sanitation, and he would think Frank had seen it all before, too.

Frank thought about the grand accommodation upstairs. From the bowels of the ship they could hear a band playing on the quayside, seeing off the happy travelers crossing the high gangplanks to the decks and ballrooms above. He wondered if Vi had read his ticket and understood his plight; whether any of his friends would find a way to be there, to rescue him, or to find a way to get a message through. But when the engines started and the ship began to move, his spirits were low.

They got lower still when the boat put in at the island off Manhattan, where disappointed would-be immigrants, denied access to America, were put onboard to be returned to Europe. Everyone had to huddle up to make room for them. Frank was appalled at the thought of spending more than a week in this stinking dump, not knowing whether there was any real hope of survival or escape. Guido thought he understood and tried to cheer him up.

"Courage, my friend," he whispered. "This is a great work we undertake. We must be proud to have been chosen."

"I know," said Frank. He hid his apprehension behind another real fear. "It's just that I'm not a great sailor." Before the end of the day he proved the truth of that, doubled over a bucket as the ship plowed into the winter waves.

Montmorency watched the mighty buildings of New York fade into the distance. He had stayed on deck while Farcett went down to sort out their cabin and meet the steward who would take care of them throughout the trip. Everyone around him seemed full of life and hope, waving to families and friends on the dock below. He spotted Vi and Tom, smiling and shouting, but he carried on scanning the crowd, looking for Mary. What was he hoping? That she would race to the quayside and beg him to stay? Or that she would at least shout her forgiveness and promise to let him write and explain? Once or twice he thought he saw her, but the elegant woman in the red coat was too tall, and the familiar hat belonged to someone too short and squat to be Mary. As the band stopped playing, and some of the well-wishers turned to go, he saw a dark figure running towards the ship. Was it her? It was definitely a woman. As she got nearer, the boat moved farther away. He would never be sure. But he had a little hope to carry with him through the journey.

Farcett approached him. "All's well down below. We should be perfectly comfortable."

"I wish I'd had a chance to see New York properly," sighed Montmorency. "This whole trip has been about missed opportunities. What have I achieved? Nothing."

"But what about Frank? He might have found out something. At the very least we can make sure he's all right."

"We don't even know if he's onboard. That would be the last straw: discovering that we've left him thousands of miles away to fend for himself. What am I going to tell George? I was supposed to be looking after him."

"Slow down! There's no reason to think we have left him behind. And remember, George has asked you to go to

Florence. Come down to the cabin where we can talk properly. I've got a plan."

The table was covered in papers.

Montmorency laughed. "Don't you ever stop working, Robert? What are you up to now?"

"It's just some stuff I've got out to show the captain. I've hit on an idea for getting down into steerage. That's where Frank will be, if he's onboard. But we can't just go looking. In fact, I've realized that *you* can't go looking at all."

"Why?"

"Because you might be recognized. Suppose he's with people who know him from Florence, or from that ice-cream factory in London. They'd know you as his friend, or even his father. I fear, Montmorency, that you are going to have to keep your head down on this trip. I will have to do most of the work."

"Suits me," said Montmorency gloomily. "But what are you going to do?"

"Well, I thought I'd ask the captain if I could do a medical study of the steerage passengers. I'll show him the work I did on the *Campania*. You know, the report on how the flu made its way around the ship. I'm going to say that the results would be greatly enhanced if I could do a medical survey of a normal ship. I'll ask to start by examining all the steerage passengers."

"It sounds pretty convincing."

"Actually, now I've had the idea, I'm quite keen on it

anyway, whether we find Frank or not. The survey could be of real interest: not just to the medical journals, but the shipping line, the immigration authorities, perhaps even to the British Government. After all, they're sending soldiers halfway around the world to fight in South Africa. I might come up with suggestions to make sure they arrive healthy and fit to fight."

"Oh, Robert, you are incorrigible. You see a career opportunity everywhere you go! But what are you going to do if Frank is down there?"

"To start with, I won't treat him any differently from the others. I'm going to see them all individually and in private, so that will give me time for at least a brief talk with Frank. Then we'll cook up something to make sure that I have regular consultations."

"And I'll just stay here and vegetate."

"No, you won't. You can help me analyze the results of my study. And if we do find Frank, you can work out exactly what we're going to do when we get off the ship back in England."

"And what about Vi and Tom?"

"Montmorency, do you really imagine that Vi will have any difficulty amusing herself in New York, surrounded by lots of new people, shops, and unlimited supplies of food and drink?"

"No, of course she won't. But I worry about Tom. He's not used to city life. But he is growing up fast, and into such a fine boy."

"Yes he is, isn't he," said Farcett, trying not to sound too proud.

"And so like his mother," said Montmorency.

"Oh yes. Very like Vi, indeed," said Farcett, changing the subject as he bundled up the papers on the table and put them under his arm. "I might as well go to see the captain straightaway. If I'm going to do this project, I haven't any time to waste."

The captain was in his cabin, having a quick drink before lunch. He liked the idea of Farcett's medical survey.

"Perhaps I should consult the ship's doctor?" Farcett suggested. "As a matter of medical etiquette. You know, operating on his patch . . ."

"Oh, no need for that," said the captain. "Onboard ship, the captain's word is law, whoever you are, and I'm delighted about your study."

He didn't say why it appealed to him so much. Farcett couldn't have known that the captain was ecstatic to have found a way to annoy the ship's doctor, who had infuriated him on the way over to New York by telling all the crew, and a good many of the passengers, about a nasty boil that had erupted on the captain's backside.

"I wonder if I might have a look at the passenger list?" asked Farcett.

The captain opened a drawer. "Of course. Here you are. We divide the steerage passengers into three groups: families, women traveling alone, and unaccompanied men. Which would you like to see first?"

The doctor in Farcett knew that the family group was the one most likely to need his attention, but Frank was more likely to be with the men. He had better start there. He made himself feel better about that by thinking of the possible military applications of his work. The men would be more like the soldiers en route to the Boer War.

"I'll start with the men."

"Very well," said the captain. "Now why don't we go straight down to tell them all what's going to happen? Then we can find you a space to do your work."

"I'd like somewhere I can talk to the patients in privacy," said Farcett. "It's important that they feel they can tell me anything without being overheard. I feel that patients have a right to confidentiality, whoever they are."

"I quite understand," said the captain, scratching his bottom. "I'm sure there's a storeroom down there that we can clear out for you."

As they climbed down a narrow ladder to the steamy atmosphere of third class, Farcett quickly cast his eyes down the list. There was no mention of Frank under Fox or Selwyn. Either he wasn't there, or he was traveling under a false name.

The crew belowdecks were surprised to see the captain, but quickly followed instructions to bring the passengers to order. They gathered in the wide low-ceilinged hall at the center of the ship. Frank and Guido squatted behind a pillar towards the back. Frank glanced around, caught a glimpse of Doctor Farcett, and fought not to show even a flicker of relief. The captain told them what was going to happen in a tone that offered no one the chance to decline a medical examination. Everyone was to go to the doctor when called, in alphabetical order.

"What should we do?" asked Guido. "Do we go along with it?"

"We'll only draw attention to ourselves if we don't," said Frank.

"You're right. And anyway, he might have something to stop you being sick!"

Frank laughed with Guido, feeling happy for the first time in days. If he could get to see Doctor Farcett on his own, there might be a way out of this nightmare.

Farcett's examinations started as soon as the crew had set up a consultation room. He brought his medical bag down from the cabin, and a notebook for recording his impressions of each patient's health. He carefully ruled columns down the page. One for the name, one for age, a wide space for his summary, and a place at the edge of the page for a cross, indicating that he should see a patient again to follow up any particular concern. Then he took off his jacket, rolled up his sleeves, and called in the first patient, a Mr. Andrews. He was a businessman who had come to America to make his fortune, failed, and was using his last — borrowed — money to get home. (The poor "friend" who had lent the money would never get it back, and never hear from Andrews again.) Mr. Andrews had not always been poor. His trip to the United States had been in second class, and he moaned to Doctor Farcett about the conditions in steerage.

As one man after another came in, Farcett learned more about the physical and emotional effects of the cramped hold, with its foul air, narrow bunks, noise, and heat. After a while he grew as angry as the passengers, and though he tried not to reveal his feelings to them, he sometimes engaged in conversation with the more articulate English speakers about what could be done to make them more comfortable. A decent supply of washrooms and water was one thing. Even so early in the trip, the passengers were filthy: especially those who had succumbed to seasickness. He commented on this to a swarthy young man with a dark black floppy fringe, who entered his room stinking of vomit. The name on the passenger list said Silvio Ermino, but it was Guido.

Farcett said a brusque "Good afternoon," and approached with his stethoscope. He pointed to stains on Ermino's shirt. "I see you are having an uncomfortable passage."

"It is not me, it is my friend. I try to help him," said Ermino. "We are so squashed together, there is nowhere for the sick to go."

"Except down your shirt!" said Farcett, wondering if the Italian would understand his joke.

He did, and he laughed as Farcett continued his examination, declaring him to be a perfectly fit young man. They carried on talking, and when Ermino left, with instructions to send in Joseph Ettles, Farcett was rather sad that he had found no reason to put a little cross in the final column, so that he could see him again, for more engaging conversation about the shortcomings of the ship.

By the time he got to the Ls, Farcett had worked out why so many of his patients stayed on to talk. Their time with the doctor was a welcome respite from the horrors of their communal accommodation. His porthole opened on to a deck, and they could breathe clean air there for the first time since they boarded. No one wanted to leave. Farcett sympathized with them, but decided to be firmer. He was halfway through the alphabet, and there was still no sign of Frank.

Down in the hold, Frank waited nervously while Guido was away. He feared that Farcett might say something that would give away their link. That he might by an unintended word or question make Guido suspicious, or that Guido might come back with advice to Frank not to go in, not to get examined. He saw Guido returning, weaving his way through the crush of fetid bodies towards their bunks.

"How was it?" asked Frank.

"He's a good man. There's nothing wrong with me. It's a shame. I would have liked to go back. You get a proper chair, you can breathe. He even let me wash my hands and face in his sink." Frank could smell the familiar odor of carbolic soap that always reminded him of Doctor Farcett.

"So you think I should go when it's my turn, then?"

"Oh yes. And try to convince him that you're ill. Then he might ask you back again!"

At last, fortune was going Frank's way. By the end of the day he would have a chance to make contact with his friends, and start planning a way out of his nightmare. It seemed ages before his false name was called. The man before him, Charles Naylor, really did look ill, and Farcett took his time with the examination. But eventually Naylor came out and called:

"Jack Newman."

Frank went in and closed the door behind him. Farcett was finishing off his notebook entry about Naylor, and spoke wearily, without looking up. "Just stand there a moment, will you?" He ruled a line across the page and copied the next name from the passenger list. "Jack Newman," he said as he wrote. "Are you Jack Newman?"

"No, Robert. It's me. Frank."

Farcett jumped up from behind his desk and hugged Frank, despite the stench of vomit and dirt. "Thank God, Frank. Thank God you are safe. We've been so worried about you."

"Are you all on the ship?"

"Just Montmorency and me. Vi and Tom are still in New York. I'll find a way to let them know that you're safe. We must get you out of this hellhole. I'll invent a reason to bring you upstairs. It's really very comfortable in first class."

"No," said Frank, lowering his voice. "I must stay here. I am not traveling alone. I have so much to tell you, but I can't afford to be treated differently from anyone else."

"Who are you with?"

"Guido . . . I mean Silvio Ermino. That's the name you'll have on your list. You saw him earlier."

Farcett looked back through his notes and remembered the charming young Italian. "He seemed a nice chap."

"He is. But he's dangerous, Robert. And he and I are on a mission we must stop. Otherwise there will be death in Italy and damage in London on a scale we have never seen before."

"Look, I'd better examine you properly," said Farcett, reaching out to Frank's face and pulling down his lower eyelids. "Put out your tongue. . . . Oh dear, Frank. You stink!" He listened to Frank's chest. "Now whether you're ill or not, I'm going to put you on the list to see me again. Tell your friend I'm worried about a rattle in your lung. Before you go now, have a wash over there, and tell me about this plot you're tied up in. I'll ask Montmorency what to do, and we'll talk again when I see you tomorrow. I'll go and tell him I've found you straightaway."

"Don't do that. Wait till you've seen some more people. Don't do anything that might draw attention to me."

So Farcett worked on, getting to the end of the Ts with a talkative man called Tomlinson before he stopped for the day.

"How did you get on?" asked Guido when Frank returned.

"He's worried about a rattle in my chest," said Frank. "He wants to see me again."

"Lucky you," said Guido. "Make the most of it!"

CHAPTER 44

≫

COUNTERPLOT

*M*ontmorency didn't appreciate quite how worried he had been about Frank until he heard the news that he was safe among the steerage passengers down below. But his relief soon turned to annoyance with Farcett, who answered only a fraction of his questions about the boy and the plot he was involved in.

"There wasn't time, Montmorency. I couldn't cover everything. And it's not as if he's going anywhere. I'm going to see him again. I'll call him in every day, and I can ask him more."

"Well, we'd better be systematic about it. Work through what we do know, and get him to fill in the gaps."

Montmorency went over to the writing desk, where the shipping line provided sheets of paper with a picture of the SS *St. Louis* at the top of each page. They drew up a list of questions, and over the next few days Farcett put them to Frank. Montmorency annotated his own scrawled notes with each new detail the doctor brought back from the consulting room. In the end only he could possibly have deciphered what they meant. But by New Year's Eve, he was sure of how everything to do with the attacks in London and Rome fit together, and he had a plan.

It was unconventional. It depended on persuading the

authorities to let Frank and Guido go ahead with preparations for the bombing exactly as instructed by Malpensa. That was the only way to prevent Frank from becoming an anarchist target himself. Montmorency could not take the chance of contacting Frank once he was in England with Guido. If Guido saw him, he might realize that Frank was a spy, and associate him once again with the Fox-Selwyns. They might all become victims in their turn. And what if Malpensa had the young idealists followed, by some trusted London operative, too cowardly to carry out the deed himself?

Whatever happened, Frank would have to disappear after January 14. But he must disappear as an anarchist hero. If the Home Secretary refused to cooperate with Montmorency, that heroism would be attained through arrest, imprisonment, or even worse. And there would be no safe way to let Frank know what was going on. Montmorency would place a vase on the windowsill of Fox-Selwyn's drawing room if the authorities had agreed to his plan. But he would never know if Frank had had the chance to see it, and in any case, Frank's instructions were the same either way.

Even if Montmorency's scheme worked flawlessly, it was high risk. It was inspired by something in Fox-Selwyn's Christmas letter. In it, George recounted the plot of Puccini's new opera *Tosca* (fittingly, thought Montmorency, a tale of political intrigue and betrayal). There was a brilliant idea in the last act. Montmorency would have to refine the details, but he thought he could make it work on the streets of

London. Farcett would go through it over and over again with Frank in his daily chats in the medical room on the boat. Frank would have to play his part perfectly if he was to get out alive. There could be no rehearsal, nor last-minute alteration to the script.

The captain invited Doctor Farcett and his friend to see in the New Year at his table in the grand restaurant. The ship's doctor gave Farcett the cold shoulder in the bar beforehand. Montmorency was happy to come out of hiding, convinced that there was no chance of his being recognized by Guido, who was safely confined below. Over dinner, the New Year joviality was interspersed with serious talk about the South African war. It was going badly for Britain, with a series of defeats and great loss of life. But when midnight came, in the middle of the Atlantic, they all stood and toasted the new century in a shower of streamers.

In Italy, two couples were walking under the stars, gazing down on the lights of Florence and planning their futures. Gus had asked Beatrice to become his new duchess. Alexander had persuaded Angelina, the police chief's daughter, that she would enjoy being the Marchioness of Rosseley. They planned a double wedding in this Italian city they all loved so much.

The post had been slow over Christmas, and they had not heard from the travelers for a while. Montmorency had sent a brief cable from New York, saying they were on their way back to Europe. But they had no details and no way of contacting Frank, the youngest member of the family, with their good news.

Lord George Fox-Selwyn was inside, playing chess with his friend Antonio Moretti, the curator of La Specola. George had grown increasingly fond of this gentle naturalist, who wore his learning so lightly, and could think of no more congenial company in which to greet the New Year. Just before midnight, Moretti got him in checkmate, and George called for a bottle of the local wine and six glasses.

Down in steerage on the SS *St. Louis,* the sick and disappointed did their best to celebrate, too.

"To the twentieth century!" said Guido, raising a cup of brackish water. "And to the year 1900. The year we will really make a difference!"

CHAPTER 45

≫

DOCTOR DETECTIVE

By halfway through the voyage, it was clear to both Farcett and Montmorency that they would have to split up when they reached land. One of them would sort things out in London, the other must go to Florence to help George foil the *Tosca* plot. They both wanted the London job.

Montmorency made his case: "Believe me, Robert, I'd love to go to Italy. I'd like nothing more than to see that opera, for one thing. But I must be the one who gets Frank through this. In any case, I already know the London police. This is going to be a tricky operation for them, and they're going to need some persuading to do it my way. Surely you understand?"

"Yes, but I have things to do as well. I've got all these articles to finish and deliver. And anyway, I want to visit Tarimond. I have to check that Maggie really has stopped the X-ray experiments, and . . ." He looked down coyly. "There's something I want to ask her."

Montmorency knew full well what Farcett was referring to. But he didn't want to talk about Robert's love life. It made him feel uncomfortable, and the other things were more important.

"Look, I can post on a letter to her. And you've got a couple of days onboard for writing up those reports. I can take them around to the publishers, too. Be reasonable. If you were handling things in London you wouldn't be able to go to Tarimond. It makes no difference to Maggie whether you're in England or Italy. Farcett, you're a great doctor, but this is my field, and I think you'll be of most use helping George."

In the end, Farcett gave way. He wrote two letters: one to Maggie, promising to visit as soon as he returned from Italy, and another to George, warning of his arrival in Florence. He didn't go into details. He wanted to deliver the worrying news about Frank in person. When he found the Florence apartment, just before lunch on the morning of January 7, he was greeted with wild waving from the balcony. An unfamiliar, disheveled figure was there, too. Professor Lombroso was back in town, and Gus had found himself unable to refuse his demand for hospitality. One reason he and Alex were so glad to see Doctor Farcett was the thought of having someone else to share the torture of living with him.

Their happy mood was soon punctured as Farcett explained Frank's plight, the dangers at home and here in Florence, too. George could hardly believe that La Specola could be at the center of political trouble once again. He offered to take Farcett there to show him how unlikely it was that the peaceful, elegant museum might be a secret arms dump. Sadly, his friend the curator was out of town, but George knew the place well enough to give Doctor Farcett a thorough tour.

He even stage-managed it a bit, taking Robert slowly through the early rooms of specimens, so like those in the

Natural History Museum at home, then building up through the big stuffed beasts and finally presenting, almost as an afterthought, the magnificent wax bodies, with their multi-colored organs, sinews, and bones. Farcett was enraptured at once, marveling at the accurate detail of the corpses, crafted more than a hundred years before. Fox-Selwyn proudly embarked on a little commentary:

"They made them for medical students to study. So they wouldn't have to do so many dissections of real human bodies. You see, they may look gruesome, but really they were inspired by the most humane of motives: education and the desire to let the dead keep their dignity. I do think that's important. It's always worried me, medical students dibbling around in real insides. I think a dead body deserves respect, don't you?"

"Indeed I do. It's one of the reasons I've been working on the Bodyscreener, to cut down the need for cadavers."

"How's that going, by the way? Was Edison a help?"

"He was tremendously helpful and generous. But he's alerted me to some possible dangers, and I may have to rethink the design. I want to get back down to it as soon as this business is cleared up."

They left the museum and set off down the stairs. George asked more about Farcett's plans, but when they got home he returned to the subject he really wanted to discuss.

"So what do you think? Did you see any sign of hidden weapons?"

"I was looking all the time we were in there," said Farcett. "I couldn't see a likely spot."

"They could be in the vaults, of course, with all the extra stock. It's wonderful down there, but it would take a very long time to give it a good search, and I'd be reluctant to start without the curator's permission."

"Are you sure he'll be back before the 14th?"

"Well, no, actually. I'm not sure how long he's away. Perhaps we should talk to whoever else is in charge."

"Is that wise? What if they're in on the plot?" asked Farcett.

"Well, what else can we do? There's nowhere else to look."

"Unless . . ."

"Unless what?"

"Unless the guns and explosives are among the displays after all. Hidden right inside them."

"What, in those glass jars? I didn't notice any revolvers floating in the preservative!"

"Not the jars. In the stuffed animals and the wax bodies."

"And how would they have got in there? You've seen how the guards watch you as you go around. If you even touch the glass they tick you off."

"Exactly. The guards are there all the time, aren't they?"

"Yes."

"And what's the one thing we know about this Guido, the anarchist who's working with Frank in London now?"

"That he was a guard at La Specola. But he's been gone for over a year. He's been away in Paterson."

"Where they manufacture . . . ?"

"I don't know. . . . Montmorency said something about silk."

"Yes, they call it Silk City, but there's something else as well. It's the place where Samuel Colt produced the first repeating revolvers. He built a gun factory there."

"And you think these anarchists would bother to send guns all this way? There must be plenty of guns in Italy."

"Maybe so. But it's illegal here for people to carry them. In America, anyone can have a gun. And here the likely suspects must think they're being watched. They can't shift arms around. How much better to send a consignment to a place that constantly gets deliveries of strangely shaped parcels from all over the world!"

"So you're suggesting . . . ?"

"I'm suggesting that someone working in La Specola has been acquiring and hiding guns and explosives ready for the big attack in Rome on Sunday. That they're planning to move them down to Rome at the last minute. They think they won't be recognized there. The police in Rome are all tied up trailing their own local suspects."

"They might be wrong about that," said Fox-Selwyn. "Most of the police from Florence have gone to Rome to help in that operation. They're down to a skeleton staff here. The police chief told me so himself before he left."

"A skeleton staff. George, you're brilliant."

"It's not a very original phrase, you know. I didn't make it up."

"No, but you've crystallized an idea that was floating around in my mind."

"Too many scientific metaphors! Robert, what are you talking about?"

"I want to X-ray those exhibits, the fat walrus, the hippo, and all those wax bodies. My guess is that someone with access to the keys has been sneaking in at night to plant the loot. It wouldn't be too difficult with the right skills and equipment. I could have done it. I could have gone in there with a scalpel, cut my way inside, then I could have stitched up after myself, or else melted the wax back together again. With enough time, I could leave the originals looking as if they were untouched."

"So, what do you think? A doctor is behind all this?"

"Not necessarily a doctor. A veterinarian, or a medical student."

"The museum is staffed by students. They do it to earn extra money."

"Well, there you are, then. I bet one of them has been going in overnight. When the museum is unguarded."

"Except that the curator lives there, you know, in a flat at the top. He'd be bound to hear something."

"Oh," said Farcett, disappointed. He had enjoyed letting his imagination run. "So the curator is always there?"

"Well, actually, now I think about it, most evenings recently the curator has been away from home."

"How do you know?"

"Because most evenings recently the curator has been with me. We play chess almost every night, and he joins us for dinner. Stays over sometimes when we've had rather a lot to drink. Oh, Robert! I may inadvertently have made it all possible."

"But we can do something about it. Get your friend the curator to let us have a look. Ask him about his staff."

"But he's away, remember. He might not be back in time."

"So we'll just have to find out for ourselves," said Farcett. "Oh, what would Montmorency do now?"

"He'd steal the keys for a start, and go and have a look himself after hours. Or he'd find a back way in, through the drains."

"Well, I don't have Montmorency's skills at thieving. And the sewers won't be much use here, the waste just runs down little gullies into the river."

"I was only joking. I don't expect you to wade through slime. But you have got other skills. You were saying so yourself only a moment ago. Do you have your doctor's bag with you? Surely there's something in it we could use to pick a lock?"

"Yes, and there's another thing in my luggage as well. Something you reminded me of when you started talking about skeletons."

"What?" said George, bemused.

"I've got one of Edison's portable fluoroscopes. If I get a few more parts to make it go, I could look right inside those exhibits. They've got electricity in there; I could wire it up easily."

"And those spare parts?"

"Nothing I shouldn't be able to get from the local hospital. I don't suppose you have any contacts there?"

"I don't. But what about our friend the professor? It's about time he did us a favor. He spends his days at the department of anatomy, analyzing the essential criminal face."

"I've heard all about Lombroso," said Farcett, casually putting a finger up his nose. "You know what a good mimic Montmorency is."

"Well, don't be misled by his bumbling habits. He's actually very eminent and well respected. And if you want him to help you get your X-ray working, you're going to have to turn on the charm."

"Don't worry, I will," said Robert.

He would do anything to find the culprits. Farcett had often wondered why Montmorency and Fox-Selwyn continued with their detective work when they could both well afford to live comfortably without it. Now that he was in the thick of one of their jobs, he understood completely.

CHAPTER 46

≫

SURGERY BY MOONLIGHT

*I*n fact, Robert didn't have to work too hard on the professor. Unlike the others, he found himself intrigued by Lombroso's ideas, and studied his book with genuine interest. The professor, in turn, wanted to hear all about Farcett's study of the steerage passengers, and they talked at length about whether the lower classes were physically distinct from the rest. Farcett didn't agree with Lombroso's theories. How could he when he knew all about Montmorency's past? But he admired the professor's methods, and happily compared them with his own. From time to time George had to take Farcett aside and remind him what they wanted to achieve. With just a few days to go, they had to smash the Florence operation before it decamped to Rome.

But Farcett was right to take his time. He won Lombroso's total trust, and in the end the professor came up trumps. He had no trouble persuading the radiologists at the hospital to lend him some equipment for his researches, and late on the night of Wednesday, January 10, he joined George and Farcett as they broke into the museum.

It was very dark. They didn't want to draw attention to themselves by turning on lights, so they crept around, lugging the X-ray equipment, finding their way between the cabinets by following George, who had been there so often that he knew where to go. The professor had to be shushed quiet as he started up one nervously random conversation after another. He almost shrieked as he saw the giant stuffed rhinoceros in front of him, outlined by the moonlight, and apparently about to charge. George had never noticed how creaky the floor was. Robert thought the pounding of his heart could have been heard miles away. They shuffled towards the end of the exhibition, to the section where the wax bodies lay in their glass cases as if asleep. Lombroso had never seen them before, and was struck with the rapture that affected most visitors when they first came. He stood stock-still and stared.

"Professor. The wire, please," whispered Farcett, who was setting up his equipment over the Venus Smantellata (the Venus who can be dismantled). "The wire, please," he repeated, holding out his hand.

Farcett looked up at the lights. They were higher than he expected, but he needed to get up there to tap the electricity supply. "Pass me that chair," he said to George, pointing towards the seat Guido had used all that time ago. Even that was not high enough, and Farcett ended up perched on George's shoulders, reaching up and calling for equipment like a surgeon in the operating room. "Pliers . . . cutters . . ." he ordered, and the professor played the role of nurse, handing them up one by one. Farcett was sweating. He wished Lombroso had a damp flannel for his forehead, like a nurse in the hospital, but he had to put up with his stinging eyes and slippery fingers, while he struggled to make the connections in the dark.

"This is really dangerous," said the professor. "You could both be killed."

"Thank you so much for letting us know," panted Fox-Selwyn, struggling to balance Farcett on his back. "We'll bear that in mind."

But somehow the wiring worked, and Farcett coaxed the fluoroscope into life. He put the eyepiece to his face, and strode towards the nearest wax model, a full-length man, whose abdomen was an explosion of intestines. The others watched Farcett in the ethereal glow. Even the professor was silent.

"Yes!" cried Farcett after what seemed like an endless pause. "There's a gun inside." He guided the viewer up the body. "And another, and another."

The others both wanted to have a turn with the new toy. Lombroso turned around to the exhibit behind: a pregnant woman who turned out to be carrying more than the full-term fetus depicted in her open womb. Fox-Selwyn took on the stuffed animals. They all seemed clear. Farcett checked after him. He was relieved. He hadn't fancied stitching up all that leathery animal skin if he'd had to operate there.

But he did need to deal with the waxworks, and he searched through his bag for a suitable scalpel. He even found himself looking around for somewhere to wash his hands. Perhaps that was a tribute to his hygienic habits. Perhaps to the artistic skills of the long-dead modelers, who had produced effigies so convincingly real that Farcett thought they should be protected from infection.

Fox-Selwyn suddenly had a private flash of panic. Perhaps the glass cases were sealed: impossible to break open without leaving a trace. He surreptitiously checked the nearest exhibit. The lid was loose. "Have you got a screwdriver?" he asked solemnly.

"No, dash it," said Farcett. "I should have thought of that."

"It's all right. You won't need one. I was only teasing," said Fox-Selwyn, lifting the lid. They all whistled with relief, and Doctor Farcett got down to work.

The wax was harder than he'd expected. He had to warm the knife in a candle flame to help it cut through. He entered each model from the side, so as to leave as little trace as possible. The professor took the viewer, and guided Farcett's maneuvers, telling him to move left, right, up, down until each weapon was exposed, and could be removed. Then Farcett softened the wax again and carefully fashioned it back into place. Fox-Selwyn had never seen Farcett in the operating room. He was amazed now at the delicacy and strength of the doctor's hands, the quiet confidence of his movements as he took his only chance to get things right before the wax hardened and defied him again. By the small hours of the morning they had collected a dozen weapons and several pounds of explosives. Fox-Selwyn did one last scan of the smaller exhibits around the walls. An oversized representation of the heart seemed to contain several small discs. Farcett cut his way in and probed with his fingers. Out came a dozen coins, and several notes that hadn't shown up on the fluoroscope.

"Looks as if we've got their train fare to Rome as well!" he announced triumphantly. "I think we should go home now."

The professor carried the sack. When the others had finished tidying up after themselves, they went back to the door, and Fox-Selwyn fiddled with the lock again so there was no sign of an intrusion.

"Where did you learn to do that?" asked Farcett.

"Montmorency doesn't do all my dirty work!" Fox-Selwyn laughed. "Actually, I taught *him* how to do it. Let's just say it's one of the tricks of the trade."

They made their way back to the apartment with the sack hidden under the professor's cape, trying to look like three men on the way home after a great night out. Fortunately there was no one to witness their overacting. Montmorency would have been appalled.

Back at home, with the lights on at last, they examined their haul.

"Let's hope we got everything," said the professor.

"They were preparing for something really horrific," said Farcett, staring down at the arsenal before him. "I can't bear to think of the suffering this lot would have caused."

"We're going to have to keep watch over La Specola from now on," said Fox-Selwyn. "Someone's going to come to collect the stuff, and they'll go mad when it's missing. With a bit of luck they'll run straight to the rest of the gang, and we'll catch the lot of them."

"Shouldn't we get the police to help us?" asked Farcett.

"Yes, but don't forget, most of them are in Rome. I expect the ones who are left will be asking *us* to help *them*."

"We'll have to take it in turns to stand guard on the museum," said Farcett. "My guess is that they'll go in at night to collect the guns, just as we did. Perhaps we can persuade Alexander to keep an eye out today, so that we can get some sleep."

And, after an exciting breakfast, where they showed the weapons to Gus and Alexander, that is exactly what they did. Farcett went first to relieve Alexander from his duties. The earnest young man had completely entered into the spirit of the thing. He had even gone inside the museum and come away with two important pieces of information. No one inside seemed to have noticed that anything was wrong. And the guard in the waxworks room, the man sitting on Guido's chair, had told the friendly British tourist all about himself. He was a medical student.

CHAPTER 47

≫

THE CORRIDOR

*F*arcett, Fox-Selwyn, and the professor took it in turns watching the museum by night. Alexander had excelled himself, and during the day had rented a room directly opposite, so they could sit in comfort and look out of the window unobserved. The police had contacted their chief in Rome, who had told them he was staying put, and urged them to be polite to the Englishman, but not to take him too seriously. The police chief couldn't risk coming back to Florence. There was still a great deal of work to be done in Rome. Only a couple of days to go until the royal opera première, and nothing had been found there yet.

"Of course it hasn't!" said Fox-Selwyn to the desk sergeant who broke the news. "It's all here. They're looking in the wrong place."

The officer shrugged and promised that he would arrange backup if Fox-Selwyn sent a message asking for help; but he didn't inspire much confidence.

"It seems we're on our own," George told the others when he got back to the lookout room. "We'll all have to stay here. One can watch, one sleep, and one run for the police when we need them."

They had a long wait, and the professor's chatter and bodily noises began to get on their nerves. It wasn't till the early hours of Friday, two days before the opera, that Farcett, on duty at the window, saw somebody stirring in the street below. He was carrying what looked like a doctor's bag. Farcett beckoned Fox-Selwyn over, and roused the snoring professor.

"I'll watch," said Fox-Selwyn. "You go for the police, Robert. You're the fittest of us. Tell them to get here as soon as they can, and not to make a noise."

Farcett set off, and the others waited. Surely the intruder must have found out by now that the guns and money were gone? Fox-Selwyn imagined the scene in the museum. The man must be cutting open each model, frantically hoping that something would be left. Perhaps he was taking time to patch up after himself, fearing capture even though he had found nothing. Perhaps when he gave up, he would run straight to his confederates, warning them that someone was on their tail.

"You wait here," Fox-Selwyn told the professor as dawn was breaking in a breathtaking rustle of pink light over the ancient rooftops. "Keep watching. I'm going down to the street so I can follow him if he comes out."

George was just in time. He had been tucked into the shadow of a doorway for less than five minutes when the medical student let himself out through the small door in La Specola's huge front gate. He looked around, and set off towards the river, across the wide open courtyard in front of the Pitti Palace. George tried to follow at a discreet distance, but there was nowhere to hide once the man was crossing the square, and to hold back would be to risk losing him. Fox-Selwyn tried to match the rhythm of his own steps to his quarry's. It didn't work. In the early morning calm every footfall echoed against the palace walls. The man looked around, saw he was being followed, and started to run.

He sped through an arch, into the vast Boboli Gardens, disappearing inside an ornamental grotto behind the palace. Fox-Selwyn went in after him, but he was blinded by the sudden darkness, and then again when his eyes had had a chance to adapt to the gloom and he spun around, chasing a sound, and found himself facing the light. The man went up a staircase, through a door, into a chamber inside the palace, then faced another door. He was held up forcing his way through, and Fox-Selwyn was gradually catching up, though his heart was thudding and his breathing short. A third door gave the student more difficulty than either of the others. Fox-Selwyn was almost upon him when it swung into the darkness ahead, and the man disappeared again. George knew they were now well above ground level. His knees had felt every tread of the stairs, and yet now the man seemed to have plunged into a dark tunnel.

George's eyes let him down again, and he could only follow the thumping footsteps in front. Fox-Selwyn was mystified. Where were they? The walls were close, the ceiling low, the floor rose and fell, and there were sudden corners, little runs of stairs as the levels shifted, but no sign of an end, a door, or an exit. At last he worked it out. The student was fleeing through Vasari's secret corridor — the passage built by the great architect in the sixteenth century so that the Medici family, the grand rulers of Florence, could get about the city without mixing with the crowds. George had tried to get in to see it as a tourist several times, but it had always been closed. How he wished he had explored it before, or at least read up in the guidebook exactly where it went. What should he do? His friends didn't know where he was, and he had no idea where he was going. Just on, relentlessly on, in the dark, with his chest aching and his skin pouring sweat.

Then, around a corner, he could smell incense and hear a distant muttering. There was an opening in one side of the wall looking down onto the interior of a church. Ahead of him, just before the gap, the student had stopped — perhaps to get his breath back, or maybe to avoid being seen by the sacristans who were preparing for an early morning service down below. So the Medici could even worship without mingling with the hoi polloi. From the balcony here they could join a service without ever leaving their homes.

George had almost caught up with the student now. But the man heard his wheezing and was off again, ducking down below the opening as he went. The sacristans were distracted by the commotion and looked up, just in time to see Fox-Selwyn thundering by.

"Call the police!" he shouted from the gallery as he sped past, back into the gloom of the passageway, feeling that his lungs were about to burst, as the corridor weaved around corners, up and down.

Then there was light. Bright morning light through round windows in the side walls. He could see the river below, far below, and just beneath him the bustle of shopkeepers setting up for a morning's trade. This must be the Ponte Vecchio: the old bridge lined with shops that he had walked across a hundred times without realizing there was another, hidden, passageway above. Perhaps they would be out soon. If the exit was here, he could shout to those shopkeepers for help. But no, the closed route continued, right, away from the bridge and along the side of the river, left, right, left, then straight on, cutting through buildings and across streets, high in the air. All the time the distance between Fox-Selwyn and the fleeing student was growing, until at last there was another door. And it was locked. The exhausted young man was unable to force it open, and lay collapsed at its foot, panting and crying. When he caught up, Fox-Selwyn's greatest handicap was instantly transformed into his best asset. He sat down on top of the skinny student, pinning him there with his enormous weight. His own chest heaved alarmingly as his body overcame the shock of such unaccustomed exercise. But after a while he was calm and still enough to take a notebook and pencil from his pocket. He started questioning the man, who suddenly looked very young and very frightened.

Fox-Selwyn thought for a moment of Frank, and wondered if he should back off and give the boy a chance to compose himself. But then he thought of the arms in the museum, of Queen Margherita at the opera in the Teatro Costanzi, and the innocent people who might lose their lives with her should she be attacked. He demanded to know the student's name. The boy lied at first, not knowing that Fox-Selwyn had already heard it, from Alexander, the day before. Fox-Selwyn challenged him, and sat a little harder on his legs, making sure it hurt. He got the real name that way, and the names and addresses of several accomplices followed.

Then there was scuffling on the other side of the door, and the terrified student pushed against Fox-Selwyn with all his might, freeing himself, and trying to run back down the passage. But his ankle had snapped, under the pressure of George's backside, and he staggered in agony. It wasn't the first time Fox-Selwyn had used unconventional methods to get results.

The big door swung back to reveal a room Fox-Selwyn had seen before. It was at the top of the Uffizi, the magnificent concoction of public offices and art galleries he had visited with Gus and Beatrice many times. The police were there, alerted by the sacristan. They were looking for the fat Englishman he had described but, after a little explanation, agreed to arrest the limping Florentine instead. The list of names turned out to be genuine. They were all picked up before breakfast, and Fox-Selwyn took great pleasure in watching the deputy chief of police dictate a cable to his boss in Rome, telling him of their triumph back home.

The professor appeared and was soon measuring and sketching the heads of all the suspects, declaring them to be criminal types to a man. Farcett watched him and began to wonder if

there might be something in this strange science of charac-
terology after all.

Back at the apartment, he got out his stethoscope and gave
Fox-Selwyn a thorough examination.

"That was quite a run, George. Take it easy for a few days
now. Doctor's orders."

"No time for that, old boy. I'm going to Rome."

"Whatever for? We've foiled the plot. You're not worried
that there's still going to be trouble, are you?"

"Not at all. I imagine that the Teatro Costanzi in Rome
will be the safest place on earth on Sunday night. The danger
is over, but the police will still be out in force to show that
they're doing their job. I'm so convinced we've crushed the
plot that I'm going to use one of these." He took two tickets
from his pocket. "Puccini sent them to me. I met him at the
contessa's before Christmas. What a shame Montmorency
isn't here to use the other one. Would you like to come
along?"

"I think I'd better, just to see that you are all right," said
Doctor Farcett. "Then I really must get back to England. I've
got important things to do."

CHAPTER 48

≫

TOSCA AND TICH

*I*n London, the days leading up to January 14 were just as tense as in Italy, but in a different way. In Florence, Farcett and Fox-Selwyn had been following hunches, and scrambling to catch the anarchists in time. In London, Montmorency, the police commissioner, and a few carefully chosen intelligence officers knew everything: the target, the timing, and the location of the armaments. But between them they had agreed on an unusual plan of action. They were all to hang back until the very last minute, ready to catch Frank and Guido in the act. Only then would more policemen be brought in, as if the operation were the result of painstaking detection, bearing fruit at just the right time. The Home Secretary personally made two decisions that would prove controversial should they ever become public. Preparations for the opening of the Hippodrome would be allowed to go ahead as planned — no one there would be warned of anything untoward. And unknown to anyone but Montmorency and himself, there would be secret marksmen on duty outside the Hippodrome on the evening of January 14. They would be under orders to be prepared to shoot to kill.

The first decision, about going ahead at the Hippodrome, was mainly political. The South African war was going badly, with news arriving of more than a thousand dead in the disaster at Ladysmith only that week. There was trouble in Ireland. There was illness. There was fog. The opening of a grand new theater, with all the opportunities it held for outpourings of patriotism, was just the tonic London needed to distract the people from their anger and gloom. To stop it, after it had been so lavishly promised in the press, would only make matters worse.

The second instruction had Montmorency's full approval: to shoot to kill. It was the only way to stop Frank's family from becoming terrorist targets for the rest of their lives.

Frank himself had bravely agreed to go along with Montmorency's plan when Farcett explained it to him on the boat. But in London, especially at night, shivering in a series of seedy backstreet rooms, he was scared. He felt trapped. At other times, fired up by Guido's political passion, he didn't want a way out. He was getting better and better at pretending he wanted to go through with this terrible crime. So good at it that he sometimes convinced himself. He enjoyed the sheer terror of creeping to dark hiding places to collect the explosives, and he valued Guido's company and support. After all, for months now, Guido had been closer to him than his family. A constant companion who trusted him completely. Yet Frank kept the promise he'd made to Doctor Farcett during their mock medical consultations. He didn't give a hint to Guido that he had already betrayed him and was powerless to stop the forces ranged against them both.

Montmorency worked closely with the police from the

moment he reached London. Frank and Guido were observed, but not overtly followed. Montmorency promised Scotland Yard the leather-bound book from the White Hart, with its details of anarchist supporters. He went around to Fox-Selwyn's house to get it, taking the key from the secret hiding place only he and George knew. He took off the dust sheets and aired the house again, ready for Vi and Tom, who were already on their way, on one of the newest and fastest ocean liners. He moved a vase into the drawing-room window — the signal to Frank that all was as planned.

Then he went through the mail that had piled up on the doormat while they had been away. Most of the letters were for George, but one, from Scotland, was for Robert. Montmorency put it in his pocket, intending to pass it on when Farcett returned from Italy. It reminded him of the various tasks he had promised to do for the doctor, and he spent much of the first week home delivering manuscripts to medical publishers, and visiting old colleagues of Farcett's with assurances that the doctor was on his way back. He wrote a cheery letter to Maggie on Tarimond, explaining why they had been gone so long, and saying that they would all visit again soon. He knew when he posted it that at this time of year it might take a long time to reach her, but he felt it was worth trying to keep in touch.

But the days dragged. He wanted to talk to Frank, to reassure him that everything was under control, and that his efforts were appreciated by the authorities, but he couldn't risk it. He was lonely. He had to console himself with a few extravagant shopping trips and some late-night drinking at Bargles, where he was staying again, now that the flu outbreak was over and they were fully staffed with Sams once more.

He walked around town, and made a point of sizing up the new Hippodrome. The massive building dominated the junction of Cranbourne Street and Charing Cross Road, near Leicester Square, not far from where he had lodged with Vi all those years ago. The builders' hoardings and scaffolding were down, and the fancy brickwork made it look more like a palace than a theater. Huge posters advertised the grand opening and the star of the evening — Little Tich — one of Montmorency's favorites. There was a life-size picture of the tiny man, no more than three feet high, who gamboled about the stage in shoes almost as long as he was tall. He did impressions, daft walks, and silly voices. Montmorency found it impossible to say why he was funny, but when he had seen him perform he had laughed until he ached. He went to the box office and bought himself a ticket for the opening night. It was a gesture of confidence in the success of his mission. But still, he didn't get seats for Vi and Tom, just in case something went wrong.

"All set for the big night?" he asked the clerk behind the ticket counter.

"Oh, they'll be panicking right up to the last minute if you ask me. But they'll get there, even if they have to rehearse around the clock."

Montmorency hoped the management would insist that

everyone should go home and get a good night's sleep on the eve of the great day. But he had a suspicion that they wouldn't, and he was worried. The anarchists were planning to blow up an empty theater, but it looked as if many lives might be at risk.

After all the waiting, suddenly it was Sunday, January 14, and everyone started getting into place. Vi was unnaturally cheery that morning, and kept referring to the welcome cable, which had reached them the night before.

ALL SAFE ITALY. GOOD LUCK LONDON. GEORGE.

"Isn't that good news!" she kept saying. "Isn't that just good news!"

Tom wanted to go with Montmorency to meet the police near the Hippodrome. He was angry when Montmorency refused.

"It might be dangerous, Tom. I don't want you going where you won't be safe. Leave this one to the experts."

"But Montmorency, I've been in on this job from the start!"

"I suppose you have, in a way," said Montmorency. "And perhaps you would like to help me properly sometime in the future. But tonight your place is here. Look after your mother for me. She's more worried than she's letting on."

"All right," said Tom. "You care about my mam, don't you?"

"I certainly do." He laughed, covering his embarrassment with a little too much jollity. "Now you take care of her."

On the ocean crossing, Vi had asked Tom about his list of Montmorency's sins, and he had confessed that it had been intended as a means of defeating Mary. She had told Montmorency, and his old, cheery relationship with the boy had picked up again. Nether he nor Vi had yet found the right moment to tell Tom the full truth, but as Montmorency set out for the Hippodrome it was with a feeling of great fondness for his son, looking forward to a time when they might go out on jobs like this together.

In Rome, the audience for the first night of *Tosca* had to fight their way through police lines and demonstrators. For a moment George was worried, but plenty of people had decided to defy the threats. The queen was there, and Puccini himself. It would seem very cowardly to pull out now. He rattled off the plot to Farcett:

"Act One: 1800. Political activist, Cavaradossi, in love with opera singer, Tosca. He's in trouble for helping rebels. She's admired by the evil ruler.

"*We have a drink.*

"Act Two: Our hero is in prison. Tosca buys his freedom by yielding to the evil ruler. She gets the tyrant's promise on paper and kills him before he can get his side of the bargain.

"*We have another drink.*

"Act Three: Tosca visits Cavaradossi on the castle battlements and explains the deal. He will be executed by firing squad, but the soldiers will be firing blanks. He just has to pretend to die, and then they can both run away when the soldiers have gone. They fire. He falls. She tries to rouse him. Discovers she's been tricked. He really is dead. She jumps off the battlements.

"*We all go home.*"

"Sounds cheery!" said Farcett. "I like the sound of the bits when we get a drink."

"And it will all be over in three hours or so. Though I'm afraid we've been invited backstage afterward to meet the queen. She wants to say thank you, apparently."

The lights went down just as Farcett started to worry about meeting royalty, and he didn't much enjoy the opening minutes of the show. But by the time he got his first drink he was buzzing, and after the second he was excited, even though he knew how the story would end. It was getting on towards eleven o'clock when the curtain rose on the final act.

In London, the lights were still burning at the Hippodrome. The dress rehearsal was running late. The builders were still finishing off inside the auditorium, and bad-tempered dancers, singers, musicians, and animal handlers could be seen darting in and out of the stage door.

Montmorency was sweating, even though his breath froze in front of his face. He had paced the local streets for hours. He wondered if any outsiders now recognized the plainclothes detectives in the area as well as he did. There was no sign of Guido and Frank. The activists named in the

White Hart logbook were being arrested all over London. Suppose word of this had somehow reached Malpensa? Suppose he had called the job off? Where was Frank? Was he in danger again? Even if he got there, would Montmorency's plan work? Would Frank remember to do everything exactly as Farcett had instructed him day after day on the boat from America?

On the stage in Rome, the tenor was singing his last great aria and when he finished, the audience went mad and he sang it all over again. From his box, Puccini acknowledged his share of the applause, and the scene continued. Tosca arrived and more lush love-singing drew more cheering from the audience. Then the orchestra started a new beat, which could mean only one thing: The firing squad was on its way.

At last Montmorency saw the unmistakable figure of Frank, walking up Charing Cross Road with another man, shorter and darker, just ahead of him. Both of them were carrying large bags. Montmorency touched his hat. It seemed as if an electric charge ran through the chain of policemen tucked in the shadows along the street as Frank and Guido joined the gaggles of performers around the stage door. This wasn't how Montmorency had pictured it when he'd made his plan. The street was supposed to be empty so late at night. It wasn't safe. A bystander might be hurt. But there was no way to signal to the hidden marksmen to hold their fire. They were struggling to get a clear view of the two suspects. The lead marksman felt his moment had come and pulled the trigger.

Frank slumped to the ground.

In the Teatro Costanzi the sound of the guns brought a gasp from the audience, and Cavaradossi fell forward to his knees and collapsed as if dead. Tosca waited excitedly for the soldiers to leave, ready to rouse her lover and run away with him.

Outside the Hippodrome the shot brought screams, and people instinctively pulled back from the scene. The dark-haired man looked down on his fallen friend. The marksmen lined their sights up again, waiting for the running civilians to clear the area. But they didn't have to shoot. Guido took his revolver from his pocket and fired it into his mouth.

It took no more than a few seconds, and a few bars of climactic music, for Tosca to realize her mistake, discover that Cavaradossi was really dead, and throw herself to her death. The London police were just as quick. Plainclothesmen moved in and scooped up the bags as uniformed officers cordoned off the area. The two corpses were swiftly removed to separate police vans and whisked away. Montmorency got in the back alongside the stretcher bearing Frank's body, and gently stroked his ashen face.

"It's all right, Frank. You can open your eyes. It worked. The marksman fired wide. It's over."

"And Guido?"

"Dead, Frank. He shot himself."

Frank looked at Montmorency. His relief soon dissolved into uncontrollable tears, and the two of them sobbed all the way to Scotland Yard.

CHAPTER 49

≫

CONGRATULATIONS

*T*he papers next morning carried brief accounts of a gun-fight between two as yet unidentified men in the West End of London. Both were dead. A couple of days later, the police released their names: the two false names Guido and Frank had used on their transatlantic journey. It was enough to satisfy Malpensa, waiting in Milan, that the job had failed, and that Frank and Guido had done the decent thing, killing themselves rather than risking capture. There was no word in the press about the explosives they'd been carrying. That didn't surprise Malpensa. The police were bound to keep that quiet. But he was alarmed at the mass arrests of his supporters in London. One of the men he'd put on Frank and Guido's trail must have been sloppy, or maybe Frank and Guido had been betrayed, nobly killing them-selves for the sake of the cause just as the police swooped. Malpensa already suspected that his organization had been penetrated by informers: How else could the collapse of the plot to bomb Rome be explained? He ceased all contact with sympathizers in Europe and disappeared to America to keep himself safe.

So no one was looking for Frank. He would have to lie low, but with time he would be able to come back into circulation as Lord Francis Fox-Selwyn. Montmorency took him back to George's house. For the first few days he was visited by policemen and government agents who wanted a full account of his experiences in the anarchist world. He told them all he knew. But he grieved for Guido more than he could ever have imagined possible, and the sound of those shots echoed in his head at random moments day and night. He had three deaths on his conscience now: those of the policeman in Florence, Rossi the ice-cream man, and Guido. The first two had died when he had been out of control: so caught up in adolescent enthusiasms that he couldn't foresee the consequences of his actions. Guido was killed when Frank was doing good, saving countless people from bloody terror. Yet it was Guido's death that troubled him most, despite the praise of friends, family, and officials for what he had done.

Montmorency went to the Hippodrome for the opening night, and roared with the rest of the audience at Little Tich. He tore a review from the paper to keep for Frank, when he was strong enough to look back on events and take pride in his achievement. It described the unprecedented spectacle, and the wild patriotism of the crowd, roused by ad libs in act after act to declare their support for the South African war. The article ended with two lines that were an unintentional tribute to Frank and his part in Montmorency's elaborate plan:

"In an event such as at the Hippodrome, much depends on the elaborate mechanism. And last night everything worked without a hitch."

In Rome, George and Robert had a wonderful time backstage after the opera. First they congratulated Puccini.

"Thank you for the tickets," said George. "We enjoyed ourselves immensely. A triumph! May I introduce Doctor Robert Farcett?"

Farcett found himself quite tongue-tied in the presence of the great man. "The opera was marvelous, sir. Very moving."

"Well, you can see it again in London in the summer. I am coming for the opening. Perhaps we can meet again then. Though I trust I will not need your detective talents there, my lord!"

George laughed with him, but Puccini's words reminded him of the dangers in London that night. He thought of Frank, facing the greatest challenge of his life so far, and of Montmorency, who would so much rather have been there, in Rome, lost in his favorite world: the opera.

"My friend Montmorency will be very sad to have missed tonight," he said. "He really is your greatest fan. Perhaps I could bring him to meet you in London?"

"I should be delighted," said the composer, moving on into the arms of his next adoring follower, who had brought him a fresh glass of champagne.

Farcett was looking sheepish, and whispered to George: "I feel guilty now, having such fun when Frank and Montmorency are up against it at home. Perhaps we should go back to the hotel, in case there's a message."

"There won't be. Not at this hour. And anyway, look, the queen is coming."

Queen Margherita, sparkling with jewels in her high hairdo and at her throat, was escorted by the theater manager, who clucked and simpered as he introduced Puccini and the stars from the cast. Then, at her request, he called forward the local police chief, who in turn brought forth his counterpart from Florence, Angelina's father, Mario Baldo, whose men had caught the plotters. Generously, Baldo gave credit to Fox-Selwyn and Farcett, who had the chance to touch the queen's long white glove as a reward while Baldo babbled on.

". . . and I'm proud to say that my daughter is marrying Lord George Fox-Selwyn's nephew, the Marquess of Rosseley!" he boasted.

"How nice," said the queen. Two words the proud policeman would never forget. She turned to George. "I believe your brother is the Duke of Monaburn?"

"Indeed, ma'am."

"I hear that he is to be married, too. Do please pass on my heartiest congratulations."

George wondered how she knew, but Beatrice's connections never failed to astound him.

He delivered the queen's message the next day, when he and Farcett returned to Florence. A cable from Montmorency was waiting when they arrived. It was deliberately terse, meaningless to anyone outside the loop, but it told them all they needed to know:

ALL OVER. BOY WELL. M

"Let's go home, George," said Farcett. "To England. It's time to get back to normal."

"You go if you want to, Robert. I've got a few loose ends to sort out here. I want to explain everything to poor old Moretti, the curator at La Specola, and I want to spend a bit more time with my family. Why don't you stay a couple of days to see Florence properly, then I'll put you on a train?"

"But I really want to get to Tarimond, and make sure Maggie got my warnings about the X-ray machines."

"Are two days really going to make such a great difference, Robert? Come on! You may never get the chance to visit Florence again. Do stay."

And so, after two days of eating, drinking, and sightseeing, during which Farcett felt he was in danger of losing his heart to Italy forever, the time came for him to leave. He said good-bye to Beatrice and Gus, Alex and Angelina, and Professor Lombroso, who promised to come and visit him in London. Then he and George took a taxi to the station. They were both tired but happy. Fox-Selwyn pressed a little packet of local sweets into his hand. "Give these to Tom," he said. "I wouldn't want him to think I was neglecting him."

What on earth does he mean? wondered Farcett. *Surely he doesn't think* he's *Tom's father?* But it was too late to ask, even if Farcett had been able to find the words. Fox-Selwyn was already walking away, tall, fat, and jolly, not looking around, but raising his arm in a sort of backward wave and twiddling his fingers in the air to say good-bye as he faded into the distance.

CHAPTER 50

≫

LOOSE ENDS

$\mathcal{F}$ox-Selwyn went straight to La Specola. The curator, Antonio Moretti, was due back that day, and George knew he would be distressed to find that his museum had once again been the victim of anarchist activity. George climbed the stairs and went straight to the waxworks room. Moretti was already there, standing in the middle. He had his back to the door, but Fox-Selwyn could tell just from the slope of his shoulders that the new outrage had hit him hard. He approached quietly, and put his hand on Moretti's arm.

"I'm so sorry, Antonio. Take heart. Nobody is blaming you."

Moretti said nothing, but pointed to one of the glass cases. Doctor Farcett had left the wax effigies with almost no scars. The medical student who had gone in afterward had done much more damage, gouging into the wax in a frantic attempt to locate the missing guns. A liver was smashed to pieces here, a brain there. A delicate tracery of blood vessels, which had survived intact for more than a century, now looked like nothing more than shards of candle grease.

"It can never be repaired," said the curator sadly. "It would cost a fortune."

Fox-Selwyn was overcome with a feeling of generosity. "I will pay, Antonio. Your city has brought my family much happiness. It will be a joy for me to do something in return. We will find a craftsman to remove every trace of this vandalism."

"Thank you," said Moretti weakly. "You are too kind. Are you going back to England now?"

"Not just yet, no. There are a couple of things that still worry me about this business. I can't help thinking that that millionaire — the one who donated you Lord Astleman's collection — didn't die naturally. I've a feeling he must have been involved with the anarchists in some way: willingly or not. I want to stay and find out more. And what about that man Lopello, Astleman's assistant who committed the theft? He's disappeared. He hasn't been caught in any of the latest police swoops, here or in England. He might be working away still, in hiding, planning some new outrage. I want to find him before it happens."

"Are you sure, George? Haven't you had enough? Why don't you just go home? We have plenty of policemen here who can do all that work. You deserve a rest, a chance to enjoy your wealth in peace."

"No, that's not me. I like action, Antonio, and I don't like to leave a job unfinished. In any case, I feel I have a duty to England here. I've read what these anarchists say about the British Empire. I know it's our queen they'll be after next. No, Antonio, I have a duty to stay."

Moretti still just stood in silence, surrounded by his injured exhibits. Fox-Selwyn tried to cheer him up.

"But we can have fun, too, Antonio. You and I can still

play chess. I'll need you to keep me sane with all the marriage preparations going on in our house! You will laugh again, and when all this mess is cleared up, this museum will be a peaceful haven for you once more. Come on! Let's go out and have a drink."

In London, Frank slept for two days. Vi thought he should be seen by a doctor after all he had been through. But she understood why Montmorency insisted that only Robert would do. She thought it would be best if they all went off to Tarimond. Frank would be safe and the fresh air would restore him. Robert could see Maggie again, and perhaps would realize after so long an absence where his heart really lay. And she could get Tom away from London, to a quieter life. She was worried that all this exposure to Montmorency was giving Tom a taste for excitement, danger, and the more dissolute side of London life. She started packing, so that they would be ready to go as soon as Doctor Farcett came back and gave the word.

He returned in good spirits, full of chatter about saving the Italian queen, and boasting about how Edison's X-ray machine had helped them find the guns. He raved about the opera, and thrilled Montmorency with Puccini's invitation to the London première in July. Montmorency had good news for Farcett, too. The editor of *The Physician* was delighted with his articles, and would be publishing them as soon as possible.

"Let's go to Bargles and celebrate," said Montmorency in the cab on the way from the station. "Then you can have a look at Frank. Vi thinks he's exhausted. She wants to take him off to Tarimond to recover."

"Sounds like a good idea. I'd like to go with them, as soon as possible. It's a very long time since I've heard anything from there. No doubt there'll be some letters waiting for me at home."

"Actually, one came for you at George's house," said Montmorency, pulling the tattered envelope from his pocket. "It's been there for a while, I think. The gossip's probably a bit out of date."

Farcett looked at the envelope. He was disappointed to see that it wasn't Maggie's handwriting. "Who do you think it's from?" he asked.

"It could be anyone. They all learn that curly script from Maggie up at the school. Open it and see."

They were turning from Trafalgar Square into Pall Mall when Farcett opened the letter. He would never forget where he was when he found out about Maggie's death. Montmorency knew at once that something was wrong, and took the paper from Farcett's hand. The news hit him almost as hard, but he knew that his friend had lost the person who meant the most to him, even though they had never talked about her in that way. Despite, or perhaps because of, their extraordinary past, the two men had never found it easy to express emotion in each other's company. But this was different. Montmorency banged on the roof and redirected the driver to Fox-Selwyn's house. Then he and Farcett fell into each other's arms and wept.

Everyone took it badly. Vi had the most to thank Maggie for. Maggie Goudie had seen Tom into the world, put a roof over their heads, and helped them find a foothold in Tarimond life. For Frank, Maggie had been a wise friend through countless summer holidays. She had tended the cuts and bruises of his childhood, and told him tales passed down the generations of her rocky island home. But Robert was hit hardest of all, and lashed out at himself for not being there when Maggie had needed him.

"I didn't even say good-bye properly when I left. I was too obsessed with America, with Edison, and that infernal X-ray."

"It's not your fault she died," said Vi.

"Yes it is," said Farcett, waving Morag's letter. "Look at the symptoms. It's just like what happened to that man in America. Edison was right. The rays are harmful. I exposed Maggie to more radiation than her constitution could bear. I burned away her life in pursuit of my ambition."

"But you were doing it for the good of others, Robert," said Montmorency. "Your Bodyscreener will transform medical education. It will save lives."

"It will do nothing of the sort. Because there isn't going to be any Bodyscreener. I'm stopping work on it now. I'm having nothing more to do with X-rays and their evil power. I'm going to Tarimond, and I'm going to carry on the work Maggie did best: quiet, humble, day-to-day medicine that makes people better. Not self-centered research that kills the best . . ."

His voice trailed off into a shudder of sobs. No one spoke. After a while he started up again, mumbling and sniffing.

"I should have stayed. I could have done more work on the flu. I should have concentrated on something like that. Something real, something where my efforts might make a difference, where I might actually have stopped patients dying. Who knows how many people are dead because I went gallivanting around the world pursuing a stupid dream?"

Montmorency slid the newspaper under the sofa with his foot. It carried the announcement of the death of John Ruskin, the writer, another victim of influenza. Farcett had treated him from time to time when he was in London. Ruskin had been a visitor to the contessa's house in Florence, too. No doubt, in his current state, Robert would imagine he could have saved him, if only he had concentrated all his energies on influenza.

Vi knew they must all get to Tarimond as quickly as they could. Montmorency helped her make the arrangements. Once or twice he tried to urge her to tell Tom he was his father, but she hid behind all the new distress, and he was none the wiser when she left.

Montmorency decided to stay in London. He wanted to

take stock in his own way, to comfort himself with the things that really made him happy, or at least numbed his sensibilities enough for him to imagine himself content. He wanted to see his friends at Bargles, go to the races, visit shows, eat fine meals, read books, and sleep. And he was determined to keep out of politics for a while. War or no war. Lord George Fox-Selwyn would be back in town soon, surely, and they could have a good time together, as they had so often before.

And then there was Mary Gibson in America. Should he write? He tried many times, but never quite found the words. In Paterson, she waited for that letter, too proud to write herself, but hoping all the time to hear from him. She grew increasingly irritated with Cecilia, who gloated in her victory over Vi, even though it had lost them both the man they wanted. She tried to recall Tom's features, to judge whether Cissie's allegation that he was Montmorency's child was correct. Had Vi's silence indicated assent or proud defiance of a bully? Should Mary have rejected the man she loved when their future had looked so good?

Down the hill in Paterson, the red-brick mills continued working, and the population kept rising, as more and more hopeful workers arrived from Europe only to be swallowed into the industrial machine. In the office of the *Question*, Gaetano Bresci worked on for his cause, even more fired up with rage against the authorities since receiving the news that Guido and Frank were dead. He had a new lodger, Erico Lopello, another of Malpensa's protégés from Florence, who had worked in London, too, for an eccentric lord who collected dead animals in bottles. They talked long into the nights about what was wrong with the world, and how to put it right. One summer evening, Bresci didn't go to the office. Like Guido and Frank before him, he was on his way to Europe. He knew what he had to do.

CHAPTER 51

≫

MORETTI'S GIFTS

*M*ontmorency enjoyed the spring and early summer, though he missed his old friend George. Time after time Fox-Selwyn wrote to say that he was about to come home, but something always came up at the last minute. George didn't go into detail in his letters, but Montmorency could tell that at any time he might be invited to go out to Italy, to join Fox-Selwyn on the trail of one more anarchist, or to undermine another plot. George's other news was of the wedding plans, which kept changing. The two couples could not agree on whether to marry in Britain or abroad. They squabbled over the style of the ceremony, and the scale of the reception afterward. They started planning separate marriages, then came together and began joint arrangements all over again. George stayed on at the apartment partly to referee all this, but also to make sure he didn't miss anything if they all decided to get it over with quickly and tie the knots quietly there and then.

By July, Montmorency had had enough. George had promised to come to London in time to introduce Montmorency to Puccini at the first performance of *Tosca* at the Opera House on the 12th. He wasn't there. Didn't even send a letter of introduction. Montmorency was at the performance, and his heart nearly exploded with the beauty of the music and the agony of the ending, but he was turned away from the stage door afterward by a rude official besieged by fans.

Fox-Selwyn knew full well that he and Montmorency had an important engagement on the 29th. Lord Astleman had sent an invitation for them to revisit his collection, now restored to its original glory thanks to their efforts. Montmorency knew how rarely the reclusive naturalist had guests. If he and George were invited, it was because Astleman really wanted to see them; and way back in June, Montmorency had written telling George all about it. George had replied, saying that he would definitely be there; but on the morning of the 29th there was still no sign of him, and Montmorency angrily set off for Dulwich on his own.

Lord Astleman greeted him with uncharacteristic exuberance, and gracefully accepted his apology for Fox-Selwyn's absence. "I'm so excited," he said, "I had no idea they were coming. And what good fortune for them to arrive today!"

The cause of all the fuss turned out to be two large gray metal containers, each about seven feet by four, sitting on the gravel path outside Astleman's barnlike museum.

"The carrier brought them this morning, quite without warning. They appear to be a gift from La Specola in Florence. There's no covering letter, but tanks this size are likely to contain something pretty special. I've got some people coming from the Natural History Museum to help me open them and work out what's inside."

Montmorency walked around the tanks. They came up as

high as his shoulders, and were sealed with huge steel clamps. Astleman was right, there were no labels, though he could see where one had once been, and the only scrap left showed part of the address of La Specola.

Montmorency tapped on the side of the nearest tank. "What do you think is in here?" he asked. "Sounds as if this one's full of water to me."

"Liquid, certainly, I think. They're pretty heavy. The people who delivered them had to use a special crane to get them down from the lorry. I told them to leave them outside in case they're full of preserving fluid. We could be knocked right out if we opened them up without ventilation."

"So, what are you expecting to find when you get the lid off? Fish?"

"Probably. Or perhaps reptiles of some sort. It really is very exciting. Perhaps it's a thank-you for my not making a fuss about those missing specimens. I imagine these are things that have come Moretti's way for which he simply doesn't have enough room."

Montmorency thought back to the crammed museum and its overflowing vaults. "It's true, they wouldn't have the space to display anything as big as this," he said.

The gravel crunched behind them, and the butler appeared, ushering four distinguished figures towards them. A maid followed with a tray of champagne. Astleman lowered his voice.

"By the way, I haven't told anyone about that business of the theft. Best if it isn't mentioned today." Then he stepped forward to meet the newcomers, and introduced them to Montmorency. They were the experts from the Natural History Museum. They examined the tanks, much as Montmorency had done.

"I have a team of workmen outside in a van," said the fattest and most eminent-looking man. "I think we'll need cutters and levers to get the tops off, and then pulleys, chains, and straps to lift out whatever is inside."

The thinnest and most timid of the group set off to look for the workmen. While he was away, Astleman proposed a toast.

"To La Specola. To its great curator, Antonio Moretti, and to whatever creatures lurk inside these surprise parcels!"

Everyone raised their drinks.

It took a fair while for the thin man to organize the opening of the first tank. Glasses were filled and refilled while they waited. Eventually the heavy lid started to budge, and the unmistakable smell of preserving fluid wafted towards them.

"Just as well you didn't take them inside!" said the head expert. "We'd be flat on our backs!"

They pressed handkerchiefs to their faces and leaned towards the tank. No one could stand the fumes for more than a few seconds, but in that time they could see a dark curled form and, gazing up at them, a glossy eye the size of a dinner plate. The head expert reeled back from the tank, coughing.

"Shark, I think, most likely. Can't say what type without a proper look. We'll have to winch it up."

Lord Astleman ordered more champagne and canapés while the workmen erected a pyramid of metal struts over the top of the tank. They set up a huge pulley with strong chains dangling from a hook. Then two of the men put on long waterproof gloves and reached down into the tub, securing leather straps under the belly of the beast. They had to do it all with their heads turned away, so that they weren't knocked out by the fumes. As soon as the straps were attached to the chains, they ran away to catch their breath.

The thin man interrupted the drinkers' high-spirited conversation. "Excuse me, gentlemen! May I have your attention? I think we are ready to lift."

Lord Astleman got as close as the fumes would allow and gave the workmen the signal to start. Two of them wound a handle, and an arc of dark gray skin broke through the top of the liquid. The dorsal fin came first.

"You're right. It is a shark," said one of the men.

"Look at the tail," said another as the fish rose higher, exposing its lighter underbelly. "Two keels. If you ask me it's a . . ."

"Porbeagle!" said the thin man, excited out of his shyness, and adding its Latin name: "*Lamna nasus!*"

The glossy shark's enormous mouth seemed to smile at the correct identification.

"Marvelous. Marvelous," said Astleman. "What a wonderful present. But how can I possibly keep it?"

"Well, if you're looking for someone to take it off your

hands!" The head expert laughed. "We would be only too pleased to oblige."

"She's yours, then!" said Astleman.

"You can come and visit her whenever you want, of course."

"You should give her a name," suggested Montmorency.

"*Lamna nasus*," said the thin man once again.

"No, I mean a pet name." He was too drunk to notice the instant disapproval of the scientists. "Something appropriate. Like . . . Florence!"

Lord Astleman started giggling, and reached up to pat his new friend.

"Hello, Florence! Welcome to England!" They all laughed. Montmorency held out his glass for a top up.

The head expert was growing impatient to see what was in the other tank. "Perhaps we'd better get her back in her bath now, and see if she's brought a friend?"

"Yes," said Astleman. "Let's seal her up and move the tackle across to the second tank." He called for more drink and some fruitcake to keep them going while the workmen dismantled the pulley and moved it across. The conversation turned to sharks: their lives, habitats, and habits. Montmorency felt he must be learning a lot, though he wasn't sure how much was actually getting from his ears to his memory. He liked the cake, and helped himself to another slice. Darwin, the giant tortoise, lumbered towards the strange party, and Montmorency made everybody laugh by sitting on his back and taking a ride with cake in one hand and champagne in the other. Then the workmen indicated that they were ready, and Astleman called for quiet again.

The second lid came off, the handkerchiefs came out, and everyone darted across for a quick look at the next exhibit. This one was slightly smaller and browner. A wave of disappointment passed through the group as they stepped away from the smell.

"Not quite as exciting, by the look of it," said Montmorency. "We're going to wish we'd opened this one first and built up to that wonderful shark."

"Wait and see," said Astleman. "Remember what our nannies taught us. The biggest presents aren't necessarily the best! This might be a real rarity."

The workmen put on their long gloves again, looped around the straps, and waited for the signal to start winding up the chains.

Astleman paused for another toast. "To Florence's ugly sister! May she surprise us all!" He lowered his arm, and the winch started to turn.

"Curious skin structure."

"Almost like tweed."

"And those darker patches, are they camouflage?"

"Is that some kind of leathery flipper, down there at the bottom?"

The fumes forced the experts back again.

"Could be a reptile?"

"Or a . . ."

There was a rushing splash as the creature broke the surface and swung, dripping, from the crane.

The skin looked like tweed because it was tweed. Just as the feet looked leathery because they were encased in leather shoes. The body of a man hung slumped in the sling, face tucked in, limp arms and legs dangling down and swinging. The dark patches on its back were no camouflage. They could only be bullet holes and bloodstains.

The men stared as the preserving fluid dripped from the corpse's beard back into the open tank.

It was a middle-aged human, of considerable height and girth.

It was Lord George Fox-Selwyn.

The only sound was of Montmorency vomiting violently into the bushes.

≫

CHAPTER 52

MONZA, ITALY, 29 JULY 1900

Gus, Beatrice, Alexander, and Angelina were on their way to Monza, where they were to be guests of King Umberto and Queen Margherita at a big sporting festival. It was hot, and they were all uncomfortable in their formal clothes. Gus was angry. Angry with George for leaving him in a difficult social situation. He had gone off on one of his mysterious trips ten days ago, and they had expected him back in time for their date with royalty. And he had let them down. They had waited as long as they could without risking compounding his rudeness with their own lateness. Now Gus would have to dream up an excuse. Typical!

The queen was gracious, if a little frosty. "This does rather upset the seating plan, but I can forgive your brother. After all, he did save my life! Beatrice, dear, you come and sit by me. We can catch up on your exciting news."

They sat through what seemed like endless races and athletic stunts in the raging sun.

"Thank goodness Frank isn't here," said Alexander. "His nose would be bright red and peeling by now!"

"How much longer?" whispered Angelina.

Alexander looked at the program. "About half an hour at least. And then we've got the prize-giving. Try to stay awake. Everyone's looking this way to see the king and queen."

"We seem to be the only people who actually have to watch the games," Angelina complained. "And do you know, the more I see, the less I care who wins."

Alexander was right. All eyes were on the royal party. Among them were the eyes of Gaetano Bresci, newly arrived in Italy from Paterson, New Jersey, where he was considered to be an upright and dependable craftsman in the silk trade. He had left behind him his wife and child, whom he loved dearly, but not as much as he loved the idea of Italian people generally, and in particular the memory of those gunned down with the king's approval in the bread riots in Milan.

He had heard Malpensa speak about that day and had offered himself to avenge the wrong King Umberto had done. Malpensa had arranged his transport to Europe, and put him on to Antonio Moretti, curator of La Specola, who for years had assisted anarchists in Florence, without a flicker of suspicion penetrating his kindly academic exterior. Moretti had supplied the gun, found the occasion, and bought the ticket to the games.

There had been only one hiccup. An inquisitive Englishman was on Bresci's heels. He had seen the tall man with the bushy beard following him more than once. He had told Moretti, and Moretti said the man would be dealt with. He was nowhere to be seen today. There was nothing to stop Gaetano Bresci now.

The king was on the podium, handing out the prizes.

Gaetano Bresci ran towards him and fired three times before the guards grabbed him and dragged him away.

The queen and her guests were rushed to safety as the king fell dead. Gus felt a blast of anger. Where was George? Why hadn't he stopped this? And then he suddenly knew. It was no surprise when the British Ambassador came to tell him about an urgent telegram from the Foreign Office in London. Gus would never see his brother again.

And no one saw Moretti either. The curator of La Specola disappeared. A few weeks later, yet another immigrant ship sailed into New York. A short, round man with a friendly face was traveling alone. His name was Agostino Grasso. He was on his way to Paterson, New Jersey, to start a new life.

CHAPTER 53

≫

MEMORIAL AND LEGACY

*I*t was agreed at the highest level that the true facts of Lord George Fox-Selwyn's death should be kept secret. An announcement was made in *The Times* that he had died suddenly on holiday abroad. His body was quietly interred in the family vault at Glendarvie as soon as the duke and his sons could get there. Cook and Chivers were both in attendance, and both in shock to have survived their master, who had always seemed so full of life.

A memorial service was arranged at St. Margaret's, Westminster, alongside the Abbey. The duke was worried that George's murderer might be watching the occasion, and he insisted that Frank should stay away. But Vi and Farcett came over from Tarimond, still wretched with grief for Maggie. Neither was laid as low as Montmorency, who could hardly bring himself to rise from his bed when he woke each morning, tortured to find that he was still alive when George — whose wonderful friendship had shaped and sustained almost his whole adult life — was not.

Farcett came up with the idea of getting Montmorency to plan the music for the memorial service, and the project probably saved his life. With the help of an inspired choirmaster, and the voices of some of Covent Garden's finest singers, he devised a program of classic hymns interspersed with his own favorites from oratorio and opera. Everyone cried through the *Lacrimosa* from Verdi's *Requiem*, and Alexander had to save Montmorency from collapsing during "Dido's Lament," at the words "Remember me, but ah! forget my fate."

The congregation included most of the members of Bargles; old school friends; leading figures from the world of racing; politicians; and some shady characters who worked, unofficially, for the government and wouldn't normally show themselves in public, but wanted to pay their respects to a colleague of impeccable integrity, wit, and courage.

Gus bravely took on the task of speaking about his twin brother. He elegantly surveyed the highlights of his life, inevitably omitting the most exciting stories, which could never be told. During the prayers, the mourners conjured in their minds' eyes their last image of George. For Montmorency and Vi, it was a hurried good-bye as they had rushed away to America. George had been right: It would have been disastrous to have ignored developments in Italy. He had saved lives by going there instead. Gus and Alex had both been asleep when George had left the apartment for the last time. Their final sight of him had been the night before, sitting at the chessboard with Antonio Moretti, whom he had thought at the time to be a dear friend. Robert Farcett closed his eyes and saw George walking away along the station platform in Florence, casually waving what turned out to be his last good-bye. Farcett had never given Tom those sweets. He'd forgotten all about them after the shock of Maggie's death and the dark rage that had driven him to smash all the X-ray equipment on Tarimond. But now he remembered George's last words about the boy. Had George really believed that he was Tom's father?

He got the answer at the offices of a leading London solicitor, who read out Fox-Selwyn's will. Apart from a few bequests to servants and five thousand pounds for Doctor Farcett to invest in a medical project of his choice, George had left his entire cash fortune to Tom. The boy looked bemused and stared questioningly at his mother, but her expression gave nothing away, even when she was bequeathed all Fox-Selwyn's property on Tarimond. George's country homes were to be shared by Gus's children. But his London house and everything in it, along with several racehorses and the contents of all his wine cellars, went to Montmorency.

That night, Cook produced a splendid meal for them all at Montmorency's new home. Each course was one of George's particular favorites. Chivers served the food, pleased that Montmorency would be keeping him on. With the memorial service behind them everyone found it easier to talk about George and to remember the very many happy times they had shared. Gus and Beatrice, Alexander and Angelina agreed that they would marry very quietly, at St. Margaret's, with Montmorency and Doctor Farcett as witnesses. Vi invited them to Tarimond for their honeymoons.

A month later they were all on the cliff top, sharing the simple delight of a calm sea and a red sunset. Montmorency looked at them. Frank was getting stronger, but still had episodes of uncontrollable remorse or fear. Tom had grown on his travels and was nearly as tall as his mother, but still unaware of the identity of his father. The newlyweds supported each other in their grief. Doctor Farcett stood apart, contemplating Maggie's grave. Each of them was indelibly marked by two years of travel, excitement, and tragedy. They would always be united by those experiences.

But they were bound together by something else as well.

An overwhelming, animal desire for revenge.